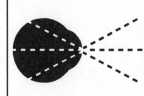

This Large Print Book carries the
Seal of Approval of N.A.V.H.

SHADOW GIRL

SHADOW GIRL

GERRY SCHMITT

THORNDIKE PRESS
A part of Gale, a Cengage Company

GALE
A Cengage Company

Farmington Hills, Mich • San Francisco • New York • Waterville, Maine
Meriden, Conn • Mason, Ohio • Chicago

LIBRARY OF CONGRESS CIP DATA ON FILE.
CATALOGUING IN PUBLICATION FOR THIS BOOK
IS AVAILABLE FROM THE LIBRARY OF CONGRESS

ISBN-13: 978-1-4328-6202-2 (hardcover)

Published in 2019 by arrangement with Berkley, an imprint of Penguin Publishing Group, a division of Penguin Random House LLC

Printed in the United States of America
1 2 3 4 5 6 7 23 22 21 20 19

SHADOW GIRL

1

Mom Chao Cherry hunched forward in a broken wicker chair and stared anxiously across the Mississippi River toward the University of Minnesota campus. Almost unrecognizable as a wealthy *khunying* from Bangkok, she wore a polyester blouse and baggy pants, cheap rubber flip-flops, and carried an eight ball of cocaine in her handbag. Only her red lacquered nails, edged in twenty-four karat gold, hinted at her ridiculous wealth.

"Time?" Mom Chao Cherry asked in an accent that probably sounded Thai or Chinese to a Westerner, but to a linguist's ear, clearly betrayed her American heritage.

"Paed nalika," Narong replied. Eight o'clock.

The corners of Mom Chao Cherry's mouth crinkled faintly, giving her aging face the appearance of a patient but ravenous crocodile. *"Di yeiym,"* she said. Most excellent.

She hadn't been back to America in more than sixty years, ever since her missionary parents had dragged her off to Asia to bring the word of Jesus to the impoverished, war-ravaged people of China. But this home-coming felt incredibly sweet. Like sweet revenge. Now, relaxing slightly, she reached into her bag and pulled out a cigarette. Lit it with a hissing lighter and inhaled deeply. She would have preferred to imbibe her drug of choice, cocaine, but that would have to wait. Right now there was wild work to be done.

Narong, who was old beyond his years at twenty-four, lifted the PF-89 rocket launcher onto his right shoulder and braced himself. Two years of compulsory service in the Royal Thai Armed Forces and another two years in the private employ of Mom Chao Cherry had taught him to truly love all forms of weaponry. He was in awe of their cold precision and the impersonal way in which they delivered death. Narong, whose name literally meant "to make war," hungered for the moment when he could sight a potential target in his crosshairs, gently squeeze the trigger, and feel the pulse-pounding rush of total destruction.

For close-up work, he was an expert in *awud mied,* or Thai knife fighting.

They'd come to this third-floor room above the Huang Sheng Noodle Factory some two hours earlier, right after they'd received the call from their hospital contact. Entering through the back door, eyes downcast, they'd pushed past the cooks and dishwashers that toiled in the hot, humid, clattering kitchen where bean sprouts littered the floors and orders were barked out in greengrocer Cantonese.

Up to the top floor they'd been led by the nervous owner, and then down a long hallway lit with bare bulbs. They'd ghosted past small cramped dormitory rooms that held two and three sets of narrow bunk beds, finally emerging in this end room with a lumpy bed and the smell of rancid cooking oil and mouse droppings. A room with a single window that afforded the perfect prospect of the slow rolling Mississippi River and, beyond it, the University of Minnesota Medical Center complex.

The helicopter swept in from the north, decelerating to approximately five knots. Two pilots in a Bell 407 who'd made this run a hundred times before. They'd just dropped out of an indigo blue sky scattered with bright stars like jacks strewn haphazardly across a lush cashmere blanket. A mile to their right, Minneapolis skyscrapers twinkled in the night — the IDS tower, Capella Tower, and the Wells Fargo Center, as well as a dozen highrise luxury condominiums. Closer still was the newly constructed football stadium, raking the skyline with its harsh, unforgiving wall of reflective glass.

The chief pilot, Captain Sam Buell, had his hands on the cyclic stick, his feet working the rudder pedals. He was carrying no emergency patients tonight, just medical cargo he'd picked up in Madison, Wisconsin. So, an easy run for Buell, who was looking forward to spending the night with his girlfriend, who lived in a nearby North Loop condo. She was an assistant producer at a TV station, a hot chick with a killer body and a healthy appetite for experimental sex. She had no clue that Buell had a pregnant wife waiting for him back home. Or if she'd figured it out, she didn't much care.

Buell's feet worked the pedals as he swung the helo around in a wide arc over the turgid Mississippi. He was preparing for their final approach. All he had to do now was coast in slowly and drop the skids. The landing zone, with its sixteen green perimeter lights, shone like a Christmas tree. No problem there.

"Looking good," his copilot, Josh Ansel, said. "Ten-degree angle, LZ dead ahead. Almost there." Ansel was young and unmarried, so he might be hitting the clubs tonight. First Avenue, where Soul Asylum and Prince had gotten their starts. Like that.

Buell hovered the Bell 407 over the dark ribbon of river as easily as if it were a giant bubble floating on a summer breeze. He was just about to throttle back and adjust his airspeed and pitch when a tiny flash, no bigger than a lightning bug, caught his eye.

Buell frowned, concerned that someone might be aiming a laser pointer directly at his windshield. There were dormitories close by, jammed right up to the edge of the towering riverbank, so there was always the chance some dumb-ass kid would pick him out as a target.

But dumb-ass kids were the least of Captain Buell's problems at this moment. The rocket slammed into his helicopter with an angry hiss, piercing the metal skin, pulverizing the gearbox, sending the bird into a perilous and lethal spin. In the darkened cockpit, with the hydraulics gone, sensor gauges, warning lights, and control switches

11

all went crazy. Ansel screamed in fear, or maybe it was pain from the raging inferno that suddenly engulfed them.

And when the big explosion came, a riotous event of incandescent shrapnel, Ansel was already gone, bones and flesh sizzled into an unrecognizable carcass. Buell had maybe a split-second longer, time for a fleeting regret about a baby he'd never see.

Two students walking back from Stoll's Bar in Stadium Village witnessed the eruption overhead. A raging, pulsing beacon that looked as if a big-ass rocket had just blown up in space.

"Holy shit!" one of the men cried as the remains of the flaming bubble jerked and throbbed in the air and then, like an angry demon cast out of the bowels of hell, hurtled downward in a furious arc, screaming directly toward them. The two men had just enough presence of mind to dive beneath a bus shelter before sheets of fire and twisted hunks of metal rained down upon them.

Nearby, on Washington Avenue, a bus was hit by an enormous fireball of white-hot metal that shattered the windshield and sent the vehicle crashing into a light standard. A rotor spun free of the plummeting debris and carved its way into the side of the chemistry building. More debris rained down as students returning from Walter Library, a Chekhov play at Northrop Auditorium, and a French film festival at the Bell Museum, all began to shriek in terror. A minute later, a dozen sirens cranked up to join the unholy cacophony.

2

It was the springtime of unrest. Of students protesting loans they claimed rendered them indentured servants for the better part of a decade. Of real estate developers paying rock-bottom prices for rat-hole boarding houses, booting out tenants, and then throwing up overpriced, high-rise dorms. Of angry people hanging around the dismal cluster of bars, retail, and restaurants directly adjacent to the University of Minnesota that was known as Dinkytown. A place that, in its heyday, had been a hub of fine bookstores, interesting head shops, and coffeehouses haunted by university intelligentsia and the ghost of Bob Dylan.

It was all different now. Nobody wore tie-dye and worried about banning the bomb or building a better world. Now students huddled over mobile devices, muttering and malcontent, never rallying together over one particular cause, but still very freaking

14

pissed off.

Family Liaison Officer Afton Tangler and Detective Max Montgomery, both of the Minneapolis Police Department, had just endured a particularly harrowing university neighborhood meeting a few blocks away at Windmere Elementary School. Afton was supposed to have delivered a quasi pep talk on victims' advocacy rights, but the meeting had quickly devolved into Max being harassed and shouted down by a gang of wild-eyed students who were across-the-board angry at what they termed "police brutality." Which basically meant they'd probably been ticketed or arrested for drunkenly racing their cars up and down University Avenue. Or smoking pot beneath the Fourteenth Avenue Bridge. Or turning a deaf ear when their girlfriends pleaded "no" during a drunken party.

"Wait until their precious BMWs get jacked," Max said, practically grinding his teeth. "Then who are they gonna call? Ghostbusters?"

They were cruising down University Avenue in Max's Hyundai Sonata, slipping past fraternity houses, copy shops, student centers, and imposing buildings with Ionic columns and donor names carved high on marble cornices. Buildings named after

15

academic superstars in chemistry, geology, and mathematics whose names and accomplishments had long since been forgotten.

"Nobody wanted to talk victim advocacy," Max grumped. "We were sent in as sacrificial lambs."

"Of course we were," Afton said. "That was the edict that came down from on high."

Afton was the more politically savvy of the two, a sociology major and family liaison officer who was used to dealing with victims and family members caught in the messy aftermath of murder and trauma. Max, on the other hand, was a hot reactor. A veteran police detective who didn't worry about decorum and political correctness. Of course, when you found yourself in a life-threatening situation — say, some asshole hopped up on bath salts was charging directly at you down a dark alley — you pretty much wanted a hot reactor on your side. A hot reactor whose Glock was loaded with hollow points.

"The police chief specified police presence at key neighborhood meetings," Afton said. "Not much we could have done except claim we never got the memo." Afton was a shade past thirty, with shaggy blond hair and the lithe, compact body of a rock climber, which was her current adrenaline-boosting sport of choice. She had the piercing blues eyes of a Siberian husky and the heart to match. Though she enjoyed being a family liaison officer, her sights were set on becoming a detective.

Max hunched over his steering wheel and searched the dark street ahead. "I gotta get this bad taste outta my mouth. Isn't there a Micky D's around here somewhere?" Max was silver-haired and in his mid-forties. Like most detectives, he was mistrustful and circumspect, with political leanings that tended to the right. He'd been married and divorced twice but was still clearly on the radar of several women who worked at their downtown headquarters.

"There's a Burger Basket in Stadium Village." Afton leaned back in the passenger seat and stared out the window. It was past nine o'clock on this Tuesday night and she was anxious to get home to her kidlins, Poppy and Tess. She was a single mom and hated being away from them on a school night. "Maybe if we . . ." Afton stopped abruptly. She'd just felt a shudder, a grinding vibration of some sort followed by a low-level explosion. It was as if the fabric of the universe had been ripped apart by something deep and threatening. She suddenly sat up straight, senses alert, antennae prickling. "Did you hear that?"

But Max was still grousing noisily. "Chief wants police presence, next time he can go by himself. See how he likes . . ." Angry static burst from Max's radio. "What the hell?" His cop instincts kicked in immediately as he dropped his diatribe and pawed at the dial. Goosing up the volume, he swerved to avoid hitting two jaywalking coeds who bounced across the street, cool as you please, in maroon hoodies and butt-twitching miniskirts.

"All available personnel . . . Explosion at Washington Avenue and Oak Street," came the dispatcher's crackly voice.

"That's right here at the U," Afton said, stunned. "Like, ten blocks away."

"Better haul ass," Max said, tromping down hard on the accelerator.

3

Owen Hacket, more often known as Hack to his lowlife friends in Duluth, was waiting a block away, exactly as he'd promised. He chomped down hard on his cigar when he saw the old lady and the kid running toward him through the darkness. They were bookin' it, even the old lady, bodies hunched forward, feet slapping the pavement loudly. Hack had heard the ominous *whomp* of the explosion — a hell of a thing — and wondered just how much time they really had before the cops and *federales* showed up. With visions of terrorists dancing in everybody's heads these days, he was positive the feds would have their shorts in a twist in no time at all.

Hack had timed out his route earlier this afternoon. Turn right on Cedar, go across the bridge, then swing left onto the ramp that circled around to 35W. Then you were pretty much in the clear. After a hard, snowy

Minnesota winter that was still coughing up an occasional spit of snow in early April, the pavement had accumulated a few potholes but was now bone-dry. Which was a very good thing. Still, a dry run was always your basic piece of cake. It's when you needed to pull it off for real that all sorts of problems reared up to bite you in the ass.

The Asian kid jerked open the rear door, shoved the old lady in, and sent her sprawling across the backseat. Then he jumped in himself, hauling his heavy weapon in after him. Hack gunned the engine and spun his way toward the green light even as the kid was still pulling the door closed. Then Hack was gripping the wheel like Dale freaking Earnhardt Jr. and making his turns — right, left, then right again.

His pulse pounding like a timpani and every nerve ending fizzing, Hack caught a quick glimpse of himself in the rearview mirror and liked what he saw. Cocksure grin across his face, eyes in a half-knowing squint, buzz-cut hair. In just the right light, he thought he kinda looked like Bruce Willis.

4

Afton and Max didn't have to go far before they came upon a scene of complete chaos. To Afton it looked like news footage that had been shot following a bombing in Lebanon or Syria. All that was missing was a grim-faced reporter in a flak jacket.

"This is bad," Max said as they coasted toward the scene.

Flames lit the night sky, throwing eerie specters of shadow on the nearby campus buildings. Chunks of unidentifiable metal stuck out like jagged tumors from the side of a concrete wall. Noxious, oily black smoke boiled from a gasoline fire that smoldered in the middle of Washington Avenue. Injured students were everywhere. The walking wounded.

"What happened?" Afton wondered. "Plane crash?"

"Or some kind of explosion."

Max ran his car up onto the sidewalk,

21

threw a POLICE card on the dashboard, and the two of them jumped out. Dozens of people were injured and dazed, and Afton spotted a nurse, on her hands and knees, frantically applying pressure to the leg of a wounded coed. More nurses and med students were pouring out of the nearby university hospital. From blocks away, sirens screamed their approach. The cavalry was coming.

Afton sprinted toward a young man in a white hoodie who was stumbling toward one of the medical buildings. As she reached him, the kid collapsed to the ground.

"Max!" she hollered. "Give me a hand."

In an instant Max was right there. They braced their arms around the kid's waist, hoisted him up, and began carrying him toward the hospital.

"What . . . ?" the kid muttered.

"You're going to be okay," Afton told him. "Just try to stay awake, try to focus."

Blood soaked Afton's shirt as the kid's head lolled against her shoulder. Her legs began to cramp with the effort of hauling the deadweight, but she and Max kept going.

"Almost there," Max huffed.

And then they were at the glass-door entrance to the hospital, where two orderlies in blue scrubs met them and hastily laid the kid on a gurney.

"Do you know what happened?" Max asked one of the orderlies.

"Helicopter crash," the orderly said as they rushed the kid off. "They were on approach to the hospital's helipad."

"Oh no," Afton said.

"Hard landing," Max grunted.

They rushed back outside to find that dozens of vehicles had arrived — ambulances, police cruisers, fire trucks, big black SUVs packed with lifesaving gear, even a BearCat armored vehicle. More doctors, nurses, and paramedics had spilled out onto the street from the various medical buildings and were tending to the wounded. Police officers were questioning dazed-looking gawkers, other officers strung up yellow crime scene tape, and firemen were uncoiling hoses to deal with the last bits of flaming wreckage.

"Thacker's here," Afton said. She'd just caught sight of the black van the Minneapolis Police Department often used as a mobile command post.

"Let's go check in," Max said. "See how we can help."

Deputy Chief Gerald Thacker was pretty much unflappable, but tonight he looked harried. He stood at the back gate of the van, a phone in each hand, barking orders. He was tall, with a commanding presence and salt-and-pepper gray hair that gave him an almost corporate look. Tonight he wore a black MPD windbreaker over blue jeans. Like so many other first responders, he'd gotten the emergency call at home.

"Anything we can do, Chief?" Max asked.

Thacker gave a slow reptilian blink when he recognized Max and Afton. "You guys got called out for this?"

"We were down the street doing a town hall," Afton said.

"Good, I can use you," Thacker said. "This is the worst damn thing since the I-35 bridge went down." His phone buzzed again and he held up an index finger. "Wait one." He lifted the phone to his ear, listened for a few moments, and said, "We don't know yet. NTSB and Crime Scene are on their way." He nodded. "Okay, sure." Dropping the phone to his side, he said, "Homeland Security is worried this might be a terrorist attack."

"What do you think happened?" Afton asked. She knew that when Thacker ventured a guess it was usually the right guess.

"Hell if I know for sure," Thacker said.

"But it was probably a malfunctioning heli-copter."

"Passengers on board?" Max asked.

Thacker shook his head. "Far as we know, it was just the two pilots."

Afton gazed at Max and lifted an eyebrow. At least some poor stroke victim hadn't been on his way in for a clot-busting dose of TPA. Still, she assumed that both pilots were goners. Looking at the twisted metal that was strewn everywhere, there was no way they could have survived such a devas-tating crash.

"Hey!" an officer called out. He was run-ning toward them in a shambling, flat-footed way, his right hand lifted in a wave. Afton recognized his uniform as that of a University of Minnesota Police reserve offi-cer. He was a young guy, maybe twenty-two at most, with brush-cut blond hair and a blond fuzz of a moustache.

"Can you see what this guy wants?" Thacker asked Max. He was talking on the phone again, trying to give directions to two different people at once.

Max nodded as he turned to meet the young officer, who'd just skidded to a halt in front of them. "What's up? You okay?"

"There's a problem in one of the dorms," the reserve officer said. "Some kid just

25

called in, said they need help real bad." He took a gulp of air. "It's just a couple blocks over."

Max gave a quick nod. "Show us."

Max and Afton ran after the young officer. They jogged down the middle of the street, hung a right at Upton, and dashed up a grassy hill, running up against a crush of frightened-looking students who had heard the sirens and been inexorably drawn to the crash scene. Afton figured that grisly photos would be plastered all over social media in a matter of milliseconds.

They followed the reserve officer across the street and up to a ten-story redbrick building that had MILBURN HALL emblazoned above the glass entrance doors. A crowd of panicked students milled about inside the lobby while alarms blared and strobe lights flashed. Some nervous Nellie had obviously pulled the fire alarm.

The reserve officer doggedly pushed his way through the crowd, Afton and Max following closely in his wake. With the elevators out of commission, they ducked into the stairwell, took the steps two at a time, and finally slammed through the crash-bar door on the sixth floor.

They banged down the hallway as students in various states of dress and undress peeked out at them, their curiosity mingled with abject fear. This was, after all, the 9/11 generation.

"Is this dorm coed?" Max asked as they jogged along. "Or are these kids just amusing themselves with a pajama party?"

"It's the new world order," Afton said.

"Hell of a thing."

"Right here," the reserve officer said, indicating a door. "Room six-twenty-three."

"Okay, we got this," Max said. "You go back to your unit and do what you can to help."

"Sure thing," the officer said.

The door was half open, so Max did a pro forma knock with his knuckles and pushed his way in. "Minneapolis Police responding to a call," he boomed out. "We're coming in."

Two frightened-looking students were inside the room — a boy and a girl. The place reeked of gasoline and smoke, just like the street below. Twin beds were pushed together, and books, pizza boxes, clothes, and computer shit were strewn everywhere. There was an enormous, gaping hole in the window that looked out toward the river, and the curtains billowed from the strong updraft. The temperature in the room had probably dropped to a chilly fifty degrees.

"Holy shit," Max said. "Are you kids okay?" He gave the kids a quick once-over and determined that they were relatively unharmed.

"You guys are cops?" the boy asked.

"Detectives," Max said. "Minneapolis PD." He pulled out his ID and held it up. "I'm Detective Max Montgomery and this is Liaison Officer Afton Tangler. We were right here on campus when we got the call." He spun on his heels and surveyed the huge jagged opening in the window. Glass shards rimmed the hole like gleaming shark's teeth. From down below came the *whoop-whoop* of ambulance and police sirens. More first responders were arriving every second.

"You're sure nobody's injured?" Afton asked. The kids were white-faced and shivering. Shock.

"We're okay," the boy said, though he didn't look okay. His eyes bulged out of their sockets and his face was flushed. His blood pressure was probably off the charts right now.

"We better call Building Services and get some guys in here with nails and big sheets of plywood right away," Max said. "Board up this window."

"We appreciate your help," the young man said. "But that's not the problem. That's not why we had our RA call the police."

Max turned to Afton. "What's an RA?"

"Resident assistant," she said. She looked at the boy. "Why did you ask him to call? What's the problem?"

"Over there," the young woman said. She pointed toward an open closet that was jammed solid with clothing, mostly jeans and plaid shirts. Another rat's nest of sneakers, boots, and pale blue towels lay on the floor. A small red-and-white cooler was canted atop a denim jacket. It stuck halfway out of the open closet.

"That cooler came flying through our window and almost conked Ashley in the head," the boy said.

Max fixed his gaze on Ashley. "Are you sure you didn't get hit?"

Ashley twisted her hands in her long sweater and nodded shyly. "When I saw the fireball out the window and heard the screams, I thought I was going to die. And then when the glass broke, I thought the whole building was going to explode."

"The cooler must have come shooting out of the helo," Afton said.

"You kids are damn lucky that you didn't get clipped," Max said. "With an explosion like that, pretty much anything and everything becomes a deadly missile. Hunks of

29

glass, metal parts from that bird, any medical junk they were transporting inside."

"Do you know why the helicopter exploded?" the boy asked.

"Not yet," Max said. "But we'll figure it out, you can count on it. For now, we'll bag your cooler and take it in as evidence. The NTSB's gonna want to look at every bit of debris that we can round up."

Ashley screwed up her face, seemingly to summon up her courage, and spoke again. "You need to look inside."

"Inside the cooler?" Afton asked. She'd detected a funny tension between the two students. Like there might be more going on here than met the eye.

"What's the problem?" Max asked, stepping across the room to stand directly over the cooler.

"Open it," said the boy.

Max leaned down and flipped open the two latches, tilting the red top away from the white bottom part.

Afton leaned forward as well, expecting . . . well, she wasn't sure what to expect.

"Jesus Christ," Max breathed.

Now they were all staring into the cooler, where an amorphous red glob wrapped in some kind of netting was surrounded by sterile cool packs.

"What is that?" Max asked.

"It's a heart," Afton said. "A human heart."

5

Hack liked to think of himself as a facilitator. Should a Panamanian tanker come steaming into Duluth Harbor and a little weed or crank needed to be offloaded privately, he could handle that. If you happened to have some excess cargo that a first mate wanted to sell on the down low, he could make that happen, too. And should you be a Greek sailor looking for some amorous female companionship — well, that was in Hack's wheelhouse as well. Besides the facilitating and the dope and the smuggling and the covert appropriation, Hack also ran a few girls out of the Silver Seas Bar in West Duluth.

Tonight, however, sitting here with the old lady and the Asian kid, Hack felt that he'd finally moved up a notch in the hierarchy of criminality, if there was such a phrase. And to tell the truth, it felt pretty damn good.

He'd driven his two contacts back to their

suite at the Hotel Itasca and was sitting with them now, adrenaline still coursing through his veins like fire as he sipped a fine, smooth whisky in a cut-glass tumbler. He was savoring the victory so to speak. The kid was sitting across from him, basically mute, must be some kind of servant, he thought. But the old lady . . . well, she was clearly a big shot who'd come all the way from Thailand just to get her kicks.

Mom Chao Cherry was staring at him now as he sprawled in a black leather club chair, sipping his liquor. Her eyes were flat, dark pools and reminded him of the eyes of a cobra he'd once seen. The snake had been smuggled in on a freighter from the Philippines and the snake's owner was trying to sell him to one or another of the various dockworkers, talking up the finer points of owning a venomous reptile.

"You performed extremely well tonight, Mr. Hacket," Mom Chao Cherry said in her somewhat clipped English.

"Hack," Hack said. "Just call me Hack." After all, they'd just done some crazy business together. And he was pretty sure there was more coming his way.

"Very well, Mr. Hack. You came highly recommended as a man who can be trusted, as well as be useful in any number of critical situations."

Hack tipped his drink toward her. "That's me, ma'am. Always happy to oblige."

Mom Chao Cherry smiled, but there was very little warmth. "I have some additional requirements that Narong will fill you in on."

Hack nodded at Narong and said, "Dude."

Narong stood up abruptly as if some sort of silent alarm had just gone off, prompting Hack to pull himself to his feet as well.

"Gonna cost you," Hack said, but there was a genial tone to his voice, no implied threat, nothing contentious. Hack was a businessman who prided himself on his strong work ethic and highly flexible morals. His attitude was: *If somebody needs dirty work and they've put cash on the table, then let's get that mother done.*

"We will speak again tomorrow," Mom Chao Cherry said. "For now . . ." She nodded at Narong, who responded with a formal half bow. Then Narong led Hack out of the suite and down the hallway to his own, much more modest room.

Mom Chao Cherry, whose long-ago given name had been Regina, after a second-century Christian martyr who'd been tortured and beheaded for her unyielding faith,

34

had changed out of her poor clothes and into a gold embroidered Roberto Cavalli caftan. Now she reclined on a white velvet chaise lounge in the bedroom of her penthouse suite.

She was musing happily about the carefully engineered helicopter crash. And the donor heart that had certainly plunged into the murky depths of the Mississippi River, serving now as a tasty banquet for the bottom-feeding fish that lived there.

She was also doing a celebratory line of coke.

The TV set flickered and blared as her glazed eyes idly watched Newswatch 7's coverage of the chaos that was still ongoing at the University of Minnesota. Jittering, wide-eyed students gave disjointed, first-hand accounts of the explosion, while police and firemen scurried around like frazzled little ants.

She barely heard Narong slip back into her suite. When he politely cleared his throat, she looked up. "You gave the man his instructions?"

"All will be prepared."

"The other," she said. "Dead?"

Narong shook his head. "Not yet."

Mom Chao Cherry's face betrayed no trace of emotion. She was still savoring the euphoria and the hot drip that trickled down the back of her throat. What dopers liked to call the burn.

Finally, she licked her lips and said, "How much time does our contact think he might have?"

"He doesn't know for sure," Narong said. "The doctors are saying perhaps a few more days." He shrugged. "Maybe only hours." Narong had been studying English for the past two years under his employer's tutelage and was excited to finally put his new language skills to work.

"That's good," Mom Chao Cherry said. When she was stoned, her voice took on the soft purr of a jungle cat. "Once we are able to take possession of our merchandise we will kill him."

"When?" Narong asked. He'd been driven to a fever pitch by tonight's wondrous and deadly explosion. Now the need for more killing was practically boiling up inside him.

"Soon. Tomorrow." She lifted a finger. "Call Sing and tell him to send three men. Make it clear that he's to put them on a plane immediately."

Narong bristled slightly. "I have weapons. I can handle any problem. Plus we have the American, Mr. Hack."

She smiled a tolerant smile. "Three men.

Just in case."

"As you wish." Narong did his half bow again, then turned and slipped out of the room.

Mom Chao Cherry smiled as she pulled a pale pink cashmere shawl around her thin shoulders. The accommodations here were better than she'd expected. A three-room suite on the top floor of the Hotel Itasca, a luxury boutique hotel that sat squarely on the Mississippi River, overlooking Lock and Dam No. 1 and the original Pillsbury A Mill. Rock stars had stayed here. Sports celebrities. One has-been movie star had even OD'd here.

Mom Chao Cherry opened her gold case and spilled out another tiny pile of white powder. She tamped it into a line, leaned forward, and, using a thin glass straw, snorted it quickly.

A hot rush exploded inside her head. She flopped back, letting the fire ripple and roar but feeling the euphoria ooze over her as well. A friend had once told her that cocaine was the selfish drug, the drug that made you love yourself more than anything in the world. She smiled lazily. That was true. But, of course, it hadn't always been that way.

She'd been fifteen years old when she and her missionary parents had been expelled from China by a new government led by the young and brash Mao Zedong. They'd packed up hymnals, crosses, and everything they owned and fled to Cambodia, where they'd set up a temporary church in the middle of a snake-infested jungle. Baby Jesus had been a tough sell to the men of the Khmer Rouge and, four months later, her parents were murdered, hacked to bits one night as they slept on their cots. A Cambodian woman she'd befriended helped smuggle her away. When they finally crossed the border into Thailand, she was put into an orphanage. That lasted only a few weeks until the head of the orphanage, an unsavory man named Kim Duk, sold her as a child prostitute to a madam in Bangkok.

Bangkok had been nothing short of bizarre — the young girls, the aberrant sexual needs of the older men, the craziness of the clattering, overcrowded city. But she had been an oddly curious girl and a sexual prodigy of sorts. With her porcelain white skin and fluent English, she soon became a favorite of the American GI's who came to Bangkok for R & R, on leave and trying to forget the horrendous, bloody fighting in Korea.

Three years later, a rising brothel star, she was confident enough to engineer her own move. She bribed her way into a higher-class brothel located in the Rattanakosin section of Bangkok. There she began to entertain men who were high up in the military and the Thai government. She learned sex tricks, improved her Thai and Chinese language skills, and became adept at flattering and charming older men. Within a few years, she met her future husband, Somchai Homhuan. He was a Thai arms dealer, smuggler, and crime boss. None of that mattered. She'd already seen and done it all. And she'd learned the most important lesson in life — that a person had to scratch and claw and kill for every single baht they earned and any sliver of respect they hoped to get.

It wasn't long before she became Homhuan's wife and, eventually, his trusted business partner. Her new Thai name, Mom Chao Cherry, which meant Her Serene Highness Princess, had started out as a private joke between the two of them. A pet name and a gentle jibe at her proclivity for first class travel, expensive jewelry, and need to spend money as wildly as the Thai royal family. Then it evolved into her given name. A decade after giving blowjobs to Japanese businessmen who traveled to Bangkok on corporate-sponsored sex trips, she'd risen to what was known in Thailand as Hi-So, or high society. It was the absolute pinnacle of success.

Three years ago, Homhuan was killed, murdered by men from the rival Kham cartel, who ruled the Golden Triangle, that sliver of land where Burma, Thailand, and Laos came together and poppies were the most prolific cash crop.

After Homhuan was gone, it seemed only right for her to step in and oversee the entire organization.

Mom Chao Cherry gazed out the window at the night sky. It was early spring, and Cassiopeia hung lazily just to the left of Draco. The lady was tipped back in her chair, a celestial goddess surveying her heavens. Mom Chao Cherry decided it was a very auspicious sign for what was yet to come.

6

"It was shot down," Deputy Chief Gerald Thacker said. "The NTSB suspects a surface-to-air missile." He was standing at the head of a long table in Conference Room A. His hair lay flat against his head, looking a little wonky, the normally razor-sharp pleat in his trousers was long gone, and Thacker's voice was raspy and hoarse. Afton recognized that Thacker was wearing some of the same clothes she'd seen him in last night, and it was readily apparent that the man was exhausted. He'd most likely spent the entire night fielding questions from every law enforcement agency, politico, and power broker in the state.

Afton didn't envy him. Thacker was generally on the front end of things, walking point and running interference. And he was good at it. He was a savvy, highly capable individual who, for the most part, was a well-liked, affable boss who wasn't afraid to grab the reins. But this crash, this explosion, had rocked him from the top of his head to the soles of his wingtip shoes. Because this type of deliberate, premeditated, terrorist-type attack just didn't happen in the Twin Cities. Which meant that Thacker, and everyone else, was justifiably on edge.

Afton sat at the far end of the table next to Max, quietly sipping her double espresso java Aftershock. Two other detectives, Dick Dillon and Andy Farmer, sat across from them. Dillon was the only non–coffee drinker in the room, preferring to get his requisite caffeine fix from the latest neon-flavored Mountain Dew.

"Terrorists?" Max asked.

"We don't know," Thacker said. "But it would be strange. Records indicate that the helicopter was a Bell 407, which I'm told is the most common type of chopper used as an air ambulance. It was making a medical delivery to the university hospital."

"What happened to the pilots?" Dillon asked. He'd come late to the party and wasn't up on all the details.

"The medical examiner is sorting that out right now," Thacker said. "What's left of them."

"Were there any passengers on board?" Dillon asked.

"Not exactly," Max said. He glanced sideways at Afton and said, "The only cargo the helicopter was carrying was a heart."

Dillon did a double take. "Human?"

"No, a chicken heart," Max said. "Of course it was a human heart. Family Liaison Officer Tangler and I found that puppy on ice right after the cooler it was packed in blew through a window into some kids' dorm room."

Afton grimaced at both the memory of the heart and at her title, *liaison officer*. More than anything else, she longed to earn the title of detective. But that, she'd been told, was still some years away. Many years, unless she figured out a tricky way to circumvent the system.

"Some poor bastard must have been awfully disappointed," Dillon said. He was a short, overweight, florid-faced cardiac patient-in-waiting. He was also a fairly decent detective, though he could be wildly inappropriate at times. This was one of those times.

"Do we know if the heart was being transported for anyone in particular?" Afton asked.

"Yes. It was earmarked for Leland Odin," Thacker replied.

"Name's familiar," Max said. "Can't place

it, though."

"He's the CEO of Diamond Shopping Network," Thacker said.

Dillon's eyes went wide. "Holy crap, that's big money!"

"All the money in the world might not buy him another donor heart," Thacker said. "Word was, Odin was prepped and waiting in an operating suite at the university hospital last evening. Waiting for that particular heart. Seems he was diagnosed with restrictive cardiomyopathy some six months ago."

Max shook his head in disbelief. "You gotta be kidding me. He was that close to getting a new heart?"

"And then it all went boom," Dillon said. He nudged Farmer with an elbow.

"And we're positive the heart was for this guy Odin?" Farmer asked.

"So the doctors tell us," Thacker said. He picked up a piece of paper and read from it. "Motorcycle accident in Madison, Wisconsin, yesterday afternoon. Twenty-two-year-old Matt Havers swerved to miss a deer, drove into a ditch, and flipped his bike three times. Mr. Havers died on his way to the hospital."

"Donor cycle," Max said under his breath.

"Is Mr. Odin still alive?" Afton asked. She

44

was getting geared up to meet with the family.

"He is," Thacker said. "Though the university hospital lists his condition as extremely critical."

"What about the heart?" Farmer asked. "Could it be saved? I mean, even if it's been sitting in the gutter for a couple of hours, it's gotta be better than what Dillon has under the hood."

Max rolled his eyes. "Oh Christ. Here we go."

But Farmer was on a tear. "I got some jumper cables in my car, maybe we can get it started again."

"Screw you, Andy," Dillon said. "This is some serious shit."

Thacker waited until the laughter died down. "I'm afraid Mr. Odin's heart was not salvageable."

Afton had recognized the name immediately. Leland Odin was the man behind Diamond Shopping Network, a home-shopping company that was headquartered out in the western burbs. He was a man who'd started a small chain of dollar stores, jumped to television with directresponse infomercials, then went multi-platform in sales and became a gazillionaire along the way.

"Wait a minute," Max said. "Was this an act of terrorism or do you think somebody shot down that helo to keep Mr. Odin from getting his heart? Why would they go to the trouble? The damn surgery is risky enough as it is."

"Terrorism . . . sabotage . . . they're both theories we're floating around," Thacker said. He pulled his mouth into a grim line.

"So two pilots killed and at least three dozen people injured by crash debris," Max said.

"It could be attempted murder as well as a double homicide," Afton said under her breath. "A crime within a crime."

Thacker heard her. "I want to keep everything under wraps for now until we get a handle on the facts."

"If someone was gunning for Leland Odin, you're not going to be able to keep it quiet for long," Afton said. "People are going to start asking questions."

"People already have," Thacker said.

"The media?" Max asked.

Thacker exhaled deeply and rocked back on his heels. "They're the least of our problems. Right now, I'm fending off inquiries from Odin's family, his business partner, and, unfortunately, two city council members, as well as our own Governor

46

Lindsay. The governor . . . well, let's just say he and Odin are good friends. They went to school together at St. Paul Academy."

"And I'm guessing that Odin probably contributed a shit load of money to Lindsay's last campaign," Max said.

"There's always going to be big-time political muck that we have to wade through," Thacker said. "So put on your rubber boots and keep your head on straight." He cocked an eye at Afton. "And when it comes to the family, you're especially going to have your work cut out for you."

"Did someone want to kill Odin? Along with two pilots?" Farmer asked.

"Helicopters don't just explode on their own," Max said. It was a statement, not a question.

"Not usually," Thacker said. "Which is why the NTSB and our Crime Scene guys have been working over the debris since eleven o'clock last night."

"What have they found so far?" Afton asked. If the family asked, she wanted to be ready.

"Like I said before, the NTSB is thinking surface-to-air missile," Thacker said.

"Fired from where?" Max asked.

"And where the hell does somebody get a freaking missile?" Afton asked.

Thacker raised both hands as if he were a preacher about to bestow a blessing. "You tell me. The missile, I don't know. Probably military, which means there's a huge security problem somewhere. As to where it was fired from, we haven't got that pinpointed. We've had patrol officers going door to door last night and first thing this morning. Plus, we've got our guys as well as two physics professors from the university analyzing copies of our videos. We're hoping they can determine some sort of trajectory path."

"How would they do that?" Afton asked.

"For one thing, we have video from three different cams," Thacker said. "They're gonna use the different angles and factor in the distance and velocity to figure out where the missile might have originated."

"No witnesses?" Farmer asked.

"Only for the actual explosion. But the tech guys down in the Batcave have a copy of a video that a kid shot on his GoPro. They're cleaning it up so we can review it."

"What about the news stations?" Afton asked. "Every one of them has some kind of weather tracking Doppler. Maybe we could use that as well."

"Good thought," Thacker said. "I'll make

a couple of calls."

Before he could say another word, a young man Afton didn't recognize entered the room with a monitor on a rolling cart. The young man had a shaved head and a bushy black beard. He was wearing a brown HAN SHOT FIRST T-shirt and faded blue jeans.

"Here we go," Max said.

"So we're going to Zapruder it?" Afton asked.

Thacker's head jerked in her direction. "What'd you say?"

Afton scrunched down in her chair. "You know, watch it frame by frame, like the Zapruder film of the Kennedy assassination. The FBI watched it frame by frame to try to figure out how many shots were fired and from what location."

"Lone gunman, my ass," Dillon hissed.

Black beard cleared his throat. He'd been plugging in cords and fiddling with a laptop computer. "Uh . . . I'm Jeremy Payne?"

"Mr. Payne," Thacker said. "Thank you. People, this is the new team leader of our IT Division."

The crew mumbled introductions, then Payne said, "We've been working on this with the NTSB. You guys ready to see the vid?"

"Let's do it," Max said as Afton jumped

up and flipped off the light switch.

"What we have here," Payne explained, "is rough footage shot via a GoPro."

Afton sat on the edge of her chair transfixed as the image on the screen came to life. There was a shot of gray clouds scudding along a dark sky as the camera made a panning motion, then the camera dipped down to show the dark river.

"The vid gets kind of muddy here," Payne said.

The footage continued to roll. The camera zoomed left, catching a row of trees, wavered a bit, and then went right. The time stamp numbers in the lower right-hand corner flashed by with each passing second.

"At least we're getting an accurate idea of time," Afton said. She watched as the camera focused on the I-94 bridge off in the distance. Headlights flew by as the camera swung shakily left and then right.

"Is the explosion even on here?" Max asked. He was getting antsy.

"Just wait," Payne said.

More seconds ticked by and then, suddenly, the helicopter came into view. It hung there for a few moments, looking practically motionless as aircraft usually do when they're coming directly at you. Then, a split-second later, the helicopter exploded, turning into random bursts of light.

"There you go," Thacker said. "Like a meteor exploding."

Afton thought it looked like old footage she'd seen of a hydrogen bomb explosion. Stark and contrasting, almost like an X-ray.

"Holy shit," Dillon said.

The camera shook for a few seconds and then refocused on what looked like vestiges of fireworks falling out of the sky. Afton knew these were parts of the helicopter. Probably parts of the pilots, too.

"What does this tell us?" Farmer asked. "Besides time of day?"

"Let me back up the vid, turn up the sound, and add some compression," Payne said as he pecked at his keyboard.

"Compression?" Afton asked.

"It's a technique that will compress or level the signal to a dynamic range where all other sounds are reduced, but the sound we want is significantly boosted," Payne said.

Max tapped a finger against the table. "And that means . . . ?"

Payne played the video again. Only this time, there was an ominous hissing sound right before the explosion!

"Holy shit!" Max exclaimed. "What was that?"

"The missile," Afton said. "Just before it hit the helicopter."

"That's exactly right," Payne said. "We isolated the frequencies to a specific range in order to locate the sound."

"Tell them why that's significant," Thacker said.

"So you noticed that the hiss got increasingly louder just before the explosion?" Payne asked.

The detectives all nodded.

"Now we can tell which direction the missile came from." Afton smiled. "Holy crap."

"Exactly," Payne said. "And based upon the duration and frequency of the audio we can estimate a general location."

"So where did it come from?" Max asked eagerly.

"We don't know exactly," Payne admitted. "We want to calibrate this video with the video from the other two cameras to pinpoint location and trajectory."

"How soon will we have that?" Thacker asked.

"We've got a dozen people working on it now," Payne said.

"So . . . hours?" Max asked.

Payne nodded. "Hopefully."

"And a kid shot this from across the river?" Max asked. The Mississippi River sliced through the heart of the University of Minnesota campus, creating an East Bank and a West Bank. Kind of like Palestine, just not so contentious.

"That's right," Payne said. "Best guess right now is that the missile was fired from the West Bank. In the Cedar-Riverside area."

"While the technicians do their part," Thacker said, "we have our work to do, too. Dillon and Farmer, I want you guys to head back to the crash site and see if anything else has turned up. Max, I want you to go talk to Sunny Odin, the victim's wife. She's not a widow yet, but it's not looking good for Leland Odin. Afton will go with you as family liaison officer."

Max nodded. "Got it."

"Look, I don't need to tell you this is high profile. The university has already beefed up security and we've got some heavy hitters looking over our shoulders. More than that, we've got an anxious public thinking that ISIS is on our doorstep. Let's leave no stone unturned."

"Is this a courtesy call to Sunny Odin or are we looking for something specific?" Max asked.

"We're looking for whatever we can turn up," Thacker said. "There are too many unanswered questions right now. We have to start somewhere, but I want you to play nice."

"How much do we know about Leland Odin?" Afton asked. "And, I guess, Sunny."

Thacker ruffled through a stack of papers that sat in front of him. "Damn, where is that stuff? I wish Angel was back." Angel was his regular administrative assistant who was out on maternity leave. "Oh, here it is." He pulled out a couple of black-and-white photos and passed them to Afton. "This is the guy, Odin."

Afton recognized Odin immediately. Large gray bushy eyebrows, crooked nose, steely eyes, and an attitude that projected power; as if he were one of the original Masters of the Universe. She'd seen him in the newspapers and on television, breaking ground for his corporate headquarters, acquiring smaller companies, cutting a ribbon for a new hospital wing.

Thacker slid the rest of his pile down to Max and Afton. "There's lots more here, too. Diamond Shopping Network is owned by Leland Odin, but he has a partner, Jay Barber, who holds a minority share. DSN is talking with underwriters about a possible IPO, which would be a very big deal for them. Plus, they've recently picked up a possible suitor. A business conglomerate in

Saudi Arabia that's interested in acquiring them."

"Saudi Arabia?" Afton said. "If the public hears Saudi Arabia, they're immediately going to think al-Qaeda was responsible for the helicopter explosion."

"Maybe so. But as you can probably guess, we don't know much about that particular connection. Yet."

"We'll get on it," Max said. He indicated the pile of research. "This is all good stuff. Where'd it come from?"

Thacker flipped him the most recent issue of *Minneapolis-St. Paul Biz News.* "It wasn't all that tricky. Seems the folks at DSN don't just love publicity, they court it. And Odin's online so much, he's like a teenage girl with an Instagram account."

"Free publicity is always better than paid advertising," Afton said.

Thacker looked at her. "Who made you a marketing guru?"

Afton shrugged. "Just paying attention to our brave new multi-platform world."

"Anyway," Thacker said, "back to DSN. They're nationwide and moving into Canadian TV. Getting bigger all the time, probably gonna give the other TV shopping networks a real run for their money."

"What do they sell besides commemorative coin sets and ShamWows?" Max asked.

"I asked my wife about that this morning," Thacker said. "She told me they hawk anything and everything. Watches, lawn furniture, turquoise jewelry, bedspreads, turtle cheesecake, socket wrench sets, fancy crystal vases." He looked tired. "You name it, they sell it."

7

Sunny Odin looked exactly as her name implied: sunny. She had flaxen blond hair, intense blue eyes that were probably enhanced by tinted contact lenses, a heart-shaped face, and a killer figure that was either the product of excellent liposuction or hard-core crunches.

She answered the front door herself, the lady of the manor who lived in an Italianate mansion complete with a hand-laid brick driveway on the west shore of Lake of the Isles. This was plum real estate in the wealthiest, classiest part of Minneapolis. Early lumber barons, timber barons, and beer barons had built their sprawling mansions here, up on a majestic hill overlooking downtown, the spot where rich folks always preferred to stake their claim no matter what the city.

"Thank God you people are investigating this," Sunny said, once Max had introduced himself and Afton. "I didn't sleep a single wink last night, knowing that Leland's life was hanging in the balance."

"Have you been able to speak with him this morning?" Afton asked.

"Yes," Sunny said. "My daughter and I were at the hospital first thing this morning, but they only let us see him for, like, half a minute. He's just so weak and he's still quite sedated."

"But your husband knows what happened?" Max asked.

"He knows he didn't get his heart, yes," Sunny said. She put a hand to her mouth and stifled a sob. "Do you know he was practically on the table? They had him all prepped and ready for the transplant surgery, a half dozen different drugs dripping into his veins. Two surgeons and their entire team were standing by."

Max raised his eyebrows at Afton, indicating that she should do her thing.

"Mrs. Odin," Afton said. "I'm here to serve as liaison between your family and the Minneapolis Police Department. If there's anything you need, anything at all, please don't hesitate to contact me." She handed Sunny one of her business cards. "I'm here to run interference for you. If you have questions, I'll do my best to find answers.

Whether it's from the MPD or the National Transportation Safety Board."

"Thank you," Sunny said, fingering the card. "Right now we're going to need all the help we can get." Her eyes fluttered rapidly, blinking back tears, then she said, "You need to come in and meet the others. I know they have questions for you."

"The others?" Afton asked.

But Sunny had already turned and was walking briskly across the white marble–tiled entryway, where an enormous bouquet of exotic flowers, purple orchids and white Oriental lilies, sat atop a white lacquered table.

"If you'll follow me," Sunny's voice floated back to them. "They're waiting anxiously in the library."

The "they" turned out to be Sunny's daughter, Terrell Carter, as well as DSN's corporate attorney, Bob Steckel, and Odin's business partner, Jay Barber. They were all seated on caramel-colored leather chairs and loveseats in a large library that was lined floor-to-ceiling with leather books.

All the classics, it looked like to Afton: the Greek tragedies, Jane Austen, Shakespeare, F. Scott Fitzgerald. She wondered if the people who lived here really read these books or if they were just for show. Placed there by a decorator who'd bought out some poor, failing bookshop for pennies on the dollar.

Once introductions were made, Sunny got down to brass tacks.

"Shooting down the helicopter . . . that wasn't just terrorism, was it? It was deliberate. Somebody *knew* that Odin's heart was on board."

"We think so, yes," Max said.

"The question is, who would do that?" Sunny asked. "How would they even know?" She was chattering nervously and kept twisting and worrying a very large diamond ring. On their way over here, Afton had read the rest of the research on Leland Odin and his wife and knew that Sunny was in her late forties, almost thirty years younger than her husband, and had been a former on-air host during the early days of DSN. They were also rich as Croesus.

Barber slid forward in his chair. With his silver-gray hair and sharply drawn features, he looked like an alert German shepherd. "You're bringing in the FBI, aren't you? Because this attack could have international ramifications."

"The FBI handles domestic issues," Afton said. "The CIA concerns itself with international threats."

"Still," Barber said, "it could have been the Saudi buyers, trying to gain some leverage in a potential sale."

"Is there a potential sale?" Max asked.

"We've been talking to a couple of interested parties," Barber said. He lifted both hands, fingers spread apart. "You know how it is. You build a business, make it as competitive and profitable as possible, and then you sit back and reap the rewards."

Afton didn't know how it was to be a corporate big shot, but Barber's words sounded fairly logical to her. She supposed many business owners had that same endgame in mind, the dream of cashing out bigtime. "So Diamond Shopping Network was actually up for sale?" she asked.

"For the right price," Barber said.

"And to the right buyer," Sunny said.

"Who were the other buyers?" Max asked.

Barber and Steckel, the attorney, exchanged meaningful glances.

"From my point of view, there was really only one serious party," Steckel said. He was in his early fifties, thin and bespectacled, and wore a three-piece suit. Afton hadn't seen a guy in a three-piece suit since she saw Elvis Costello in concert.

"And who was that?" Max asked.

"We took a meeting with Consolidated Sports a few weeks ago," Steckel said. "They'd put out tentative feelers, so we sat down and talked with them."

"They're a pretty big operation," Afton said. She knew Consolidated Sports owned a chain of sporting goods stores, Sport Gear Plus, that were located all over the Midwest. She'd even bought bikes and helmets for Poppy and Tess at their south Minneapolis store.

"Yes," Steckel said. "Consolidated is a good outfit looking to expand. They see the future fairly clearly and know that it's not going to be in brick-and-mortar stores. Retail is going online." He glanced at Sunny. "It's all going online."

"But you had an amicable meeting with Consolidated Sports, am I right?" Max asked. "You don't think they'd . . . *do* anything. To weaken your stance or try to force your hand?"

"I can't imagine they would," Barber said. "I've known their CEO, Jeremy Shank, for a number of years. He wouldn't . . . well, he just wouldn't."

"Who knew about Mr. Odin's heart transplant surgery?" Afton asked.

"Everyone," Barber said. "It's all Leland's been talking about ever since his docs diagnosed his cardiomyopathy."

Max flipped open a small spiral notebook. "So that would be . . . ?"

"Well, quite a few of his friends at the Metropolitan Club downtown," Steckel said. He raised his brows and threw Afton a sideways glance. "That's a *private* club."

"Yes, thank you," Afton said. "We have that information." She could spot a put-down a mile away.

"Who else knew about Mr. Odin's heart transplant surgery?" Max asked.

Sunny glanced around at Barber, Steckel, and Terrell. "Who else knew?" she asked brightly.

"Probably all the guys at his golf club," Terrell said without looking up. She was a languid-looking dishwater blonde in a pair of faded designer jeans and a beige cashmere sweater. She hadn't said anything until now and was busy picking at her nails and adjusting an armload of colorful, jangling bracelets. Afton wondered if the bracelets had come from DSN. Somehow she didn't think so. Terrell struck her as a fairly high-maintenance young woman with a taste for luxury goods rather than mass market. Class not mass.

"Leland golfs at Minnewashta Hills," Sunny said. "He sits on their board of directors, too." She thought for a minute. "Oh, and he's on the board of the Northern Plains Foundation and the Children's Cupid Charity, too."

"How about the people at Diamond Shopping Network?" Afton asked. "That's going to be our next stop. How much did they know about Mr. Odin's transplant operation?"

Sunny put a hand to her cheek. "I honestly don't know. I mean, they certainly knew that Leland was sick and all. He'd dramatically cut back on his hours these last couple of months."

"They knew he was *ailing*," Barber said, as if that somehow lessened the seriousness of Odin's cardiac issue. "We tried to contain that aspect as much as possible."

"Leland was very optimistic about the transplant," Steckel said. "He was making bold plans for the future. And then yesterday, when we found out there was a donor heart available . . ." His throat seemed to constrict and go dry. "We were all simply overwhelmed with joy."

"What's puzzling," Sunny said, tapping an index finger against a white marble coffee table, "is that the people at DSN and most of Leland's contacts *weren't* privy to that particular information. They didn't know there'd been a fatal motorcycle crash in Madison and that a donor heart had been matched and harvested. They didn't *know* it was being flown in last night. So who could have . . . ?" Her words hung in the air.

Max aimed a pen in the general direction of Sunny and her entourage. "Everybody here knew."

Sunny's expression remained frozen. "I suppose that's true."

"Does that mean we're all suspects?" Barber asked.

"Persons of interest," Max said.

Steckel's jaw tightened. "We don't need threats; we need you people to do your jobs."

"You don't think one of *us* hired an assassin, do you?" Terrell asked. She was lounging in an eight-thousand-dollar leather Eames chair, her legs casually crossed, and didn't look one bit nervous. In fact, she looked moderately interested. As if this little Q & A session had broken up what could have been a long, boring morning for her. "Goodness, I wouldn't know where to look for an assassin. Maybe . . . Craigslist?"

"You'd be surprised how easy it is to have someone killed," Afton said. It wasn't really, but it shut Terrell up and put thoughtful looks on the faces of everyone else.

"Okay, let me ask you folks this," Max said. "Can anybody give me the name of someone who *didn't* want Mr. Odin to receive a new heart?"

Those were the magic words, of course. But nobody spoke up. Sunny cupped a hand under her chin and, despite the Botox, tried to pinch her forehead together in a thoughtful, hard-working expression. Barber looked down at his shoes, which Afton decided might be Tod's. Terrell continued to study her fingernails, as if she might be contemplating a new manicure. Steckel just looked unhappy.

"Mr. Odin had enemies?" Max prompted. Afton thought he sounded like a sports coach, trying to hustle up some school spirit. No dice. They all just shrugged and stared at one another some more.

"Come on, people," Max said. "Mr. Odin must have had some enemies."

"I suppose he did," Sunny said slowly. She looked pointedly at Barber, then at Steckel, but they were no help. They cleared their throats, they studied the god-awful modern artwork that hung on the far wall, they did everything but shuffle their toes in the dirt and murmur a collective *Gee, I dunno.*

Finally, Steckel stepped in. "Is there a possibility it was the cygnus opponents?"

Max lifted his pen in anticipation. Now they were getting somewhere. "Who are they, please?"

"Sunny heads a neighborhood group that is concerned with ridding Lake of the Isles of the myriad flocks of Canada geese," Steckel explained. "The situation is really quite dreadful. I live two blocks from here and I can personally vouch for how bad it's gotten. Although some people — well, a lot of people who don't actually *reside* in this neighborhood — claim to love the geese."

"The problem," Sunny said, "is that these geese randomly waddle around our walking paths and lawns and freely deposit their droppings."

"Excuse me?" Max said. He put a hand to his head as if he feared his brains would blow out his ears.

"We've been lobbying the local residents to go along with the relocation of the Canada geese," Sunny said. "And then we'd replace them with a lovely flock of trumpeter swans."

"How's that working for you?" Afton asked.

Sunny looked unhappy. "So far our neighbors have been quite resistant."

8

"She's worried about goose poop," Max said, "while her husband is laying in the hospital with a bum ticker that could implode any moment." He swung over into the right lane without bothering to flip on his turn signal. They were barreling west on Highway 394, passing Ridgedale Shopping Center, heading for the headquarters of the Diamond Shopping Network.

"Maybe if you lived in Sunny's neighborhood," Afton said, tongue planted firmly in cheek, "you'd begin to appreciate the magnitude of her goose dilemma." She gripped the door handle as Max rocketed past a large tanker trunk. He was a notorious speed demon, and his driving was giving her a unique brand of heart palpitations.

"If I lived in a house like that I wouldn't have *any* problems at all. Especially not Canada geese, French-Canadian geese, or any other nationality of geese. If that was my zip code, it would mean I was fat-and-sassy rich."

"Rich people have problems, too," Afton said. "They're like everybody else." Her ex-husband, Mickey Craig, owned two luxury car dealerships and was fairly well-to-do. He was also on his third girlfriend in eight months and was nursing a nasty Oxycontin habit.

"The thing is," Max said, "rich people always have the option of buying their way out of a bad situation. If they get sick, they can high-ho themselves to a really good specialist. If they're feeling stressed or burned out, they can whip out their American Express Gold Card and jet off to a sunny beach in Maui. If their kid is flunking geometry, they can hire a private tutor." He stopped abruptly.

Afton shifted in her seat to look at him. "Is one of your boys flunking geometry?" Max had two boys, Jake and Tyler. Jake, his oldest son, was a hockey all-star, but struggled to keep up his GPA.

"Let me put it this way," Max said. "The only pi that Jake is intimately familiar with right now is the thick-crust variety that comes from Domino's."

"Sounds like you're pretty worried about him."

"Probably because I work too many hours and don't spend enough time with either of my boys." Max worried endlessly about his kids, who were the loves of his life.

"You could cut back," Afton said.

"Two words," Max said. "College tuition. Jake's less than stellar GPA is going to hurt any chance he has of getting a hockey scholarship, so I need to keep logging the hours. Tyler . . . well, he's just my little gremlin guy." He turned off onto Hillson Parkway. "And right now I'm so hungry I could chew my own foot off. In case you haven't noticed, my deductive reasoning goes to shit when I'm hungry."

"So let's stop and get something to eat."

"But nothing too healthy. None of that fro-yo crap or wheat shooters in a juice box."

"I hear you."

Afton knew that Max, like most other cops, didn't like dealing with crime victims' families. They wanted to focus on the crime itself, not the messy aftermath. But Afton was interested in all aspects: the crime, the victim, the collateral damage, as well as the hunt for the killer, kidnapper, perpetrator, whatever. The whole thing fascinated her and tugged at her. Sometimes, when she was brushing Poppy's hair or helping Tess

70

put together a costume for her dance class, her mind would drift to a certain case, and she'd analyze the evidence they'd gathered so far. And think, *What if we just went off in this direction?* Yeah, she liked her job as family liaison officer just fine. For now.

They drove on another couple of blocks until Max said, "Okay, here we go," and aimed the car into the drive-through of a Burger King. "Nothing a tasty flame-broiled Whopper can't cure."

"If I had to choose, I'd say I'm more partial to the Big Mac," Afton said.

Max fairly chortled. "For years those guys have been trying to conjure up a Mac with mayo. What you'd call your Whopper stopper. So far it's been a miserable failure."

"I hear these guys are testing out a Whopper taco."

"Bad idea," Max said. "If I were their new product guru, I'd put the kibosh on that idea. You want a burger, you buy a burger. You want a taco, you head over to El Lancer in West Saint Paul and get the real deal."

They got their burgers and Cokes, then sat in the parking lot eating. Nobody worried about messing up Max's car. It was already a mosh pit of empty Pepsi and Red Bull cans, candy wrappers, dirty socks, hockey breezers, and various pieces of sports equipment. The aroma from all that mess was exactly what you'd think it would be, your basic *eau de teenage boys.*

"What'd you think about our meeting with Sunny?" Max asked as he popped a French fry into his mouth.

"I think it's strange that she didn't have any idea concerning her husband's possible enemies," Afton said. "Usually, the spouse of a victim or intended victim goes a little bit berserk. They make wild assertions, point fingers, see potential suspects lurking behind every rock."

"Is it possible Sunny wants her husband dead?"

"You think?" Afton said.

"If she could profit from it, why not? Or if something else was going on. You never know what dark forces are at work in a marriage." Max glanced at her. "You oughta know all about that — you've been divorced. Twice."

"Thanks so much for reminding me."

Diamond Drive was a narrow lane sandwiched between rows of silver maple trees. They were perfectly manicured, perfectly spaced, and must have been gorgeous when they flared red and orange in fall. Up ahead, the road widened to reveal a sprawling white

72

building in a parklike setting. World head-quarters for Diamond Shopping Network.

"This is a big-ass operation," Max said.

"I looked them up online," Afton said. "This building is something like eighty-five thousand square feet and houses the whole enchilada: three TV studios, all the executive offices and the buyers' offices, a warehouse, and a call center."

"Call center for . . . ?"

"It's where customers call in and place their orders for stuff they don't really need."

"How much you think a company like this is worth?" Max asked.

"A shit load."

Max pulled into a visitor's parking spot right near the front door. "I mean, what's it worth to the heirs?"

"Hundreds of millions?" Afton speculated. "Half a billion?"

"Exactly."

"You think we're going to find something here?"

"You never know," Max said. "But we gotta look for some kind of thread. And then give it a tug and see where it leads."

Angus Wagner, the general manager of DSN, met them at the front door.

"Welcome," Wagner said. "Sunny called a

little while ago and said you'd be dropping by."

"Nice of her to call," Max said. He made hasty introductions, and then Wagner led them to the front desk, where they signed in and were issued clip-on ID badges.

"Hell of a thing, isn't it?" Wagner said. He was balding, round-shouldered, and slightly pear-shaped on the bottom. The cut of his bespoke suit was the only thing that saved him from being a dead ringer for Tweedledum. But his hangdog face was friendly and his tone carried great concern.

"You're close to Mr. Odin?" Max asked.

"Close enough," Wagner said. "Here at DSN we like to think of ourselves as a close-knit family. A lot of us were here from the very beginning, when we were just a small import company. We built this company together, and Mr. Odin has never forgotten that. We have a generous pension and profit-sharing plan in place, and employees receive very good benefits."

"I assume that everyone who works here is aware of the helicopter crash last night?" Afton asked. "They know that Mr. Odin's heart was lost?"

"They pretty much know," Wagner said. "The rumors have been rampant, and folks have . . ." He checked himself and switched tack. "But I have to say I'm proud as hell that everyone is carrying on with nary a hiccup. There are a lot of good people here."

"I'm sure there are," Afton said. They were standing in a large lobby with a shiny white tile floor and white walls like an art gallery. On those walls were enormous color photos of Diamond Shopping Network hosts posing with some of the various products that DSN sold on air. Watches, colored cookware, bath gel, tins of brownie bites, fluffy towels.

"You're here to ask questions?" Wagner asked. "Where do you want to start?"

"Actually, we're on a fairly general fact-finding mission right now, so we'd like a tour of your place if that's possible," Max said. "Hopefully that will give us a feel for how things are run. Which, in turn, might prompt a few questions."

"Fine," Wagner said. "That's just fine. If you want to follow me . . ."

He led them down a wide, carpeted hallway that featured an even more densely packed mosaic of DSN product photos.

"We might look like a big, complacent established conglomerate," Wagner began. "But DSN is a company that runs lean and mean. We're selective about the products and brands we sell, and if a product doesn't perform, then it's axed. There's a very fine art to running a TV shopping network."

"There is?" Afton said.

"Yeah, tell us about that," Max said.

Wagner turned and squinted at them. "At DSN, direct-to-consumer marketing is a carefully orchestrated chain of events. We buy large amounts of excess inventory, get it on the air as fast as possible, and try to sell it at an irresistible price."

"That's your magic formula?" Max said. "Isn't that what any smart retailer tries to do?"

"Not exactly," Wagner said. "For one thing, DSN spills directly into our customers' homes, so we literally insinuate ourselves into their living rooms and bedrooms. Our skillful on-air hosts use demos, explanations, and testimonials to build a high degree of trust and rapport and make DSN a truly personal shopping experience. And because our customers can't actually see or touch the merchandise, there's a critical psychology that comes into play."

"What's that?" Afton asked.

Wagner grinned. "For one thing, we need to sell the sizzle. We need to tell our customers exactly how a product feels, smells, and tastes. We have to give them an emotional rationale on how it will improve their lives and make them feel better. In other words, we give them a good, strong reason to buy. We strive to communicate what psychologists call *permission* to buy. DSN does this right down to the letter, and we do it very, very well."

"This is fascinating stuff," Afton said. She'd never thought about the psychology behind direct-response marketing before, and she decided it wasn't all that different from the hucksters at the state fair who sold lemon juicers and Ginsu knives.

"Have you folks ever been in a studio before?" Wagner asked.

"Never," Afton said, although she'd actually visited two different TV studios when she'd been invited to give quick sound bites for their evening news programs. "We'd love to see what goes on."

"Follow me," Wagner said. He led them down another wide corridor, where dozens of people buzzed about. They passed the wing where offices for all the various buyers were located, and then, as they drew closer to the actual studios, they peered into glass-walled control rooms. Afton also noted the hair-and-makeup studio, wardrobe room, and lounge for on-air hosts.

"And we can go into one of these studios?" Afton asked.

"Yes," Wagner said. "Just remember that we're live on the air. In fact, we're always on air, twenty-four/seven. So try to be as quiet as possible." He pulled open a door, there was a suck of cool air, and then they stepped into darkness.

Afton blinked. The studio was dimly lit and enormous, with a smooth polished floor, dozens of technicians moving cameras and dollies about, and hundreds of klieg lights hanging overhead. There were, in fact, three different sets. The set in the middle, what appeared to be a large frosted pink-glass desk that practically mimicked a counter at an upscale jewelry store, was lit with impossibly bright lights. A dark-haired woman sat there holding up various pieces of jewelry and talking animatedly into a camera. The other two sets were dark, but people in rubber-soled shoes hovered around them, presumably setting up for the next product presentation.

Wagner waved them forward. "Come on," he whispered. "We can get closer if you'd like. Stand right behind Reggie, our floor director."

Afton and Max crept closer and closer, until they were standing right behind the floor director. Reggie wore a set of head-phones, held another set in his hands, and was dividing his time between two large color monitors and a computer console. The first monitor, Afton ascertained, was a direct feed from the camera that captured the show host doing her live on-air presentation. They were using a two-camera setup, cutting back and forth from close-ups to medium-wide shots. The second monitor was filled with all sorts of stats and numbers.

"That's Fan Ling doing her presentation on Dreamweaver gold jewelry," Wagner whispered in Afton's ear. "Fan is one of our premier show hosts."

Afton peered across the studio at Fan Ling. She was a beautiful young Chinese woman with fine almond eyes and a sweep of dark, lush hair. As petite as she was, her excitement could barely be contained as she cooed over a gold necklace with a moonstone pendant.

"And . . . we're going to break in ten," Reggie said into his microphone.

Fan Ling held up the necklace again, said a few more words, and then smiled winningly into the camera.

"And we're out," the floor director said.

On the monitor, a promo for next hour's Confetti Cookware show began to play.

Reggie moved forward toward Fan Ling, who watched him approach with pursed lips and narrowed eyes. "Watch the nipples, Fan," he said. "We're starting to show a little pink."

Fan Ling gave a halfhearted tug at her low-cut black silk blouse, but didn't seem to make any noticeable adjustment.

"Makeup," she said. "Where is makeup?"

A young woman with frizzy red hair rushed onto the set and twirled a brush against Fan Ling's cheek.

"Reggie," Fan Ling said, a note of authority coloring her voice, "what have you heard about Leland?"

"Only that he's still holding his own," Reggie said.

Fan Ling pushed the makeup artist's hand away from her face and peered at Reggie. "Do my eyes look red?"

Reggie shook his head. "No. You're looking good. Everything's reading great on camera."

"You look gorgeous," the red-haired woman practically drooled. Fan Ling turned her head and continued to ignore her.

"What's the story with your on-air host?" Max asked from their spot behind the cameras and lights.

"Oh, you don't know?" Wagner said. "Fan Ling is one of Mr. Odin's discoveries. He was over in China, about a year ago on one of his buying trips. I think he was buying solar-powered garden lights from a repurposed Chinese tractor factory or something like that. Anyway, he got to this shit-hole factory town and apparently Fan Ling was the one bright spot on the entire landscape, the designated English-speaking cupcake. Fan Ling did the dutiful bowing and scraping thing, introduced Odin all around, and translated for him. She ended up ordering his meals, picking him up at his hotel, and sitting in on all his business meetings. She even helped with some of the negotiations, or so the story goes. Anyway, Fan Ling ended up coming back to the Twin Cities with Odin on a private jet."

"Lucky girl," Afton said.

"Four months later, after the voice coaches, makeup artists, and media experts were finished with her, she stepped out of the wings and onto the air," Wagner said.

"Is she good?" Max asked.

Wagner gave a faint smile. "Just watch for a minute."

They watched. Fan Ling was back on the air now. She slid a thick gold bangle onto her wrist, smiled brightly, and shook her wrist enticingly.

"Now take a look at this," Wagner said. He poked a button on the second monitor and suddenly the entire call center appeared. The bank of over two hundred phones had just lit up and operators were bending their heads forward as calls poured in. Murmuring encouragement to customers, they typed credit card numbers and shipping information into their computer terminals as fast as they could.

"Jeez," Max said. "There's a shit load of women calling in to order that bracelet? Just off her little sales pitch?"

Wagner looked pleased. "She's one of our best."

"We need to talk to her," Afton said.

"Not now you can't," Wagner said. "She's live on air for four more hours."

9

Narong sat cross-legged on the floor of his hotel room in a half-lotus position. He'd just finished his meditation, a mindfulness-of-breathing exercise that calmed his thoughts and lowered his heart rate while still helping him sharpen his inner energies. He'd lit a stick of sandalwood incense, and now he relaxed as he inhaled the fragrant scent that reminded him so much of home. Of his small apartment on the Rat Buranda Road just a block from the Chao Phraya River.

His employer, Mom Chao Cherry, had no use for meditation, yet she enjoyed burning a special Chinese sandalwood incense. She was constantly lighting sticks of it and placing them before tiny little statues that she carried around in her designer handbags. Narong didn't know if she was religious, looking for an ancestor to worship, or just a coked-up pseudo Buddhist.

It didn't matter. They were here in America now, with a job to do, and he was determined to do it well.

When he was just a teenager, before his military service, Narong had worked for Mom Chao Cherry's husband. Then the old man had been murdered in some sort of drug war. Narong had heard that Mom Chao Cherry had gone hysterical, pulling out her hair, slashing at her face, swearing to avenge her husband's death.

And he guessed that she probably had, many times over. Mom Chao Cherry was Hi-So, or high society, which meant she had numerous connections with important people and government officials. She was even a personal friend of General Prayuth Chan-ocha, who'd staged a coup d'état in 2014. He was a powerful man who, with one simple order, could send battalions of soldiers into the jungle to wipe out an entire village or gang, or assassinate a drug lord. Or lock down an entire province.

Now Mom Chao Cherry was focused on this man Leland Odin, a man she claimed had stolen great wealth from her. And she was determined to exact revenge in her own careful and creative way.

Narong didn't know how Mom Chao Cherry had learned about Leland Odin's heart, but somehow she had. Her spy net-work, he supposed. Or perhaps even her business network. If you didn't reside near a large port city, didn't come into contact with manufacturing and shipping industries, you would never know that 420 million shipping containers crossed the world's oceans every year. That accounted for bil-lions and billions worth of baht, yuan, dol-lars, yen, drachmas, and euros. It also spun a huge world of contacts (some honest, most not), and led to an enormous degree of theft.

The killing would come soon, Narong thought as he smiled to himself. Drifting into a reverie about guns and soldiers, he was reminded of gun battles in the provinces of Yala and Pattani. Driven into a frenzy by the smell of cordite and blood, their army had fought off insurgents in the hot jungle.

After a while, there was a knock on the door. Narong sprang to his feet and opened the door. Accepted a package delivered by a man in a brown uniform.

He carried the package to his bed and pulled off the wrapping paper. Opened the box and saw what was inside. There was a set of blue scrubs, a white coat, a stetho-scope, and a university hospital ID. And something else that made Narong smile. A set of stainless steel surgical scalpels.

Yes, there was more work to be done. And soon.

10

Thacker was on the prowl. Like a jungle cat looking to sink his teeth into the neck of a nice, tasty springbok, he paced back and forth in the squad room. None of the detectives — or the staff, for that matter — wanted to be his next meal.

"I need information, people," Thacker said in a driving, staccato voice. "Tell me what's going on."

He'd herded Max, Afton, Dick Dillon, and Andy Farmer into a small conference room again. The temperature in the room must have been eighty degrees, the building's old boiler not seeming to be aware of the rising afternoon temps outside. The tension was palpable.

Thacker's head swiveled like a periscope. "Max?"

Max cleared his throat. "We met with Odin's wife, stepdaughter, attorney, and business partner. They all claimed to be clueless. They have no idea who might have been behind the attack on the helicopter."

"Unacceptable," Thacker said. "We need to interview each one separately."

"What they did mention," Max said, "were two potential buyers for DSN."

"The Saudi company and who else?"

Max explained to Thacker, Dillon, and Farmer about Consolidated Sports.

"Dillon," Thacker said, "see what you can find out about this company. Call up the CEO and take a meeting."

"Yes sir," Dillon said.

"And don't be squawking to the media," Thacker said. "Be sure that any questions those jackals ask, and there will be plenty, are routed through our media specialist."

Farmer made a face. Nobody liked Gene Hensen, their media specialist. He had an MBA in mass communications and never let you forget it. He was roundly regarded in the squad room as a horse's ass.

"Now," Thacker said, focusing on Afton and Max, "what'd you guys find out from your talk with Sunny and your trip to DSN headquarters?"

"Not much," Max said. "Everyone seems to be as much in the dark as we are."

"Is it possible we're looking at a case of domestic terrorism?" Dillon asked. "That shooting down the helo was completely unrelated to Leland Odin?"

"Doubtful," Thacker said. "It feels too planned, too premeditated." He glanced at Afton. "I understand that you've already checked with St. Stephen's Medical Center in Madison? Where they harvested the heart?"

"I just spoke to their administrator," Afton said. "A Mr. Hal Boniwell. He claims that only a limited number of medical personnel knew about the heart." She consulted her notes. "Um . . . Dr. Smathers, the attending physician, Dr. Winchester, the surgeon who harvested the heart, two surgical nurses, and an on-staff psychologist who walked the family through the donor process."

Thacker shook his head. "Not good enough. Somebody knew that heart was on its way here."

"But how did they know it was earmarked for Odin?" Dillon wondered out loud.

"Somebody at the university hospital tipped the shooter?" Max said.

"Could have," Thacker said. "We need to get a list of medical personnel who were on last night."

"I already tried that," Farmer said. "It's like pulling teeth."

"Try harder."

"What about the heart-database people?" Afton asked. "The transplant network?"

Thacker pointed at her, snapping his fingers. "Get on that, will you?"

"I'm not supposed to be involved in actual investigations, remember?" Afton said. "You told me I should function only as family liaison officer. And help keep Max's notes straight."

"I said that? Well, let's set that issue aside for now," Thacker said. "The problem is, we're up to our ass in alligators and you happen to be the only person here who has a data-entry background. That means you're the one who's most knowledgeable about researching this transplant-network business." He glanced over at Max. "Max still types with two fingers like he's trying to poke out somebody's eyes. Dillon over there . . . well, don't even ask."

"I'm on it," Afton said.

Afton went back to her cubicle and plopped down in her chair. Researching the transplant network wasn't exactly a plum job, but it's what she'd been assigned. That and keeping Max's notes straight. Max had a laptop that he never used, preferring instead to scratch notes on legal pads, Post-it notes, and paper drink coasters.

She'd found it was easier to gather up his paperwork and retype everything into a more meaningful, cohesive format. Incident report, victim, injuries, witnesses, interviews, probable cause.

Hmm. Probable cause.

Afton wondered why someone would purposely shoot down a helicopter that was transporting a human heart? To destroy that heart? It seemed like a roundabout way of getting to Odin. Then again, if you wanted to drive home a point, there was nothing better than a helo going boom in the night sky. And now four different law enforcement agencies were coming after the perpetrators with as much force as they could muster.

Even though Afton thought the basic underlying motive felt shaky, she knew that motive always lay there like a slumbering beast in the dark basement of the human mind. Anger, greed, money, revenge, political ideology — they were all good contenders for being the prime motivator.

Forcing herself to set thoughts of motive aside, Afton got busy with her research. She clicked through the website for the official transplant organization called OPTN, the Organ Procurement and Transplantation Network. She printed out as much information as she could on that group, then switched over to organizing Max's notes. Once that was done, she went to the website for Consolidated Sports, found their investor relations section, and printed out that information.

Then Afton stood up, stretched, thought about what she'd fix for dinner tonight — maybe hot dogs and beans? — and headed back to Homicide. She sidled up to Max, who was just hanging up his phone, and said, "I've got your notes . . ."

Suddenly, Dick Dillon, who'd stepped out to do god knew what, came racing into the room. Red-faced and bursting with excitement, he yelled out, "The University of Minnesota Police just called. They're pretty sure they've located the shooter's nest!"

Thacker appeared in the doorway like a manic critter who'd just jumped out of a Whac-a-Mole game. "Where is it? Where's the nest?"

"Top floor of some place called the Huang Sheng Noodle Factory," Dillon said. "Over on the West Bank, just off Cedar Avenue."

"Max, you're lead detective," Thacker said. "You take this."

"I know that location," Afton said. "It's right next to the Chelsea Bar." She remembered Huang Sheng as a greasy spoon Chinese restaurant — really a greasy chopstick — that dished up passable Moo Goo Gai Pan and was frequented by U of M students. The fact that it was called a noodle factory was meaningless.

Max jumped up from his chair, almost upending it. "If you know the area, then you're coming along."

"Don't think you two are going to cowboy in all by your lonesome," Thacker warned. "I'm gonna get the Tactical Rescue Squad cranking on this, too. We'll have them gear up and go in first for the initial takedown. Then we'll need the Crime Scene guys. *Then* you guys can go in." He paused. "You say it's a noodle company? Better call INS, too. Have them meet you there. And keep me informed every damn step of the way!"

By the time Afton and Max arrived, it was a full-scale bugout. Tactical's shiny black SUVs crisscrossed the narrow back alley behind the noodle factory, and the crime squad van was there, too. Two uniformed officers and two guys in plain clothes, possibly agents from INS, were conferring with a group of people, probably the kitchen workers. A few women and some kids milled around as well.

"I hope we didn't miss all the fun," Max said as they jumped out of his car. The alley was long and narrow, riddled with potholes. Rusted green Dumpsters with the words JIMBO'S SANITATION stenciled on them stood everywhere. The place smelled of rotting garbage, sour bean sprouts, and old cooking oil. Parked in close to the back door of the restaurant was a bright red BMW 550i with a gold tassel hanging from the rearview mirror.

At the exact moment Afton and Max climbed from the car, a young man suddenly exploded from the group and ran, arms pumping like pistons, full speed down the back alley.

"Whoa!" Max yelled out. "We've got a runner."

The younger of the two uniformed officers turned and took off after the guy and charged down the alley. He disappeared around the side of a redbrick building that had an old-timey label of Busker Czech-Style Pilsner painted on the side.

"What's going on?" Max asked the officer who was left behind. He had a handlebar moustache that probably skirted the bounds of regulations, and his name tag said L. JUSTER.

"Is this the shooter's nest?" Afton asked.

"That's the word I'm hearing," Juster said.

"Can we take a look upstairs?" Afton

asked Max. No need to be blasé. She was dying to go up and see for herself. This type of investigation was brand-new to her, and she found it exhilarating as hell.

"Let's see if they're ready for us," Max said.

"Hey, Randy," Juster called out from behind them. "Looks like you just got your ass handed to you."

Randy, the young officer who'd taken off after the runner, was limping back all by himself. His shoulders were hunched forward and his tongue was hanging out. He looked like he'd just run the thousand-yard dash against Usain Bolt. And lost.

Sergeant Gene Scheffler from the University of Minnesota Police Department met them at the second-floor landing. After handshakes and hasty introductions Max said, "What'd you find?"

"Your tech guys are the ones who narrowed down the trajectory and pinpointed this place," Scheffler said. "We had it figured down to about five blocks either way. But you know, we're not exactly Imperial Storm-troopers who can go crashing in anywhere we want. We let your tactical guys have that honor."

"They're up there now?" Max asked.

Scheffler nodded. "Yup. Tactical and Crime Scene. Anyway, UMPD got here first because we were closer; our Transportation and Safety Building is just across the river. We sat on this place until your guys arrived."

"You think this is right?" Max asked. He was jittery and bursting with excitement. "That this is where the assassin shot from?"

"Oh, yeah," Scheffler said. "No doubt about it. When tactical went in first and cleared the place, they figured it out right away."

"The people milling around out back," Afton said. "They all live here?"

"I guess," Scheffler said. "Tactical herded a few women and a bunch of kids down from the second and third floors. I think most of the men work at the restaurant downstairs. Or maybe they showed up from someplace else. Who knows?"

"And the shooter's nest?" Max asked.

"Third floor, room at the end of the hall," Scheffler said.

"Now can we take a look?" Afton asked. She was as antsy as Max.

"Crime Scene's been in there for a while, so it's probably okay," Scheffler said. "But lemme go ask."

Scheffler was back a minute later. "It's

cool," he said. "Go on up."

Afton and Max walked up another flight of steps, then down a hallway lit with bright lights on stanchions that the Crime Scene guys had brought in. Along the way, Afton peered into what looked like bunkrooms. They were all tiny, cramped, and dirty.

Joe Jelenick, one of the crime scene analysts, met them at the door. He was a skinny, redheaded guy, a marathon runner who was constantly training and always anxious to discuss split times and running strategies. LSD, he'd once advised Afton when she'd expressed interest in running. Long, slow distances; that's where it was at. He'd run Grandma's Marathon in Duluth and the Twin Cities Marathon, and he talked constantly about running the Boston Marathon. Got misty-eyed, in fact, when he spoke about Heartbreak Hill.

"This is it?" Max asked Jelenick. They were old friends and had worked together on any number of cases.

Jelenick walked to the window and flapped a scarecrow hand. "We think the rocket was fired from right here. We can't prove it, of course, but some pretty smart math geeks worked on this, and that's what the trajectory seemed to indicate. And take a look out this window. You see how there's a perfect view across the river to the helipad?"

Afton and Max took turns peering out the window.

"It is perfect," Max said.

"This is it. This is the place," Afton said. The window afforded a bird's-eye view directly across the slow-moving river, right up a leafy green riverbank to the University of Minnesota Medical Center and their private helicopter landing pad. She turned to Jelenick. "Did you find anything? Any evidence that can be linked to the shooters? Cartridges? Gunpowder residue?"

"Candy wrappers?" Max asked. He'd once linked a fingerprint on a Snickers bar to a late-night stick-up guy.

"The window slides up and down, slick as shit," Jelenick said. "So it's been greased. There are fingerprints on the frame, so we'll take those and run them through the FBI's IAFIS. As far as any other stuff, it was pretty clean in here." He chuckled softly. "Well, clean if you don't count the dust balls, mouse droppings, and various bits of crud we scraped up. We didn't find anything that said X marks the spot, but there's usually *something* left behind. Gotta be powder residue with an explosion like that, so we'll be collecting some of that. And we did find a cigarette butt out in the hallway."

"Cigarette butt," Max said. "Might not amount to much. Could belong to anybody." He was clearly disappointed by the lack of actionable evidence.

"Then again, it could be useful," Afton said. "You never know."

"Either way," Jelenick said, "we'll take it all back and have it tested." Jelenick was a testing freak. He loved his electron microscope, his DNA sequencer, and his mass spectrometer, and he had affectionately named his bloodstain and spatter viewer Bloody Mary.

Afton stood at the window and thought about the shooter, who'd aimed his rocket launcher out this same window just last night. More than a dozen years ago, long before Poppy and Tess had arrived, she'd been knocking around the Gunflint Trail, teaching outdoor survival and guiding canoe trips. She'd worked with a guy there, an outfitter named Roy Donaldson, who'd been trained at the U.S. Army Sniper School at Fort Benning in Georgia. Roy had taken her out to a range once and taught her a few shooting basics. Schooled her in battlefield intelligence, stalking, and long-range precision firing. Ever since then she'd figured that if somebody *wanted* to shoot you, and they possessed the basic skills, there was nothing you could do about it. Like it or not, Kevlar vest or not, you were gonna get nailed.

"We have to go downstairs and put the screws to those kitchen workers," Max said. "See how much they know."

"If they know anything," Jelenick said. He subscribed to the theory that witnesses were completely unreliable, and that blood spatter, gunpowder residue, and trace evidence were what broke cases and won convictions.

11

The owner of the Huang Sheng Noodle Factory, a smiley, round-faced guy named Zhang, didn't much want to talk. He crossed his arms across his bright green sport shirt, rocked back on his heels, and, for all practical purposes, zipped his lips.

"No problem," Max told him. "You don't want to cooperate with us, we can arrest you right now as an accomplice to murder. Then you can cool your heels in jail for a couple of days while we sort this out."

"Under arrest?" Zhang's reserve suddenly crumpled and his face pinched into a worried expression. "No, that can't be."

"Sure it can," Max said in a friendly voice. "Face it, pal, you're going down."

Zhang shook his head and tried to smile back. "No."

Max did a Groucho Marx with his eyebrows. "Exactly which part of this don't you understand?"

Zhang touched a hand to his chest. "I'm a businessman. I run a restaurant."

"While you were whipping up a pot of Kung Pao Chicken, you were also aiding and abetting a couple of murderers."

"No murder," Zhang said.

"Don't forget the flophouse," Afton said.

"Thank you," Max said. He turned back to Zhang. "And you're running an illegal flophouse upstairs."

"Hotel," Zhang said. "It's no secret. We advertise in the *Southeast Asian Times.*"

"Okay," Max said. "So it's not a secret. But it's still illegal."

"Wait, please, wait one minute," Zhang said.

"Yes?" Max said.

"We can help each other, right?"

"I think he wants to deal," Afton said.

"That's right, a deal," Zhang said, bobbing his head.

"First you have to tell us everything," Max said. "Then we'll see what kind of, um, accommodation we're willing to make. So . . . last night. Your so-called hotel had a couple of guests."

"Two people," Zhang said. "One young, one old." He lifted his shoulders in a gesture almost akin to an apology. "All I know is they wanted to stay one night. Top floor, end room. That's it."

"But these people didn't stay the night, did they?" Max said.

Zhang shrugged again. "I don't know when they left. I don't keep track."

"Maybe right after that big helicopter fell out of the sky and went boom?" Afton said.

Zhang furrowed his brow, pretending to think. "My memory is not so good, and we were very busy last night."

"Were these people armed?" Max asked. "Do you know if they carried weapons?"

"Like a rocket launcher?" Afton pantomimed a rocket launcher.

Zhang understood the reference right away. He nodded and smiled. "Bang," he said. "Bang bang."

"Yeah, right," Afton said.

"So a young guy and an old guy," Max said.

Zhang frowned. "No, a young man and an old woman."

"An old *woman*?" Max said, suddenly caught off guard. He turned to face Afton. "A woman? How the hell would that figure in?"

"The shooter's mother?" Afton said. "He's a dutiful son who takes mom along on jobs? Who knows?"

"Were they Caucasian or Asian?" Max asked.

"I think Asian," Zhang said. "But I didn't get a good look at the woman."

"And you don't know who these people were?" Max asked. "Mr. Zhang, you're going to have to do a whole lot better than that. We need to get some kind of identification on these two shooters and we need it right away. They killed two men and caused a huge accident that severely injured several people."

"How did these two people get here?" Afton asked. "Did they come in a car or did they just show up on foot?"

"I don't know," Zhang said. "I really don't know."

"Do you have a security camera?" Afton asked.

Zhang looked at her as if she were nuts. "What for? Because one of my kitchen workers might steal a ten-pound block of tofu?" He wandered away, looking unhappy and put out.

"Excuse me." Someone tapped Afton on the shoulder. She turned to find a young Chinese man in a golf shirt and stone-washed jeans gazing at her.

"Yes?" she said. "Who are you?"

"I'm Sammy Mah," he said. "I wash

104

dishes and help prep some of the food here." He glanced sideways and eyeballed Zhang. "Except I'm guessing that, after I talk to you, I'm probably out of a job."

"You know anything about what went on here last night?" Afton asked as Max sidled in to join them.

"A little bit," Sammy said. "More than he does anyway." He nodded in the direction of the owner, Zhang. "I don't give a crap about that guy. He's been screwing me blind. Screwing all the people who work here. Most of us are enrolled in school, at the University of Minnesota or Augsburg. The others have green cards, so we're legal. But this *piyan* . . ."

"What's a *piyan*?" Afton asked.

Sammy grinned. "An asshole."

"That's a word that seems to translate fairly well in any language," Max said.

"He's been paying us off the books," Sammy said. "Paying us shit."

"Did you see the two people who were here last night?" Afton asked. "The man and the woman?"

"I didn't see their faces," Sammy said. "But after I dropped a couple bags of garbage into the Dumpster on my way home, I might have caught a look at their car."

"Why didn't you speak up sooner?" Max asked. "We had squads running all over this neighborhood last night."

"Because I wasn't here last night. I left around seven." Sammy looked worried. "I didn't hear about the helicopter crash until this afternoon."

"But you think you might have seen their car," Afton said. "How is that possible? You say you walked past it as you were leaving?"

"I catch the bus just up on Cedar Avenue, and I saw a car with a driver sitting at the curb. The driver gave off this kind of nervous attitude, as if he was waiting for someone." Sammy held up his hands in a cautionary gesture. "I'm making an assumption now that the car was waiting for the two people you're asking about."

"Can you describe the driver?" Max asked.

Sammy shook his head. "I never really saw his face."

"What did the car look like?" Afton asked.

"Midsize sedan, red in color. But faded red, like it had been left out in the sun too much and the paint had oxidized."

"That's it?" Max asked. "There must be a million beat-up red cars on the road. Was it a Ford, a Buick, a . . . ?"

"It just caught my eye for a couple of seconds," Sammy said. "So I don't know the make or model."

"Not so fast," Afton said. "There must have been something about it that made you take a longer look at it."

"I don't think so," Sammy said. "I think I remember it just because it was parked there. And the driver was kind of jittering around inside."

"Maybe the license plate?" Afton pressed. "A sequence of numbers that caught your eye? Maybe a bumper sticker or something?"

Sammy's brows puckered. "I could have seen . . . I saw . . . what would you call it, on the back window? A sticky? A sticker?"

"A decal?" Max said.

Sammy shot a finger at him. "Yes, I think maybe so."

"What was the design?" Afton asked. "Like, maybe from one of the colleges? Or one of the hospitals?" There were a university, two colleges, and four different hospitals in the surrounding area, and she figured they all issued decals for access to their parking facilities.

But Sammy was shaking his head. "No, it wasn't a university or hospital design. It didn't have that academic look to it. It was more . . . artsy."

"Artsy?" Max said. "What's that supposed

to mean?"

"What kind of artsy?" Afton asked. "Can you describe it?"

Sammy closed his eyes as if trying to reconstruct the image. Finally, he said, "Maybe blue? With wings?"

"Blue with wings," Max said. "Air force?"

"I don't know," Sammy said.

"We need to get with the FBI," Afton said to Max. "They maintain a database of all sorts of logos, insignias, symbols, and hallmarks."

"How do we get in touch with you?" Max asked. "If we need you to look at a couple of images? Maybe even as early as tomorrow?"

"Mobile phone," Sammy said. "Here, I'll give you my number."

They sent Zhang downtown in a squad car. Not because he was under arrest, but because they wanted to hook him up with a sketch artist while his memory was still relatively fresh and he would hopefully recall a few more details.

Max got on the phone and called Thacker, told him all about the raid, Zhang the restaurant owner, and Sammy Mah. When Afton climbed into Max's car, he said, "I'd like to take a run over to that high-rise apartment. The one where the student who shot the video lives. His name is . . ." He squeezed his eyes shut, trying to conjure it up.

"Jason Wold. He's getting his master's degree in computer science."

"And you have the address?" Max asked.

Afton riffled through her notebook. "Yeah, I got it right here. And I want to go along."

"Awright," Max said. "Why not?"

Just as Max started up his engine, another van rolled in. This one was shiny white with a large dish on top and a red swath across its side that read NEWSWATCH 7.

"So, what are we waiting for?" Afton asked. She shoved her notebook in her bag, glanced up, noticed the TV van, and muttered, "Crap."

Portia Bourgoyne, a features reporter for Channel 7, had just jumped out of the passenger seat and was looking around for someone to nail. Afton and Max had had run-ins with Portia before, and they hadn't been pleasant. Portia had the temperament of a pit viper.

Portia saw Max easing his car forward and made a beeline for him just as he tried to sneak past her van without being spotted. Too late. Portia was already tapping on his side window, smiling her fake newsperson smile.

"Portia's like a T. rex," Afton said. "A genuine man-eater. But if you don't move, she can't see you."

"Detective. Oh, Detective," Portia called out. She was wearing a stylish white wool skirt suit and had her long blond hair done up in a messy topknot. On anyone else, that hairdo would look legitimately messy; on Portia it looked like she'd tumbled out of bed, fresh from a lusty encounter. Which, of course, was the perfect pseudo-sexy look for any female TV reporter who was hot on the heels of a good story.

"Shit. I think she can see me," Max said. "So much for the T. rex theory."

"Tell her we're in a hurry."

Max's window slid down an inch. "I can't talk right now," he told Portia. "Something on our case just broke." He eased his car forward another few inches.

"What you're breaking is my ass," Portia spit out. "I missed the five and probably the six. At least throw me *something* for the ten o'clock."

"No can do," Max said.

"Your media guy, Gene Hensen, told me to . . ."

"Screw Gene Hensen," Max said as he slid

110

the window back up. Then he put his car in reverse and slowly backed down the alley. They could see Portia's lips moving as they pulled away. The girl could swear like the proverbial sailor.

"Look, Portia's nostrils are flaring," Afton said. "That girl is mad as hell."

"She can sit and spin," Max said. He backed all the way down the narrow alley, made a K-turn, and then sped down the block. "So can Gene Hensen." He stopped at a stop sign before turning onto Riverside. "Which way?"

"Left. About ten blocks down. You'll know it when you see it. It's a fancy-schmancy high-rise. Got a doorman and everything."

"This is some place," Max said when Jason Wold let them into his eighteenth-floor apartment. Wold's place wasn't your typical grad student abode; it looked more like a corporate executive lived there. Swoopy, designer-style furniture, an Aubusson carpet that had to have run at least two grand, bookcases with hardbound books instead of dog-eared paperbacks.

"Just out of curiosity," Max said, "how can you afford a nice apartment like this?"

Afton was impressed, too. When she was going to school, she'd lived with three other girls in a scuzzy old pile-of-rocks apartment near the Tenth Avenue Bridge that they called the Anthill.

"My dad is rich," Wold said matter-of-factly, as if he was talking about the sky being blue.

"Must be nice," Max said.

"Yeah, it is," Wold said. He was twenty-two, serious looking, and outfitted head-to-toe in Tommy Hilfiger.

Afton and Max stepped out onto his balcony and gazed across the wide blue ribbon that formed the Mississippi River. Wold's balcony afforded a sweeping, unobstructed view of the university hospital's complex, which was composed of a series of several different buildings, all set at differing heights. There was a good view of the helicopter pad, too, tucked right in the middle of it all.

An afternoon sun, as bright and bitter as a Seville orange, burned low in the western sky, its lengthening rays lighting up the windows of the hospital like golden tiles.

"Jeez," Max grunted. "No wonder his video captured the whole damn thing."

"You know what we should do now, don't you?" Max asked when they were back in his car.

"Go home and drink ourselves into a stupor?" Afton said. "Oh, wait. Silly me. I've got book club tonight."

"Knowing you, you probably talked your book club ladies into reading some true crime."

"You're one to talk. You bought the boxed DVD set of *Criminal Minds.*" Afton paused. "But you were saying . . ."

Max stared at her. "I think we should take a side trip over to the university hospital."

"To talk to . . . ?"

"Leland Odin."

"I thought Odin was dying," Afton said. "I thought his heart was on its final blip, like an old Frogger video game that was low on battery power."

"Look," Max said. "The guy might be on life support, but who better for us to question than the victim himself? Think about it. If we can ask him directly who his number one enemy is, maybe we can figure out this whole thing."

"And you want me along for the victim's-advocate part? The sensitivity part?"

"That, and because you're smart," Max said, a slight harshness coloring his voice. "I think someday you're going to make a hell of a good detective."

"Look, I'm flattered by your high hopes

for my career trajectory. But it's getting late. I gotta go home and fix dinner for my kids."

"Isn't your sister there?" Max asked. "Can't she handle it?"

Afton thought for a couple of moments. "I suppose." She knew this *could* yield some critical information. She pulled out her phone and dialed her home number. When her sister, Alisha, answered, she said, "I'm going to be late tonight. Can you make burgers for the little muggles?"

Next to her, Max lifted an eyebrow. "Muggles?"

Afton ignored him. "Yeah, it's been defrosting in the fridge. Okay, thanks. I'll be home as soon as I can."

12

Leland Odin felt like a five-hundred-pound weight was pressing down on his chest. Every time he took a breath, it hurt. Every time he tried to move, it hurt even worse. Lying on his back, his eyes misting over with tears, he couldn't believe how his life had spiraled downward. He was an invalid now, probably a dying man, trapped in a web of nonstop pain.

How could this be happening to him? He was Leland Odin, for Christ's sake, a powerful man, a power broker. He'd sat in the boardrooms of Fortune 500 companies and traded dirty jokes with the Twin Cities' most elite movers and shakers. He'd knocked back thirty-year-old Scotch like it was Hires root beer and smoked Cohibas smuggled in from Cuba, compliments of Raul. He belonged to Minnewashta Country Club, an uptight, white-bread Episcopalian golf club where you practically had to be *born* into upper-crust Wayzata society to be considered for membership.

So what if his father had been a postal clerk and his mother a homemaker? He himself had worked two jobs to pay his way through the University of Minnesota, eventually graduating with a degree in business. He'd climbed corporate ladders, then struck out on his own and built a multimillion-dollar enterprise.

He was a rock god of retail, for crying out loud. Not some stupid, pathetic invalid with a plastic bag full of urine hanging off the side of his bed.

The heart transplant had been his one big shining hope. The entire time they'd been prepping him last night, he'd been planning his triumphant return. His second coming.

And when the news came that the helicopter had crashed and his heart had been lost, all hopes were dashed. As the orderlies were wheeling him back to his room, he'd overheard them talking, whispering among themselves that the helicopter had possibly been *shot down.*

That's when he knew. As sure as shit, Leland Odin knew who was responsible for his heart being destroyed. Dr. Graham had come to him last night to tell him the terrible news in person. And even though Odin had been bleary from drugs and gagging against the pain, he'd known immediately who had masterminded the helicopter crash. Who had crushed his hopes of ever being made whole again.

Odin shifted his shoulders slightly and every nerve and fiber within his chest strummed with pain. It felt like a demon was crouching inside his chest, barbecuing his ribs and pouring on the hot sauce.

He cursed that bitch. Wished he hadn't stupidly dismissed her as just another crazy, addle-headed woman. But he'd made a move against her, against her organization. Now she was coming after him like some kind of evil black scorpion that had crawled out of a steaming hot jungle.

What could he do? Nothing. How could he defend himself? He couldn't. Certainly not like this. There was security on the floor, but that meant nothing these days. Just some half-assed rent-a-cop.

And what about Barber? Odin wondered. Now Barber was in just as deep as he was. Would the hell bitch come after Barber, too?

What to do about it? Warn his partner? Or hope that . . .

"Mr. Odin."

Someone was standing over him. Talking to him in a soft, patient voice. He turned his head and cracked open his eyes. They felt sticky and rimmed with grit.

"You have a visitor," the nurse said.

He fought to make his lips form an oval. "Who?"

Then, like a vision from a Botticelli painting, Fan Ling tiptoed into his room. She touched a cool hand to his forehead and said, "I'm here, darling."

"You've got two minutes," the nurse whispered. "You shouldn't even be here."

Odin watched as Fan Ling's hand dipped into her handbag, pulled out a wad of bills, and passed them to the nurse. He waited until the door closed behind her, then he crooked a gnarled finger at Fan Ling. She leaned over his bed.

Odin's spindly white fingers crawled across the blanket to touch Fan Ling on her arm. "You're so beautiful," he croaked.

"I love you, darling," Fan Ling whispered to him. "You are my everything."

"God forbid . . ." Odin tapped his chest weakly. "If there isn't another heart . . ." He stopped abruptly. The look of sadness that swept across Fan Ling's face told him all he needed to know. There probably wouldn't be another heart. Not one that would arrive in time anyway. He'd been told there were something like three thousand people on the general transplant list in Minnesota alone. He didn't know how the logistics worked. Had he been kicked to the back of the line now? He wanted to ask his doctor for an answer, but was deathly afraid of what that answer would be.

"Listen to me," Odin whispered. It took all his strength. His head was spinning as he gasped for air, his vision narrowing and going dark.

"What is it?" Fan Ling sounded so sorrowful as her face hovered above him.

"If I should . . ." Odin gasped in pain. "You need . . . account number."

Fan Ling leaned forward and pursed her lips. "Account number?" Her voice was suddenly a shade brighter.

"Lockbox," Odin wheezed.

"Nothing's going to happen to you," Fan Ling whispered. "You must never think the worst." But she leaned in even closer as Odin gasped out the numbers, hastily committing them to memory, making sure they were etched permanently in her brain.

13

Afton followed Max through the sliding glass entrance doors of the university hospital. The place was less than two blocks from the street where so many people had been injured the previous night, and the scars of that conflict were still evident: flapping yellow police tape, scorch marks on the pavement, upturned earth from where emergency vehicles had slewed to a stop and their nubby tires had dug in.

"It's getting late," Afton said. "Won't visiting hours be over?"

"When you're rich like Leland Odin, the same rules don't apply," Max said.

"Must be nice."

They paused at the information desk, where a middle-aged woman with short curly hair, bright red cat's-eye glasses, and a name tag that read MAVIS was talking on the phone.

". . . you take the Huron exit off I-94, then

go north until you get to Fulton," Mavis explained. She smiled nervously when she noticed Afton and Max watching her. Held up a finger as she continued to give directions.

Afton shifted from one foot to the other. Now that they were here, now that she'd agreed to come along with Max, she was more than a little impatient to talk to Leland Odin. From everything she knew, time was critical. What's more, Odin's family and business associates seemed to know little to nothing about any enemies that Odin had made — or maybe they just weren't telling. Afton was beginning to suspect the latter. It seemed nearly impossible that Odin wouldn't have stepped on more than a few toes, or even crushed a few people like bugs. If he was that big a player, chances were he was also a corporate thug.

"Yes?" Mavis said. Max was holding up his police ID and she was beginning to look nervous.

"We're here to see Leland Odin," Max said.

Mavis shook her head and pursed her lips together like a good bureaucrat. "We're not allowed to give out that information," she said. "It's confidential."

"This is a police investigation," Max said.

He showed her his ID, then slid a business card out of his wallet and handed it to her. "Perhaps you'd care to call downtown and speak to my supervisor, Deputy Chief Gerald Thacker . . ."

"Or even the city attorney," Afton offered. "I know he's taken a personal interest in this case." There was nothing like a good tag-team act to bump open a few doors.

Mavis flicked the card between her thumb and forefinger as she thought for a second. Then she said, "The VIP floor is on eleven."

Max smiled. "Thank you."

"They have a VIP floor?" Afton asked as they rode up in the elevator.

"Yup. Fat cats have their own area in the hospital. I guess senators and CEOs don't care to share a room or shuffle down the hallway with their asses hanging out the backs of their hospital gowns."

The elevator dinged, the doors slid open, and Afton stepped out onto a hospital floor that she never dreamed existed. The floors were covered in thick dove gray carpeting instead of durable linoleum, the walls were hung with colorful original artwork, and the lighting was low and inviting, much like in an elegant restaurant. A six-foot-high water fountain dribbled water over copper water lilies as it tinkled out calming notes.

"This feels more like a spa than a hospital," Afton said.

"There's even room service," Max said. "You can order a cup of tea and crumpets instead of settling for Jell-O and oatmeal served on metal cafeteria trays."

"You've been here before."

"Just once. When one of our illustrious pro athletes shot himself in the leg with his own gun right in the middle of the dance floor at Glow. You remember that swanky night club down by the Target Center where all the beautiful people went to dance and snort blow?"

"Can't say I ever made it to that place." Although Afton figured her ex-husband Mickey probably had. Numerous times.

At the nurses' station, directly in front of them, a pair of young women dressed in identical light blue scrubs sat behind the desk. They were talking in hushed tones as they both pecked away at keyboards.

As Afton and Max approached the nurses' desk, a security guard came out of a nearby room and stepped in front of them. "Help you?" he said. He was carrying a steaming cup of coffee and looked like he might be on break.

Max pivoted toward the guard and pulled out his ID once again. "I'm Detective Max

Montgomery and this is Family Liaison Officer Afton Tangler. We just dropped by to see if we could speak to Leland Odin."

The guard, a behemoth with brush cut hair, blew on his hot coffee. "I understand the man's pretty sick. Not sure the docs want him disturbed."

"We're not going to disturb him," Afton said in a pleasant voice. "We're just checking on him as part of our ongoing investigation into the helicopter crash."

The guard, who looked like he'd probably played pro football at one time, nodded. "You think somebody engineered that crash on purpose? That's the scuttlebutt I've been hearing around here."

"We think that's exactly what happened," Max said.

One of the nurses at the desk glanced up and said, "Do you need me, Joey?"

"No, I got this," the guard said. He tipped his cup at Max in a friendly manner. "Lots of investigating going on tonight," he said in a quiet voice.

"Excuse me?" Max said.

"Your guy, Odin. He just had a visitor an hour or so ago."

"Who was it?" Afton asked.

The guard shrugged. "Girlfriend?"

"You sure it wasn't his wife?" Afton asked.

"Or his stepdaughter?"

"Mmn . . . pretty sure."

"What did this girlfriend look like?" Max asked.

"Pretty Asian lady. Maybe Chinese."

Afton stared at Max. "Fan Ling," she said.

"And she was here when?" Max asked.

"Like I said, about an hour ago."

"Mr. Odin was awake then?" Afton asked.

Joey shook his head. "I don't know. I don't generally go into the patient rooms. Access is only for the docs and the nurses. And, I guess, for visitors."

"You're on break right now?" Max asked.

Joey nodded. "Just came off break."

Max glanced over at the nurses' desk, where they seemed to be busy again. "Maybe you could stretch it out a little bit? And you wouldn't mind if we wandered in and tried to talk to our guy?"

Joey thought for a moment and then said, "I guess that'd be okay. Not much going on here anyway. Just don't let the docs catch you."

"Which room is Odin in?" Afton asked.

"Eleven-E," Joey said. "Um . . . that Fan Ling woman, she's very good-looking."

"She works for Odin," Max said.

Joey grinned. "I had a feeling she does more than work for him."

■ ■ ■ ■

Afton and Max headed down a long, softly lit corridor that ended at an exit door. Carpet whispered under their feet, mahogany doors opened into hospital suites that were twice the size of standard hospital rooms. In fact, when they peeked into a door that had been left ajar, the room looked like something you'd find at a five-star hotel.

"Which room did he say?" Max asked. They'd just passed 11-B.

"Eleven-E," Afton said. She was glancing at the artwork that hung on the walls as they walked along. "Holy smokes," she said, stopping in front of a photo. "Look at this."

Max peered at the large, framed color photo. "It's the cherry and spoon sculpture from the Walker's sculpture garden. So?"

Afton tapped a finger against the glass. "This particular photo was shot by a very famous architectural photographer. His work hangs in the Minneapolis Institute of Art."

"Yeah? You're a photo aficionado?"

"Like I keep telling my kids, art nourishes the soul," Afton said. "But what I really can't believe is that they have . . . what?

One, two, three of his photos here."

"Maybe they're all on loan," Max said.

"Or maybe the university's decorator spared no expense. No wonder they keep jacking up the tuition. By the time Tess and Poppy get here, it'll probably be a hundred grand a semester."

"I wonder if Jake will *ever* get here," Max said.

Just as they reached Suite 11-E, a man in a pristine white coat came sliding out of the door. He wore a stethoscope around his neck and looked grimly serious.

"Excuse me, doc?" Max said. He hastily showed the doctor his identification and then asked, "How's Mr. Odin doing?"

The doctor turned his concerned look on them. His name tag read DR. SANCHEZ. CARDIOLOGY.

"Mr. Odin is a very sick man," Sanchez said, shaking his head. "We just put him on a dobutamine drip and now he's sleeping. I'm going to have a private nurse sit with him to make sure his respiration and heart rate don't escalate any further."

"Is there any way we can get in there and ask him a question or two?"

"Not at this time," the doctor said. "I'm afraid any undue stress or disturbance could be fatal. And if his pulse rises above one

127

hundred and twenty beats a minute, we'll need to halt inotropic therapy."

Max squinted at him. "That all translates to . . . ?"

"We're giving him meds to make his heartbeat stronger and keep his kidneys functioning," Dr. Sanchez said.

Max nodded. "Gotcha."

"Thank you, Doctor," Afton said.

They turned, walked back in the direction of the nurse's station, and stopped. Afton glanced back over her shoulder. "Hold it."

"What?" Max asked. "What are you thinking?" He knew darned well what she was thinking but he had to ask anyway.

"Maybe a tiny peek wouldn't hurt?"

"You sure about that?" Max asked.

"No, but if he's been talking to a hoochie momma like Fan Ling, apparently the old boy's not dead yet. Who knows? Maybe he's been reinvigorated thanks to her ministrations. Or maybe that doctor stuck him full of some miracle drug."

Afton and Max backtracked down the hallway.

"Where'd that doctor disappear to anyway?" Afton asked.

"Must have gone in some other fat cat's room."

They paused outside the door to Odin's

room. The private nurse was nowhere in sight yet.

"This was your idea, you know," Afton said. "I mean, initially."

"So you're going to blame me if we kill him? If we jolt him into having a heart attack?"

"No, we'll share equally."

"Okay. Deal."

Afton put a hand on the doorknob and pushed the door open slowly. "Mr. Odin?" she said in a soft voice. "Hello?"

The inside of the room was hushed and dim. Odin was lying in bed motionless under a pile of white blankets. Large machines surrounded his bed, blinking and beeping, flashing numbers, producing ragged green lines that blipped across a screen, disappeared, then came back across the screen again.

"Mr. Odin?" Afton said.

"Looks like he really is asleep," Max whispered.

They stood there for a few seconds, but Odin didn't move. Didn't twitch a muscle.

"At least we gave it a fair shot," Max said. "C'mon, this guy's all doped up. We won't get anything out of him tonight."

Afton hesitated. Something felt wrong. What was it? She wasn't sure, but deep down in her psyche she felt a tickle of unease. Odin seemed quiet enough, but she'd detected a strange, low hissing sound. One of the machines, perhaps?

"Come on," Max whispered. He was silhouetted in the doorway.

"It feels like . . . Is he really okay?" Afton asked.

As if triggered by Afton's sudden apprehension, one of the machines began to beep. Seconds later, it brayed out a high-pitched, urgent warning sound.

"What the hell?" Max said, taking a step into the room.

Her heart in her throat, Afton gazed in terror at the screeching machine. Numbers — were these supposed to indicate Odin's heart rate? — flashed by in rapid succession. Forty-six, then thirty-eight, then thirty-two, descending ever lower, tumbling quickly, ticking off like a digital clock at an Olympic time trial. *What's happening?* Afton wondered. Was Odin's heart rate in free fall even as they were standing here?

"I think he's . . ." Max began, but Afton had already taken a step closer to Odin's bed.

And that's when she saw it. Something dark and wet and sticky pooling right beneath his head!

Afton ripped back the covers just as Odin lifted his head and great gluts of blood began to spray like a faucet.

"Jesus," Afton gasped. "He's been cut."

Odin's eyes were half-open now, forming dark pools of pain. His lips were pulled back in a bizarre rictus and even though the machines were still going crazy, there was a steady, low hiss, like air being let out of a balloon.

"Son of a bitch!" Max yelped. He sprang forward and placed his hands against the thin red line that continued to spurt blood, trying to apply some pressure.

"We gotta get help," Afton barked as she grappled for the buzzer to call the nurse. "Have them get a crash cart in here. A doctor." She hesitated a split-second as comprehension finally dawned. "I think that doctor . . ." Then Afton spun past Max and pounded down the hallway. "I'm gonna go after . . ." Her words floated back to Max. ". . . that son of a bitch Sanchez."

She saw the crash cart heading for Odin's room, saw the grim, determined looks on the two nurses' faces. Then she turned left and headed for the exit door. She was making a guess, one she knew could be off base, but she decided to take that chance anyway. She burst through the door at the end of the hallway and threw herself into the narrow stairwell.

Had he gone this way?

Afton paused to listen. Maybe three or four flights below her, she could hear loud footsteps banging down the metal stairs. Going like crazy. *Yes! It has to be him!*

Afton hammered down the steps two at a time, sending up her own echo that reverberated loudly in the cement stairwell. Her knees absorbed the shock as she rushed down the first four flights, then started to protest. Her thighs began to burn and she gasped for breath. Her hand clutched the rail at each numbered landing as she flung herself around to the left and continued to descend. Just like Odin's heart rate, the numbers painted on the inside of the stairwell doors got lower and lower.

Minutes later, Afton burst out of the door at the bottom of the stairwell and staggered into a large maintenance room. It was jammed with gray plastic carts and large green Dumpsters. Overhead fluorescent lights illuminated the cinderblock room with a harsh, jaundiced glare. She surveyed the room.

Nobody here.

Her heart hammered inside her chest as a fresh jolt of adrenaline flooded her veins and urged her to keep going.

Gonna catch this son of a bitch!

Bolting past the Dumpsters, Afton saw a bunch of tools leaning against the wall. She grabbed a cultivating rake that had a long handle and four curved metal tines as she rushed past, then pushed open another exit door and found herself on a large cement loading dock. A cool wind whooshed around her, and stars sparkled in the black sky overhead. She lifted the rake above her head and did a clumsy pirouette, scanning in all directions. That's when she saw the two men standing there, dressed in blue scrubs and smoking cigarettes. The red tips of the cigarettes glowed like beacons in the night.

"Did a man just come flying out this door?" she barked at them.

A tall, stooped-shouldered man with a surgeon's paper cap on his head gave her a curious, detached look and nodded tiredly as he lifted an arm in the direction of the main campus. "Yeah, he took off that way."

14

Narong glanced back over his shoulder as he ran toward campus. He'd already stripped off the white coat and balled it up in his hands. Now he stepped out onto Washington Avenue, dodged a city bus and then a red Prius, and finally skipped his way across the busy street. A cement garbage can sat on the sidewalk dead ahead of him. Excellent. He swerved to a stop, stuffed the lab coat into the trash can, and breathed a sigh of relief.

But no.

He glanced back and there she was. That stupid woman. Caught like a rabbit in the headlights of a bus that had just pulled to the curb. The woman who'd clattered after him all the way down the stairwell. He could see her now across the street, balancing some kind of stick in her hands, bobbing and weaving her way through a throng of people who'd just piled off the bus. He thought he'd lost her, but there she was. Foolish to follow him.

Narong knew exactly what he would do. Kill her. Slit her throat from ear to ear just like he'd done with the old man. He'd killed several women in his short career as an assassin, so there wasn't any kind of ethical decision to make. He just had to lure her into a dark place. His skill and knife work would take care of the rest.

Afton sprinted across the front lawn of the hospital, bounded into the street, and skidded to a stop. A blaring horn sounded as a speeding car blew past her, almost clipping her.

"What the hell, lady?" the driver shouted back.

Afton didn't care. As soon as the car passed, she darted across the street and headed into the darkness that was the Northrop Mall. Passing the chemistry building, she glanced left and then right. It was quiet here in this massive greenway that was filled with trees and lined with enormous stone buildings around the perimeter. Not much was moving except for a couple of bikes that rolled silently toward her, their headlights poking through the darkness like weak flashlights. Maybe she'd lost him? The fake doctor.

But no, that had to be him just up ahead. Zigzagging, running lightly, almost effortlessly on the balls of his feet, glancing back over his shoulder to see if she was following him. Of course she was following him. And when she caught up with him she was going to . . . what?

Scream her head off? Poke him in the eye with the rake handle? Or use the claw end . . . and do what?

Checking her speed, Afton figured that Max had already raised a red alert, had screamed bloody blue murder and got the University Police Department rolling out to search the campus. That knowledge gave her some degree of comfort as she kept going.

Long shadows lengthened as Afton kept the runner in sight. All was silent save for a chill wind that snaked through the treetops overhead. Because it was still early spring, the oaks and maples hadn't fully leafed out yet, so bare branches rubbed against each other, creaking and clacking like dry bones.

Suddenly, the silence was broken by the scream of a siren.

Excellent. Help was on the way. Now if she could just . . .

Up ahead, her runner — her madman

killer — dodged left and disappeared into a copse of trees. Were those trees just outside Wilson Library? She couldn't remember; it had been a long time since she'd gone to school here.

Creeping forward, Afton's head was on a swivel, trying to sense where the guy was hiding. The big question, the hard-assed question, was — was he trying to evade her? Or was he lying in wait for her?

Afton's heart pounded in her chest as a fresh shot of adrenaline coursed through her veins. Where were the university cops? Where were the yapping dogs and searchlights? Why had that siren faded away to nothing? Was help coming or not?

Off to her left a branch snapped. Afton's stomach dropped and her skin prickled. He was close. And all she had was a stupid, flimsy weapon. What to do? Turn tail and run?

Cowardly, she told herself. *That would be cowardly.*

Time seemed to crawl as her world condensed to the cluster of trees just up ahead.

Suddenly, the guy burst out of the trees like a greyhound leaping from a starting gate to charge after a mechanical rabbit. He flew across the quadrangle in the direction of Morrill Hall.

That was all Afton needed. She poured on the speed, running after him, hoping to drive him out onto one of the paved streets that crisscrossed the campus. Drive him out to a waiting cruiser where there'd be officers with drawn guns waiting for him.

Afton flung herself around the corner of Morrill Hall and was rocked to the core to find the man right there, his arm swinging toward her in an arc, knife blade flashing. She literally slammed on the brakes and ended up standing on her tiptoes and sucking in her gut as his knife slashed past, missing her by a fraction of an inch.

Damn, that was close!

She took a hasty step backward, dodging and ducking as he came at her again.

"Help!" Afton shrieked at the top of her lungs as she tried to manipulate the rake in front of her. "Police!"

He slashed again as she danced to her right. Then, just as he missed a second time, just as he was thrown slightly off balance, she jabbed at him with the rake, a swift, dead-on jab that packed as much power as she could muster.

And she connected! Poking him right in the eye!

Her adversary exploded with an angry string of words in a language she didn't understand while she let out another shrill scream for help.

Then he was rushing at her again. And this time Afton was stunned at how strong he was. She tried to parry him with the rake handle, but he dove in close, whipping right up against her, his chest butting her chest while he enveloped her in his arms. A split-second later, he tipped his head back and then brought it forward with horrific force, slamming her in the forehead.

An entire constellation of stars exploded before Afton's eyes and she let out a cry of pain as his right foot crashed into her right knee, causing her to crumple to the ground.

Struggling for breath and trying desperately to remain conscious, Afton struck out wildly. She jabbed the rake upward and, through sheer luck, connected solidly with the man's elbow. That was the single break she needed. The knife went flying from his hand and landed with a dull, metallic clatter a few feet away.

They both scrambled for the knife, Afton wrenching herself across the sidewalk on all fours, the man diving desperately for his knife. They fought and rolled, a pig pile of grappling hands, flying spit, and gnashing teeth.

In Afton's vision of herself as an Amazonian warrior, she grabbed the knife, twisted around to her attacker, and sank it deep in his chest.

Didn't happen that way.

The guy wrapped his hand around the knife and slashed out wildly as Afton's left arm came at him. She'd lost the rake somewhere, so she pulled her hands into claws, hoping against hope to jab him in the eye and rip the hell out of it. But when the knife suddenly sliced into her, the pain was so excruciating, so acutely sharp, that she lost all sense of purpose.

Cut me? I'm cut?

Her brain blipped out a warning to the rest of her jangled nerve endings that something had gone horribly wrong.

Afton rolled away from the man, kicking frantically as she did. Her arm was going numb and she knew her feet were her best and only weapon now.

Gotta kick him hard and then get back on my feet.

But everything was happening in slow motion. She wasn't moving as fast as she hoped.

I think I'm in big trouble.

Just as she was about to scream for help, a shuffle of footsteps on pavement sounded just behind her. And a young man called out in a querulous voice, "Are you okay?"

A faint light poked at Afton and her attacker. A flashlight? No, the light from a cell phone.

"Of course she's not okay," a girl answered in a disdainful voice. "She's squirming around on the ground with that guy. Does she *look* okay?"

"Watch out!" Afton croaked, as her attacker, momentarily startled by the intrusion, took a step forward, thought better of it, and then drew back. He peered angrily at the two young students who'd just emerged from the darkness, then seemed to make a hard, anguished calculation and took off running.

"Help her up," said the young woman, suddenly taking charge. "C'mon, give her a hand."

Together, the two students pulled Afton to her feet.

"Phone?" Afton said. She was having trouble making her words coherent. As if there was a faulty connection between her brain and her mouth. Signal interrupted.

The young woman held out her phone. "Who do you want to call?"

"Jeez, are you cut?" the young man yelped. His eyes practically bulged out of their sockets as he stared at the wet, dark stain that was spreading on Afton's jacket.

"Nine-one-one," Afton gasped. "Police." She was on her feet now, legs feeling like rubber, arm hanging useless at her side. Then she mustered her inner fortitude, spun around, and lurched away from them.

"Hey, where are you going?" the young man called out.

"Hospital," Afton said over her shoulder.

It was five blocks back to the university hospital and Afton figured that she could make it. It would be better than just lying on the ground, waiting for the University Police (who *still* hadn't come!) while blood oozed out of her arm.

Her arm. How bad was it? Well, it hurt like hell, so that gave her some kind of clue. And there was a sticky mess from the cut on her upper arm all the way down to her wrist, so she was definitely losing blood.

No, don't think about that right now. Just focus on Poppy and Tess. Get patched up so you can go home. Live to fight another day.

Her kids needed her, and there was no way she was going to let that son of a bitch get the better of her. It just wasn't in the playbook. But as she walked along, a strange sense of warmth began to creep over her. She could literally feel warm blood trickling down her arm, then spilling over her fingers to drip on the ground as she walked along. Just like Hansel and Gretel, she thought, leaving a trail.

Or like a wounded animal.

Just a few more steps, Afton told herself as she kept moving, stumbling along toward the bright lights of the hospital off in the distance. But now darkness was beginning to cloud her vision and she could feel her knees begin to quiver like jelly.

A few more steps.

There were more sirens now. Off in the distance and close by, too.

That's good, Afton told herself. *They're gonna catch that asshole. Make him pay.*

But it was getting more and more difficult to focus. To keep putting one foot in front of the other.

Just as Afton emerged into a puddle of light on Washington Avenue, a loud buzzing sounded in her ears, like a nest of bees gone wild, and she felt her vision begin to close in on her.

Like walking down a long, dark tunnel, she thought. *Just gotta keep going, no matter what.*

Afton stopped and blinked. Realized that she wasn't making any forward progress.

Then her next thought was, *I think I'm going to fall.*

Someone screeched loudly in her ear. A god-awful noise that sent her mind reeling.

Shh. I'm way too tired for that.

"Oh my God, Afton!" Max cried.

Max?

"I got ya! I got ya!" He scooped her up in his arms and started running. "Doctor," he said. "Gotta get you to the ER."

Afton felt herself being carried along. Her mind drifted peacefully but her body felt like it was being jostled like crazy. *That's Max,* she told herself. And she could hear him screaming for help.

Max nearly stumbled as he carried her out into the street, but he managed to catch his balance and regain his footing. Afton heard him grunt loudly as he hoisted her back up in his arms.

A siren screamed. The volume increasing as it drew closer and closer.

Through half-opened eyes Afton saw approaching headlights and a galaxy of flashing red and blue lights. Then a cruiser squealed to a stop and Max shouted, "Gotta get her to the hospital. She's lost some blood."

Afton could feel herself being placed gently in the backseat of a cruiser, then Max

144

slid in alongside of her.

"I lost him," she murmured in apology. "Got away."

"Faster," Max said to the cop who was driving. "Lights and siren all the way."

Two minutes later they screeched to a halt outside the ER. Afton felt practiced hands reach in and carefully lift her up. She was gently placed on a gurney, felt it go bump bump bump through some sort of doorway, and then they were speeding smoothly down a long hallway, lights flashing by overhead.

"Max?" she called out.

"Right here. I got your back."

She was wheeled behind a pair of billowing white curtains.

"Sleepy," Afton murmured. Then she felt a slight pinprick and really did go to sleep.

When Afton woke up, she was propped upright in bed with an IV in her right hand. There was a bandage on her right upper arm and a large, beeping machine on her left. Max was sitting next to the bed in a lounge chair reading an issue of the *Minnesota Daily*.

"Max," she whispered.

That startled him. He jerked his head up and practically dropped the paper. "Holy shit," he said. "You're awake."

"Odin?" she asked.

"Dead," Max said.

"Damn. Did they get the guy?"

Max stared at her. "No."

"No? All that for . . . ?" Afton exhaled slowly and focused on trying to get her bearings. "How long was I out?"

Max got to his feet. "I don't know." He checked his watch hastily. "Maybe thirty minutes? You needed a couple of stitches."

"How many?"

"Six."

"Not so bad."

"Oh, hell no," Max said. He was jabbering now, burning off pent-up nervous energy. "You remember Petrie, who used to work in Robbery? He tangled with a pit bull once and had to get twenty-two stitches in one leg."

"That was no pit bull," Afton said. "He banged himself with a Weedwacker."

"They were still stiches," Max said. When he saw she was back with the living and tracking fairly well, his face clouded over and he said, "You shouldn't have done that."

"What?" Afton said. "Gone after him?" She shook her head. "We should have known right away. That guy's name tag read Sanchez, but he was no Sanchez. He was an Asian guy. Probably the guy who fired the

146

rocket last night. And, Max, I was freaking *on* him until he cut me!"

"Jeez, Afton, you went after an armed guy without benefit of a weapon or radio."

"You gonna issue me a citation?" she mumbled.

"Something like that." Max pulled out his phone and punched in a number.

"Oh no," Afton said. "You're calling Uncle Thacker." Just what she *didn't* want to happen.

"Already talked to him once. I told him this was partially my fault, since I let you come along. He wanted me to call back once you woke up."

Afton cringed as she listened to Max's one-sided conversation. From what she could glean, Thacker was sending a crime-scene team over to the hospital and had already called Sunny to notify her that her husband had been murdered. Max and Thacker went back and forth for a few minutes and then Max finally fell silent and seemed to just be listening. Then he threw Afton a meaningful glance.

"Is he talking about me?" Afton asked. She thought she was whispering but she was really talking loudly.

Max looked away from her, the phone still pressed to his ear. "Yeah, she's hanging in there." He hunched his shoulders. "I don't know. I don't think so. Well . . . maybe." Then he handed the phone over to Afton. "Thacker wants to talk to you."

Afton hesitated. "Is he going to yell at me?"

Max sighed. "Just talk to him, okay?"

When Afton came on the line, Thacker didn't waste a single breath. "Are you okay?"

"I think so."

"That was a very foolish stunt you just pulled."

"I'm sorry," she said, not really meaning it.

Thacker berated her a little. Max as well, but not too much. And every time Afton attempted to croak out an explanation, he overtalked her.

"Max should never have taken you along tonight," Thacker said.

"Yeah, but the good thing is . . ."

Thacker interrupted her again. "There's actually a good thing?"

"Even though it was dark, I got a fairly decent look at the guy."

There was a soft intake of breath. "You think you could do an Identi-Kit?" Thacker asked.

"I could do one right now if you thought it would help."

"You go home first and get some rest."

Thacker talked to her a little longer and then they both hung up.

"What'd he say?" Max asked.

"He told me to take it easy."

"You should do that."

"Maybe." Afton gazed at the white bandage that was wrapped around her arm and saw that a bright red line had already begun to seep through. It was growing now, like a random blob on a Rorschach test. "But not if I want payback, I won't," she growled.

15

Mom Chao Cherry sat at a low table across from Hack. Candles flickered while music, something low and mournful, oozed out from the suite's sound system. At first glance, the two of them looked as if they might be playing a friendly game of mahjongg, one of the old lady's favorite pastimes. But no. When Narong looked more closely, he saw that they were each doing a line of coke.

Of course they were.

He didn't disapprove of his employer's drug use, but he didn't completely approve of her fraternizing with Hack. The man was her employee and a temporary one at that. He knew that, if they were not in America, a woman so highly placed as Mom Chao Cherry would never associate with a man who was a thug and common dockworker.

When Mom Chao Cherry heard Narong enter her suite, she turned and fixed him with a questioning gaze. "Did the old man tell you where my drugs are being held?" she asked.

Narong shook his head. "No." Then he dropped his head slightly to show a small amount of contrition. "I used my knife, but he held out. Long time he held out." He trembled slightly, keenly afraid that he'd disappointed her. That was the last thing Narong wanted to do, especially after she'd brought him to America and opened his eyes to this strange new way of life.

She licked her lips. "His heart gave out?"

Narong nodded. "As was expected. He was very sick."

"And the *coup de grâce*?"

"Yes, of course." She'd meant the blood-letting, the final act of slitting Odin's throat. She'd insisted on that. She'd made him promise, said it would make for good theater.

"That pig and his associates stole from me," Mom Chao Cherry spat out. "My merchandise, coming in through Vancouver, trucked across Canada, hijacked before Thunder Bay. He must have paid off many people."

"Yes," Narong said. He didn't really want to know the details, just wanted to work with his guns and knives.

"We have been talking," Mom Chao Cherry said, nodding at Hack. "Formulating an alternate plan." She turned a meaningful gaze on Narong. "Perhaps an easier and more clever plan."

"Of course," Narong said.

Mom Chao Cherry held out her hand. "Telephone, please."

Narong picked up a mobile phone from the side table and handed it to her. He'd already decided there was no need to tell his employer about the chase with the policewoman. He would take care of the woman himself once they recovered Mom Chao Cherry's goods. It would be his pleasure.

The old lady dialed a number from memory. When the phone was answered, she said, "We have business?" She listened for a few moments and then said, "Yes, it will be available to you shortly." Her eyes slid over to Narong. "Of course," she continued. "We look forward to making the exchange. I will be in touch." She stabbed at the Off button, silencing the voice on the other end of the line. She smiled to herself as she set down the phone and leaned back in her chair. Tonight she was wearing slim black slacks, a black leather jacket of supple lambskin over a hot pink silk blouse, and diamonds.

It was the height of Thai chic, and a style especially copied by the younger women who frequented upper-crust nightclubs in Bangkok.

"Our reinforcements are on the way?" she asked.

"Yes," Narong said. "I have been in touch. The three men you requested will arrive soon."

Mom Chao Cherry lifted a hand as she gazed around the luxurious suite. "Time to move."

"When?" Narong asked.

"Soon."

"Where?"

"Mr. Hack has already found a place for us." Mom Chao Cherry smiled across the table at Hack. She was growing fond of this insane redneck who liked to toot up as much as she did. "A building that is deserted and very much private."

"Someplace we won't be disturbed?" Narong asked. He knew that this time he could not fail. This time he must extricate the information from his subject.

"I've already inspected the place," Hack said as a wide grin split his face, an expression that was both mirthful and terrifying. "Nobody will be able to hear a single scream."

16

Afton's sister, Lish, met her at the door.

"You okay?" Lish asked. She was a no-nonsense type of girl who shrugged off most problems. But tonight, along with her Minnesota Wild sweatshirt, black leggings, and fuzzy socks, she wore a very worried look.

"Max called you?" Afton shut the door behind her and felt instant relief, as if a weight had been lifted from her shoulders. She was finally back home in her little craftsman-style bungalow in South Minneapolis with the saggy couch, faux Tiffany lamps, and bookcase full of well-read books and old-timey games like Clue, Candy Land, and Monopoly.

"Well, yeah, he called," Lish said in a flat, almost Valley girl voice. "With all the pertinent nasty details. He also told me to send you directly to bed. Do not pass Go, do not collect two hundred dollars."

Afton shrugged out of her coat. "How are

the kids?"

"I fed 'em, read to them, and then tucked them into bed," Lish said. She was like a second mom to the girls, and they dearly loved their aunt Lish. She could whip up a mean pepperoni pizza, had taught the kids how to line dance, and loved to sprawl on the floor with them and play board games. Lish worked a short shift as a medical reporting analyst at CareView Medical, so she was always there when the kids came home from school.

"Did you tell them what happened? That I got cut and had to have stitches?"

"Uh, no," Lish said, cocking her head to one side. "I thought you might want to tell them about that yourself. You know, about how stupid and impulsive you were? Or maybe you want to sugarcoat it and make it sound like an exciting war story."

"I think I'll just play it straight," Afton said. "Anyway, thanks for waiting up." It was getting late and she could hear Jimmy Fallon cackling away in the next room making some sort of joke about the Kardashians.

"I just finished watching the news." Lish finally smiled. "It's always a relief when I don't see your face on Newswatch Seven."

"I did my best to score some face time tonight. But no such luck."

"Max said you chased this guy right through campus?"

"I'm afraid so."

Lish's brows knit together. "What were you thinking? Never mind — I know exactly what you were thinking. But you can't *do* that sort of stupid stuff. You've got responsibilities. And not nearly enough life insurance." She paused. "So how bad is the arm?"

Afton slid up her sleeve to reveal her bandage. "Not too bad."

"Hurts though?"

"Hardly at all." Her arm was throbbing as if somebody were sitting inside and wailing away on a big bass drum. "But I'm tired."

"You want a glass of wine? I opened a bottle of that rosé that the ladies in your book club were raving about."

In response, Afton pulled an amber vial from her pocket and rattled the pills.

"Oh. Guess not."

The phone in the kitchen suddenly rang.

"I'll get it," Afton said. She limped in, picked up the receiver. "Hello?"

"This is Steve Lynch from the *Minneapolis Courier,*" came an eager voice. "Is it true you were just involved in . . . ?"

Afton dropped the phone back on the hook. "If it rings again, don't answer it," she told Lish.

Lish nodded. "Got it."

Lish fussed around downstairs, turning off the TV and shutting off lights, while Afton started up the stairs. Five steps from the top she saw a pair of shiny eyes peering out of the dark at her. Bonaparte.

"Hey, buddy," Afton said. Bonaparte was a French bulldog she'd helped rescue this past winter after he'd been dumped down a steep embankment on the Mississippi. Bonaparte wagged his tail and stretched his squarish head out, eager for a scratch, and his ears flicked forward, huge and alert. Afton obliged. "You're a good little guy, aren't you?" she said. Bonaparte was doing his little prance dance now, looking like a circus dog dressed in a black-and-white fur tuxedo.

A door snicked open, then a little voice called out, "Mommy?"

"It's me, honey," Afton replied. "I'm home now." Tess, her ten-year-old, had crawled out of bed and was creeping down the hallway to greet her. Her long blond hair was pinned up and she wore a long sleep shirt along with a curious, almost adult expression. Two more years and she'd be a heartbreaker. "But keep your voice down; we don't want to wake your sister."

"I'm awake," a sleepy voice called. Now

Poppy, her six-year-old, was toddling toward her, a miniature version of Tess, looking adorable in her terry cloth jammies.

Afton grabbed both girls and pulled them into a tight embrace. "Hey, kids. I'm sorry to be so late."

Poppy stared at her with big eyes. "Did you have to work late?"

But Tess wasn't so gullible. "I heard Aunt Lish talking to somebody on the phone," she said. "Did you get hurt?"

"You got *hurt*?" Poppy's voice rose in fear.

Afton squeezed her kids again. "No, no, just a scratch. Nothing to worry about. It's kind of like when you fall off your bike or scooter."

"What happened?" Tess asked. She was wide-awake now and wanted answers. Would probably demand answers.

"You know that part of my job is to help catch bad guys, right?" Afton asked.

They both nodded solemnly. They'd had this talk before.

"Sometimes the bad guys don't want to be caught, so you have to chase after them."

"Did you chase him and catch him?" Poppy asked.

Afton hesitated. She tried never to lie to her kids. "No, not exactly. Tonight the bad guy got away."

"So you didn't lock him up in jail?" Tess asked.

"Not yet."

"What if he tries to find you?" Poppy asked.

Afton gripped both girls tighter. "That's not going to happen. The bad guy doesn't even know who I am or where I live."

Tess put a hand to her chest and gave a theatrical sigh. "Thank goodness."

"Now you guys crawl back into bed, okay?" Afton nodded at Bonaparte. "Bonaparte, you're on dream duty. I want you to chase away any bad dreams and make sure that Poppy and Tess only have sweet dreams tonight."

Bonaparte gave a little bark and wagged his tail so hard his entire back end shook.

"Atta boy," Afton said.

"Mommy," Tess said, "are we still taking Bonaparte to the dog walk on Sunday?"

Afton tilted her head as if deep in thought. "Well, let me think about that." Poppy and Tess had been collecting pledges for the Furry Friends Animal Shelter and were looking forward to taking Bonaparte to their Jog Your Dog event. "I think . . . yes!"

Ten minutes later, Afton was snuggled under a puffy down coverlet. As she lay in

159

the dark, trying to relax and drift off to sleep, her mind kept skittering back haphazardly to some of the crazier times in her life. Her wild college days, dropping out and then bumming around as an adventure guide and rock climber, two boyfriends that both became ex-husbands before she'd turned thirty.

Yeah, her dad had warned her (he was always quick to warn) that she was throwing her life away when she'd married Chad, ex-husband number one. And he'd been both right and wrong in his pronouncement. He was right because Chad had turned out to be a lazy, self-centered slug, whose idea of a good time was drinking beer and racing his truck. And wrong because out of that marriage had come Poppy and Tess.

Thinking about her sweet girls, Afton fell asleep with a smile on her face. But as she tumbled deeper and deeper into sleep, her dreams grew troubled. Until finally she dreamt of an Asian man with lightning-fast hands and a razor-sharp knife.

17

Jay Barber needed to clear his head. Had to escape his house before he lost his freaking mind. Before his wife, Shelly, started asking too many questions. Which explained why he was jogging around Lake Harriet at 6:00 A.M., shivering his ass off as a thin ray of sunlight peeped over the horizon.

He'd received the call from Sunny at four fifteen this morning. The *briiing* of the phone slicing through his REM sleep and giving his heart one hell of a nasty jolt. Then Sunny was on the line, babbling wildly about how some maniac had snuck into Odin's hospital room last night and slit his throat.

That did it for Barber. No more sleep for him. Odin butchered like a pig in a slaughterhouse? Even though he'd been parked in a luxury suite in a major hospital? Jay had immediately called Bob Steckel and set up an emergency meeting for ten o'clock at

DSN. Said all the empathic things a shocked business partner might be expected to say.

Except Barber wasn't just shocked, he was scared shitless. He knew about the hijacked drugs. Had figured that, when the helicopter was shot down, someone was sending Odin a very clear and distinct message.

Odin. Sweet Jesus. The old fart had gotten crazier and crazier over the last couple of years. The dope and the women and all that other stuff. No wonder he'd needed a new ticker. And this last hijacking — holy crap! When Odin had told him about it, whispered it to him only a matter of weeks ago, Barber had just about burst a blood vessel. This wasn't the business they were supposed to be in. This was the kind of dangerous crap that Chinese triads and South American cartels got involved in.

And now Odin was dead, killed by an unknown assassin. Probably the same one who'd taken down the helicopter.

Barber knew he'd been dealt a dirty hand. Now he was the one who was left to clean up the mess. Barber might have some ideas about that, of course. But first . . . first he had to quell the fear that rose like dirty bubbles in his brain and try to think.

His feet slapped loudly on the deserted jogging path as he ran along halfheartedly, the cell phone he'd clipped on the inside of his sweatshirt pocket poking into his ribs. A thin mist had settled over the middle of the lake, giving it an ethereal feel. Like some kind of ominous, creeping fog out of a Stephen King novel.

There were questions he had to figure out. How much did Sunny know about Odin's deal? Did she know anything at all? How exactly could he unload the merchandise — and how fast? And, most important, was he in mortal danger? Would these maniacs, whoever they were, come after him?

Barber figured they might, and he made a mental note to hire a personal security detail ASAP. Like, really good security guys who packed serious weapons and weren't afraid to use them.

As Barber jogged along he also thought about the money. Couldn't help it. There was so much to be gained if he played this just right. There was the sale of the merchandise, of course. The key-partner insurance that would come his way now that Odin was dead. And the enormous profit he'd reap if he convinced the board — and it wouldn't be so very difficult — to sell Diamond Shopping Network to Consolidated or the Saudi company.

Maybe the best thing to do would be to

cash out completely. Barber took a gulp of
air as he rounded the turn by the bandstand
and let his fantasy run a little wild. Leave
the wife, who'd become a pain in the ass
anyway, move to Bora Bora, wear a loin-
cloth, and walk the beach. Drink tropical
drinks and make love to island women.
Probably not a bad way to live. Not much
stress.

On the other hand, there were glittering,
cosmopolitan cities where he could live in
unfettered luxury: London, Paris, Rio,
Dubai.

Luxury. Somehow luxury sounded far
more inviting than primitive hedonism.
Good. That was one decision nailed down.
Now all he had to do was . . .

Something small and sharp slapped him
hard in the back of his neck.

Shocked by the ferocity of the sting,
Barber stumbled, his arms windmilling out
to his sides. Then he caught himself and
regained his stride, but just barely. What the
hell was that? A hornet? Had he just been
stung by a damn hornet?

Barber slowed to a shambling pace, feeling angry, out of sorts, and a little light-
headed. Before he could think what to do
— go home and swallow a Benadryl? —
there was another sharp stab in the back of

his right thigh.

What the hell is this?

Now he felt as if he were moving in slow motion, picking his way through molasses, his vision and hearing all going a little bit woozy.

He reached back reflexively to touch his thigh and his fumbling fingers felt a stick-like thing, what his reeling mind suddenly realized must be a tiny dart, hanging off him.

Barber staggered off the path and onto the still-damp grass, heading for a dense copse of poplars and fir trees. The limbic portion of his brain, the part that controlled the fight-or-flight response, was beeping out a warning signal, telling him he had to get out of sight and hunker down. That danger was imminent. But as his knees wobbled, as his steps became a jittering shuffle, he began to collapse. He flailed wildly for a few moments, hoping to somehow recover, but the ground was suddenly rushing up at him way too quickly. His chin struck the turf with a molar-shattering impact and he felt a distinct pop in his nose. Barber groaned in pain and tried to roll himself over even as his mouth filled with blood. As he shifted onto his left shoulder, spitting blood and a hunk of broken tooth, almost retching from the pain, his eyes fluttered open.

Two men peered down at him.

Barber blinked, his eyes goggling as he tried desperately to pull everything into focus. He stared up at them, his lips working soundlessly until he finally managed a garbled "Gugh?" One man was a serious-looking Asian with a blue snake tattoo that was visible on his neck just above his black windbreaker. The other was a tough-looking hillbilly wearing a camouflaged army jacket and missing a front tooth.

"Say now," Hack said. He pulled a thin piece of wire out of his jacket pocket and slipped it around Barber's neck. Caught him, like a rabbit in a snare.

Then the two men got their hands under Barber and carried him awkwardly across the uneven ground. Barber's feet paddled helplessly as if they had a mind of their own and still hoped to make a belated getaway. Then one toe stubbed on a tree root and his running shoe went flying off. And even though Barber's eyes were still open, his wonked-out brain still trying to puzzle out what was happening to him, he didn't seem to feel a thing when they tossed him into the back of a cargo van. Then the door rolled shut and he descended into complete unconsciousness.

Hack drove with Narong riding shotgun. They sped down Lake Harriet Boulevard, cut over on Thirty-ninth Street, and then rounded the east side of Lake Calhoun. There was a chain of four lakes that ran right up the gut of Minneapolis: Cedar, Isles, Calhoun, and Harriet. They were hooked together by narrow waterways, bridges, and trails; rimmed with beautiful parkland; and mostly lined with expensive homes. The vision of all these splendid homes reminded Hack of Superior Street back in Duluth, just past the old Fitger's Brewhouse. There were fancy mansions up there, too. Like Glensheen Mansion, where old lady Congdon had been smothered to death. Now the University of Minnesota owned Glensheen and led tours through the place, all the visitors ponying up their thirty-five dollars to look for restless, wandering spirits, though UMD tour guides always seemed to downplay that particular part of the mansion's heritage. Still, he'd taken the tour himself and really grooved on the place. Especially the old lady's bedroom, where she'd died.

"Slick as shit through a goose," Hack said

gleefully as they turned down Hennepin Avenue to join the early birds who were grinding their way through early morning rush hour traffic. One lane was closed up ahead because of perpetual road construction around Loring Park. "We really pulled this off."

Hack was fairly crowing as he drove along, pleased with himself, pleased at how well things had worked out with Barber. Unlike Narong, who'd screwed the pooch last night, he'd engineered this morning's capture to go off without a hitch.

Narong, on the other hand, was beginning to suspect that Hack was crazy. Or maybe even possessed by demons. Thailand was populated by Buddhists and Hindus, but most everyone still clung to the old legends that were passed down. And the demons in those legends, like the ten-faced Thotsakan or his brother, Kumphakan, were not to be trifled with. Perhaps it would be prudent to wear an amulet for protection.

"How's he doing back there?" Hack asked. Every once in a while they heard a dull, metallic thump coming from the back of the van. It wouldn't pay to have Barber wake up and start banging around in a drug-addled stupor. You stop at a red light, you never know what nosy person might hear a suspicious *clunk* or *thunk.* Everybody was paranoid these days, ready to point a finger and call the cops.

"He's fine," Narong said. "Still sleeping."

"He's not sleeping, he's *out,* man. He's, like, unconscious," Hack said. "You practically gorked him with that dart. What the hell drug was that anyway? Maybe I should get me some."

Narong glanced over at Hack, who was driving one-handed now while he pulled a twist of foil from the pocket of his jeans. When they stopped at a red light, Hack unwrapped it, bent his head forward, and snorted a tiny mound of coke from the foil packet. "Whoo-ee, this is good stuff," he said, his voice going high and reedy. "You want a toot? I got another twist here someplace."

Holding up his hand to wave off the offer, Narong smiled to himself. There was still more work to be done. He needed to prove himself to Mom Chao Cherry. But that would happen; he was quite sure of it. All he needed to do was sharpen his knife and refine his interrogation technique.

18

"You're not supposed to be here." Max scowled at Afton. It was Thursday morning, forty minutes before Thacker's big emergency meeting was scheduled to start. Everybody in Homicide was walking on eggshells, shoulders hunched all the way up to their ears, feeling the pressure. They'd already been briefed about last night.

Now Afton's presence seemed to ratchet up the pressure even more.

"I had to come in and do the Identi-Kit," Afton said. "Remember?"

"So do it." Max was sitting at one of the communal desks in Homicide, making scratches on a yellow notepad. Those notes would be added to a large binder Afton had been keeping on the Odin case. Max preferred to work old-school, with yellow pads and rollerball pens. Computers were great for accessing databases and doing all sorts of research, but paper notes were easier for him to sort through. Easier to keep straight in his head.

"I already worked on the sketch," Afton said. "We should have laser copies by the time the meeting starts."

Max aimed a finger at her. "You're not coming to that meeting. If you showed up, Thacker would shit a brick."

"I have to come."

"Why? Everybody already knows about your chasing the guy, about how you got cut."

"Maybe I can give some additional input."

"You're killing me," Max said. "You know that?"

Afton slapped a hand against his shoulder. "Come on, you know you love it."

"Aw, jeez . . ." Max made another note, threw down his pen. "So how's the arm?"

Afton shrugged. "Okay. Hurts a little." Truth be told, it hurt like hell. When she woke up this morning she'd had to wrap another layer of gauze around her arm to hide the bleeding. It wouldn't do to scare the kids while they were busy snarfing down their Apple Cinnamon Cheerios.

"I'm not surprised you're still feeling it," Max said. "You really got stuck."

"Nah, I'm fine. Comes with the territory."

"Wasn't supposed to be your territory,"

Max said. He wanted to scream and holler at her, but it was the best reprimand he could manage at the moment. Maybe later, when they were alone, he could really unload.

"Face it, I'm younger and faster," Afton said, trying to make a joke of it. "It was logical that I go after him."

Max spun in his chair to face her. "You mean younger and dumber," he said, and this time his voice rose in genuine anger. "And even if you perceive me as being somewhat — and I said *somewhat* — older and slower, never forget . . . I'm the guy what carries the gun."

Dillon looked up from one of the desks, where he was digging into a bag of Cheetos. "With a license to kill. Hey, did you guys happen to catch the all-star press conference on TV this morning?"

"No," Afton said. "What happened?"

"The press pretty much crucified the chief and the mayor." Dillon stuck another handful of orange glop in his mouth.

"Wonderful," Afton said in a slightly acerbic tone. "Did anybody else join in with the torches and pitchforks?"

"Some of us kind of thought Sunny Odin would be screaming her ass off, but so far there's been no sign of her," Dillon said.

"She's in shock," Max said. "Gotta be brutal for her. The rocket attack and now this."

"At least she's got closure," Dillon said. He held out his bag of Cheetos. "Want some?"

Afton shook her head. "No thanks." Dillon's wife was always nagging him to lose weight, trying to get him to eat only protein along with small servings of fruit. Looks like he'd fallen hard off the protein wagon.

"Has there been a preliminary report from the medical examiner?" Afton asked.

"Yeah, but nothing interesting," Dillon said, still crunching loudly. "Other than the fact that the killer practically sliced Odin's head off."

They met in the large conference room. The one where the chief of police held press conferences and the mayor was known to pose with whichever officers were being either praised or excoriated, depending on the political winds of change. The group this morning consisted of Max, Afton, Andy Farmer, Dick Dillon, Kip Wheeler and Joe Jelenick from Crime Scene, and Deputy Chief Gerald Thacker.

Thacker didn't look happy. "Now Odin's been murdered," he said, stating the obvious. "And we're still no closer to catching the people who shot down that helicopter."

"Has to be the same guy," Dillon asked. "The one who blasted that copter with a rocket and the guy who slipped in last night to kill Odin."

"I'd say the odds are about ninety-five percent," Max said. "And whoever the asshole is, he's still one step ahead of us."

"So what's with the Asian connection?" Farmer asked. "The two people who were at the noodle factory Tuesday night, the guy who posed as a doctor last night. What's that all about?"

"We don't know yet," Max said. "But I'll tell you one thing: With Fan Ling popping in to visit Odin at the hospital less than an hour before he was killed, we need to take a serious look at her."

"Is she Odin's mistress?" Jelenick asked.

"Probably," Max said.

"Then she's a serious suspect," Farmer said.

"If Fan Ling was Odin's mistress," Afton said, "then Sunny is also a suspect. Sunny could have had her husband killed out of sheer rage."

"Wait a minute," Thacker said. He gazed at Afton as if he was just seeing her for the first time. "Tangler. What are you doing here? You're supposed to be home resting."

"I had to meet with Steve Drury first thing and do the Identi-Kit," Afton explained. Drury was the resident sketch artist for the MPD, although now everything was done on computer and Drury mostly manipulated a plug-and-play program.

"So you're still tailing Max around?"

"That's what you asked me to do," Afton said. "You wanted me to take notes and organize all the information." Police officers, detectives, even deputy chiefs all loathed writing reports. It was the one common denominator that was a prickly thorn in their side. Afton, on the other hand, was a whiz at writing reports and could whip them out with all the necessary details. She could "subject claimed" this and "incident" that circles around the rest of them. Which was one of the reasons the homicide detectives loved her and secretly (and not so secretly) allowed her access to their cases.

"I must be losing my mind," Thacker said. "If Chief Peters knew I was letting you sit in on this meeting, he'd serve my head on a silver platter to the city council."

"Tasty," Dillon chuckled.

"You know what the governor asked me?" Thacker said, focusing on Afton.

"No sir," Afton said.

"He called me at six o'clock this morning, before I even had benefit of my morning caffeine, and said, 'What's this I hear about a chase last night?' "

"That's good," Max said with a straight face. "It means he's showing some serious interest in our case."

"It is *not* good," Thacker snapped. "It means he's going to rattle some cages in city hall. And you know what that means. When it comes time for funding . . ."

"We'll be shit out of luck," Dillon said. "So what else is new?"

"Just so they keep their hooks off my pension," Farmer muttered.

Thacker ran his hands through his hair and then seemed to pull himself together. "All right, people. We have to focus." He turned toward Wheeler. "Was there anything you guys picked up at either scene? The shooter's nest or the hospital?"

Wheeler shrugged. "We lifted a partial print from the doorjamb at the hospital, but it doesn't match anything we've got so far. We have some other stuff, too, but we're still busy processing."

"So who are these killers?" Thacker asked. "And where are they holed up? We have basic descriptions — we're fairly sure it's a man and an older woman — so we need to get this information out immediately. We need to alert every unit in Minneapolis, Saint Paul, and the surrounding suburbs, as well as all the TV and print media. The airport for sure, in case they decide to make a run for it, and even hotels they might be staying at. The whole enchilada."

The door opened and a tentative female voice called out, "Deputy Chief?"

"What?" Thacker yelled.

Darlene Allman, Thacker's temporary administrative assistant, came creeping in. She looked like she was about fourteen years old and acted as if Thacker jabbed her with an electric cattle prod every time she ventured near him. "Chief Thacker, um, excuse me, but I have those composites you asked for?"

"Good. Thank you, Darlene." Thacker held up one of the sheets for everyone to see. "This is the suspect we're looking for. Afton refined the initial descriptions we got from that guy Zhang and Sammy Mah. So now we have a fairly decent composite." He looked at the group. "Who wants to honcho this, get it out ASAP?"

"I'm on it," Farmer said.

"Getting back to Sunny," Afton said. "What are the chances she hired some sort of Chinese assassin?"

"I don't know," Max said. "Maybe twenty to one?"

"Maybe Fan Ling hired the assassin," Thacker said.

"That's always a possibility," Max said. "Which means we better go jack her up. Push her hard to see if she gives us anything." He drummed his fingers against the table. "The other thing we need to do is have a talk with Jay Barber, Odin's partner at DSN. The way I see it, he's the man in charge now."

"Do it," Thacker said. "In fact, let's do him first."

"I'll get Barber on the line," Afton said. She grabbed her notes, jumped up, and walked to the back of the room, where a bunch of landlines were located. As she dialed the number at DSN, she could hear Thacker ranting about a call he'd taken earlier from Governor Lindsay. He was relating all the ugly details and didn't seem one bit happy.

When Afton reached the receptionist at DSN, she said, "Could you please put me through to Mr. Jay Barber's office? You can tell his secretary that Detective Max Montgomery would like to set up a meeting with Mr. Barber."

"Tell her we'd like to meet with him

around eleven," Max called out to her.

But when Afton was routed through to Barber's secretary, she was told that he wasn't in yet. "He's not?" she said. "Well, have you heard from him? Nothing?" She dropped the phone to her chest. "Barber's not at his office yet and nobody's heard from him."

"Not even his secretary?" Max asked.

"That's who I'm talking to right now."

"Better call him at home."

"Gotcha," Afton said. She checked her notes for Barber's home number, dialed it, and when it rang, heard it snatched up immediately.

"Is that you?" a woman asked urgently.

"This is Liaison Officer Afton Tangler from the Minneapolis Police Department. Is this Mrs. Barber?"

"Yes?" said a querulous voice.

"We're trying to get hold of your husband."

"So am I," Mrs. Barber cried, and now there was real anguish in her voice. "He hasn't come home and I'm worried sick!"

That set the wheels in motion for Afton and Max to make a quick trip over to Jay Barber's home. It was located on a prosperous-looking block just west of Lake Harriet.

Though it was still early spring, a few crocuses and tulips bloomed in front yard gardens.

"Nice place," Max said as they pulled up in front of Barber's modified Tudor-style home. The place had decorative half timbers, stone masonry, casement windows, and a slate roof. Afton figured it had to go for at least a million dollars in this tony neighborhood.

Barber's wife, Shelly, met them at the front door along with an aging brown dachshund with sad eyes.

"Are you the police?" she asked. Then, before they could answer, she said, "Come on in." Shelly Barber was in her early forties with short brown hair that had been streaked a honey blond, striking green eyes, pointed chin, and what was probably a pretty good figure camouflaged inside a slightly-too-large brown velour tracksuit.

Shelly led them through a small music room, where a Steinway baby grand sat collecting dust, and into a large, well-furnished family room, which contained a flagstone fireplace, two expensive-looking red brocade sofas, four leather chairs, and a gaming table. She settled in one of the chairs with the dog on her lap and indicated for Afton and Max to take a seat, too. Afton noticed that the dog's fur matched the color of Mrs. Barber's tracksuit.

"So where do you think your husband went?" Max asked. Driving over here, he and Afton had entertained the possibility that, for whatever reason — fear, business problems, sheer craziness — Barber might have just bolted.

Shelly Barber blinked. "The lake?"

"Wait. What?" Max said. "You mean . . . ?"

Shelly gestured frantically. "Lake Harriet. Two blocks over. Jay went for a jog first thing this morning, right after he got the phone call about Odin being killed. He was very upset and wanted to go somewhere by himself and clear his head. He was wearing shorts and his blue Macalester sweatshirt, so I don't think he planned to go anyplace else."

Afton threw a startled look at Max. No way had Barber just boogied on out of town on his own.

"Not good," Max said.

"Not good?" Shelly said. "What does that mean? You're scaring me."

"I'll call this in and get a couple of squads rolling," Afton said. "Have them circle the lake and then fan out into the neighborhood."

"You think he's gone?" Shelly asked. The

181

terrible reality of the situation was starting to sink in for her.

Max stretched a hand out to her. "Give us a minute."

Shelly waited nervously while Afton made her call. Max, meanwhile, put in another call to DSN, just in case Barber had turned up there. No dice. Barber hadn't come storming into his office dressed in his jogging clothes.

"We need to ask you a few questions," Afton said gently, once they'd made their calls and put things in motion.

"Like what?"

"Like does your husband go running every morning?"

"Maybe three times a week. Otherwise he does Nautilus at the Calhoun Club. I called over there to the front desk, but they said they hadn't seen him this morning."

"When he goes for a run, how long is he usually gone?" Max asked.

Shelly squinted one eye closed. "Jay's more of a plodder, so . . . maybe fifty minutes? Certainly not this long. I mean, it's been almost four hours!"

"Do you think your husband could have taken another route?" Afton asked. "I mean, after hearing about Mr. Odin's murder, your husband could have been feeling extremely upset and decided to take a longer run. Maybe he needed time to think, to pull his thoughts together." She knew her rationalization sounded weak even as she said it.

Shelly shook her head. "No, I don't think so." Her lower lip trembled. "I have to tell you, after hearing what happened to Leland, I'm worried sick. I mean, something terrible might have happened to Jay, too." She rocked back and forth, cradling the dachshund, who gazed up at her with its sad, rheumy eyes as if to confirm that he was worried, too.

As they were leaving Barber's house, a black-and-white squad car rolled up to the curb. They walked down to meet it as the two officers climbed out.

"Pogue and Gilliam," Max said. "Good guys." Then a little louder, "You see any sign of our guy?"

Gilliam, the older, gray-haired officer who'd been driving, shook his head. "Not yet. But we haven't finished looking, and a couple more units have been called in. We'll keep searching for him."

Pogue was younger. Tall and rangy, cheekbones that jutted out like the edge of a knife blade. He poked a finger at Afton. "Are you the one who chased that shitheel through campus last night?"

"That was me," Afton said. Was he going to give her a lecture, too? But no, he wore a faint trace of a smile on his face.

"Too bad you weren't carrying," Pogue said. "Save us all a lot of trouble."

"Not that she didn't want to," Max said. "C'mon." He and Afton walked back toward his car. "Mmn, look at you," he said under his breath. "Got some swagger going, huh?"

"Thacker's mad at me, but those guys think I did okay," Afton said.

"Yeah, well . . ."

"What do you think?" she asked. "Now that you've cooled down some." Max's opinion was the one that mattered to her. She was thrilled to have been assigned to him and knew she could learn a lot from him.

"Don't tell anybody I said this, but . . . you did okay. Still, you gotta be careful not to overstep your bounds. You're not even technically on the force, not even a rookie."

As Afton pulled her seat belt across she said, "Where do you think Barber is? Besides out there in the wind?"

"I don't know," Max said. "But I'm worried as hell. These people — whoever these people are — don't screw around. They might have taken him. And if they have him, for whatever reason, it's probably not going to end well."

"What about Sunny?"

"What about her?"

"What if we went over there and pushed her hard? Maybe she knows more than she let on. Maybe she knows *why* her husband was killed and Barber was . . . kidnapped?"

"You want to beat up a woman less than twelve hours after her husband was murdered?" Max asked.

"If I can get beat up, so can she," Afton said. "Besides, if Sunny wants us to find Odin's killer, she's going to have to dazzle us with some serious information. Not just some bullshit about a bunch of marauding geese."

19

Sunny wasn't home.

"She went to the funeral home to make the arrangements," Terrell said. "Wenger and Wainwright Funeral Home over on Hennepin." She touched a tissue to her nose and sniffled loudly. "Jesus, this is terrible. Just so damn depressing."

"You think murder is depressing?" Max asked. "Really?" He was feeling the pressure and coming on a little too strong.

"Hey," Terrell said, her eyes flashing, her mouth pinched into an unflattering grimace. "I don't have to take any crap from you. I happen to know you guys were *there* last night. At the university hospital. And that you didn't do squat to stop that murdering asshole. That you can't even figure out who's causing all this misery!"

"Are you freaking nuts?" Max cried. "Afton got *hurt* chasing that asshole."

They were standing in the foyer, shouting,

practically hissing and spitting in each other's faces. Even in the heat of the moment, Afton noted that Terrell was wearing a well-tailored jacket, designer jeans, and Manolo Blahnik heels. She looked like she was ready to jump in her Mercedes and hit the Mall of America for a serious shop.

Afton held up a hand. "Let's all take a deep breath here, okay? We all want the same thing. We want to catch these crazies as soon as possible and put an end to this nightmare."

"Whoever's behind this really is crazy," Terrell said. She suddenly looked sorrowful and was slowly backing down from her hissy fit.

"We need to talk to you about a few things," Max said. Now his tone was lighter and much more reasonable as well. "We have a few questions for you."

Terrell put her hands on her hips and cocked her head. "What now? What the hell else has gone wrong?"

"Maybe we could come in and sit down?" Afton asked. "Let us fill you in on some . . . recent developments."

They followed Terrell into a solarium that looked like it had been built as an addition to the house. A long, wooden trestle table held ceramic pots filled with orchids, birds of paradise, and bromeliads. A banana plant in a large blue-green Chinese pot sat in one corner. Wicker chairs were upholstered in butter yellow cushions. A bored-looking matching yellow parakeet sat in a tall gilded cage.

"This is a lovely room," Afton said. Except, of course, for the parakeet. She didn't believe in putting birds in cages. Didn't like the idea of *any* animal existing within the confines of a cage.

"It's nice now, but not so great in summer," Terrell said. "Then this room heats up too much." She'd taken a seat in a reclining chair, but wasn't particularly relaxed. She crossed her legs and jiggled a foot. "So. What's going on?"

Max glanced at Afton.

"We're sorry to have to tell you this," Afton said in her best sensitive-family-liaison-officer voice, "but Jay Barber disappeared this morning."

Terrell bounced forward in her chair with a sharp intake of breath. "What do you mean Jay's missing? What happened to him?"

Afton gave a quick explanation about how Barber had learned of Leland Odin's death, then gone for a jog around the lake, presumably to clear his head. And then hadn't returned home.

"Where do you think Barber is?" Terrell asked. "I mean, did he suddenly lose all his marbles and decide to pull some wacky Forrest Gump stunt? Run across the country and back again?"

"We don't think he's out running," Afton said. She said it slowly and with meaning.

"Ah," Terrell said. "So you're thinking the worst. That Barber's been murdered, too?"

"We don't have any evidence that points to a homicide," Max said. "So we don't want to jump to any conclusions just yet."

"But you've got guys out looking for him?"

"There are a number of squads searching the immediate area, yes," Afton said.

Terrell frowned and then blew out a glut of air. "Well, that's just plain nuts. Jay disappearing like that."

"Do you know a woman named Fan Ling?" Afton asked.

"Sure." Terrell bobbed her head. "She works at DSN."

"But do you know her personally?"

Terrell gave a delicate snort. "You really think I hang out with those people?"

"What exactly do you mean by *those people*?" Max asked.

"The on-air people. You know, the worker bees."

"You don't spend any time at DSN?" Afton asked.

"Why would I?"

"Maybe because your stepfather was DSN's founder and CEO?" Afton said.

"Not only do I not spend any time there," Terrell said, "I don't spend any money there. Seriously, do I look like the kind of girl who carries a vinyl handbag and wears low-heeled orthopedic shoes?"

Snob, Afton thought. *You might shop there if you didn't have a whole lot of money. And had a couple of mouths to feed.*

"Clearly," Max said, "whatever's going on is somehow tied to DSN. We don't know how that shakes out exactly, but with two top executives involved . . ."

"You're looking at me as if I have an answer," Terrell said. She looked resentful as she folded her arms across her chest. "I don't."

"But you might know something," Afton said, trying not to hate this woman, trying to stuff down the fact that Terrell was an arrogant, judgmental airhead whose very existence depended on her stepfather's money. "You might not know exactly what it is, but you might be privy to some information, some sliver of knowledge that can point us in the right direction."

"Trust me," Terrell said. "I don't know anything."

Afton decided to try another line of questioning, one that wasn't quite so direct. "Tell us about Leland Odin and Jay Barber's relationship. As you saw it."

"That's pretty simple," Terrell said. "Leland was always the big-picture guy while Jay Barber was more operations."

"Big-picture, meaning . . . ?"

"Leland always had the corporate vision. He imagined what DSN could grow to be, what its future would be, so he was the one who developed the five-year and ten-year plans. Plus, he completely oversaw the marketing, merchandising, and hiring of on-air talent."

"And operations . . . ?" Afton said.

"Jay Barber dealt with the accountants, attorneys, and all the facilities management. You know, the day-to-day running of the company. Warehousing, shipping, delivery, that sort of thing."

"But both men certainly delegated most of the day-to-day tasks," Afton said.

"Oh, absolutely," Terrell said. "They had vice presidents, divisional merchandise managers, marketing execs, and warehouse managers up the wazoo."

"And Leland Odin and Jay Barber held

equal shares in DSN stock?"

Terrell shook her head. "Not quite. Leland held sixty percent, Jay had forty percent."

"And now Barber . . . gets it all?" Afton asked.

"If you find Barber . . . then *maybe* he's in charge of the whole thing," Terrell said. She waved a hand in the air as if to erase that thought. "But I don't know the exact answer to that. I have no idea what's been stipulated in their buy-sell agreement. Which party gets what or who inherits what or if any shares get ceded to some of their top executives. I guess you'd have to talk to Bob Steckel; he's corporate counsel."

"Actually," Max said. "For someone who professes not to be interested, you seem to know an awful lot about DSN."

"Mostly I know about the import side of the business," Terrell admitted. "Because I studied it in school."

"Such as?" Afton said.

"Oh, you know, goods come in through a port of entry, where the cargo is cleared and duties are collected, then they're entered for warehousing. Of course, some of DSN's goods go to a designated Foreign-Trade Zone."

"What's that?" Afton asked.

"It's no big deal," Terrell said. "Just one

of many locations in the U.S. where import-
ers can store, assemble, manufacture, or
process goods." She shrugged. "It's kind of
like a tax break. DSN often uses our local
Foreign-Trade Zones so they can delay payment of duties."

"So it's just a way to help manage cash
flow," said Max.

Terrell nodded. "Something like that."

They questioned Terrell for another five
minutes but didn't come up with anything
significant. Toward the end of the conversation, she started to get a little weepy.

"Leland was a good guy, you know?" Terrell said. "It's not fair that this happened to
him." And when she walked them to the
door and Afton pressed her business card
into Terrell's hand with the admonition to
call her anytime, day or night, Terrell said,
"Please find Leland's killer, will you? I don't
think my mom can take much more of this."

When they were back in Max's car, Afton
said, "Well, that went fairly well after all."

"Still, Terrell's a tough cookie," Max said.

"She's also a woman with a secret."

Max swiveled in the front seat to face Afton. "What do you mean? You think she
knows why Odin was killed? That she knows
where Barber is?"

"I wouldn't go that far, but it felt like

something was going on."

"Yeah . . . ?" Max sounded skeptical.

"For one thing, I don't think Terrell was giving us the full story. And she acts all tough and snotty, but deep down she's insecure and lacks self-confidence."

"With all that money wrapped around her?" Max said. "I'd say she probably feels extremely secure."

"But it's not *her* money," Afton said. "At least not yet anyway."

"You have a very suspicious mind, you know that?"

"Isn't that the hallmark of a good investigator?"

"Huh," Max said. "You never stop, do you? Always with the body punches."

"You got that right."

Max pawed through the discarded fast food wrappers in the bin between the two front seats and pulled out his phone. "Gotta check in with downtown." His thumb worked the keypad. "See what's . . . Who's this, Farmer?" he barked into his phone. "Yeah, we talked to Barber's old lady and then went over to the Odin residence. Naw, not much. Just the daughter was home. What's going on with you guys?" He listened for a couple more minutes and then hung up. "Not much happening except they

194

got that updated sketch out to all the media, suburban police departments, area hotels, airports, and cab companies."

"That's something," Afton said.

"And Farmer spoke with the heart doctor who was going to do Odin's transplant surgery. He's apparently got a small window in his schedule, so he could talk to us if we want."

"Is that what we want?" Afton asked.

"Couldn't hurt to meet with him."

"When?"

Max turned his key in the ignition. "Right now."

Dr. Malcolm Graham, the cardiothoracic surgeon who would have been the team leader on Odin's transplant surgery, was young, intense, and restless. He wore green scrubs and booties over his shoes as if he'd just stepped out of a surgical suite, which he probably had. His hair was short and blond, his head slightly egg-shaped, and he had the antsy demeanor of a serious type A. They met him in the visitors' lounge on the lower-level surgical floor of the Minneapolis Heart Institute–Crosby, one of three hospitals that made up the University of Minnesota Medical Center complex. The room was sterile and cold, with a gray vinyl couch, three molded plastic chairs arranged around a round table, and a stack of dog-eared, year-old *Hospital Today* magazines.

"Cheery," Afton said once they'd all introduced themselves. "But without that overdone decorator touch you see on the VIP floor."

"Afton," Max said with a warning tone. But he was struggling to keep a straight face.

"I can only give you ten minutes," Graham said, glancing at a black rubber band that circled his left wrist. Afton figured it was either a cardiac monitor, pulse oximeter, stopwatch, phone, personal CT scanner, or some hybrid of all five. Or, glory be, maybe it even told time.

"We'll make this quick," Max said.

Graham nodded but basically ignored him. "I have a PCI at twelve," he said glancing at the door as if hoping for a quick getaway.

"What exactly does that mean?" Max asked.

"It's a percutaneous coronary intervention on a patient with severe ischemic heart disease."

"Sounds serious," Afton said.

"Believe me, it is." Dr. Graham placed his hands flat against the table. "Now . . . what? What's this all about?"

"The Leland Odin case," Max said. "Remember him?"

Dr. Graham pursed his lips and looked suddenly unhappy. "Oh. Well. Perhaps if you spoke with our corporate counsel . . ."

"We're not here to grill you about security breaches or medical malfeasance or anything like that," Afton said. Once again, Max was making like Conan the Interrogator.

"Then what do you want to know?"

"Can you tell us a little bit about the circumstances surrounding the donor-heart process?" Afton asked. "Like how does this whole organ-transplant thing work?"

"It's fairly straightforward," Dr. Graham said. "Mr. Odin's name and specific organ request was listed with the Organ Procurement and Transplantation Network. In other words, he was on the OPTN heart waiting list."

"And that's a long list?" Max asked.

"There are eleven regions in the country," Dr. Graham explained. "And we're in region seven. That includes Minnesota, the Dakotas, Iowa, and Wisconsin." He leaned forward now and gestured with his hands. "The thing is, some organs, particularly a heart, can only survive outside the body for four to seven hours. After that, it's generally not viable."

"So that's why there are different regions," Afton said.

"Exactly," Dr. Graham said. "When a donor organ becomes available, the regional waiting list always takes precedence. If there's no good match, they start to look farther away. But then it becomes much more of a gamble. Will the organ even be viable?"

"Which is why Odin's heart was coming from Madison," Max said. "They're in the same region, this hospital was fairly close by. Hence, you could rush it here via helicopter."

"Yes," Dr. Graham said. "My team was on point and ready to roll. The entire process went like clockwork right up until the end."

"When it all went boom," Max said.

"Beyond my control," Dr. Graham said.

"Would there have been another heart for Mr. Odin?" Afton asked. "If he'd managed to survive last night?"

Dr. Graham shrugged. "Who knows?"

"Would he have gone back to the top of the list?" Afton asked.

This time Dr. Graham didn't meet her eyes. "Probably not."

20

"I haven't seen food this crappy since I was in the army," Max grumbled.

After meeting with Dr. Graham, they'd wandered into a nearby cafeteria and, trays in hand, shuffled their way through the food line.

"It's hospital food," Afton said. There was a rainbow assortment of pink, green, and yellow gelatins. Some plain, some spiked with diced fruit that had probably come straight from a twenty-gallon can. "What are you gonna do?"

"Try to find something edible?"

Afton slid her tray down a metal railing past several different food stations. Here there were red neon signs that announced PIZZA, PASTA, and BURGERS. But nothing that said SALAD. Or even EAT ME, I'M SLIGHTLY MORE HEALTHY.

Afton finally settled on a bowl of tomato soup while Max opted for a grilled cheese sandwich. They grabbed a Diet Coke for Afton and a cup of coffee for Max and then sat down at one of the tables.

"Did you ever notice how most hospitals serve really awful food?" Max asked. "I mean unhealthy food." He picked up his cheese sandwich. "Take this for example — it's loaded with grease. And did you see they were serving fries up there, too? And gooey pizza?"

"Your point being?"

"You'd think they would at least run their menu past a dietician."

"This place is staffed by a bunch of eight-dollar-an-hour cafeteria ladies, not Gordon Ramsay."

But Max couldn't let it go. "Have you ever been to that hospital over on Chicago Avenue? Do you know what they have right there on the first floor? A Micky D's. Can you believe it?"

"You love Micky D's."

"I know, but that's beside the point. See, I'm guessing that particular franchise is owned by a bunch of heart surgeons who are hoping to attract a bunch of new clients."

"I guess that's the price of having a free market economy," Afton said.

Max took another bite of sandwich and

chewed thoughtfully. "So. What do you think? When your mouth is pulled tight like it is right now, you're usually trying to work out a problem."

Afton leaned forward across the cafeteria table. "Know what I think? I think someone knew that Odin's heart was winging its way from Madison. That someone was watching out for it."

"Yeah?" Despite his health rant, Max had already polished off half his sandwich.

"I think somebody right here at this hospital knew exactly which heart was earmarked for Leland Odin."

"Huh. You're saying we should forget about the Madison hospital and focus all our energy here?" Yesterday Max had spoken with two Madison detectives, who'd promised to look into things.

"Yes, I do. Somebody who was working Tuesday night must have known that Odin was being prepped for surgery. Which means they also knew his heart would be arriving via helicopter. If they were on the lookout for it, they could have . . . alerted the shooter. Or shooters."

"You mean someone was bribed to keep an eye out?"

"Maybe. Probably."

Max lifted an eyebrow, giving her a cockeyed look that said she must be plum crazy. "As in a conspiracy?"

"Yes." Now a finger of doubt had crept in and Afton thought she might have gone too far. Was she completely off base with her conspiracy theory? Was this what cops referred to as the proverbial grassy knoll?

Then Max squinted at her and said, "You know what? That makes sense to me, too."

Afton sat back and relaxed. She hadn't expected him to be so quick on the buy-in. "So what do we do next?"

Max popped the last of his sandwich into his mouth and took a slug of coffee. He chewed, swallowed hard, and said, "Let's find out who was working in the cardiac unit that night."

Ten minutes later they were sitting across an enormous oak desk from Anne Manchester, RN. She was the chief administrator tasked with scheduling the surgical teams along with the nurses, orderlies, med techs, and, probably, janitorial staff. Manchester had steel-gray eyes, matching steel-gray hair that was scraped back into a tight bun, and reading glasses that dangled on a chain around her neck. She wore an oatmeal-colored cardigan sweater over a polyester white blouse with a floppy pussycat bow at her neck. And she was frowning. Big-time.

"Your request is highly unusual," Manchester said. Afton had spent five minutes recapping all that had happened and laying the logical groundwork for their records request.

"Actually this is rather routine," Max replied. He had slid down in his chair and the toe of his shoe was knocking against the corner leg of her desk — *thunk, thunk, thunk* — clearly annoying her. Afton wasn't sure if it was deliberate or if Max was just plain bored. Or maybe he'd developed a gas bubble from wolfing down his sandwich so fast.

"It's certainly not routine for us," Manchester shot back. "Those records are private; we rarely allow anyone access to that kind of information."

"They're *scheduling* records," Afton said. "We're not asking for anybody's blood type, pay grade, or if they've ever been affiliated with the Communist Party. We just want to know who was working here that night."

"And we need to know what they were doing that night," Max said. "I mean, if they were in surgery, had their hands inside somebody's guts, then we can probably eliminate them as a suspect."

Manchester offered them a wintery smile. "I'm afraid my hands are tied. The hospital rules are quite clear."

"You realize," Max said, "this is a police investigation. Three people have *died* here at your hospital." His shoe moved again. *Thunk, thunk, thunk.*

Manchester shook her head. "It's simply not possible." Now she sounded cranky, veering toward snippy.

Max looked over at Afton and lifted a shoulder. "Here we go again."

"Who do you think I should call first?" Afton asked. "The president of the university, Governor Lindsay, or . . . who's the director here again?"

"A guy named Todd Edwards," Max said.

They'd both pulled out their phones and were talking casually, as if Manchester didn't even exist.

"Or do you want to make this exciting and play a little Russian roulette?" Max asked. "You take the university president, I'll do the governor, and we'll see who gets through first."

Manchester held up a hand. "Stop. The records are yours. Just take them and leave."

21

Hack was tipped back on a rickety black folding chair, smoking an unfiltered Camel cigarette and sucking down a can of Red Bull when his burner phone buzzed.

"Huh?" He fished the phone out of his shirt pocket and looked at the screen. Well, well, his contact at the hospital was calling him. Imagine that. He stabbed the On button. "Yeah?"

"Do you know who this is?" his contact asked.

"Course I do. It's Zach, right? We met over at the Triangle Bar a couple of nights ago."

"Um . . . what?"

"Relax, buddy, I'm just messin' with your head. Sure, I know who this is. Now what the hell do you want?"

"As you might imagine, the police have been all over this place, pulling people aside, asking questions."

"I'm sure they have. What did you think

was going to happen, big-ass explosion like that?"

"Yes, well . . . you didn't give me any warning about the *other* thing. The incident last night." The man's voice had gone hard and almost petulant. "There are serious consequences now. The police have obtained a list of all the people who were on duty Tuesday night as well as last night. They're working through it, questioning every nurse or doctor who was on the transplant team, as well as talking to all the techs and support staff who worked in or around the OR and on the VIP floor."

"Life sucks and then you die," Hack said. He snorted, turned his head, and spat a phlegmy glob onto the cement at his feet.

"The reason I called . . . I'm going to require another payment."

"I don't know," Hack said. "I'm a cash-and-carry kind of guy. I give you cash, you carry out the job. That's it. The way I see it, our arrangement is a done deal."

"The thing is, I may have to lay low for a while. Or explore other job opportunities."

"Can you do that?" Hack tried to sound concerned. "Lay low for a while? Because now that you mention it, that might be best for everyone involved."

"I can do that, yeah," the contact said.

"But, like I said, I'm gonna need some more money."

"How much more?"

"Another twenty grand." There was no hinting, there was no hedging. The man just spit out the number as if he'd been rehearsing his request for the last hour and a half.

Hack let loose a low whistle. "Big number. This ain't carte blanche, my friend. Your request for additional funds is gonna require an executive decision. I'll have to clear it with my boss. I need to — how do you say it? — take a meeting."

"When can you do that?"

"Soon. Now. So hows about you call me back in ten or fifteen minutes? Can you do that?"

"Of course, yes."

Hack punched the Off button on his phone and tucked it back into his shirt pocket. He lit up another cigarette and watched as a freight train lumbered past, not more than fifty yards from the loading dock where he was perched. It was a big sucker with four green-and-yellow locomotives pulling god knew how many grungy-looking, oil-streaked tanker cars. Reminded him of how it used to be on the docks in Duluth. Years back, in the good old taconite mining days, there were lots of trains coming and going at all hours of the day and night. Now activity had dwindled to just a few grain and coal trains.

Twelve minutes later, Hack's phone rang. He thumbed it on and said, "Yeah?"

"It's me again."

No shit. Hack tried to inject a spark of excitement into his voice. "Guess what, buddy? This is your lucky day. I talked to my employer and she approved your extra twenty grand."

"She did? That's great."

"But make no mistake about it, this is your final payment. After this you can never come back to us again. Agreed?"

"Sure, sure, that's no problem."

Hack knew it would definitely be a problem if they gave this asshole what he wanted. He would always be back . . . cajoling, threatening. But Hack let his contact rattle on anyway.

"So, will you FedEx the money or . . . ?"

"No, no," Hack said. "I'm gonna give you an address . . . You got a pencil and paper so you can write this all down?"

"Yes, of course."

"Okay, I'm gonna give you an address and you're gonna meet me there tonight at nine o'clock."

"Can we make it ten? I have to work."

"Sure, that's okay. So you'll get your money then — I'll make sure of it." Hack gave him the address, enunciating slowly and carefully as he watched the tail end of the train disappear slowly down the tracks.

"Thank you. I'll see you tonight."

Hack grinned. "I look forward to finishing up our business." Was he ever.

22

The list of names Afton and Max brought back from the hospital created a nice stir of optimism.

"These are all the people who were working Tuesday night?" Farmer asked. He was sitting at a communal desk in the middle of Homicide, pecking away at a computer. Another detective, Walter Hostetler, was going over the NTSB report. Looking for any nit or nat they could possibly use.

"That's right," Afton said. "The lady at the university was thrilled to hand it over. Delighted to help us in any way possible."

"I'll bet she was," Farmer said. He grabbed the list out of Afton's hands and scanned it quickly. "We gotta tear this thing apart and interview everybody and his brother-in-law. Everybody and his house cat. We should have been on this like stink on a skunk yesterday."

"What's with the animal metaphors?" Afton asked.

Farmer barely heard her. "Huh?"

"Hey, dufus," Max said. "That guy Sammy who spotted the decal on the red car. Did he come in yet?"

"Oh, yeah," Farmer said.

"Did you get anywhere with that?"

"Me and Hostetler showed him a whole bunch of possibilities. You know, emblems, gang signs, logos, graffiti tags, the works," Farmer said.

"Everything we had in our database," Hostetler said, jumping into the conversation. "But Sammy didn't seem to flash on any of them."

"You're going to keep working that angle though, right?" Afton asked. "Maybe access the FBI database or the BCA's?" The BCA was Minnesota's Bureau of Criminal Apprehension. "They might have something that we don't."

"Sure," Farmer said. "Whatever." He stuck a red pen in the corner of his mouth and chewed at it. "What about your guy Barber? Still no sign of him?"

"Not yet. Anybody here got anything?" Afton asked.

Farmer shook his head. "Haven't heard a thing. So I'm thinking . . . the worst?"

"You can't ever think that way," Afton

211

said. "We have to stay positive."

"Excuse me," Farmer said, "but do you really think you're cut out for law enforcement? I mean, what's with this rah-rah cheerleader-positivity business?"

"She has to stay positive," Hostetler said. "She usually works with crime victims."

"Oh, yeah," Farmer said. "I forgot that." He poked a finger at Afton. "You hang around Max so much, I figured you already scored a gold shield."

"She's helping me keep track of my notes and correlate reports," Max grunted. "Now. Can we please get back to business?"

"I thought we were," Farmer said.

"What baffles me about this whole thing," Max said, "is motive. Are these two attacks personal or is someone trying to take down the entire company?"

"Hard to take down an entire corporation," Afton said. "There have been instances where two or three top executives of a company were killed in a small plane crash and the company still keeps going. In manufacturing or retail, once everything's set in motion, the entity more or less runs itself."

"You been reading *Forbes*?" Farmer asked. "Getting your MBA in night school?"

Afton gave him a crooked grin. "You never know."

"Maybe that shopping network has been juicing the numbers," Max said. "Trying to make the profits look better than they really are. And somebody got wise to it."

They got to work then, calling the names on the list, setting up interview times. Afton went back to her own cubicle and made a couple of calls. Checking in with the families of victims that she'd worked with previously. One woman, Flossie Tyler, had just lost her son, a fourteen-year-old who had been slowly going deaf. Her son had taught himself American Sign Language and, one night on a street corner, a gang of local thugs misinterpreted his hand motions and thought he was making gang signs. They'd shot him at point-blank range. Heartbreaking.

Afton talked to Flossie, fighting to hold back tears, then made two more calls. One was to a guy, Chip Anderson, to break a date for Friday night. Chip was an okay guy who she'd been halfheartedly seeing. Problem was, he constantly referred to himself as a foodie and was forever extolling the virtues of Minneapolis as a, quote, foodie town. He'd informed her that San Francisco and Chicago were having semi-foodie moments, too, but Minneapolis was far superior since it wasn't nearly as snobby as San Francisco and definitely not as blue collar as Chicago. Afton had good friends in San Francisco and had once enjoyed a memorable dinner at Alinea in Chicago, so she was pretty sure good old Chip was full of crap. Besides, he seemed lukewarm about her kids. Yeah, that definitely made for a deal breaker. Her daughters trumped a dinner of charcuterie, sunchoke velouté, and Kobe beef any day.

Just as Afton was feeling bored and making angry doodles on a yellow pad, she was struck with an idea.

Hotfooting it into the break room, she deposited four quarters into the coffee machine and waited until a cup of burnt, too-strong coffee poured out. Then she carried it in to Max and set it down next to him.

Max looked up from his desk and sniffed like a hungry wolf. "Mmn. Crispy jitter juice — my favorite. You must want something."

"We should put a tap on Jay Barber's home phone," Afton said.

"What brought this on?"

"What if Barber isn't the innocent victim we think he is? What if Barber staged his own kidnapping? What if the little woman is in on it?"

Max picked up his cup of coffee, took a sip, and grinned at the bitter taste. "Interesting concept. Why would he do that?"

"Maybe Barber is somehow involved in this mess. Maybe he's the one who masterminded the helicopter crash to get rid of Odin. Maybe he's a slimy guy who's just trying to capitalize on Odin's death." Afton stopped and took a breath. "Anyway, think about how it could play out. Barber disappears for a while, then turns up eventually looking all bedraggled and spouting some cock-and-bull story about being held prisoner in some dark dungeon. A story that will deflect the investigation away from himself."

"Now you're starting to think like a criminal, you know that?"

"Thank you."

They batted ideas back and forth for another fifteen minutes. When Darlene, Thacker's temp, walked through, Afton said, "Is he treating you okay?"

"He claims he can't find anything," Darlene said. "Like *I'm* supposed to magically know what's in his files."

"He's just stressed," Afton said, "because his regular assistant is on maternity leave. Give him a chance."

"Yeah, yeah."

Afton glanced through Dillon's notes on Consolidated Sports, but he didn't think there was anything there.

Then, just as they all started to run low on energy, a sort of mid-afternoon slump, Dillon came hustling in, the legs of his cheap polyester slacks rubbing together and whistling like a demented tea kettle.

"Got something," Dillon said, his voice rising with excitement.

Max sat up in his chair. "What is it?"

"Test results on that cigarette filter that Joe Jelenick picked up at the noodle factory."

"So it didn't turn out to be your generic Marlboro?" Afton said.

"Not at all," Dillon said, looking pleased. "On a hunch, Jelenick e-mailed some photos of the filter to the San Francisco FBI office. We figured their crime-lab guys might be able to get a handle on it. We got their answer back a few minutes ago."

Max lifted an eyebrow. "So, what is it?"

"The filter's from a cigarette called Double Happiness, a brand that's manufactured in China and sold widely across Asia. I'm talking China, South Korea, Thailand, places like that."

"Is it sold here?" Afton asked.

216

"Here in the Twin Cities?" Dillon said. "No, we don't believe so. We just checked with the few smoke shops that are still in business and none of those places carry them. But Double Happiness cigarettes are definitely sold on the West Coast in a few specialized smoke shops, especially the ones located in major cities where there's a high concentration of Asian-Americans. Like LA and San Francisco. Maybe Vancouver."

"Still, that butt could have belonged to one of the cooks at the noodle factory," Max said.

Dillon shook his head. "I don't think so. We received word from INS that those guys are fine, all perfectly legal. Plus, they've all been here, working in this country, for at least six to eight months. Unless they brought in a containerized freight–load of cigarettes, that butt probably wasn't theirs." He paused. "There's another aspect to this cigarette business."

"What's that?" Afton asked.

"Turns out Double Happiness cigarettes are expensive. Our West Coast guy tells me they cost something like a hundred and thirty yuan a pack."

"How much is that?" Max asked.

"Approximately twenty dollars in Chinese currency."

"So twenty bucks a pack," Afton said. "That's an expensive pack of cigarettes. Probably more than the average kitchen worker can afford."

"More than most people can afford," Max said.

"Apparently Mao used to smoke them," Dillon said.

Farmer squinted at him. "Who dat?"

"Chairman Mao," Dillon said. "You know, that Cultural Revolution guy? The one Andy Warhol did all the colored portraits of?"

"Oh, that guy."

Afton was running down names and addresses on the shared computer when Thacker burst into the room. "Listen up!" he shouted. "We got a couple of breaks here." He looked excited. The collar of his jacket was askew and his tie had flown back over one shoulder. As if he'd come rocketing down the hallway.

Everyone turned to face him.

"What's up?" Dillon asked. "Please tell me we got a line on that crackhead who keeps setting Dumpster fires."

"Better than that," Thacker said. "One of our units located what they believe is one of Jay Barber's running shoes."

"Bingo," Max said.

"Where'd they find it?" Afton asked.

"In a bunch of bushes near Lake Harriet," Thacker said. "A size eleven blue-and-white Saucony running shoe."

"Did they show the shoe to his wife?" Afton asked.

"They're running it over to her right now," Thacker said. "But there's no question that it's his. The unit called her right away and she remembered that Barber was wearing those particular shoes this morning."

"Hot damn," Max said. "So somebody took him for sure."

"There's more," Thacker said. "And this is big. We just got a hit on the suspect description we sent out this morning. Personnel manager from the Hotel Itasca called. She's pretty sure two of their hotel guests match our description — an Asian man and an older American woman. They've been staying there for a couple of days, occupying one of the larger suites."

"That has to be them," Afton said.

"Which hotel did you say?" Max asked.

"Hotel Itasca," Thacker said. "Over on the river near all those new condos. Just down from the Guthrie Theater."

"That's a pretty fancy place," Afton said.

"Are the two people still there?" Max asked.

"The caller didn't say. This lady was in a blind panic. She was hyperventilating and babbling about how she had to notify her security guy."

"Let's go!" Max yelled. Everybody jumped to their feet in a mad rush, eager to be in on a possible bust.

Thacker held up a finger. "Wait one."

"Wait for what?" Afton asked. "If they're still there, we've got them."

"Nobody's taking a step inside that hotel lobby unless an entry team goes in first."

23

"What the hell?" the desk clerk cried out when he saw four SWAT officers charging across the contemporary and very minimalist lobby of the Hotel Itasca. The SWAT guys wore full body armor and tinted face shields, and looked as if they were ready to engage in a gun battle in the streets of Fallujah. "What's the meaning of this?" he sputtered. "Who are you people?"

Max elbowed his way to the front of the pack and skidded to a stop in front of the registration desk. He held up his ID. "Detective Max Montgomery, accompanied by Liaison Officer Afton Tangler and four of our very capable and heavily armed SWAT officers. Pleased to make your acquaintance. And you are . . . ?"

"Kyle Dalman, hotel manager."

"General manager?" Afton asked.

"Well . . . day manager."

"Just the man we need to see," Max said.

Dalman was a nervous-looking skinny guy with slicked-back hair. He wore a slim-fitting black suit that was probably supposed to be very hipster and European, but Afton thought his pants just looked way too short. A man's socks shouldn't show *that* much, should they?

"We're looking for two people who are or have been staying at your hotel. One Asian man, one American-looking older woman," Max said. "We put an alert out on them and your personnel manager, Miss Lucy Ronson, called us?"

"Ms. Ronson's not here," Dalman said. "I just tried to ring her office."

"What about your two hotel guests?" Afton asked. "Are they here?" She was chafing at the bit, ready to bust the asshole who'd killed Odin and slashed her arm last night. He must be one of the guests. *Had* to be.

"You just missed them," Dalman said. "They checked out."

"What!" Max said.

"When?" Afton asked.

"Today. Late morning. The usual."

"Crap on a cracker." Max's hand slammed down hard against the front desk. "Do you know where they went?"

Dalman looked pained. "No, I don't. Why do you . . . ? I'm sorry, I was just made aware of this issue a few moments ago."

"We think they masterminded a helicopter crash two nights ago," Max said. "And murdered someone last night."

"And possibly kidnapped another man this morning," Afton added.

Dalman turned pale. "Oh . . . oh my goodness."

Afton asked Dalman the same question she'd asked Zhang last night: "Do you have a security camera?"

"Just at the front and back doors," Dalman said. "We're a high-end hotel and we pride ourselves on being discreet."

"We'll need to look at that footage," Max said.

"And I'll bet you have their credit cards on file," Afton said. "If you do, we need to take a look."

"Let me check." Dalman hit a few keys on his computer. "Yes, of course. Here it is. We require a credit card on file even though they paid with traveler's checks."

"What card did they use?" she asked.

"A Visa card from the Standard Chartered Bank of Thailand."

"Thailand," Afton said. She had the odd sense that things might start to fall into place. "Did you get Xerox copies of their passports as well?"

"This is America," Dalman said. "Guests aren't required to present their passports when checking in. That's only when Americans travel to foreign countries."

"That's some stupid policy," Max snarled. "What about IDs?"

"Well, we have their names."

"Give them to us, please," Afton said.

Dalman hit more keys and then a sheet spit out of his printer. He pushed it across the counter as if he were handling a dead rat.

Afton grabbed the sheet and read it out loud. "Victoria Achara and Michael Piwat." She bit her lip and gazed at Max. "You think these are their real names?"

"No," Max said. "But we'll run them through the system anyway, just to be sure."

"Got it. And we need to look at their room."

Dalman's brows pinched together. "But the guests have left. Housekeeping has already cleaned the rooms."

"Nevertheless, we still need to take a look," Afton said. "It's very important."

"Yes. Fine," Dalman said. He slid a key card across the counter. "Suite Twelve-B. The penthouse. Please don't disturb anything."

"Before we go up, is there anything else

you can tell us?" Afton asked. "Did they order room service, entertain any guests, anything like that?"

Dalman squinted at his computer screen again. "They were fairly quiet as guests go. Checked in five days ago, checked out this morning. No special requests or anything like that. Oh, they did receive a phone call. Looks like it was long distance."

"Is it possible to check your log?" Afton asked. "Determine where the call came from?"

Max squinted at Dalman. "Long distance, huh? Like from what part of the country? California? New York?"

Dalman shook his head as he studied the screen. "No. It looks like . . . Thailand."

"They got a call from Thailand?" Afton asked. She leaned forward and gripped the counter with both hands. "And you have that number?"

"Not offhand, but I think I can locate it if I . . ." Dalman bent over his computer again and hit a few keys. "Maybe if I . . . Okay, I have that number. Do you want it?"

"Please," Afton said. She wrote down the number carefully and then looked at Max. "Can you get through to a foreign country with your cell phone?"

■ ■ ■ ■

Turned out he could. Not only that, they did a quick calculation and discovered that it was nine o'clock in the morning in Thailand. Then they found the international calling code for Thailand — 66 — and Max made the call.

Afton stood in the sitting room of Suite 12-B watching the SWAT guys poke through closets and look under furniture, as they waited for Max's call to go through. One of the SWAT guys was eyeing a bronze statue of a naked woman.

"Can you put your call on speaker?" Afton asked.

Max nodded and pressed a button. There was a hollow, crackling sound and then a polite voice, a woman's voice, answered with, "Good morning, Kantana Industrial Group."

"Yes," Max said. "I'm calling about one of your people." Max looked at Afton and shrugged. He was winging it all the way. "One of your employees."

"I'm sorry, what is your inquiry about?" came the receptionist's precise, clipped voice. She pronounced it in-*quire*-y.

"Mr. Michael Piwat," Max said. "The man

who's in Minneapolis, Minnesota, right now. Traveling on business?"

"I'm sorry," the receptionist replied. "I have no knowledge of that person."

"Ask for her supervisor," Afton whispered.

"May I speak with your supervisor?" Max asked. "With your boss?"

"Most certainly," said the receptionist.

This time a young man came on the phone. English-speaking but with an accent. "May I help you?"

"I'm calling about Michael Piwat. He's in Minneapolis, Minnesota, right now on business?"

"We have no one by that name in our company."

"How about a Victoria Achara? I believe she's traveling with him."

"I'm sorry, no."

"Are you sure?" Max asked. "Because I'm standing in the suite the two of them vacated this morning at the Hotel Itasca." He bobbled his head back and forth, as if trying to come up with a credible cover story.

"They left something behind," Afton hissed.

"And the problem is," Max said, "some of their papers were inadvertently left behind. In the hotel room. I'm afraid our cleaning staff just found them. They appear to be important business papers and we'd like to get them back to Mr. Piwat and Miss Achara as soon as possible. So if you could tell me where they are, that would be a great help."

"Who am I speaking with, please?"

"Uh, this is the concierge at the Hotel Itasca. In Minneapolis. Where are you located?"

"Bangkok, Thailand. But as I just told you, we have no Michael Piwat or Victoria Achara working at Kantana Industrial."

"You're sure of that?"

"Quite sure."

"Okay," Max said. "Thanks." He pushed the Off button. "Struck out."

"No, we didn't," Afton said. "Somebody at this Kantana Industrial place called these people, so we know there's a definite connection." She glanced around the suite, saw the bed with its sumptuous silk duvet, the side table with a small collection of Chinese cloisonné.

"Problem is, our jurisdiction doesn't extend to Thailand." Max hesitated. "Unless . . ."

"What are you thinking?"

"Let me make another call."

Max called back to headquarters, asked for Jelenick and his Crime Scene team to be sent over, and then had his call routed to Deputy Chief Thacker. He gave Thacker a quick rundown on what they'd learned so far. The names of the two people, the phone call from Thailand, the fabulous hotel suite. Then he listened for a couple of minutes, nodding as if he agreed with everything Thacker was saying.

"What?" Afton asked once Max was off the phone.

"Thacker says he's going to get in touch with both Interpol and the CIA. See if they have anything on a Michael Piwat or Victoria Achara as well as a Kantana Industrial Group in Bangkok."

"Did he say if there's been any sign of Jay Barber yet?"

"He said they still only have the running shoe." Max shook his head. "A stupid shoe. Not much to go on. Nothing to go on."

"So that's it?" Afton felt suddenly deflated. They'd come rushing over to the Hotel Itasca to hopefully make an arrest, only to find they were one step behind yet again.

"Thacker did say one thing."

"What's that?"

"He thought we got some pretty decent intel."

"Let's just hope we can make something pop," Afton said. She looked around the suite, at the leather chairs, velvet cushions, crystal chandelier, thick swags of drapery, naked-lady statue, sitting room, bar, and separate bedroom. "So this is how the other half lives."

"Pretty swanky," Max agreed. "Wonder if I could rent this joint for Tyler and Jake? They'd go bonkers if they could have a pizza party here and invite all their friends."

"The hotel would probably ask for a serious damage deposit."

"Probably because there'd be serious damage," Max said.

"Did you find anything?" a voice behind them called out.

Afton and Max both turned to find Dalman, the manager, standing in the doorway.

"No," Max said. "Not much of anything."

"Told you so," said Dalman.

"But Crime Scene is still going to come over and check the room," Afton said.

Dalman bristled. "They'd better not leave a mess."

"Perhaps you should oversee them," Afton said. She was sure Jelenick and his team would love that.

"This is a nice suite you have here," Max said. Afton was pretty sure he was trying to make nice and smooth any ruffled feathers.

"This is basically four-star," Dalman said.

"Although we were given three stars by the *Michelin Guide.*"

"That's good?" Max asked.

"That's the best," Dalman said.

Afton took in the amenities once again. Better than the last Holiday Inn she'd stayed in, and a whole lot fancier than her own home. And that white velvet chaise lounge looked . . . exquisite.

"Excuse me," she said to Dalman. "This is where the man, Piwat, stayed?"

Dalman shook his head. "No, the woman stayed here. Miss Achara."

"The *woman* stayed here," Afton repeated.

"Yes," Dalman said absently, drifting back out the door. "Please do take care, will you? Close the door when you leave?"

"She's the important one," Afton said to Max once they were alone.

"You think?"

"Has to be. She's the one in charge, she's the one calling the shots."

"What does that mean?" Max asked.

"I don't know," Afton said. She walked to the windows and looked out. The view was magnificent. The Mississippi River made a leisurely S-curve below. Directly across the river were two terra-cotta-colored condominiums. Each one featured a large terrace and each unit was stepped back from the one below it so everyone enjoyed a full view of sun and sky. A little farther upstream, another luxury hotel sat on a small island, like its own unique principality, connected to the east river bank by an old-fashioned ironwork trestle bridge.

Afton drifted back toward the door, trailing her fingers along a black lacquered table that was smooth as polished obsidian.

"Afton?" Max said. "We should get back."

Afton tilted her head back, almost like a coyote testing the wind. The suite carried the faint mingled aromas of Chanel No. 5 perfume, furniture polish, and . . . something else. Could it be a hint of burnt wood?

24

Afton and Max went back to headquarters armed with Xerox copies of the two IDs that Dalman had given them.

"They were definitely using fake IDs," Thacker said. "We already ran those two names and found out they're both stolen identities that were probably purchased on some black market website."

"So the names are a dead end," Afton said. She was still noodling around the idea of the woman being in charge.

"Did you get anything on Kantana Industrial Group?" Max asked.

"No," Thacker said. "I talked to a friend of a friend who works at Interpol in Singapore and nothing about that particular company had ever come across his desk. In fact, the only thing he knew about Bangkok was that human trafficking is rampant there, and the CIA once set up some sort of black ops site at Don Mueang Airport where they interrogated al-Qaeda suspects."

"Now what do we do?" Afton asked.

"Keep checking through those names you got from the university hospital," Thacker said. "Work that angle."

"Sure," Max said while Afton just made a face at him from behind Thacker's back.

"There's got to be some way we can run a check on Kantana Industrial," Afton said to Max. She'd worked at her own desk for twenty minutes and then, feeling antsy as hell, had come creeping back to talk to Max.

"Short of buying an airline ticket to Bangkok, I don't know what it would be," Max said.

"What if they're still here?" Afton asked. "What if they're not finished with whatever they came to do?"

"More killing?" Max said.

"I don't know. Maybe we should stake out the local Thai restaurants."

"Somehow, I don't think that's the answer."

Afton doodled some x's and o's on a legal pad for a few minutes. "When I worked in Data Entry, there was a guy there who was married to a woman from Thailand."

"You want to go pester some guy's wife? About . . . what exactly?"

"The thing is," Afton said, "I seem to recall that the wife's brother worked as a cop in Bangkok."

"Bangkok."

"I know it might be a long shot, but . . ."

"But you want to try this angle anyway."

Afton shrugged. "Hey, it's all I can think of at the moment."

Max stood up and stretched. "Okay, but if your guy gets all ticked off at us, don't come crying to me."

Don Martin still worked in Data Entry on the third floor. He was a twenty-eight-year-old guy who'd worked at Chulalongkorn University in Bangkok for two years teaching English. It was where he'd met his wife and earned a few credits to put toward his master's degree. Now he was chipping away at his PhD at Metropolitan State University. Martin remembered Afton and seemed genuinely pleased to see her.

Once Max and Martin were introduced, they moved into a small break room that had a Formica table, chairs, Coke and candy bar machines, and a small refrigerator. The refrigerator had an angry handwritten note stuck on the door that said, *Stop stealing my soup — I know who you are and I'm watching you!*

"Afton's one of our success stories," Martin said to Max. "She moved upstairs while I'm still here."

"The difference is," Afton said, "you're doing this to earn a living so you can springboard your way into some Fortune 500 company as an executive VP, while I'm trying to be a cop."

"So how can I help you?" Martin asked.

"You're still married?" Afton asked.

Martin looked a little startled. "Sure. Sami and I have been married four years now." He smiled. "In fact, we're thinking about starting a family."

"We've got a case we're working on," Max said. He glanced at Afton. "Why don't you run through it for him?"

Afton quickly outlined the broad strokes of the Leland Odin case, then told him about chasing the suspect last night, putting together the Identi-Kit, and going to the Hotel Itasca and finding out about the two possible suspects. Then she told him about Max's phone call to Kantana Industrial Group in Bangkok.

"That's all rather chilling," Martin said, looking a little nervous. "But what does it have to do with me?"

"Nothing," Afton said. "But we were

wondering if we could possibly talk to your wife."

"To Sami?"

"If I recall, her brother is a Bangkok police officer."

"With the RTP, the Royal Thai Police." Martin leaned back in his chair and looked thoughtful. "I suppose I see where this is heading."

Sami Martin worked as a paralegal at the Winder and Josten law firm in the IDS Center in downtown Minneapolis. Her husband had phoned ahead and told her that Afton and Max would be stopping by. Sami, a serious-looking woman with dark hair, golden complexion, and beautiful smile, wearing a serious-looking navy blue skirt suit, met them at the front desk. She led them into a wood-paneled conference room and closed the door, and they all sat down at a polished mahogany table. From the looks of things, Sami was doing well.

"Don called me," Sami said. "He said you were interested in speaking with my brother Kai Pak?"

"That's right," Afton said. "We're trying to get a handle on a certain Bangkok company. You heard about the helicopter crash over at the university?"

Sami nodded.

"There have been several more developments since then," Afton said. She took a few minutes to update Sami on the events thus far.

"Oh," Sami said, looking surprised. "It's like a manhunt."

"It is a manhunt," Max said.

"Anyway," Afton continued, "we've surmised that the people involved in that crash, and who were staying at the Hotel Itasca, have ties to a particular Bangkok company."

"Which company would that be?" Sami asked.

"Kantana Industrial Group," Afton said.

Sami's eyes widened slightly. "You know this for a fact?"

"Pretty much," Max said. "Problem is, we're two thousand miles away from Bangkok, so it's hard to gather any sort of decent intelligence."

"I have heard of Kantana Industrial," Sami said.

"Seriously?" Afton said. "Then are you familiar with the names Michael Piwat and Victoria Achara?"

Sami shook her head. "No. I'm afraid not."

"But Kantana Industrial. Do you know what they . . . ?"

"Kantana Industrial is a ship-building

company. But they are also rumored to be a front for a criminal organization."

"What!" Afton said.

"Criminal how?" Max asked.

Sami looked serious. "Guns, drugs, and the sex trade."

"Holy shit," Max said. "These are bad guys."

"You have no idea," Sami said.

"Would it be, um, feasible to talk to your brother about this company?" Afton asked. "To maybe get a little local information?"

Sami considered the request for a few moments. Then she said, "Perhaps it would not be in his best interest. Some members of the Royal Thai Police have, shall we say . . . connections to various entities. It's not always easy to determine who is an ally and who cannot be trusted."

"I see," Afton said.

"I'm very sorry," Sami said. "But my brother could be in danger if . . ."

"It's okay," Afton said to Sami. "I think we picked up some valuable information just talking to you."

"What does this all sound like?" Max asked. It was four in the afternoon and they were walking down Marquette Avenue, shouldering their way through a bunch of early commuters.

"Just off the top of my head, it sounds like Diamond Shopping Network might have been involved in something really nasty and illegal," Afton said. "I think I read somewhere that DSN imports, like, ninety percent of the goods that are sold on the air."

"Imports them from Thailand?"

"Probably from all over China, Southeast Asia, and India," Afton said.

"So they're a shopping network and also a front for something else?"

"I don't know. That sounds awfully farfetched."

"Hold on a minute," Max said. He broke away from Afton and walked over to a red-and-yellow food truck that was parked at the curb. "Two tacos, please," he said to the clerk at the window counter. He glanced back at Afton. "You want a taco, don't you?"

"Why not?"

"Two pulled-pork tacos," Max said. "With chilies and cheese sauce."

They munched tacos in little tinfoil wrappers as they strolled along.

"Now we know there's a Bangkok connection," Max said. "The case isn't exactly coming together, but we know a little bit more than we did before."

"Except who those two people really are. And where Jay Barber disappeared to."

"I didn't say we cracked the case," Max said. "Far from it."

"What if the people from the hotel, Piwat and Achara, have another set of IDs and they're already on a plane that's halfway across the Pacific by now?"

"Then we're not going to catch them. Then we're shit out of luck."

"So we follow the Jay Barber connection," Afton said slowly.

"We follow up with Sunny, that lawyer Steckel, and the folks at Diamond Shopping Network."

"What do you think we should do first?" Afton asked.

"None of the above," Max said. "It's quittin' time. For you, anyway. I'm going to work the phones for a little while and give this a last-ditch effort, see if there's anybody we can plug into internationally."

"I don't want to go home. We've done some really good work. We're on a hot streak."

"Ah, you're just dehydrated."

"Max . . ."

"I mean it," Max said. "You're still recovering from last night. You should go home, put on a pair of fuzzy slippers, and watch *Wheel of Fortune.* Eat something bad."

"I'm already wolfing down a street taco. I'm probably going to get heartburn."

"I meant eat something really bad. Like Chunky Chip cookies or Nutty Monkey Ice Cream."

"I'll tell you what we should do," Afton said. "We should go out to Diamond Shopping Network and put the screws to Fan Ling."

"You don't like her, do you?"

"I don't know her enough to dislike her. But, right now, I don't trust anybody out there."

Max stared at her. "You really want to do that?"

"More than anything."

25

Because Max had called ahead, Angus Wagner, the general manager, met them at the front door.

"Is this about Mr. Odin or Mr. Barber?" Wagner asked. He looked somber, as if he'd been breaking bad news to people all day long. Which he probably had.

"Why?" Afton asked. "Don't tell me Barber finally showed up?"

Wagner shook his head. "Afraid not. Nobody's seen him or even heard from him. We're all extremely worried."

"I think you should be," Max said. "One of his running shoes was found near Lake Harriet around eleven o'clock this morning."

Wagner looked astonished. "That's it? Just his shoe?" He touched a hand to his forehead. "What does that mean?"

"We're not entirely sure," Afton said. "But if he was blown clear out of his sneakers, it might mean that somebody snatched him."

"He was kidnapped?" Wagner's face crumpled with worry. "Holy smokes. What's going on? First Mr. Odin is murdered in his sleep, now Mr. Barber is missing." He looked miserable. "Does someone have it in for our company? Are they trying to destroy us?"

"That's what we're trying to figure out," Max said.

"Well, figure harder if you can."

"Mr. Wagner," Afton said, "are you familiar with a company by the name of Kantana Industrial Group that's located in Bangkok, Thailand?"

Wagner shook his head. "No, I'm not."

"You don't think your company might do business with them? Or has in the past?"

"We really need to nail down a possible connection," Max said.

"Are they the people who killed Mr. Odin?" Wagner asked.

"We don't know that. We're following up on several leads," Max said.

"I suppose we could go talk to the buyers," Wagner said. Then he frowned, shook his head, and said, "No, I'm not thinking straight today. Too much bad news. If anything, it would be better if we went and talked to Janine."

"Who's Janine?" Afton asked.

"She's our controller," Wagner said. "Every contract, purchase order, or invoice that has to do with our vendors passes directly through her hands."

"Then let's go talk to Janine," Max said.

Janine Worley was a plump fifty-year-old woman who looked like she should stay home and bake cookies and banana bread. But to everyone at DSN she was a tough corporate autocrat who you took care never to cross. From her spacious private office, she reigned over a dozen bookkeepers, accountants, and administrative assistants who sat in a bullpen just outside her door. When Angus explained to Janine what Afton and Max were looking for, she pursed her fleshy lips and the corners of her mouth turned downward. "Does this have something to do with Mr. Odin getting killed?" she asked.

Afton noticed that Worley didn't bother to get up. She made no motion to shake hands. She just sat behind her desk like the Queen of Sheba.

"We're following up on several leads," Max said, knowing he was beginning to sound like a broken record.

"What was that name again?"

"Kantana Industrial Group."

"Doesn't ring a bell," Janine said. She swiveled her desk chair around and faced one of two computer screens. "But let me check." As her manicured fingers flew over the keys, searching her database of vendors, her upper arms jiggled. "No," she said after a minute or so. "I don't see any company with that name."

"Could Kantana Industrial be listed under a different identifier?" Afton asked.

Janine turned heavy-lidded eyes toward Afton. "Such as?"

"I don't know."

Janine gazed at Wagner. "Do you know when Mr. Odin's funeral is going to be held?"

"Friday," Wagner said. "That's what I'm hearing."

"Has Mr. Barber been located yet?"

"I'm afraid not," Wagner said.

"Do you think he's dead, too?" Janine asked. She scanned Wagner's face and then moved on to Afton and Max.

Nobody said anything.

Janine finally cracked. She slid open a desk drawer, pulled out a Kleenex tissue, and dabbed at her eyes. Then she stared directly at Max. "You people have to find this killer," she said. "Before he rips our company to shreds."

"Believe me, we're trying," Max said. "We're doing everything we can."

"Janine's been with us since the very beginning," Wagner said. "She's very loyal."

Janine looked back at her computer and sniffled. "I wish I could help you in some way."

"DSN imports merchandise from Thailand, am I right?" Afton asked.

"We probably import from fifty different countries," Janine said. "But the bulk of our merchandise is purchased through wholesalers, so we don't always know the exact company or country of origin."

"Isn't everything clearly marked?" Afton asked.

"Yes, of course," Janine said. "But when you go into a big, fancy department store and the dress label says MADE IN PARIS, I can tell you unequivocally that's not always the case. So you can imagine what we deal with here." She raised her penciled brows as if to say, *What can you do?*

"Caveat emptor," Afton said.

"Excuse me?" Janine said.

Wagner knew what the phrase meant and gave a sad smile. "Let the buyer beware."

Fan Ling was at the top of their list to be jacked up, but it turned out she was in a particularly uncooperative mood. Correction: She was in a horrible mood.

Fan Ling sat in her private dressing room wearing a pink silk robe and curled up in a yellow tub chair, her feet tucked daintily beneath her. Her hair was clipped into a high, loose ponytail and copious tears streamed down her soft cheeks.

"Why are you questioning me?" she sobbed. "Why can't you just leave me alone!"

"Fan Ling," Max said in a fairly gentle tone, "we need to know why you were at the university hospital last night? Less than an hour before Leland Odin was murdered."

She turned wild eyes on Max, Afton, and Wagner. "You think *I* murdered Mr. Odin? My special *benefactor*?" This brought on a fresh onslaught of tears accompanied by loud hiccups.

"We're not accusing you of anything," Max said. "We just need answers to a few simple questions."

Fan Ling threw up an arm as if to ward off a serious blow. "No questions," she shouted. "I know my rights. I don't have to answer any questions." Her tears had caused her eye makeup to smear horribly, and now she looked like a sad raccoon.

Max turned an imploring look on Afton.

248

A look that said, *Maybe you can talk some sense into Fan Ling?*

Oh dear, Afton thought. She crept closer to Fan Ling and went down on one knee directly in front of her. "Ms. Ling? We're trying to *catch* Mr. Odin's killer. Do you understand that?"

Fan Ling shook her head vigorously. "You will not catch him by questioning me!"

"Look," Afton said, "all we want to know is: Why did you visit Mr. Odin at the hospital last night?"

Fan Ling reached up and unclipped her hair. It spread like a dark curtain around her shoulders. "Because Mr. Odin was very special to me."

"Because he discovered you?" Afton asked. "Because he was the one who gave you a job in this company?"

Fan Ling turned away from Afton and stared at the wall. "So insensitive," she muttered. "Mr. Odin would never let you treat me this way."

"I certainly don't mean to treat you with any disrespect," Afton said. "Or accuse you of any crime or wrongdoing. The thing is, you were close to Mr. Odin, so you might know something. It's possible that a small — maybe even incidental — bit of information could point us in the right direction, could help us apprehend Mr. Odin's killer."

"This is crazy. You're making me crazy," Fan Ling said. "I must go on live television in forty minutes." She pronounced it *four-tee.*

"I realize that," Afton said. "And we certainly don't mean to upset you. But you realize that Mr. Barber is also missing?"

Fan Ling curled a lip. "You think *I* took him?"

"No, no, of course not," Afton said. "But I'm sure you can understand that a lot of people are being hurt. And that this company — your company — is in trouble."

Fan Ling just shook her head.

Afton stared at her, wondering if Fan Ling gave everybody this much grief or if she was just a poor, young girl who was scared to death. Whatever the reason, they weren't making any forward progress.

"Fan Ling," Wagner said, speaking up for the first time, "if you think of anything that might be of help, we'd really appreciate it."

But Fan Ling just crossed her arms and refused to talk.

Afton sighed. So much for exploring that avenue.

"I don't think she'll be able to go on air today," Wagner murmured, half to himself.

Fan Ling's eyes blazed. "I will go on."

26

It was a little past six o'clock when Afton finally arrived home. Bonaparte met her at the front door, eyes liquid and bright, toenails clicking against the parquet floor in the entryway.

"Bonaparte." Afton knelt down and gave the dog a gentle hug. Bonaparte pressed himself up against her, his tail working overtime. "That's my boy." It felt good to embrace a sweet living thing after the day she'd had. After the week she'd had.

"Mommy?" a squeaky voice called out.

Afton got to her feet, shrugged off her jacket, and headed into the kitchen. Poppy and Tess were sitting at the table finishing up their homework. The table was already set with her mom's old Fiestaware, and Lish was just pulling a pan of lasagna from the oven.

"If it isn't our own 007," Lish said. "And such perfect timing, too."

"Hey, guys," Afton said. She kissed each girl on the top of her head and flashed an enthusiastic smile at Lish. "That lasagna looks fantastic. Smells good, too."

"Doesn't it?" Lish said. She set the pan on top of the stove and pulled off her oven mitts. "It's from a recipe I clipped out of the Taste section. You use Roma tomatoes, ricotta cheese, and pecorino cheese."

"Sounds like it's almost made from scratch."

Lish smiled. "Almost."

Tess squirmed around in her chair to look at Afton. "Mommy, what happens if you put a marshmallow in the microwave?"

"I don't know," Afton said, squeezing the girl's shoulders. "But maybe we shouldn't find out."

"You got a call about your car today," Lish said.

"Oh, yeah?" Afton said. She'd gotten a Jaguar XK-E and a Lincoln Navigator as part of her recent divorce settlement from Mickey Craig, ex-husband number two. Now she was trying to sell the Jag.

"It was a dealer from Rochester," Lish said. "And he sounded very interested."

"Excellent," Afton said. "Because I'm more than interested."

"Why do we have to sell the Jag?" Tess

252

asked. She was old enough to know it was a cool ride.

Afton smiled at her. "Because our family only needs one car, and we can invest the proceeds of the sale to help pay for your college education."

"I got an A on my spelling quiz today," Poppy said.

"That's fantastic," Afton said. "Sounds like you're already on the way to acing your SATs. Maybe you can even get a scholarship." She gathered up the kids' books and papers and placed everything on a side table. "Are we ready to eat?"

Lish nodded. "Let's do it."

"I'm probably going to be a famous author someday," Poppy said as Lish placed a square of lasagna on everyone's plate, followed by a scoop of mixed green salad. "Like Henningway."

"Hemingway," Tess corrected. Then she added, "He's dead."

"When did that happen?" Poppy asked innocently. Which made everybody laugh.

After dinner, Lish went upstairs to give herself a pedicure while Afton, Poppy, and Tess cleaned up in the kitchen. The girls stacked the dirty dishes in the dishwasher while Afton wiped down the counters, stove,

253

and refrigerator — it was amazing how far red sauce could spatter.

She paused in front of the refrigerator. Along with a bunch of drawings and restaurant coupons held on with magnets, there was a photo of a cute little blond toddler. It was Elizabeth Ann Darden, a child she'd helped rescue from kidnappers a few months ago. According to the girl's mother, Susan, Elizabeth Ann was now thriving and things were getting back to normal. Except, of course, for Susan's divorce from her cheating husband, Richard.

"Mommy," Poppy said, "you know that red shirt with the black polka dots that you bought me?"

Afton punched the On button for the dishwasher, turned, and said, "You mean the one we got at the Kids General Store? That one?"

"Uh-huh. Do you think it makes me look like a ladybug?"

"Well, uh . . . no. Not really." Afton knew that if she said yes, Poppy would never wear that particular blouse again.

"Oh. Good," Poppy said.

"Is it okay if I get my paints out?" Tess asked. She'd gotten a starter set of acrylic paints for her birthday and was beginning to experiment.

"Homework all done?"

"Yup."

"Okay, then, sure. We can put down some newspapers and you can paint right here at the table," Afton said.

Once Tess was painting — she'd decided to try her hand at portraiture and had gotten Bonaparte to sit still, for now — Afton joined Poppy on the couch, where she was curled up with a book but not really reading it.

"What's up?" Afton asked. "Doing a book review? Checking out the competition author-wise?"

Poppy laid her book flat on her lap. "Should we be worried?" she asked.

"About what, honey?"

"Oh . . . things."

"Could you be more specific?" Afton asked.

"Dinosaurs aren't really real, are they?"

"No. The ones you see in movies look real but they're computer generated. You know, like cartoons."

"Okay."

Afton sensed there was more. "What else are you worried about, Poppy?"

"The zombie apocalypse?"

"There's no such thing." Afton knew damn well that there were real monsters roving around out there, but she wasn't about to explain that to her baby girl. No way. Keep her kids safe for as long as it takes. Forever, if it came to that.

"So the TV ones are cartoons, too?" Poppy asked. "The zombie people?"

"I think those are mostly actors with lots of goopy makeup on their faces to make them look all green and moldy." Afton hesitated. "Anything else?"

"Do you think I could have a Rice Krispies bar?"

"I think that could be arranged."

Tess looked up from her painting. "Just don't leave it sitting on the table by the TV or Bonaparte will get it." She shook her head. "You can't trust dogs to watch your food."

By nine o'clock the kids were tucked into bed. At ten o'clock Afton decided she could do with some serious z's herself. Still, what she'd come to think of as the Leland Odin mess continued to swirl around in her brain. When she was with the girls, it was fairly easy to quiet her mind and set aside the pressure of the workday. But when she was alone, when she wanted to find some inner solace and peace, then the questions and what-ifs reared their ugly heads: What if the killers had already left the country? What if Sunny had contracted for these killers? How was Fan Ling involved? Or was she?

Afton crawled into bed and punched on the tiny TV set that sat at the foot of her bed. She scanned the news channels but, thankfully, found nothing that was related to her case. Then, out of curiosity, she switched over to the Diamond Shopping Network.

She watched with a faint degree of curiosity as an enthusiastic on-air host named Jeffrey held up a bright red frying pan and urged viewers to stay tuned for the Confetti Cookware show coming up next hour. Then Jeffrey's twinkling eyes and dulcet tones reminded her that they were only halfway through their Treasures of Asia show and that there were lots of exciting things just ahead.

Jeffrey — clearly she was on a first name basis with him now — held up a decorative butterfly pillow and began to extoll its virtues as the perfect accent piece for your bed or sofa. Then he moved on to a blue-and-white Chinese vase, a matched pair of ceramic foo dogs (cute but expensive), a tea set decorated with swirls of pink peonies, and a jade-colored incense burner.

Afton frowned and sat up a little straighter in bed.

Incense. That's what she'd smelled in that fancy suite at the Hotel Itasca. Someone had been burning incense.

But what did it mean? Maybe nothing.

Maybe something.

She snapped off the TV and turned out the light. For some reason she felt like calling Max. But no. It was too late to call. Have to catch him first thing tomorrow morning. Let her brain stew on all this crap while she slept. She yawned deeply. Maybe figure something out. But for now . . . *zzzzz.*

27

The Callahan Casket Company, located a few blocks west of Central Avenue in northeast Minneapolis, had shut down some twenty years ago when the funeral industry downshifted into what's now generally accepted as the cremation industry. Cremation caught on big-time because it proved to be cheaper than traditional burial, was much more environmentally friendly than a leaky tomb, and neatly solved the problem of overcrowded cemeteries. Plus, baby boomers loved it. To them, cremation sounded more like an *alternative concept,* which meant they could avoid thinking about the harsh realities of dying. At least for a while.

After the casket factory shuttered its doors, the enormous redbrick monolith of a building stood empty for ten years until a hopeful group of artists, painters, potters, and photographers tried to carve out studio space inside of it. But somehow, the giant hooks in the ceiling, the metal tracks that led out to the loading dock, the catacomb-like atmosphere, just hadn't been all that conducive to creativity. Or to attracting a flurry of wealthy, artsy people who wanted to attend their studio openings.

Now the artists were scattered all throughout northeast Minneapolis in cheery, sunlit studios while the empty casket factory still hunkered next to a jumble of railroad tracks, looking gloomier and more deserted than ever.

Except the building wasn't deserted.

On this chilly Thursday night, Mom Chao Cherry, Narong, and Hack were gathered in the basement. Narong had built a charcoal-and-wood fire on the stone floor and now that small blaze illuminated their faces as well as the body of the man stretched out on the floor in front of them. Unfortunately, the fire did nothing to penetrate the darkness of that enormous subterranean room.

Jay Barber came awake in several stages. First he realized that he was dreaming and allowed himself to slide back into the gray zone where he'd been hovering for what felt like many, many hours.

Then he decided it must be very early

morning, but he could still sneak in another hour of shut-eye.

Finally, his thinking became slightly more cogent and he really did begin to wake up. But he was feeling irritated by his wife, Shelly, who kept yapping in his ear.

"Where is it?" Shelly yapped.

"Where is what?" Barber mumbled back to her.

"Where is it?" she asked again.

"Shut up," Barber said.

A man's voice suddenly sliced through the fabric of Barber's dream, shocking him and rousing him to almost total consciousness.

"The blow," Hack snarled. "Where'd you people stash the blow?"

What? Barber peeped open a single eyelid, only to discover a man standing over him. He was also shocked and totally discombobulated when he realized he wasn't in his own bed and that it wasn't his wife who was screeching at him. It was . . .

"I know you," Barber said in a dry, scratchy voice. He tried to swallow, but his stomach clenched in a painful knot and his throat suddenly felt like sandpaper. It was all coming back to him in a blinding flash, like a fast-forwarded horror movie on his DVR. He remembered running along Lake Harriet Boulevard and then . . . the slap of something painful? Tumbling down hard and seeing two men's faces?

"That's good," Hack said. "You look like you're finally starting to track. You've been out like a light for almost sixteen hours." He turned to Narong and said, "Gotta get me some of that tranquilizer shit."

"Water," Barber gasped. "I need water."

"No problem," Hack said. "So long as you cooperate."

"What?" Barber asked. He looked confused.

"Where's the shit?" Hack asked.

"Shit?" Barber was even more awake now, a look of panic lighting his face as he realized that his arms and legs were tied down. That he was lying spread-eagled on a cold stone floor in a dank basement somewhere.

"That's right," Hack said amiably. "The white lady. The gutter glitter. You know, the stuff you people stole from this fine lady." At this casual introduction, Mom Chao Cherry and Narong both stepped forward to stare down at Barber.

"Stick him now?" Narong asked. He was anxious to get going.

"Oh shit," Barber said in an anguished tone. "Oh shit." Comprehension was dawning at lightning speed. They were looking

262

for the drug shipment that Leland had hijacked. He began to cry, softly at first, then in loud desperate sobs that turned to guttural cries. "Don't hurt me," he pleaded. "You don't have to do this."

"Sure we do," Hack said. "In fact, we can do anything we want. Tables are turned, pal. We make the rules."

"You have my drugs," Mom Chao Cherry said with barely an inflection in her voice. She could have been talking coolly about breakfast cereal. Or an expensive new handbag.

"I didn't take your drugs," Barber moaned. "That was my . . ."

"We understand," Mom Chao Cherry said. She waved a hand as if she were waving a scepter. "That is old business. We already dealt with your partner, Mr. Odin. Now we do business with you." She took a step back and nodded to Narong.

Narong moved forward, knife blade extended.

Barber saw the flash of the knife and screamed loudly before the point even touched the center of his chest. But when Narong did slice him from sternum to belly button, his eyes popped, his nostrils flared, and he howled like a crazed animal caught in a trap.

From out of the darkness came Mom Chao Cherry's voice: "You will tell us everything there is to know about my hijacked shipment. You will tell us exactly where it is."

"Pleeeeeease." Barber's scream echoed off the brick walls. "We can make a deal!"

Mom Chao Cherry sighed. She was immune to Barber's screams and pleadings. She'd overseen plenty of interrogations much like this one. Some of the men had been innocent, some not. But this man, this partner of Leland Odin, was clearly guilty. He was an accomplice. "Again," she said to Narong.

Narong probed with his knife and, right on cue, Barber screamed.

"Untie me and I'll tell you where the drugs are," Barber moaned. "Wait, I'll *show* you. I'll take you there."

"Maybe deeper?" Mom Chao Cherry suggested helpfully. She wished she'd brought along one of her native venomous brown spiders. Once, in a long-ago brothel where she'd been forced to work, a man had abused her horribly. Then, two weeks later, he'd come scrabbling back, grinning sheepishly and offering her a bag of candy, acting as if nothing had happened. She'd bowed deeply like the madam had taught her and led the customer upstairs. After they'd had sex on her sad, flat pallet of a bed, the man had fallen asleep. She'd crept down into the basement, caught a fat brown spider in a jar, and carried it back to her room. When death came for the snoring man, it was very painful.

"I've got an idea," Hack said to Narong. "Why don't you try . . ." He turned and ambled back a few steps, dug through his duffel bag. "Here," he said. "Maybe this will give our boy some incentive." He handed Narong a long, wicked-looking knife, basically a Bowie knife, with a curved fifteen-inch sawtooth steel blade and rubber handle.

Narong accepted the knife with pleasure. "What is this?"

"Call it a pig sticker," Hack said.

"Very nice."

Hack flicked a wrist. "Give 'er a shot."

Narong went to work on Jay Barber's left thumb, which produced another sequence of high-pitched screams.

"Good," Mom Chao Cherry said. "Now we must . . ."

"Hold everything," Hack said. He glanced at his watch. "I gotta meet a guy upstairs."

"Here? Now?" Mom Chao Cherry asked.

"Just takin' care of business," Hack said. "You know, that asshole from the university."

Mom Chao Cherry pulled her mouth into a tight smile. "Yes. Of course. The greedy one."

Out on the front steps, pounding on a front door that was covered with decade-old graffiti, Gary Toft figured he must certainly be in the wrong place. It was the exact address that he'd been given, all right, but this five-story brick building — really more like the shell of an old factory — looked utterly deserted.

"This sucks," Toft muttered. He was a hospital orderly, Hack's lookout, for lack of a better description, who'd been bounced out of nursing school for cheating on a test. And right now he was pretty sure he was being jacked around, that Hack was trying to screw him royally on the twenty grand. But just as he turned to leave, the front door snicked open and a smiling Hack said, "Hey there, Toft."

Toft turned around. "I'm here for my money." Now that Hack was standing right in front of him, Toft didn't feel quite so confident in shaking him down.

"Sure thing," Hack said. "Come on in and

I'll grab it for you."

Toft hesitated. Something felt fishy. "What is this place?" he asked. "You live here?"

"I own it," Hack said with some pride in his voice. "Got a grant from the Minnesota State Arts Board to turn this place into artists' lofts."

Toft nodded. He'd read about this kind of thing in a local arts magazine. Shit-hole buildings being rehabbed for use as artists' studios and even small repertory theatres. "Cool."

"Come on, let me show you around."

"Okay," Toft said. And with that he stepped inside and sealed his fate.

"Down here," Hack said as they descended a long flight of narrow steps. The beam of his flashlight bounced along, probing the way.

"Down here?" Toft said. This did seem awfully strange. "You got an office down here?"

"Something like that." Hack waited until they were all the way downstairs. *Use the gun or the snare?* he wondered. *The gun. Easier and more industrial.*

He turned to Toft and said, casually, "We got our own little torture chamber set up down here."

"What? *What?*" Toft's face drained white

and he made a motion to turn and run, but was stopped abruptly in his tracks. Hack had just stuck a snub-nosed revolver one inch from his nose.

"Get over there and shut up," Hack said, giving Toft a push. There was no sense in fooling around or keeping up any sort of pretense.

"Jesus H. Christ," Toft said when he saw Jay Barber spread-eagled on the floor, sobbing and leaking blood. "What did you people *do* to that guy? Who is he?"

"Aw, we were just having a friendly bull session," Hack said. He pushed Toft closer into the circle. "Come on, meet the gang you signed on to help. Don't be shy."

Toft turned a wild-eyed gaze on Mom Chao Cherry and Hack. "You people are crazy. This right here is torture!"

"Torture, yes," Narong said. He seemed to be enjoying himself for the first time in several days.

Hack gave Toft a rough shove that forced him down into a sitting position. "Shut up and watch. You might get a kick out of this." He gestured at Narong. "Go ahead, Narong. Get to work."

Barber squealed continually as Narong worked on him, first with his knives and then with a small blowtorch. It was the kind a five-star chef might use to glaze the top of a meringue.

"Now he is fearful," Mom Chao Cherry said. "Now he'll tell us what we want to know."

Hack nodded. "Dude knows you're serious. Make him sing like Pavarotti on a warm day."

Toft was weeping and moaning, rocking back and forth as if he couldn't stand the pain himself. A sour smell was coming off him. "This is so wrong!" he roared. "Somebody's got to come and *stop* this. Somebody's got to *hear* this."

"Shut up," Hack said. He lifted his arm, aimed the gun at Toft, and shot him square in the forehead. Toft looked momentarily surprised. His mouth formed a perfect O as his scream died on his lips. Then he rocked backward for a final time. When his head hit the stone floor, it sounded like the *splat* of a watermelon being dropped.

"He was starting to get on my nerves," Hack said.

"Can anyone hear us?" Mom Chao Cherry asked. It was the first time she sounded nervous.

"No," Hack said. "Walls are too thick. If you heard anything at all, you'd just think it was a trick of the wind." He took a step forward and looked down at Barber. "You gonna tell us where to find the drugs?"

"You're never going to let me go," Barber moaned. He'd tried to deal and they'd scorned him. Now he was running his chances through his mind and the endgame didn't look good.

"Stick him again," Hack said.

Two minutes later, Barber was barely able to grunt, let alone form actual words.

"Shit, I think something tore inside his throat," Hack said. "He's just making grunts and groans."

"Untie him and give him a pen and paper," Mom Chao Cherry said. "He will tell us."

Narong untied Barber and sat him up, which was no easy feat. Barber flopped and sagged so much, it seemed as if his spine was broken. Then, finally, when Barber was staring at them, dark-eyed and numb with pain, Hack put a pen in the man's good hand and placed a sheet of paper on the floor.

"Go ahead," Hack said. "Write it down. Tell us where the drugs are."

Barber's head lolled on his shoulders and some white froth dribbled out one corner of his mouth. The pen dropped out of his hand.

"Uh-oh," Hack said. "He might have some brain issues."

"Stick him again?" Narong asked.

"No, no, he's gonna be able to pull it together," Hack said. He leaned down and put the pen back in Barber's hand. "Aren't you, buddy?" He clapped Barber on the shoulder. "Go ahead, you can do it."

Barber stared at the pen in his hand, as if he couldn't quite comprehend what was expected of him. Finally, he leaned forward and, with painstaking effort, scribbled three letters. *FTZ.*

Narong's face convulsed with anger. "What does that mean? It is just letters. Nonsense." He was anxious to torture Barber some more.

Hack stared at Barber's scribbling and smiled. He understood perfectly well what Barber had written. "It's cool, Narong, you don't have to torture him anymore."

Narong looked at Hack expectantly. "We have our answer?"

"Sure do. Now you can go ahead and just finish him off."

271

28

A thick gray bank of clouds scudded across a crescent moon, shielding the loading dock in a bank of shadows.

"This is good," Hack said as he and Narong hauled the two dead bodies out to the rental van. "Nobody around to see what's going on." Hack knew that when the screaming and begging stopped, the real work began.

And he was prepared. The back compartment of the van looked like a hazmat truck, every square inch lined with thick plastic stitched together with duct tape.

"Piece of advice you can take to the bank," Hack said. "Gotta use at least six-mil plastic sheeting. Anything else is crap, and you'll spend the rest of the night with a bunch of bleach and paper towels trying to clean up a mess."

"Okay," Narong said. They shoved the two bodies in headfirst and slammed the doors.

"Now we gotta make these guys disappear," Hack said, sounding reasonably upbeat.

"How?" Narong asked. "Where?"

Hack swiped a hand across his forehead. "If we was up in Duluth, I'd say we could dump 'em in the Devil's Cauldron."

"What is Devil's Cauldron?" Narong asked.

"Way up near the Canadian border, there's this state park where the Brule River comes roaring down like thunder. The current hits this particular rock formation . . ." He gestured with his hand. "And makes the river split. Half of the river tumbles down a waterfall and keeps going in this long stream, while the other half disappears into this long stone tunnel they call the Devil's Cauldron."

"And it comes out in your Superior Lake?" Narong asked.

"In Lake Superior? That's the crazy part. It doesn't. They've dropped dye down that stone tunnel, ping-pong balls, rubber ducks, all sorts of things, and nothing's ever come out in Lake Superior."

Narong was fascinated. "So where does the water go?"

"Nobody knows." Hack shrugged. "That's why it's a perfect place to dump a body."

Narong had a mental picture of Jay Barber's rubber-limbed body being sucked down into the pit of roaring water and shooting straight down a dark stone tunnel to end up . . . where? Maybe in a lava tube? Or an underground cave, where his spirit could possibly gather strength? The concept was slightly disturbing. "But we're not going there," Narong said hopefully. "It's too far."

"I got another place," Hack said. "Works just as good."

Hack kept the truck at a steady fifty-five miles per hour as they drove down 35W, their tires humming against the road. Despite the late hour, they still shared the road with lots of other vehicles. And the weather had turned cold, testing the light jackets they had on. In fact, the weather lady on Channel 7 had predicted a light frost.

"Your weather," Narong said. "Very cold."

"It can be a bitch sometimes," Hack agreed. "But this is nothing compared to January in Duluth. The temp drops to twenty below and the whole damn harbor freezes up. Part of the lake does, too. You go outside in the morning to start your car and your engine is practically frozen. You gotta have what they call a block heater. Plug it into the electrical."

"That heats the car?"

"Well, the engine block anyway." Hack took the exit to westbound I-494 and accelerated past a patrol car that was parked there. Probably just finished up with a traffic stop. It was a good reminder to pay close attention and not risk being pulled over, especially when you were transporting dead bodies. "It's still colder than hell when you crawl in your car. Freeze your ass off in a matter of minutes if you're not dressed proper." He glanced at Narong. "If you decide to stay here, you're gonna want to get yourself some proper gear. Maybe a down parka, some pac boots for sure."

"We must go back home soon," Narong said. "But I'd like to visit again. This is an interesting place, like nothing I've seen before."

"You come back, we'll do some fishing."

"That I would enjoy."

"I like the tat you got." Hack tapped the side of his neck. "You know, your blue snake. Does it mean anything in particular? It don't look like any prison tattoo. Is it your gang sign?"

"Naga," Narong said. "A divine serpent in Thailand. Naga controls the rain and affects prosperity."

"Huh." Hack wasn't sure what snakes had to do with prosperity. But he was starting to enjoy Narong's company. "So you got a lot of snakes in Thailand?"

"Over two hundred different kinds, sixty of which are venomous."

"No kidding. Sixty poison snakes, that's really something." He took the turn off Highway 169 that led to Highway 21. "I saw a baby cobra once. Back in Duluth."

"We have cobras," Narong said. "Pit vipers, kraits, coral snakes. But mostly in Thailand we have pythons. Huge pythons. Some are six meters long."

"I never did get the hang of that metric shit. How long is that in good old American feet?"

"Over nineteen feet long."

"Holy shit! That's one damn big freaking snake. Are those things worth anything? I mean if you shipped a bunch of them over here and tried to sell them, could you make a few bucks?"

"Maybe," Narong said. "Possibly. But it's a long trip, and if the snakes were shipped in containerized freight, they might not all make it."

Hack nodded. "That would be a bummer."

■ ■ ■ ■

Twenty minutes later, they left the lights and the last of the suburban sprawl behind. Now the land on either side of the mostly deserted road opened up. Dark fields, not yet plowed and planted, stretched off into the distance.

"What is this?" Narong asked as Hack turned down a narrow gravel road.

"Farm country." Hacked opened a window partway and the aromas of fresh air mingled with damp soil and a tang of manure. "Now, that's what Minnesota smells like."

Narong's nose twitched. "It smells a little like shit."

"It is shit," Hack laughed. "It's all shit, man."

One more long S-turn and Hack slowed the van. Then he cut his headlights and said, "We gotta be careful from here on."

"Where are we going?" Narong whispered.

"Just a little bit farther. A place I like to think of as Minnesota recycling."

Hack passed a solitary mailbox and then turned down a tree-lined driveway. Up ahead, a farmstead appeared out of the darkness. A two-story white house with a blue pickup truck parked in front of it. No dogs barking, no lights in the house.

"Lookin' good," Hack said. He drove an eighth of a mile past the house and stopped the van. There was a tall, hip-roofed barn surrounded by four large buildings with rounded roofs. Almost like greenhouses but not quite, because they were enclosed and had a series of fences. "We're here."

"What is here?" Narong asked.

"Come on. See for yourself." Hack jumped out of the van and pulled open the door. Grabbing Barber's feet, he pulled him out, Narong quickly leaning in to help. Together, they carried Barber toward a wooden fence. "On the count of three, we pitch him over the fence," Hack said. "One . . . two . . . three." The body went sailing and landed with a satisfying wet plop in a sea of mud. Toft's body went in a half minute later.

Narong peered over the fence just in time to see two dozen large black hogs come snuffling over to investigate the body. "Pigs," he whispered.

"Berkshire hogs," Hack said. He grabbed a twenty-pound sack of Nutrena pig feed from the van, leaned over the fence, and sprinkled it over the two bodies. The pigs came closer, keenly interested now. They

278

had shiny black coats and delicate cream-colored hooves. One hog nosed the men gently with her pink, bristly snout and then gave a delighted snort. The others moved in, quickly deciding this gift from the gods might make a tasty midnight snack.

A mile from the farm, Hack pulled the van to the side of the road. He cut the engine and said to Narong, "Time to congratulate ourselves for a job well done. Maybe do a short pop." Reaching into the glove box, he retrieved a small leather pouch. Inside were two disposable plastic syringes, a metal spoon, and a glassine bag filled with white powder. It was only a minute before they had a lighter hissing under the spoon and a mixture of powder and plain water bubbling away.

When Hack pushed the needle into his arm and released the plunger, he moaned with pleasure. It was like a Roman candle going off in his veins. Every hair on his arm stood up straight and a deep warmth crept from his feet to his skull, then slammed crazily into his brain. Gasping loudly, he felt his vision swim before his eyes. Nothing mattered. All was well. Everything seemed so simple and bright. He managed to turn his head and look over at Narong, who was grinning. His right hand held an empty syringe, his left hand was slowly swimming in tiny, tight circles.

A time later — Hack wasn't sure how long it was — he fired up the truck and swung back onto the county road. He drove slowly as the road swayed and undulated before his eyes, concentrating hard to keep the truck pointed straight ahead. It wouldn't pay to end up in the ditch now, especially when so much was at stake.

"What now?" Narong slurred in the passenger seat.

"We make another stop," Hack said. The warmth was still coursing through him. "We're just getting started."

29

Afton stirred in her sleep. She was having one of her climbing dreams. Halfway up a rock wall near Goosebury Falls, she'd just inched her way up a narrow chimney and negotiated a careful traverse over to a burly pillar. The nubbins, or small handholds, had been pretty decent, but now she'd run out of cracks and was having difficulty finding good toeholds. Now she was dangling there in her harness, feeling frustrated and unable to find a way up and over the crux of the wall.

"Tonya?" she murmured. Tonya was one of her Women on the Ropes climbing partners. But when she looked up, the cliff loomed smooth and dangerous overhead but nobody was there with the rope. Tonya had been her belayer, but now Tonya had disappeared. And Afton had a horrible feeling that she was about to fall . . .

Clenching her teeth, Afton fought to rouse

herself from her dream, to pull herself out of its murky, frightening depths. She knew, deep down in her subconscious, that this wasn't reality. The reptile portion of her brain was probably overstimulated and playing nasty tricks on her.

A hand touched her thigh.

No, it's nothing. Nothing's there, Afton told herself with a sharp intake of breath.

Then a slightly more urgent touch.

Afton's eyes flew open as she shot up in bed, her hands twitching and fumbling for something, anything, to defend herself with.

"Mommy?" came a plaintive voice.

Afton blinked. "Poppy?"

"I had a bad dream," Poppy moaned.

"You had a bad dream?" Afton was still fighting to clear her head as her heart thudded heavily inside her chest.

"There were bugs flying around my nightlight."

"Oh, honey. You know they're not really there."

"I know," Poppy said. She touched a hand to her head. "But they were in my dream and I'm really scared. Can I please sleep with you?"

"Of course." Afton pulled the covers back and let Poppy crawl in next to her. "Better?" Poppy didn't say a word, just snuggled in close, but Afton could feel the girl nodding her head. "Okay, you just relax and drift back to sleep, honey. I'll stay awake and watch over you for a while."

And she did, staring into the darkness, trying to calm her own jangled night fears. Thinking about . . . what else? The two killers who so far had eluded them every step of the way. They were out there — Afton could feel it — but where were they? Who were they?

Afton had taken Poppy and Tess to the Blue Dragon Children's Theatre a few months ago to see a show of Indonesian shadow puppets. It had been fascinating, these small, flat cutouts made huge by the light projected behind them. Like chimeras, these shadow-puppet figures had flitted and danced around as the narrator wove a charming story.

That's how this case felt. Shadowy and deceptive. Maybe even the stuff nightmares were made of.

It was only when she heard her daughter's steady, measured breathing that Afton allowed herself to relax and fall back asleep.

30

Hack bumped down a back alley in a shabby Richfield neighborhood. This was an area of small, aging bungalows stuck almost directly in the flight path of every plane that thundered off the runway at Minneapolis–Saint Paul International Airport. Noisy. But quiet in its own way, too, because most everybody was a renter and nobody much cared.

"What is this place?" Narong asked as Hack swung the van onto a patch of hardpan. Six other cars were parked there, too, hunkered beside a broken swing set.

"Just a place to hang out after the bars close," Hack said. "For a lot of folks that 2:00 A.M. last call comes way too early."

"We drink?" Narong said. He sounded interested.

They climbed out of the van and eased their way onto a sagging back porch. Hack knocked on the door and waited a few moments. The door opened a crack and a burly biker-type guy peered out at them.

"Whadya want?" the biker asked. He had a shaved head and a hoop earring.

Pirate, Hack thought dreamily. *Hanging out with pirates.* "Is Roseanne home?" That was the password. At least it was last time he was here.

"Who wants to know?"

He shrugged. "A friend."

The biker pulled open the door and took a step back. "Come on in and behave yourselves."

As bad as the house was outside, it was even worse inside. Large holes had been punched in the walls; the carpet was torn up in places, exposing the subfloor; a sound system warbled uneasily. But the living and dining rooms held a bar with a buzzing blue Coors sign and a dingy, mismatched array of furniture. And the drinks seemed to be flowing freely.

"It sure ain't Studio 54," Hack said, "but at least you can wet your whistle here."

Hack and Narong elbowed their way past a dozen or so unsteady customers. A heavy-lidded, graying blond woman in a Lynyrd Skynyrd concert tee barely looked up as they vied for elbowroom at the scuffed wooden bar.

"Two whiskies," Hack told her. When

Narong made a motion to pull out some money, Hack waved a hand and said, "No, I got this." They got their drinks, served in red Solo cups, and settled onto a rump-sprung sofa.

Narong looked around. "We drink here?"

"Drink? Hell, yes," Hack said. "Do whatever you want, really, if you got enough cash."

"Women?" Narong was eyeing a blue-haired woman who normally worked as a waitress but was sitting on the biker's lap, sipping a beer and smiling lazily.

Hack stifled outright laughter. "I don't know if you'd call old Donna over there a grade-A prime female supermodel, but, yeah, she'll entertain you all right if you slip her a twenty." Hack winked. "Slip her a lot more."

31

The sun was barely up and Gene Schreiber had already had a busy day. His dairy herd was already milked and, after that, he'd zeroed the row unit and drained the air-storage tanks on his planter. It wasn't going to be planting season for a few weeks yet — as evidenced by the fresh blanket of frost that coated almost everything in sight — but Gene liked to stay ahead of his chores as much as possible. Gene was what his neighbors would call "farm strong." Five feet eight inches in height in his work boots, and barely over a hundred seventy pounds the day after Thanksgiving. Gene wasn't imposing, but his muscles and body had been forged through a lifetime of hard work and near constant activity. Right now, hauling two twenty-gallon buckets overflowing with greens, grain, and kitchen scraps from his barn to his pen was easy because he'd done it nearly every day for thirty-five years.

Pausing outside the barn, Gene listened to the soft cooing of nesting doves overhead. Their song was as soothing and welcome as the noises made by all his animals — especially his hogs. Gene was bragging-rights proud of his hogs. Two of them weighed well over three-hundred-and-fifty pounds and one sow had taken a blue ribbon at the Scott County Fair last year.

The hogs were expecting him, half of them lined up at the fence like anxious customers in a deli.

"Hey pig, hey pig," Gene called to them. He flipped the latch and stepped into the pen. Dumping the first bucket into their trough, he noticed that not all his hogs had lined up for breakfast. Four of them were rooting around on the other side of the pen. Snuffling, tearing at something.

"Get over here, piggies," he called. Dropping his other bucket, he squinted in the half light. Something was sticking up out of the mud.

What the hell is that?

Gene took ten steps across the pen and, when his heart jolted clear up into his throat, decided it had to be a prank. Please God, let it be a prank, because a bloody arm sticking right up out of the mud was so bad. A joke, right? Perpetrated by that crazy

Perry Gunderson who worked for him as a hired hand.

But no, two of the fingers were missing. Gnawed off.

A sick, sour feeling swept over him. Of course Gene had heard stories of pigs attacking humans, but *his* pigs? And what human?

He retched suddenly and violently, hot spittle spurting from his mouth. Frightened, suddenly feeling as if tiny pig eyes were focused on him, he backed away and almost tripped. He spun around fearfully and saw a partially eaten leg, the shoe still on, half-buried in the mud.

Farm strong or not, Gene couldn't help himself from screaming.

Dan Fuller, a senior deputy with the Scott County Sheriff's Office wasn't happy. Neither were the three police officers from Prior Lake. It was their case and their jurisdiction and they wanted to work it. Nothing this exciting had ever happened on their watch.

"Problem is, guys," Max said, "Jay Barber belongs to us." He was fairly sure it was Barber because a blue Saucony running shoe was still attached to one mangled foot.

Fuller, who resembled a khaki-clad Captain Kangaroo, said, "I knew when I called it in that this was going to slide right through our fingers." He glanced over at the pen, where two more deputies, wearing fishing waders, were stomping around toward the front of the pen, where the body had been found. They were working under two light stanchions that had been hurriedly set up and now flooded the mud with an eerie glow. Needless to say, the pigs had been moved into one of the barns.

"You can still work the scene," Max said. "We'll ship the body . . . well, what's left of it anyway . . . to the ME in Minneapolis. But if you guys could canvass the neighbors, see if anybody saw cars coming and going or anything suspicious, that would be a tremendous help."

"Especially if they saw a red car," Afton said. She was thinking of the car that Sammy Mah had identified.

Fuller and the three cops nodded as they exchanged glances.

"We can do that," Fuller said. "We'll do that for sure."

"Who found the cell phone?" Max asked. That's how the initial identification had been made.

One of the Prior Lake officers raised his hand. "I was first on the scene," he said. "I guess pigs don't like the taste of plastic."

"And the farmer was pretty upset?" Afton asked.

The officer, whose name tag read DOBSON, nodded. "Mr. Schreiber was crying. So was his wife. Nothing like this has ever happened to them before. I was pretty shocked myself, which is why I sent out an alert to area law enforcement."

"It's lucky that Deke Henley was on the Homicide desk this morning," Max said to Afton, "and kicked it right over to me. He knew I was working a homicide and a missing persons."

"This is a pretty damn gruesome scene," Fuller said. "I've known the Schreibers for going on fifteen years. Good people. Shame this had to happen to them." He glanced sideways. "Speaking of which . . ."

A thin woman with a blue paisley shawl clutched around her shoulders was ghosting toward the barn. But instead of going into the barn, she veered left toward the hog pen.

"Excuse me, ma'am," Afton said. She hurried over to intercept her. "Are you Mrs. Schreiber?"

Wild-eyed and white-faced, the woman bobbed her head. "Yes," she whispered.

"This is a police investigation," Afton said. "We need a little space right now, so if you could go back inside your home, we'll come over and talk to you in a bit, answer any questions you might have. Okay?"

Mrs. Schreiber nodded, but continued on her path toward the hog pen.

"Mrs. Schreiber?" Afton said, her voice louder this time. "We need you to . . ."

"Holy hell!" a voice inside the pigpen suddenly roared. Then, "Oh no!"

Afton grabbed the woman by the elbow and turned to stare at the screaming man at the same time. One of the sheriff's deputies, who'd moved toward the rear of the pen, was leaning on his shovel for support and looking utterly forlorn.

"What is it?" Max went rushing over. "What's going on?"

"We're gonna need your Crime Scene unit pronto," the deputy in the pen stammered out. "I think we just uncovered" — he swallowed hard, as if he was trying not to lose his breakfast — "a second body."

Fifteen minutes later, Jim Klopp, the Scott County ME, showed up. He was a barrel-chested man with graying hair, and he wore trendy Clark Kent glasses. He said hello to the assemblage of local law enforcement, shook Max's hand, gave Afton a solemn nod, and proceeded to pull on a pair of leather gloves as well as Orvis hip boots.

"Might ruin those nice hip boots," Deputy Fuller pointed out.

"Ah," Klopp said, "I haven't made it over to the Brule for a couple of years anyway."

"Good trout fishing on the Brule River," Officer Dobson observed as Klopp entered the pigpen. "Brown trout and speckled."

Klopp squished his way through the muck, then set to work with the two deputies to carefully disinter the second body. "This one in back is fairly well intact," he called to everyone who was watching. "Pigs seem to have trampled it rather than lunched on it. You want to come in here and take a look at him? See if it's anyone you recognize? Detectives?" He looked directly at Max and Afton. "Probably pertinent to your case."

Afton and Max stepped gingerly into the pen, trying to avoid the stinkier, muddier parts, which was all but impossible. They bent over the mangled body and studied it.

"Nobody I know," Max said.

"Same here," Afton said.

Deputy Fuller came over and took a good, hard look. "Nope. Me neither."

The ME took photos, bagged the head and hands, and then carefully dug into the dead guy's pockets. Slowly, he extricated a black leather case and dropped it into a clear plastic baggy.

"Got an ID here," one of the deputies called out.

Everyone crowded in again.

"What's it say?" Max asked.

Klopp slowly worked the wallet open inside the plastic bag. "Looks like we've got a Minnesota driver's license here as well as a University of Minnesota Medical Center ID card." He gazed at everyone, then looked back down at the two IDs. "This second victim's name is Gary Toft."

"He worked at the University of Minnesota Medical Center?" Max said.

"Holy crap," Afton said. "There's your inside man right there. The guy who knew when Odin's heart was coming and alerted the shooters."

"You think?" Max said.

"Gotta call that hospital lady we talked to. See if we can confirm his employment and find out if he was working that night."

Max squinted at Afton. "Mrs. . . . ?"

"Mrs. Manchester," Afton said, glancing up at a riffle of pink clouds as morning painted the sky.

Max held up an index finger. "I'll make the call. Give me five."

Like a heat-seeking missile, Sharon Schreiber emerged from her house again, looking just as distressed and distracted. Afton once again cut her off at the proverbial pass and, amid her pleadings and protests, herded her back indoors.

Max looked grim when he came back and joined the group.

"What?" Afton asked.

"I talked to that woman, Manchester," Max said. "She confirmed that Gary Toft was indeed an employee at the university hospital."

"What else?" Afton asked. She could tell from the look on Max's face that there was more.

"Toft was working there the night the helicopter was shot down," Max said.

"Holy shit," Deputy Fuller said. He spread his feet apart and placed his hands on his ample hips, the better to make his point. "From all the background you've given us, it looks like you've got yourself a genuine class A murder mystery."

"Jeez," one of the other deputies said. "Does that mean you're looking for a serial killer?"

Max grimaced. "It's a five-body pileup anyway."

Afton and Max were leaning against Max's car and talking quietly.

"At least we know this hospital guy, Toft, wasn't about to call in sick and take off running," Max said.

"No," Afton said, shivering in the early morning cold. "He called in dead."

"It certainly looks as though Toft was somehow connected to the shooters, to the killers," Max said. "But how is he connected to Barber?"

"Maybe our friends from Bangkok killed them both," Afton said. "Toft to clean up any loose ends, Barber because he was Odin's partner."

"Okay. But how are our killers connected to DSN?"

"There's got to be something going on with DSN that these guys are after," Afton said. She glanced over at the pigpen, saw one of the deputies stringing up yellow-and-black tape.

"Contraband of some kind," Max agreed. "Weapons? Dope?"

"Most of the stuff they sell on DSN comes from Asia. Maybe they're importing something illegal along with the regular stuff."

"What if this isn't DSN-related?" Max asked.

Afton considered Max's words as, off in the background, some sort of motor revved up. "Then it's directly related to Leland

Odin," she said. She was aware of the noise growing louder and raised her voice a notch. "Maybe some kind of sideline that Odin had going."

Max looked up and said, "Oh man, the vultures are circling."

A bright blue helicopter with the words NEWSWATCH 7 painted on its side blew by overhead. It circled the farmyard twice, hovered — probably looking for a choice landing spot — and then headed for a nearby field. Dust and flotsam from the morning's frost spun up like miniature tornadoes. Then the chopper settled on its skids and, a few moments later, two figures jumped out. A man shouldering a camera and a blond woman in a bright red blazer and skirt.

"That woman keeps turning up like a bad penny," Max said under his breath.

"It's Portia?"

"Oh, yeah," Max said. He sounded pained, as if he'd just been slugged in the jaw.

Despite wearing three-inch stiletto heels, Portia managed to run through the dirt and ruts to outpace her cameraman. When she skidded to a stop directly in front of Max, she wasn't the least bit winded after her long sprint.

Pilates, Afton thought. *The chick's in shape.*

Portia lifted the microphone up to her mouth just as her cameraman arrived and started shooting. "Portia Bourgoyne," she said, "reporting for Newswatch Seven." Now she assumed her serious face. "I've just arrived at the Gene Schreiber farm in rural Prior Lake, where I've been told the dead, mutilated body of DSN executive Jay Barber has been discovered." Now she stuck the microphone in Max's face. "Detective Max Montgomery, can you fill our viewers in on exactly what happened here?"

"I'm afraid we're unable to release any details right now," Max said in a fairly even tone.

Portia was unfazed. "Tell me, Detective, is it true that Mr. Barber's body was partially consumed by pigs?"

Max clenched his fists but managed to keep his cool. "Again, I'm unable to comment on anything until after the scene is processed and the bodies are transported to the medical examiner's office."

"You said *bodies,*" Portia said, pouncing on his words. "Are you talking about *two* dead bodies? Because if you are . . ."

Max shook his head and walked away. He'd tangled with Portia before and it had never ended well.

Nonplussed, Portia started to follow Max, jerking her head at her cameraman, indicating that he should follow along.

Afton stepped in front of them and said, "I wouldn't do that if I were you."

"But I'm not you," Portia said in a snarky tone. "And why, pray tell, do you continue to photobomb my shots?" She waved a hand breezily as if she were shooing away an annoying, buzzing fly. "Aren't you supposed to be a crime victim's hand-holder? Of course you are. So why on earth would the Minneapolis Police Department allow you to be present at what has to be one of the most horrific crimes scenes ever?" Portia curled her lip as she brushed past Afton and hurried after Max.

Afton stood there, feeling powerless, insulted, and put down. Part of her even wondered if Portia was right. If she couldn't be of help, what was she doing here?

32

"There has to be a solid connection," Max said, "between DSN and the people from Bangkok. We knew it three days ago, but those crazy killers have had us chasing all over the place like a pack of hungry wolves. Now Barber is dead and that university guy, too." He and Afton were back from the body dump site and had just given Deputy Chief Thacker a blow-by-blow description.

Thacker stared at Afton and Max across the raft of desks in the Homicide division as if he almost didn't believe them. "The university guy," he repeated.

"Uh . . ." Max twirled a finger.

"Toft," Afton said, filling in the blanks. "Gary Toft."

"And he was shot?" Thacker asked.

"Shot in the head," Afton said.

"And Barber?"

"Appeared to be mostly stabbed and burned," Max said. "And eaten."

Thacker flinched. "Mrs. Barber's been notified, but nobody's told her about *that.*"

"Yeah," Afton said. "It wasn't good."

"Hard way to go," Max said.

"But we still haven't nailed down a motive," Thacker said. "Or figured out the connection between the killers and DSN."

"It's sure not the Saudi buyers," Max said. "Or Consolidated Sports."

"Something must have happened in Thailand between Leland Odin and these people to bring them right here to our doorstep," Afton said. "To send them on this mission of destruction."

"But what?" Thacker asked.

"Drugs?" Max said. "A drug cartel?"

Thacker looked puzzled. "You think Odin and his people stumbled into something?"

"I doubt it was quite that innocent," Afton said. "At least it doesn't feel that way. These people, these killers, are on a major revenge trip. Something big went down."

They let Afton's words rumble around in their heads for a few moments, until Dillon walked in.

"Happy days, huh?" Dillon said. "You know there's a media shit-storm going on out there, don't you?"

"I'm guessing you saw the footage that Newswatch Seven shot," Afton said.

"I did and it was stellar stuff," Dillon said. "You guys are very photogenic, even though Max was making with his Easter Island impression." He took off a brown suede jacket and hung it on a peg. Pulled out a bottle of Mountain Dew. "Now what?" He uncapped the bottle and took a slug.

"That's what we're trying to figure out," Max said. "How to locate this mysterious woman."

"If it was up to me, I'd go to a bunch of Thai restaurants and order as much pad thai and green curry as I could eat," Dillon said. He touched a hand to his chest, let go a loud burp. "Or hang out at the airport? The old lady's got to leave the country sooner or later, unless she intends to kill every living soul who works at DSN."

"Maybe she's already gone," Max said. "After last night's killing spree she could have hopped on a plane. Delta and United had half a dozen flights leaving for the West Coast and beyond. I checked."

"But TSA and airport security have the composites," Dillon said. "And they've been on TV."

"We looped everybody in right away," Thacker said. "As soon as we had composites and got the fake identities from the Hotel Itasca people. We figured the killers might make a run for it."

"I'm guessing they probably have another full set of IDs," Afton said. "With credit cards to match. Especially the old lady. She could put on a wig and a pair of dark glasses and — bam. She's out of here. Hell, she could probably stroll down Nicollet Mall and nobody would even take notice."

"What do we really know about this woman?" Thacker asked. "Besides the fact that she appears to be an American living in Thailand."

"She's rich," Afton said. She spoke so softly that Max was the only one who heard her.

"What?" Max said. He held up a hand to still the conversation. "Wait a minute," he said to Thacker and Dillon. "Listen to this for a minute."

Thacker frowned. "Listen to what?"

"Go ahead," Max said.

"I think this woman, the woman we think might be the mastermind behind all these killings, is extremely wealthy," Afton said. She took a deep breath and continued. "Look at the facts so far. She's stayed in a fifteen-hundred-dollar-a-night penthouse suite for almost a week and she smokes cigarettes that cost twenty dollars a pack."

Thacker was staring at her. "Go on."

"The hotel people said she dressed well, spared no expense on room service, and . . . well, I think she wore Chanel perfume."

"Huh," Thacker said. "You could tell that?"

"The woman could be a highly paid assassin," Dillon said.

"She could be," Afton agreed. "But it doesn't feel right. She probably didn't fire the rocket launcher, because she's also small-statured and older. Someone else did the actual shooting. But she went along — she was right there."

"Because she wanted the job done correctly," Max said slowly. "The old woman went along to make sure everything was carried out to her exact specifications."

"She's used to giving orders," Afton said. "And taking risks. I think she might be some sort of . . ." She struggled to find the right words. "Some sort of kingpin."

"And affiliated with Kantana Industrial Group in Bangkok?" Dillon asked.

"Son of a bitch," Thacker said. "This has to be a drug cartel, yes?"

"Yeah," Dillon said. "But what drugs and which cartel?"

"We have to go back and talk to Sunny," Afton said. "She has to know more than she's been letting on."

Thacker glanced at his watch. "Dicey move. The woman's attending her own husband's funeral right now."

"Then we'll talk to her afterward," Afton said. "Catch her on the way out."

"I got another idea," Max said. "The DEA's already dialed into this, so why don't we get a couple of drug-sniffing dogs to go through DSN's warehouse? See if anything unusual turns up."

"It's an interesting thought," Thacker said slowly. "I could make a call."

Afton turned to Max. "Looks like we're off to a funeral. Ain't it lucky that I wore black?"

"Yeah," Max said. "But, unfortunately, you still got pig poop on the soles of your shoes."

They caught the tail end of Leland Odin's funeral, which was being held at St. Philip's church. This gray granite bastion of Protestantism and old money was located on Hennepin Avenue, adjacent to Loring Park and just down the block from the Walker Art Center.

"This place looks like a movie set," Afton said as they climbed the low marble steps. At least ten black limousines were parked outside and she could hear the strains of

Johann Sebastian Bach's "Prelude No. 1" hammering out from a pipe organ.

"Yeah," Max said. "Like they're shooting one of the final scenes from *The Godfather.* So if you hear any *real* shooting, get low."

Inside, the enormous church was practically packed with mourners. Candles flickered on the altar, prisms of light shone through an enormous stained glass window, and the minister was just stepping back to the podium. Dozens of extravagant floral bouquets adorned the altar, while small bouquets of white lilies were looped on the end of each pew, making the whole place smell like a flower shop.

"This is a big deal," Max whispered as he looked around. "I see, like, major politicos in attendance. The governor, a couple of state senators, even a judge or two."

"There's probably a huge contingent from DSN, too," Afton said.

They slipped into a pew at the very back of the church.

"There's no casket," Afton said, staring up at the altar. "Do you suppose Odin's already been cremated?"

"If he was, it was better than Barber got. And that other poor shlub."

They studied the guests while the organ played, the choir sang, and the minister delivered a somber, heartfelt eulogy, making a big point of calling it a *memorial* rather than a funeral. Afton couldn't help but wonder if the killer or killers might be here right now. Probably not the Asian man, but the older woman could have easily slipped in unnoticed. If she was intent on bringing DSN to its knees, then she may very well have come to gloat and survey her handiwork. Sitting there in the dark, cool church, she was chilled by the notion.

Because they'd arrived so late, they hadn't been forced to sit through the entire service. Now, as the minister said his final words, a less somber tune rang out from the choir loft overhead. Afton recognized it as Mozart's "Sanctus."

Max nudged her with his elbow. Sunny and Terrell had stood up and were walking down the aisle now. Both of the women wore stunning black outfits and jaunty black hats. And, sure enough, Sunny had a shiny bronze urn cradled tenderly in her arms.

Sunny and Terrell were followed by the attorney, Bob Steckel, who walked alongside Governor Mark Lindsay. The governor was accompanied by what had to be two press secretaries, since they'd already pulled out their mobile devices and were tip-tapping away. Then there was another contingent of at least four dozen people, all dressed in black, but very stylish, Neiman Marcus–type black.

There was a gate-crasher, too. Hack sat on the opposite side of the church from Afton and Max, perched in the second to last row. He'd pretty much slept through the long, boring service, but now that the processional was taking place, he was suddenly alert. His eyes followed Sunny and Terrell as they walked somberly down the aisle, and he took a good long look at them. Both women struck him as being extremely classy and moneyed, especially Terrell, the daughter. She was young, very attractive, and projected that rich-bitch up-your-ass attitude, a not-so-subtle warning that she thought she was better than everybody else. Hack studied the women carefully and wondered what use they might be to him. Not right now, but perhaps eventually.

"Whoa," Max whispered in Afton's ear as they scanned the exiting crowd. "There's Fan Ling."

Dressed in a skintight black sheath dress and carrying her coat, Fan Ling was ghosting her way down the side aisle just to their right.

"Let's stop her," Afton said, jumping to

her feet. "Talk to her again." She was out of the pew and ducking around the back of the church, dodging a marble baptismal font and grabbing Fan Ling by the elbow just as the girl was about to escape out the side door.

"What do you want now?" Fan Ling hissed.

"Please. Just a quick conversation," Afton said as Max hastily joined them. They stepped outside into cool sunshine and Afton said, "You heard about Jay Barber?"

"Yes," Fan Ling said, looking fearful. "It's terrible." Then she seemed to muster her anger and said, "Can't you people catch these killers?"

"We're working very hard at doing exactly that," Max said.

Fan Ling's jaw tightened. "Work harder."

"What's going on at DSN?" Afton asked. "Are they taking any extra precautions?"

"If you're so concerned, why don't you take it up with the security detail out there?" Fan Ling said. She pulled away from them and tossed her coat on over her shoulders. "Now please stop pestering me. I have to go on the air in two hours."

"That was productive," Afton said. Fan Ling had given them nothing. Then again, her expectations had been low. Did Fan

Ling have anything new to give them? Probably not. Just more attitude.

"Let's hurry up and grab Sunny," Max said.

"Shake her up a little," Afton said.

They pushed their way through a crowd of mourners over to where the line of black limos was parked. Two limos were already pulling away and Afton surmised that the governor and his contingent were being whisked off to some important meeting. Or maybe it was just lunch.

Sunny was standing next to a stretch limo, getting ready to climb inside.

"Excuse me!" Afton called out. She stuck an arm up and waved at her.

Sunny hesitated, then turned and looked. In her black sheath dress, black cashmere wrap, and dark glasses, she looked impressively widowed. She also wore a large-brimmed black hat that looked like something Alexis or Krystle would have worn in the old TV show *Dynasty.*

"Mrs. Odin," Afton said, "may we have a word with you?"

Sunny practically snarled. *"Now?"*

"Please," Afton said.

"You want to talk to me on the day of my husband's funeral?"

"It's pertinent to the case," Max said.

"Which case?" Sunny asked. "The helicopter crash or my husband's murder?" She slid her sunglasses up onto her forehead and stared at them with red-rimmed eyes. "Or maybe you're talking about Jay Barber's murder, which I just found out about a few hours ago. Have you solved either of those murders yet?"

"Not yet," Max said. "If we could just ask you a few more questions . . . ?"

Sunny put a hand to her throat. "Can't you see that I'm absolutely heartbroken? My husband is dead and now I learn that poor Jay's body was discovered at some horrible pig farm!"

"There was another body found there, too," Afton said.

Sunny looked stunned. "What?"

"It was discovered very close to Barber's body. We're fairly sure this person worked at the university hospital. That he might have been the inside man, the one who alerted the shooters as to when the helicopter was coming in for a landing."

"You mean this person might have been a kind of lookout?" Sunny asked.

"That's right."

"And now he's dead?"

"Yes, ma'am," Afton said.

"Well, good." Sunny's mouth twisted

harshly. "It sounds like he deserved to die."

"Momma?" Terrell called from inside the limousine. "Come on, we need to get going." She sounded both annoyed and bored.

"Please," Afton said, reaching out to gently touch Sunny's shoulder to try to connect with her. "We really need to talk to you. It's important."

"Today?" Sunny asked. She looked completely unstrung. "Now?"

"If you could manage it, yes."

"All right." Sunny heaved a loud sigh. "Follow along to the house, then. We're having a catered luncheon for family and friends. You can . . ." She gave a tired finger wave. "Whatever. Come along and I guess we'll find someplace to talk." From her expression, Sunny looked as though she'd rather gargle strychnine than talk to them.

33

Sunny seemed genuinely surprised when Afton and Max showed up on her doorstep.

"Oh," she said, meeting them at the door. "You did come after all."

"We appreciate your taking time to speak with us again," Afton said.

Sunny fingered the strand of baroque pearls at her neck and frowned, as if she'd just had second thoughts. Then she (not very graciously) invited them to come inside.

"We'll try not to take up too much of your time," Max said, looking around. "Since it looks as if you have a fairly large group to entertain."

"Friends," Sunny said of the fifty or so people who were crowded into her home. They were all talking animatedly and sipping drinks. "Some of Leland's coworkers are here, too."

Sunny's hands fluttered nervously as she

led them through a crush of people and into the library, where an enormous buffet table had been set up. Because there were so many people milling around, Sunny was doing her best to put on a fake cordial face.

"And please, Detectives, do help yourself to a bite of lunch," she trilled. "La Dolce handled all the catering, and they're particularly known for their fabulous scones, smoked salmon, and goat cheese quiche."

"Appreciate it," Afton said. "But we're really here to talk." It was as if Sunny had popped a Xanax or something. A happy pill. Five people were dead and she was suddenly smiling, acting like the bountiful lady of the manor.

"If we could go somewhere a little more private?" Max suggested.

Sunny got a little less happy. "I suppose."

They moved from the library into a crowded sitting room, finally ending up in the butler's pantry amid shelves lined with Rosenthal china and Waterford crystal.

"Mrs. Odin," Max said. "First your husband was murdered and now Jay Barber. Someone seems to be picking DSN apart piece by piece."

"We're worried that you could be next," Afton said.

Sunny looked panicked. "Me? Why would

I be next?"

"If you were somehow complicit," Max said.

"Excuse me?" Her blue eyes shone with fear. "What are you talking about?"

Afton decided to go in for the kill. "Mrs. Odin, did you set your husband up to be murdered?"

Sunny was practically speechless. "Wha— Absolutely not! Why would I do a dreadful thing like that? I . . . I loved Odin."

"Even though he was bopping Fan Ling?" Max asked, rather inelegantly. "You know she visited your husband at the hospital the night he was killed."

From the look on Sunny's face, Afton could see that this information came as no great shock to her.

"That bitch!" Sunny said, her face transforming into a feral snarl. "I'm going to have her fired. For all I know, she's the one who killed Leland."

"We don't think so," Afton said. "But we still believe *you* might be privy to some important information."

"What are you talking about?" Sunny asked.

"Is there something stored in the DSN warehouse that we should know about?"

"Like what?"

"Drugs?" Afton said. "It could be the reason why your husband was killed, why Jay Barber was kidnapped and murdered."

"How would I know anything about that?" Sunny cried. Then, "Drugs? Leland wouldn't have anything to do with drugs. Believe me, he was a straight arrow. Just last year he contributed over a hundred thousand dollars to the Republican Party."

"We think there's some sort of connection with Asia," Afton said, a little more gently this time. "With a company called Kantana Industrial Group in Thailand."

Sunny looked puzzled. "Thailand? We traveled there once, but that was years ago."

"If you can think of anyone at all who might be behind this. A business contact in Asia perhaps?"

"I suppose it could be anyone my husband did business with," Sunny said. "He flew to China, India, and Thailand at least seven, maybe eight, times a year. Right up until the time he got really sick and his doctors wouldn't allow him to travel anymore."

"Did he ever mention any problems that he encountered in Thailand?" Afton asked.

Sunny pressed her lips together tightly, then said, "Everything in Asia was a problem."

"You mean there was a disgruntled vendor?" Max asked.

Sunny made a rude noise. "They were all disgruntled. Always on the take. Leland used to fly over there with duffel bags full of gifts. Rolex watches, Louis Vuitton wallets, Cartier pens. It's called *guanxi* in China. I don't know what they call it in Thailand and India, but I know it exists there, too."

"Excuse me, ma'am," Afton said. "What is that? What exactly does *guanxi* mean?"

"Tea money," Sunny said. "A bribe. The price for doing business."

Max did a sort of double take. "Your husband had to bribe people?"

"He had to bribe *everyone* just to do business. Government officials, factory owners, factory foreman . . . they were all on the take."

"I had no idea," Afton said.

"No . . . well," Sunny said. "Maybe we were just used to it." She gave a small, involuntary shudder and said, "Now I'm really getting scared. Everything you're telling me . . . this is really bad. I'm starting to fear for my life. For my daughter's life, too."

"We're going to park a plainclothes officer outside your house for the time being," Max said. "Until we catch these people."

"Not on the boulevard," Sunny said. "You

317

can't park on the boulevard."

Max rolled his eyes. "We'll work it out."

Afton and Max also wanted to talk to Terrell. They found her at the buffet table high-grading the chicken salad, picking out the most tender bits of chicken and the plumpest pecans.

"If we could have a minute with you?" Afton asked.

"Now?" Terrell said. "In case you didn't notice, this is a *funeral* luncheon. With guests." She glared at them. "Besides, I'm busy eating right now."

"This won't take long."

"Whatever." Balancing her plate, Terrell led them into the living room, heading for the solarium.

"Is there someplace more private that we can talk?" Afton asked.

"Not really."

Afton nodded toward a closed door. "What's in there?"

"I don't think . . ." Terrell began.

Afton pushed the door open to find a small, well-furnished office, what she figured had to be Leland Odin's home office. "Okay," she said. "This looks perfect."

"Sure," Terrell said. "Whatever trips your trigger." She slipped past Afton and plopped herself down behind a large rosewood desk that had papers strewn all over it. She tidied the papers into a stack and set them aside. "Now. What's so damn important that it can't wait?"

Max went through his routine, asking her the same basic questions he'd just asked her mother. Had she ever heard of Kantana Industrial, blah, blah, blah.

Terrell gave mostly monosyllabic answers, scraping at her plate, never really meeting his eyes.

"So you don't know nothin' about nothin'," Max said finally.

Terrell put one elbow on the desk and cupped her chin. "That's about right."

"You're quite positive?" Afton asked. "Because the bodies are starting to pile up."

Terrell gazed at them, the insolent look of a poor little rich girl. "And you think that's my fault?"

"No," Max said. "Certainly not."

"Then get back out there, will you, and . . ."

"Let me guess," Max said. "And do my job."

"Whatever."

Back in Max's car, they cruised around Lake of the Isles Parkway. Lake of the Isles was basically a swampy, soggy parcel of land that had been drained back in the eighteen hundreds. Today it shimmered in the faint midday sun with two small islands poking up in the middle of the lake. Refuges for returning birds.

"Terrell's a pain," Afton said. "But Sunny was a lot nicer to us today, don't you think?"

"Maybe she thought we were pro-swan."

"Cygnus," Afton said.

Max turned up Kenwood Parkway, driving past a fountain that was dedicated as a memorial to the horses that died in World War I, then past the much-photographed mansion that would forever be known as the Mary Tyler Moore house.

"Do you think I should get some of that Grecian Formula stuff?" Max asked.

"What?" Afton said. This had come shooting out of the blue. "You mean for your hair?" She turned to look at him, thinking he must be making a joke, but seeing that he was dead serious.

"No, for my armpits. Of course for my hair. I'm worried that I'm starting to bear a slight resemblance to Father Time."

"Trust me, you don't." Afton wondered what had prompted *that* concern? Max was much more into humor than vanity.

"My kids told me I looked old."

"Not at all. You look . . . seasoned," Afton said. Max was what she'd call a scratch-and-dent kind of guy. A little banged up on the outside, but still plenty of life packed inside him. He'd be a great catch for a woman who liked a certain type of silver fox and didn't mind the baggage of stinky teenaged boys.

Max cut over to Hennepin Avenue and hooked a right on Twenty-fourth Street. "Listen, I've got an idea."

"What's that?"

"I want to stop at Sampson's Bar."

"Okay," Afton said. "Just as long as we don't have to actually eat there."

Sampson's was a dive bar on Lyndale Avenue. The kitchen hadn't passed inspection by the Board of Health since 1995, the floor was sticky from sixty years of spilled drinks, and a bunch of lowlifes hung out at the bar. The menu at Sampson's was dependent on a microwave oven and a refrigerator full of prepackaged sandwiches. The kind you bought and heated up yourself at an all-night gas station.

Max pulled up in front of Sampson's Bar, parked in the handicapped zone, and threw a card that said OFFICIAL POLICE BUSINESS on his dashboard.

"We're going to talk to your friend?" Afton asked.

"The Scrounger," Max said.
"You think he's here?"
"He's always here."

34

The interior of Sampson's was darker than a Kentucky coal mine. Definitely well below the regulation lumens required by the liquor licensing board. Still, Afton was able to make out the studded red plastic lamps dangling on bare cords over the bar, the cat-urine-yellow carpeting, and the half dozen temporarily unemployed men who were slumped over their refreshing afternoon beverages.

Max gave the bar a once-over and headed for the dining room. This somewhat improved part of Sampson's consisted of a few Formica tables, a bandstand with an old Mendini drum set, and an unattended pull-tab booth that was shrouded with chicken wire.

Seated at one of the tables watching an episode of *The Jerry Springer Show* and sipping an amber-colored drink was Max's friend The Scrounger. He spotted them immediately and tipped his drink toward them. "If it isn't Minneapolis's version of Starsky and Hutch. How do."

Afton and Max sat down at The Scrounger's table. They'd done this before.

"Got something for you," Max said.

"Oh, yeah?" The Scrounger's eyes were pinpricks of intensity. He wore a jean jacket with frayed holes at the elbows, brown workman's pants, and Red Wing steel-toed boots. His ginger-colored hair was pulled back in a ponytail and he had a scruffy beard. Afton thought he could pass for either a stoner or somebody whose poetry had just been published by the Des Moines Writer's Workshop.

The Scrounger lived in a dilapidated duplex in Minneapolis's Wedge neighborhood and made a living scrounging. That is, he drove up and down alleys in his beat-up Ford pickup looking for stuff. *Stuff* being anything remotely useful that someone had thrown out. The Scrounger preferred metals such as aluminum, brass, copper, and steel, since those could go directly to the metal recycling plant on Washington Avenue North and he could earn between a dollar and a dollar forty-eight per pound. Of course, he wasn't averse to picking up lamps, mattresses, chairs, and sofas. These he hauled to a self-storage locker out on Highway 55 where impromptu (also known as illegal) flea markets were staged.

"So whatcha got cookin'?" The Scrounger asked.

"I'd like you to do surveillance on a girl," Max said.

"Ah." The Scrounger leaned back in his chair. "A covert operation."

"Something like that."

He smiled at Afton. "Are we investigating a friend of yours? Perhaps an attractive young woman who's been stepping out on her husband? Some of those Edina ladies are plenty frisky." Edina was one of Minneapolis's wealthier suburbs.

"Nice try," Afton said. "But I'm not from Edina."

"With your good looks you should be," he said, his voice silky smooth.

"Cut the crap," Max said. "This is some serious shit here."

"I'm with you, man." The Scrounger pulled an unfiltered Camel cigarette out of a pack and twiddled it between his fingers. "So what's up?"

"You heard about that helicopter crash?" Afton asked. "At the U?"

"Sure. Hell yes."

"Okay, then." Afton gave him the three-minute Cliffs Notes version of what they'd been dealing with.

When she'd finished, The Scrounger said, "So you said a woman. Are you asking me to tag after that guy Odin's widow?"

"No," Afton said. "It's someone else who's peripherally involved."

"You have a photo?" The Scrounger asked.

Max grabbed the remote control and turned the TV channel to the Diamond Shopping Network. There, up on the flat-screen, was Fan Ling. She was sitting on a pink chair behind a glass table, smiling sweetly at the camera while she hocked women's gold wristwatches.

"Oh, that chick." The Scrounger nodded to himself as he grabbed a handful of raw peanuts from a bowl and popped them into his mouth. "Sure, I know who she is."

"Good," Max said. "Then you won't have any trouble tailing her." He opened his wallet and placed four twenty-dollar bills on the table. They disappeared faster than a white dove in David Copperfield's opening act. "Okay, then, we're set."

But The Scrounger was still staring at the TV screen, looking almost mesmerized as he chewed his peanuts. "You know, I bought a food processor from that chick a few months back." He tilted back lazily in his chair. "Hell of a thing."

While Afton and Max were communing with The Scrounger, Hack and Narong were glued to a small TV set, too. The discovery of the bodies out in Prior Lake was all over the twelve o'clock news.

"Damn it," Hack said. "I thought for sure the pigs would make fast work of those guys and there wouldn't be nothin' left. Maybe just a few bones or unpalatable bits. Like . . . knuckles or something. Teeth."

"This is trouble?" Narong asked. They were both functioning in a slight haze even though it was late morning.

Hack considered this. "Oh, probably not."

They watched some more, then a commercial for Tide came on, so they clicked over to Channel 7. More coverage. This time there was shaky camera work that showed a beautiful blond woman in a red blazer as she ran toward the hog pen waving a microphone.

"Good-looking chick," Hack said. He'd always considered himself a connoisseur of women.

"Look, look!" Narong cried suddenly. The station was showing footage of a slim woman turning away from the camera, her right hand thrown up in a don't-film-me gesture. "You see that woman who is trying to run away? That is the woman policeman who chased me the other night. That is the exact woman!" He was red-faced and angry, spitting out his words, his dark hair practically standing up on end.

Hack peered at the footage. She didn't look like any kind of cop he'd ever seen, but you never could tell. What she *did* look like was athletic, defiant, and fairly intense. He studied her image. He liked intense.

"That woman," Narong said. "My feeling is . . . she is some kind of evil spirit."

"Take it easy, she's just some random chick."

"No," Narong said, touching a hand to his chest. "I can feel her thinking about me, crouching in the shadows to come after me. That's why we must find her first and kill her."

"Chill, buddy, we got to stick with the program."

But Narong was insistent. "No, you must help me find this woman so I can kill her. So I can slit her throat. You must do this for me so I can have my peace."

Hack handed Narong a can of Red Bull and said, "Let me think about it."

35

"I'm so sick of driving back and forth to this place, I'm ready to start popping Dramamine tablets," Max said. They'd just made the turn off the freeway and were headed for Diamond Shopping Network's headquarters.

"I hear you," Afton said. "Still, we're lucky that Thacker managed to line up those dogs."

Max gave an unintelligible grunt.

"Maybe we'll find something. Maybe you can close your case."

"You mean our case. You have just as much stake in this as I do."

"I appreciate the sentiment. In fact, I'm a little dumbfounded that Thacker's let me tail you around as much as he has."

"He likes you and he trusts you."

"And he's overextended right now with the Harrison killing, the robbery at the new stadium, and the fact that a gang of Eastern

329

European jackholes installed skimmers in the pumps at a chain of H&R gas stations."

"There's that, yeah."

"But he's never going to wave his magic wand and make me a detective."

"What do I keep telling you?" Max said. "Ya gotta follow protocol. These things don't just happen overnight."

"No," Afton muttered. "Only bad things happen at night."

"Ah," Max lifted a hand off the steering wheel and gave a dismissive wave. "So have you been playing Spider-Woman lately?"

"I had planned to head down to Winona and climb Sugar Loaf, but with this arm . . . I think that's going to have to wait a few weeks." Afton wasn't one bit picky when it came to climbing. She enjoyed rock climbing, bouldering, and even hacking her way up the occasional frozen waterfall.

"I've heard about that thing in Winona," Max said. "It's up on a bluff? Supposed to look like a miniature Devils Tower?"

"The bluff is about five hundred feet above the Mississippi River, and then the limestone rock pinnacle is another eighty-five feet. Not so tall."

"Are you serious? That'd scare the shit out of me."

"Actually," Afton said, "that kind of climbing is more a mental exercise in serenity."

The drug-sniffing dogs were waiting for them when they pulled up in front of Diamond Shopping Network's headquarters. Two black-and-tan German shepherds, along with their handler, a guy named Dan Ritter who looked like he could be a rugged, outdoorsy model for the L.L. Bean catalog.

"Thanks for helping out," Max said, once they'd all introduced themselves.

"Not a problem," Ritter said. "The dogs always love a good search. It helps keep them on their toes."

One of the dogs stuck his neck out to sniff Afton's outstretched hand. "And who is this?" she asked.

"That's Stryker," Ritter said. "And the other one is Shiloh, a female."

"Nice dogs," Max said.

Stryker continued to sniff Afton's hand. Then the dog's eyes flicked up to connect with hers and the hard intelligence that shone in them made it feel as if Stryker's brain was doing a very careful assessment. Afton decided this was the kind of dog that probably would have enjoyed working for the Nazis. A dog that was all teeth and business with very little emotional need to please his master.

They all trooped inside, where Angus Wagner, looking nervous and distraught, met them in the reception area. "I can't believe this is happening," he said. "Mr. Barber murdered as well? This is just unbelievable."

"You have our condolences," Afton said, handing him one of her business cards for the second time. "If you need me to help answer any questions or run interference . . ."

"Yes, yes," Wagner said, practically blinking back tears. "You know, our employees are absolutely terrified. We've had more people call in sick today than ever before. I guess most of them saw the news this morning." He looked pointedly at Afton.

"And you've increased your security?" Max asked.

"Of course."

This time they didn't bother to sign in. Rather, Wagner led them hurriedly down a long hallway, through two sets of locked doors, and into the large DSN warehouse. The place was humming with activity. Workers holding mobile devices buzzed up and down aisles, pushing hand trucks and utility carts. Forklifts hoisted pallets that were stacked high with cardboard boxes.

"A lot of our merchandise is drop-shipped," Wagner explained. "In other words, when a customer orders from us, we send their order on to the manufacturer or, in some cases, the wholesaler. Then it's shipped out from there. But as you can see, DSN warehouses a huge amount of our merchandise right here on premises."

"And you ship it out from here?" Afton asked. "I mean, to your customers?" Stryker's ears were pitched forward, listening to every word that was said. She felt like the dog was following the conversation.

"That's right," Wagner said.

"So if you have shipping then you also have receiving," Afton said.

"I guess that's why you brought the dogs out, huh?" Wagner said.

"We believe there's a possibility that Mr. Odin and Mr. Barber were murdered over drugs," Max said.

"And you think you might find drugs here?" Wagner sounded incredulous, as if he could barely entertain the possibility. "That someone shipped drugs to us?"

"That's what we're trying to figure out," Max said.

"It'd be good if you cleared your people out of here," Ritter said. "The dogs function much better without a lot of distractions."

Wagner nodded. "Yes, we told our warehouse people they could expect a fairly lengthy break."

Ritter pulled a red rubber ball from the pocket of his vest and waved it around. Instantly, both dogs came to attention and focused on the ball.

"This is their cue," Ritter said. "The dogs see this and they know they'll receive a fun reward for all their hard work. Okay." Now he focused on the dogs. "Search." He led Stryker and Shiloh down one of the aisles, their harnesses and leashes jingling. The dogs walked along slowly, heads held low, moving in a fluid motion, noses fairly twitching. Afton, Max, and Wagner followed well behind them.

Ritter and the dogs walked along, the dogs sniffing and occasionally stopping. When they finished one aisle, they turned and then went down a second aisle.

"This could take a while, huh?" Wagner asked.

"Give it a chance," Afton said. She was keeping her fingers crossed.

"The thing is," Wagner said, "I have a meeting with Mr. Steckel, our corporate attorney. I guess you could call it an emergency meeting."

Twenty minutes went by, then thirty, then forty. The dogs continued to cruise up and down the aisles. By now Wagner was repeatedly glancing at his watch, looking more than a little impatient.

"Maybe the place is clean," Max said.

"Of course it's clean," Wagner said. "DSN is a reputable business. There are no drugs here."

Then Shiloh stopped. And Stryker stopped right beside her. They sniffed, then sniffed again, looking more than a little excited. Shiloh looked directly at Ritter and whined.

"Got something," Max said under his breath.

"Impossible," Wagner said.

"We got a hit," Ritter called out. "Can you get some of your workers to come over here and" — he gestured with his hands — "pull open these boxes?"

Wagner motioned to a group of men who were standing way at the end of the building. "Bobby? Jose? Could you please come over here and lend a hand?"

Bobby and Jose came over and pulled out an enormous wooden crate. Then Jose bent forward and slipped a crowbar under a wooden strut, bent into it, and popped the entire top of the box off.

The dogs whirled about in a frenzied circle until Ritter pulled them away.

"I don't believe it," Wagner said.

Afton and Max edged closer and slipped on latex gloves.

"Take care, now," Max cautioned. They scooped out handfuls of white foam peanuts. Below the peanuts lay a thick sheet of cardboard. That was lifted out to reveal more peanuts. They scooped again until a yellowed hunk of plastic appeared. "Got something here," Max said. Everybody leaned in while Max pulled out the top item that was carefully wrapped in plastic.

"What is it?" Afton asked.

"Looks like . . ." He peeled back the plastic gingerly. "A pair of leather sandals."

"Got some freeloaders in there," Ritter said. He'd moved back to check out the box.

"What?" Afton said. She didn't catch his meaning at first.

"Bugs," Ritter said. "You see those little uglies crawling around inside? Probably roaches. Or maybe even beetles."

Afton saw a scurrying movement and took a giant step backward. Bugs were not her friends. But Bobby and Jose moved in closer.

"Bugs," Jose said. "We get that sometimes."

"Here?" Wagner said. He seemed offended.

"Oh, yeah," Jose said. "Most of the time the shipments of clothes or whatever have been sprayed down with formaldehyde. But when they're not . . ." He made a face.

"At least the dogs got some practice in," Ritter said. He pulled two rubber balls from his pocket and tossed one to each dog. "Good dogs. Good job." Tails wagging, each dog caught a ball in its mouth like a trained circus seal.

"When cartons are shipped from a warm, moist climate," Ritter continued, "you find all sorts of insect life nesting in the foam pellets and cardboard. Heck, they even dine out on the cardboard. Makes that ocean crossing so much more enjoyable."

"You see this all the time?" Afton asked.

"Lots of times," Ritter said.

Jose nodded. "Us, too."

"So we got nothin'," Max said, turning away, disappointment evident on his face.

"You got bugs." Ritter leaned down and gave Stryker a pat on the shoulder. "Good dog." Stryker was already over the red ball. Now he just looked bored.

■ ■ ■ ■

Back in the car, Max said, "At least we gave it a shot."

"Maybe it's not drugs," Afton said.

"Then what could it be?"

Afton gazed out the window as they whipped past a line of bare trees. "I don't know," she whispered.

36

Hack and Narong walked into Louie's Liquor Lounge, directly across the street from the Gemini Truck Terminal in Roseville, just north of Saint Paul.

Louie's was your classic trucker dive bar, a plain brick façade with no real windows to speak of and a neon sign that had its letters stacked vertically so it was difficult to read without cocking your head.

Whatever. Inside, the place was dark and discreet and nobody much wanted to poke their nose into anybody else's business. A ratty pool table sat in the corner, but nobody was playing. A hot dog grill sat on the bar but the dogs looked dry and unappetizing, like they'd been cooking for a week.

"The sun's about ready to set over the yardarm," Hack said. "So we might as well hoist one."

"We drink again?" Narong asked. He was

beginning to think that, besides the frequent drug use, Hack might be an alcoholic.

"It's the friendly thing to do," Hack said. "Just until Bowser shows up."

"That is his name? Bowser?"

"His name's Matt Bowser. We used to work together at the Duluth Seaway Port Authority. Until he got fired anyway." The waitress came by and Hack said, "Two whiskies." Then to Narong: "You really have to be a screw-up to get fired from a job on the docks."

Narong smiled. "In Thailand, if people who work on Khlong Toei wharf screw up, we kill them and dump their bodies in the ocean." Khlong Toei was the critical hub of Thailand's export economy.

Hack hoisted his glass. "That sounds like a fine solution, my friend. Maybe we should institute that exact same procedure."

Bowser walked in some ten minutes later, a big guy with frizzled red hair and a bushy beard, wearing a plaid shirt. He and Hack made an elaborate show of slapping hands and bumping knuckles. Then Hack introduced his friend to Narong.

"Pleased to meet you," Narong said.

Bowser sucked air in through his front teeth. "You're a polite one, ain't you?" Then he ambled over to the bar, got himself a longneck, and came back and settled at their table. "Surprised to hear from you," Bowser said to Hack. "Been busy?"

"Can't complain," Hack said. "Same old, same old. Still in Duluth. Of course, I do the occasional freelance job like I mentioned to you on the phone." He leaned forward. "You still in the paper business?" By paper, Hack meant forged documents.

"Do a little of that now and then," Bowser said. He was being modest. Bowser had a lock on fake IDs, car registrations, and concert tickets. And should someone want a will changed to reflect a more substantial inheritance, Bowser could handle that, too.

Hack turned to Narong and said, "In case you're wondering, our friend Bowser used to work at the Foreign-Trade Zone in Duluth."

"Foreign-Trade Zone," Narong repeated. "What is . . . ?" Then the lightbulb slowly turned on. "FTZ? Does that mean . . . the same?"

"You got it," Hack said. "And our pal Bowser's gonna get us in there, slick as snot."

"How?" Narong asked.

"You know which FTZ?" Bowser asked Hack.

"Gotta be the Mid-City Industrial Park

zone. That's the most logical. Eagan's too small and there's no way they'd ship that shit to the airport. Way too dangerous."

"There you go," Bowser said. "All you need is the paperwork and a truck."

"We got the truck," Hack said. He turned to Narong. "And Bowser will get us the proper documents."

Bowser scratched at his beard. "I got a new kid that I been using. He works at a big-time ad agency in downtown Minneapolis, what they call a graphic design firm. He's a genius with typography and printing. Prints IDs, insurance claims, deeds of sale, even had him print what you'd call your papers of provenance for a painting that this rich dude I know smuggled in from Europe. This designer kid created a bill of sale that looked like it was straight from the eighteenth century. Like some fine English lord had sat at his desk and written it out with a quill pen. My designer used linen paper and stained it with tea to make it look old-timey. Hell of a thing."

"Was the painting really old?" Hack asked.

"Oh no. Hell no. The paint was barely dry."

"Your designer sounds like our man," Hack said. "So what's this going to cost?"

"Five grand for the kid, thirty grand for

me," Bowser said.

"Steep," Hack said, even though he knew the old lady would pay it.

Bowser took a sip of beer and a cagey look stole across his face. "And if you're going to pick up what I think you're going to pick up, I want a Big Eight for myself." He meant an eighth of a kilo, or one hundred and twenty-five grams.

"You drive a mighty hard bargain," Hack said. "But we can make that happen. So when can we get the papers?"

"You give me the basic poop, I'll have the papers for you first thing tomorrow. I've got FTZ documents my guy can work from and he can probably steal DSN's logo right off their website."

"This is . . . amazing," Narong said.

"It's the American way," Hack said. "Fake it 'til you make it."

"And the best thing is," Bowser continued, "if you hit up the FTZ on a Saturday or Sunday, it'll be staffed by a bunch of jerk-offs. They don't just have the B or C team working then; they got the Z team. You just kind of wave your customs forms under their noses and you're in like Flynn."

37

Friday night dinner at Afton's house was a combination of food, jokes, and family togetherness. With no school tomorrow and no homework looming on the horizon, Poppy and Tess were all jacked up about watching a movie. The only question up for debate was — would it be *Frozen* or *Finding Nemo?*

"I vote *Finding Nemo,*" Poppy said. "But this family is a democracy, so everybody gets a vote." She looked hopefully at Tess and then at Lish, Afton, and Bonaparte. "What do you guys think we should watch?"

Tess glanced across the table at Afton and made a big show of giving a conspiratorial wink. She had become such a good big sister, kind and nurturing. Afton was so proud of her.

"I vote *Finding Nemo,* too," Tess said.

Afton bent down and smiled at Bonaparte. "What?" she said. "You want to watch that

344

movie, too?"

Poppy threw her hands up in the air. "Yay! It's unaminous."

"Unanimous," Tess corrected. "But I got dibs on the big chair."

"Then I get the Spider-Man sleeping bag," Poppy called out.

All the while Afton was listening to her kids, she was thinking about finding Jay Barber's body and Leland Odin's throat being slashed. The black blood had come spurting out like some kind of unholy fountain, reminding her of a passage in Upton Sinclair's *The Jungle.* About how the men had labored on the kill floor all day long, slashing the throats of cattle as they were driven down wooden chutes, bawling loudly, eyes rolling with fear. Just awful.

Any person who could kill like that today, slitting throats and torturing in an impersonal, almost industrial sort of way, had to be completely and utterly deranged. Which meant he should be put in a steel-tempered cage the size of a phone booth and never allowed out. Or maybe someday capital punishment would make a return engagement. Whatever.

Afton was just wiping down the stove when the phone rang.

"Hello?"

It was Max.

"What are you doing right now?" he asked.

"Scraping refried bean crud off the stove. Taco Tuesday was on Friday this week and my kids helped with the cooking." Afton paused, the cleaning rag in her hand. "Wait, why are you asking me this?"

"Because I'm sitting outside your house."

"What? Seriously?" Afton's first impulse was to run to the front window and look out. Instead, her heart beating a little faster, she said, "What's going on? What happened?"

"Grab your coat, we're going for a joyride."

"Come on, Max, I can't just up and leave my kids. I need to know why. Was there a break in the case?"

"You're going out?" Lish called from the living room, where the movie had just started.

"Maybe," Afton called back. "Is that okay with you?"

Lish nodded. The kids were already staring at the screen, captivated by the music and the colorful animation.

"Hey, are you still there?" Max asked.

"Yeah."

"You know that plainclothes officer we

stationed outside Sunny's house this afternoon?" Max asked.

"Uh-huh."

"He just called. The daughter, Terrell, took off a half hour ago and he followed her."

Afton had already stepped to the coat closet and was twining a scarf around her neck. "Followed her where?"

"I got the address. It's a house in Saint Paul that's owned by a guy named Lester Snell." He paused. "I'm thinking boyfriend."

Afton slipped into her coat just as Poppy came running up to her. "Bye, Mommy," she said. Afton touched her daughter's head and said into the phone, "If Terrell has a hot date, why is that our concern?"

"Hot date," Poppy said, smiling.

"Oh, maybe because he lives in what appears to be a crack house over in Frogtown," Max said. Frogtown was a blue-collar neighborhood near the state capital that was bordered by a tangle of railroad tracks.

"Does this guy have a record? Has he ever been popped?"

"Funny you should ask. Yes, he has. He's got a fairly long sheet that includes dope and some B&E. Goes by the street name of Mello Snello."

"I see. That's his professional name, I take

it. So what is Terrell doing with a lowlife like him? I mean, she's rich. Shouldn't she be swanning around a fancy country club on the arm of some Yalie or Harvard guy?"

"That's what's weird about this. That's what we need to find out."

Afton hung up the phone, bid a quick good-bye to Lish and the kids, and then hurried out to Max's car and jumped in. "So what's the deal?" she asked him. "You cruise around on Friday nights like Batman? Looking for evildoers?"

"If you must know, I had a date."

"You? Had a date?" Afton instantly regretted the surprise that colored her voice.

"Don't look so surprised. There are still a few women in the northern hemisphere who consider me a fairly decent catch."

"Well . . ." Afton stopped. She knew Max had a social life, she just didn't know to what extent. This was a whole new insight into his fairly low-key outside-of-work persona. Maybe this was why he'd asked her about Grecian Formula. She studied the back of his head. Nope, still salt and pepper. Didn't look like he'd made any major commitment yet. "So you had to cancel it? Your date, I mean?"

"Mmn . . . yup."

"Is this someone that you're serious . . . ?"

"How am I supposed to get serious with somebody when I'm out chasing bad guys all the time?" Max said as he gunned the engine and blasted through a yellow light just as it winked red. "And babysitting you."

They crept down Thomas Street, past a few ramshackle houses that looked as if they were either crack houses or HUD houses that young couples had bought on the cheap and were trying to rehab.

"Another neighborhood in transition," Afton said. "Lot of that going on these days."

"The old folks move out and the young folks move in," Max said. "Or the dope dealers."

"Young dope dealers," Afton said. "Don't need low-interest loans or government mortgages because they're making a killing selling crack to the neighborhood kids. So. You have a bad feeling about this guy Snell?"

"I don't exactly have a good feeling."

Max switched off his lights and eased his car past a dilapidated-looking Victorian home. Paint blistered off its finials, balustrades, and banisters, but the bones of the place looked solid. "There," he said. "That's the house."

Sliding forward in her seat, Afton looked

out. A plain brown car, your basic unmarked cop car, sat across the street from a small, story-and-a-half house that was painted slate gray. A rattletrap pickup truck and a silver Mercedes SL550 sat directly in front of the house. Excitement nipped at Afton. "Is that Terrell's car?" she asked. "The Mercedes?" Afton knew a bit about cars from her ex, Mickey. And she knew that particular model of Mercedes probably went for a cool eighty-five grand.

"It's registered to her, yes," Max said. "Though I'm guessing she probably didn't make the payments on it."

"So what's a rich girl doing over here?" Afton wondered out loud.

"Frankie," Max murmured into his phone, "you can take off now, I got this." There was a burst of static and Max said, "Thanks, but I don't think we're gonna need backup. I got my pit bull riding with me."

"Pit bull? Is that what you think of me?" Afton asked.

"If the shoe fits."

The brown car started up, the headlights flashed on, and it slid past them in the dark. Max eased his car forward and parked directly behind the Mercedes. "Okay, now."

Together, Afton and Max walked up the cracked sidewalk and knocked on the front

Snell shrugged. "Suppose you could call it that."

"Because if you two are in a committed relationship, then we missed your shining presence at the funeral this morning," Afton said to Snell.

"Funerals bum me out, man," Snell whined.

"I can just imagine," Afton said. She was getting a weird vibe from Snell. He came across as anxious and more than a little flustered. She suddenly wondered if he could have somehow played a role in Odin's and Barber's murders.

Max was obviously thinking along the same lines, because he turned to Snell and said, "But you haven't been too stoned out of your noggin to know what's been going on, right? The murder of your girlfriend's stepfather as well as his partner, Jay Barber?"

Snell bobbed his head. "Heard all about it. Weird shit, man. Must be some real crazies running around out there, maybe along the lines of that Manson gang."

"Charlie Manson's been in prison for forty-six years," Afton said. "So I doubt it was him."

Max focused a mirthless grin on Snell and said, in a conversational tone, "Tell us about

353

the old lady." He meant the suspected ringleader, the woman from the hotel.

That stopped Snell in his tracks. "What? *My* old lady?" He shook his head as if to clear it and looked genuinely confused. "She's long gone. We've been divorced for over a year. She hated my guts, man. Couldn't wait to get away."

"Don't get cute," Max said.

"Come on, man, it's all nice and legal. I can show you the papers. They're here . . ." Snell looked around at what passed for a living room. "Somewhere."

"I'm talking about the other old lady," Max said. "The one who was staying at the Hotel Itasca, the one who engineered the helicopter crash. We know the two of you were in on the whole thing."

"What?" Snell whooped. His mouth gaped open like a fish gasping for air, revealing a set of yellow teeth. Then he whirled to face Terrell, who also looked completely blindsided. "Do you know what this guy's talking about?"

"You're accusing *us* of murder?" Terrell shrieked. She didn't sound stoned anymore, she sounded furious. As if she'd just hit DEFCON 1.

Like a boxer who wouldn't quit, Max kept pummeling away at Snell. Asking him about the people from Thailand, the luxury hotel, the helicopter crash, slitting Odin's throat, the kidnapping of Barber, the whole ball of wax.

Terrell kept screaming like a stuck pig and Snell's eyes got wild as he suddenly seemed to come awake and realize how serious these accusations were. Afton wondered if the neighbors would hear the awful commotion and call the Saint Paul police.

"Whoa, whoa, whoa," Snell said, rings of sweat dampening his T-shirt. "What is this crap anyway? The plot for a new Jack Reacher novel? I don't know shit about what you're talking about." His pleading eyes bounced from Max to Afton and back to Max again. "Really I don't! Ya gotta believe me!"

Max pushed him a little more but then finally backed off. He didn't have any real evidence and Snell looked like he was about ready to have a brain hemorrhage and collapse. There was no need to bring a couple of EMTs into the situation.

"I'm going to have an unmarked car park right here on your block," Max told Snell and Terrell. "So don't anybody get creative. Don't get any weird ideas about another murder."

"Get out," Terrell shouted. She was on

her feet and screaming in Max's face. Her face was beet red, her teeth were bared, and Afton could see spittle flying from her mouth. "Get out of here before I call my lawyer and have your stupid little badge pulled!"

They got out. Max drove to a McDonald's over on Rice Street and they went through the drive-through. Max ordered coffee; Afton got a Diet Coke.

"What do you think?" Max asked as they sat in the parking lot, the golden arches casting a curve of light on the hood of his car.

"Snell is plenty skeevy," Afton said. "But I don't think he's smart enough to engineer three murders. Well, five if you're counting the surface-to-air rocket that killed the helicopter pilots."

"Yeah, I pushed him pretty hard."

"And he stuck to his story," Afton said. "Even though his brain cells seem pretty well sautéed."

Max blew on his coffee. "There's that."

"I suppose the possibility exists that Snell could have hired someone. That he got one of his lowlife friends to do his dirty work."

"Why?" Max asked. "Because Terrell asked him to?

"Maybe."

"What does she see in him?"

"I don't know," Afton said. "Drugs? He's her drug connection? Or she likes to go slumming . . . hang out with bad boys? Probably some rich girls get a big kick out of that."

Max sipped his coffee while he digested Afton's words. "Do you think Terrell could be the brains behind all of this?"

"What? You mean the murders?" Afton shook her head. "No, I don't think Terrell is the brains of the organization. She'd be more like . . ."

"The asshole?" Max said.

Afton let loose an indelicate snort. "That sounds about right."

38

"I appreciate the fact that you were all able to come in this morning," Thacker said.

It was Saturday morning and the team — Thacker, Max, Afton, Dillon, and Farmer — were all dressed casually. Jeans, sweatshirts, sneakers. Only Thacker was wearing pressed khaki slacks and a navy pullover sweater.

"And we're grateful for the damage control you've been able to do," Max said. "You managed to fend off most of the media jackals."

"Mmn," Thacker said, not quite ready to accept Max's praise. "We're managing, not mitigating. There are a number of hair-raising stories out there and the public is starting to collectively squirm. Just way too many dead bodies." He looked around, said, "Damn, where is that press release Darlene just gave me?"

"So, what's the game plan?" Dillon asked.

He was perched on a straight wooden chair unwrapping a package of Hostess Twinkies. Afton figured it must be his breakfast. So much for a healthy egg white omelet.

"Let me bring you all up to date," Max said. He proceeded to give a quick rundown on the two dogs searching the DSN warehouse for drugs, then segued into last night's shakedown on Odin's stepdaughter's boyfriend.

"The common denominator in all this has to be drugs," Farmer said. He cast a wistful eye toward Dillon's Twinkies.

"If it's drugs," Afton said, "we don't know where they came from or who has them."

"Or where they're headed," Max said.

"Maybe Barber had all those answers and was forced to come clean," Dillon said. He licked frosting from a finger. "I mean, he was tortured pretty bad, right? That generally means the torturer is trying to extricate a fair amount of information from the torturee."

"Genius," Farmer murmured.

Thacker ignored him. "Are we assuming the two shooters, the old lady and the younger Asian man, were the torturers? Do we think they're still here in town?"

"We don't know that for a fact," Max said. "But it feels like they are."

"Then we keep doing what we've been doing," Thacker said. "And we especially keep an eye on Sunny Odin and her daughter, Terrell."

"What about Barber's wife?" Dillon asked.

"Her, too," Thacker said. "We work harder and smarter and keep trying to find those shooters. Try to track down the window sticker Sammy Mah spotted on that red car. We should also keep in touch with law enforcement out in Prior Lake, swing back to the Hotel Itasca for a follow-up interview, maybe even go back and hit that noodle factory. And we for sure need to huddle with the medical examiner. Max, you should pay him a visit and see if anything new has turned up. Trace evidence, fingerprints, any sort of unusual signature that can be linked to another killing. You're lead detective — you know the drill."

"Put me to work, boss," Dillon said. He picked up one of his Twinkies and passed it to Farmer, who said, "Ooh."

Max went back to his desk, scratched out a few notes, and then dragged a whiteboard into the bullpen. He had Afton draw up a chart — her penmanship was way better than his, better than anybody's there — outlining what they'd already done and what they still needed to do. Then he quickly doled out assignments.

As everyone got busy, Afton said to Max, "Do you mind if I tag along to the ME's office?"

"You really want to?"

She shrugged, knowing there'd be metal tables, clanking pipes, shiny instruments, and dead bodies. The stuff of nightmares. "It might be . . . enlightening."

"Okay, but don't . . ." His mobile phone shrilled suddenly. "Hang on," he told Afton. He punched the On button and said, "Yeah? Montgomery here."

"That chick you wanted me to tail?" The Scrounger said. "She's on the move."

"What are you talking about?" Max asked. "Oh . . . jeez. You mean Fan Ling?"

"First she made a loop around Lake of the Isles, then she doubled back to Lake and Hennepin, went through a parking ramp without parking, and then drove downtown."

"She thinks she's being followed," Max said. "Which means she's gotta be up to something. Did she make you?"

"I don't think so. She just waltzed into First Federal," The Scrounger said. "The main bank, the one on Sixth and Marquette."

Max was so startled, he could barely

answer. "She's there now?"

"And get this — she's all dolled up in a floppy hat and big, bug-eyed sunglasses. Like old movie stars used to wear."

"Disguised." This wasn't good. "Can you see what she's up to?"

"She went in and started chatting with one of those assholes in a three-piece suit that you always see twiddling their thumbs behind a nice, clean desk. Then they both disappeared into a back room. Right now I'm thinking safe deposit box. With stacks of hundred dollar bills inside."

"Keep an eye on her," Max shouted. "We'll be right over."

"What?" Afton said when Max hung up. He looked so wild-eyed and excited that she knew something must have broken.

"Fan Ling's over at the bank."

"The bank?"

"First Federal," Max said. "Come on, let's go."

They jogged the six blocks to First Federal and found The Scrounger waiting outside, leaning up against a marble pillar. He was smoking a Camel cigarette and looking like a street person in his ratty army jacket and camo pants.

"Is she still in there?" Max asked.

The Scrounger nodded. "Unless she made her getaway via the back door."

"What are we doing?" Afton asked. As far as she knew, Fan Ling hadn't committed any sort of crime. Hell, maybe she'd come here to take out a home equity loan. On the other hand . . .

"Fan Ling took a circuitous route, as though she was afraid of being followed," Max said. "And she's wearing sunglasses and a big hat."

"Maybe on her way to Miami Beach?" Afton said. But she didn't think so. No, Fan Ling was definitely up to something. And Afton's best guess was that it had something to do with Leland Odin's money. After all, Fan Ling had been his last real visitor.

Max led the way through a set of brass-and-glass revolving doors with Afton following right on his heels. In the expansive lobby, at least half a dozen customers were sitting at various desks conversing with bank officers. A whole bunch more customers were lined up at the teller windows. But there was no Fan Ling in sight.

Max walked to the nearest teller window, cut in line, and said, "Excuse me, I need to get into my safe deposit box."

The teller glared at him from behind her metal scrollwork. "Sir, I'm helping someone right now," she said.

A guy with a cash envelope said, "Yeah, she's helping me."

"The safe deposit boxes?" Max said again.

"Oh, for goodness's sake," the disgruntled teller said. She waved a hand and said, "They're just to your left over there. Mr. Sandager can help you."

Max showed a hint of teeth. "Thank you."

Afton and Max walked across a plush blue carpet and skirted around a low counter. Afton figured they must be in the private banking area — everything was so hushed and subdued. They were just about to speak with a receptionist when Fan Ling emerged through a set of double doors carrying a Louis Vuitton duffel bag.

From the way the designer duffel sagged, Afton figured Fan Ling must have just emptied out a safe deposit box and filled it with . . . what? Fifty-dollar bills, a coin collection, stock certificates, first edition Batman comic books and a Captain Midnight decoder ring?

"Fan Ling," Max said. He used his serious voice.

Fan Ling stopped in her tracks, causing the man walking behind her to practically stumble into her. "You!" she said. She didn't look happy. In fact, she looked stunned.

"Making a small withdrawal?" Max asked her.

"Maybe not so small," Afton said.

"Excuse me," the man accompanying Fan Ling said. "What's going on, please?"

"Are you Mr. Sandager?" Max asked.

Sandager nodded politely. Her wore a chalk gray pinstripe suit, a pair of horn-rimmed glasses, and looked like central casting's version of a banker. "Arthur Sandager, yes. Is there a problem?"

"Police," Afton said.

Nonplussed, Sandager said, "May I please see some form of identification?"

Max flipped open his ID. "This work for you?"

Sandager studied it. "Thank you."

"You're welcome. Now. Do you have a spare office we could use?"

Sandager hesitated for the briefest moment and then said, "Of course, Detective. Right this way."

Max grabbed a protesting Fan Ling firmly by the arm and pulled her along, Afton following on their heels. When Sandager showed them into a small conference room, Max said, "Thank you." Then Max, Fan Ling, and Afton went in, along with a very curious Sandager.

"What is this?" Fan Ling demanded. She rolled her eyes, flipped her hair, and did everything but stomp her foot.

"Suppose you tell us," Afton said in a conversational tone.

"This is where I do my banking," Fan Ling said stubbornly. "I am taking care of business."

"Sure," Max said. "You're here to open a checking account, buy traveler's checks, whatever." He glanced at Sandager. "Does the young woman have an account here?"

Sandager hesitated for a moment and then said, "No."

"It's none of your business what I'm doing."

Max pointed to the duffel clutched tightly in her hand. "We'd appreciate if you'd cooperate and show us what you have concealed in your bag."

"This is just to put our minds at ease," Afton offered. "To eliminate you as any sort of suspect. We certainly wouldn't want you to get inadvertently mixed up in the Leland Odin murder."

"Or the Jay Barber murder," Max said.

"You can't do this to me," Fan Ling protested.

Afton smiled. "The bag? Would you open it, please?"

"No," Fan Ling said.

Max reached out, grabbed the bag from her, and plopped it onto the table. "Thank you."

"You are going to be so sorry you did this," Fan Ling said. "I am going to get an attorney!"

"Where have we heard that before?" Afton said.

Max unzipped the duffel bag and pulled it open. It was loaded — literally loaded — with stacks of hundred-dollar bills.

"Not traveler's checks," Afton said. "More like traveling money."

"Taking a trip?" Max asked. "Planning to leave the country?"

Fan Ling narrowed her eyes. "No."

"Come on," Max said. "I doubt if Diamond Shopping Network pays you quite that well. And in cash yet."

"So where'd you get the money?" Afton asked.

Fan Ling bit her lip. "It was a gift."

"Sure," Max said. "A tax-free gift."

"It was!" she shrieked.

Afton glanced at Sandager. "We're guessing that this money — you did know this duffel bag is filled with money, didn't you?" Afton said.

Sandager peered carefully into the bag,

then pushed his glasses up on his nose. "Well, not exactly. All our customers are afforded complete privacy when they retrieve the contents of their safe deposit boxes."

"But you know who this particular safe deposit box belongs to, don't you?"

"Well, yes. But this young lady did have the proper account number."

"That's okay," Max said. "We don't want to get you in trouble for anything. We only want to confirm who the safe deposit box, and its contents, belong to."

Sandager licked his lips. "Yes, well, the young woman was accessing Mr. Leland Odin's safe deposit box."

Afton smiled. "Thank you."

They let Fan Ling go with a stern warning not to leave town and handed the duffel bag full of money over to Mr. Sandager.

"For safekeeping," Afton said. "Is there some process by which you can hold this money, like, in escrow or something?"

"Limbo?" said Max.

"That can certainly be arranged," Mr. Sandager said. "We just need to sign some papers . . ."

"Perfect," Afton said.

Back out on the street, The Scrounger had drifted away, and a young guy with a guitar had taken his place. His guitar case was open and a scattering of dimes and quarters lay inside. He was whanging away at the strings, struggling through a bad rendition of "Layla." He was never going to give Eric Clapton a run for his money.

"There's only one thing to do now," Afton said. She dug in her jacket pocket, found a crumpled dollar bill, and tossed it into the open guitar case.

"Bless you," said the guitar player.

"What's that?" Max asked.

"Stir the pot. Go talk to Sunny. Tell her what just happened here."

Max grinned crookedly. "I like how you think."

39

"What on earth?" were Sunny's first words when she opened her front door and found Afton and Max standing there.

"Sorry to bother you," Afton said. "But there have been some new developments that we need to run by you." They'd rehearsed their dog and pony show in the car on the way over and Max wanted Afton to take the lead. He felt that Sunny would feel far less threatened by her. Afton felt that Sunny would probably feel contemptuous of her.

"What are you talking about?" Sunny asked. She wore a lime green sweater and white slacks with a stunning line of diamonds encircling her neck. "Is this about Leland? Or Jay?"

Afton managed her best earnest smile. "If we could just come in? Have a few moments of your time?"

Grudging now. "I suppose." Sunny

stepped back and let them come into her house, then closed the door with an audible sigh. "So, what's going on?"

"Perhaps we could go somewhere and sit down?" Afton said. She figured that when Sunny found out about Fan Ling raiding her husband's safe deposit box, she'd fall right off that high horse of hers.

Another sigh. "Yes. Whatever," Sunny said. She led them into the library, where several large floral arrangements graced the cocktail table and end tables. Afton figured they were funeral arrangements that had been pulled apart and reworked so they didn't look quite so . . . funereal.

When they were all seated, Afton said, "A slight problem has cropped up."

Sunny gazed at her with an apprehensive look. "What now? Please don't tell me there's been *another* murder."

"No, thank goodness," Afton said.

Max cleared his throat. "About an hour ago, Miss Fan Ling went into First Federal bank, the main office in downtown Minneapolis, and emptied out your husband's safe deposit box."

Sunny's eyes bulged and she gripped the arms of her chair until her knuckles went white. *"What?"*

"Your husband's employee from DSN

went into . . ."

"His *safe deposit box*!" Sunny screeched. "Odin had a box at . . . where did you say?" She wasn't just upset; she was practically apoplectic.

"First Federal," Max said.

Sunny started to shake so hard that the gold bangle bracelets on her wrist actually began to jangle. Then her voice began to shake as well. "That sneaky bastard. And you say Fan Ling had *access* to it? She had the code or the key or whatever it was?"

Afton nodded. "Yes, ma'am. She had removed a good deal of money from the box . . . probably all that was in there . . . when we intervened."

"How much?" Sunny asked.

"Fifty thousand dollars," Afton said. "All in neatly bound packs of hundred-dollar bills. The bank personnel counted it out for us."

"That thieving bitch," Sunny said. "That scabrous, ungrateful bitch. My husband brings her over here from China, gives her a high-profile job, and this is how we're repaid . . . ?" She was so angry, she was practically grinding her teeth together.

Tell us how you really feel, Afton thought to herself.

"Where's the money now?" Sunny asked.

"It's safe," Afton said. "It's being held at First Federal."

Sunny's jaw jutted out. "You know that's *my* money."

"Well, it certainly may well be," Max said. "But that's an issue for your attorneys to sort out with the bank or your estate or whatever."

"Of course," Sunny said. "But you're telling me you stopped her?"

"Yes, we did," Max said.

"How did you . . . Oh. You had her followed?"

"That's right," Afton said.

"Thank you," Sunny said. She touched a hand to her chest. "I am so grateful for that."

Of course you are, Afton thought. She'd come to realize that rich people, seriously wealthy people, felt actual physical pain whenever they were forced to part with money.

"There's something else we need to discuss," Max said.

Sunny looked anxious again. "What is it? *More* problems with Fan Ling?"

Max glanced at Afton. "Tell her."

"This concerns your daughter," Afton said.

"My daughter?"

"Your daughter spent last evening at her boyfriend's house," Afton said, putting a little flint into her voice. "A man named Lester Snell. You might know him as a dirtbag who lives in a duplex over in the Frogtown neighborhood."

"What?" Sunny looked stunned all over again. She shook her head hard, her long gold earrings battering at her neck. "No, that's impossible. Terrell doesn't see that man anymore."

"We were there," Afton said. "We talked to them."

"Bring her in here and ask her," Max said.

"She isn't here," Sunny said. "She went out last night and hasn't returned home yet."

"I'm confused," Afton said. "Terrell seemed quite content being with Mr. Snell. So why *wouldn't* you think she was spending time at his house?"

Sunny's hands fluttered. "It's complicated."

"Because . . . ?" Afton prompted.

Sunny's face went through a series of contortions. "My husband paid that horrible man to stay away from Terrell," she blurted out.

"He bribed him?" Max said.

Sunny dropped her head into her hands

and said in a muffled voice, "This is the exact thing Leland worried about. That something would happen to him and Terrell and . . . that *person* . . . would cash in on some of the inheritance."

"Excuse me," Afton said. This all seemed slightly complicated to her. "So your husband didn't like Terrell's boyfriend?"

"*Didn't like* isn't strong enough," Sunny said. "When Terrell started seeing him, Leland had the man investigated. He has a record, you know."

"We know that," Max said. "We are the Minneapolis Police, you realize."

"Yes, well . . ."

"You say your daughter's not home yet," Afton said. "Have you tried calling her?"

"I have, but Terrell's not answering her phone."

Max lifted an eyebrow. He figured Terrell was either still getting stoned or sleeping it off.

"Do you want us to have the Saint Paul police check on her? On them?" Afton asked.

"No," Sunny said. She rubbed her eyes and her shoulders sagged. She suddenly looked as if she'd aged ten years. "I'm sure she'll turn up eventually."

40

The noonday sun was burning a hole through the clouds and finally warming the day to a tolerable fifty degrees. Inside the old casket factory, Mom Chao Cherry's reinforcements had arrived and were setting up camp. The three men, who'd just endured a thirty-six-hour plane ride in cramped coach seats, didn't seem to mind that the place was dark and dank and infested with scuttling rodents. They stowed their gear beneath the cots that Hack and Narong had brought in for them, chatted in Thai with Narong, and generally took it easy.

These were Mom Chao Cherry's own men, recruited from Klong Toei, Bangkok's most notorious slum, and they'd done her bidding many times before. This trip, though tiring, was also exciting for them. A new country, new sights, a new opportunity to earn money.

Hack was ready to run out to the nearest Burger King and bring in a mess of food and drinks, but Narong stopped him. Instead, Narong and the three men hooked up a hot plate to a car battery, boiled a pot of water, and cooked up a batch of noodles.

Mom Chao Cherry, who'd been camped out in a room upstairs, came down to greet the men. They clustered around her, happy to see her and hear what she had to say. She was, besides being the boss lady, a benefactor of sorts. Working for her, dirty though the jobs might have been, had lifted them out of poverty.

She spoke to them in rapid Thai, thanking them for coming, telling them that she needed them for some very important work. They would have to help her move some merchandise to a place called Michigan, she said. Maybe a ten- or eleven-hour journey. They would ride in a truck armed with weapons. All this, she told them, would happen tomorrow night, so they should rest up from their trip and be ready.

All the men nodded agreeably, then hunkered around the hot plate, talking and finishing their noodles. After a while they broke out some *ya-ba* — pink meth tablets that smelled a little like cotton candy — and smoked for a while, laughing and telling jokes.

They got a good high cranking before they settled back in their bunks and fell asleep.

"Now we must be concerned about our important meeting tonight," Mom Chao Cherry told Hack and Narong. "In two hours I must meet with my buyers from Detroit."

Hack lifted a finger. "Problem, ma'am. We don't exactly have the stuff in hand yet."

She gazed at him through half-lidded eyes. "But you will obtain my merchandise tomorrow, yes?" she said. "You told me everything was in order, every detail carefully worked out."

"Yeah, I did," Hack said. "And I meant it." He scratched his head as if deep in thought. "But don't you want to leave a little wiggle room?"

"No wiggle, no room," Mom Chao Cherry said. "Now. I think we will not arrive in your automobile. We must have something more comfortable. More suitable."

"You want me to call a cab?" Hack asked. Their meeting was to take place at a fancy hotel in the town of Stillwater, right on the banks of the Saint Croix River, some thirty miles away. So a cab ride would cost a pretty penny. On the other hand, he wasn't the one footing the bill.

Mom Chao Cherry smiled. "A limousine would be best."

Hack bobbed his head. "Consider it done." He walked outside onto the loading dock, checked his phone directory, and found the number for a limo company he'd used before for some other clients.

"Mr. Hack," Narong said behind him.

Hack spun around. "Yeah? What's up?"

"The woman," Narong said. "The woman who chased me . . ."

Hack smiled. "I got that covered, kid. You know that news story they did on Channel Seven? When the cops found the two bodies?"

"Yes?" Narong sounded unsure.

"I called that news reporter up, Portia somebody, and told her I had some information for her. Details that police chick was withholding from her. Know what the news lady said?"

Narong shook his head.

"She said, 'Oh, you mean Afton Tangler?' And I said, 'Was that the chick that was running away from you?' And she said, 'Yeah.' "

Narong stared at him.

"And then I said, 'Thank you very much' and hung up."

"You got her name," Narong said.

"Better than that, buddy. I know where she lives." He put an arm around Narong's shoulders. "Hey, you can trust old Hack to come through for you, right?"

The meeting was held in the Lumber Baron Room at the Tamarack Hotel in downtown Stillwater. Mom Chao Cherry sat at the head of the table dressed in a tasteful black Chanel jacket and slacks. Hack and Narong flanked her on either side. They'd ordered pots of jasmine and Darjeeling tea and Narong did the honors, pouring small cups of steaming hot tea for everyone and then sitting back down.

The drug buyers were a strange pair. A Caucasian man in a white suit with bad, bumpy skin, and his partner, a dark-haired, dark-complexioned man who could have been Pakistani, Italian, or even Hispanic. Whatever, he seemed to be the big wheel in the operation, though no names were exchanged.

"You remind me of that famous writer," Hack told the man in the white suit.

The guy curled a lip. "You mean Tom Wolfe?"

Hack shook his head. "I was thinking more of Mark Twain."

Mom Chao Cherry took a cigarette from a gold case, lit it, and smoked it using a tiny, jeweled holder that looked like a modified roach clip. When everyone had settled down and all eyes were on her, she said, "I have procured the merchandise."

"Took you long enough," the dark-haired guy said.

"There were unforeseen circumstances," she said. "That has all been taken care of."

"You will deliver the shipment directly to us?" white suit asked.

Mom Chao Cherry nodded serenely, then waved a hand at Hack and then Narong. "These men will arrive with my merchandise Monday morning."

"Don't you mean *my* merchandise?" the dark-haired guy said.

"It only becomes yours when you make the payment," Mom Chao Cherry said, her eyes filling with a predatory glow. "Once that takes place, our business will be concluded."

"Right," white suit said. "Got it." He pulled out a wallet and withdrew a blank white card, scribbled a hasty note on it. "Here's the address. It's a warehouse on the edge of Detroit. The number below is an emergency phone number." He slid the card down the table. "If your people do not arrive at this address Monday morning — noon at the very latest — none of this information will be valid. We'll be gone. The deal goes up in smoke." He made a sound like *phfft* with his lips.

Mom Chao Cherry smiled even though she found the two buyers loathsome and disgusting. "My men will be there. No problem."

41

Afton and Max were just coming out of the medical examiner's office, squinting in the fading sunlight, trying to shake off the chill of the basement labs and the stink of formalin and formaldehyde, when Max's mobile phone rang.

"Yello," he said. Then he bent over abruptly, as if someone had just jammed a live wire up against his spine. "What? Where?" Max cocked his head and gazed openmouthed at Afton.

"What's wrong?" she asked.

"What was the name again?" Max asked. "Cosmonaut? Oh, Cosmopolitan?" He listened for another forty seconds and then punched his phone off. "A limousine company just called in to the Homicide desk. Seems one of their drivers just came back from a run to Stillwater."

"Yeah?"

"When the driver walked into the dispatcher's office, he recognized his fare from the flyers we sent out the other day to all the hotels, cab services, airlines . . . well, you know."

"And it was them?" Afton asked. "The old woman and the Asian man?"

"The driver's pretty sure it was them."

"What are we waiting for? We gotta talk to that driver."

Afton and Max crowded into the Cosmopolitan Limousine Service's small office. It was located on the first floor of a former warehouse that had been converted to luxury condos two years earlier. It was surrounded by other conversions, mostly warehouses to condos, as well as some brand-new condo buildings that had been dropped like Legoland buildings in surface parking lots. It was the new North Loop, what developers were calling NoLo, hoping desperately for the name to catch on.

They met with the dispatcher, a guy name Ricky Chase, and the driver, an older African-American guy named David Huntley. Chase had watery blue eyes and a phlegmy voice, and he handled bookings and dispatches in the office. He looked and dressed like a disreputable grad student. Huntley wore a gray suit with a white shirt and red tie, and he held a jaunty cap in his hands.

"Just to be clear," Afton said, "you picked up a young Asian man and an older woman."

Huntley shook his head. "There were three passengers."

"Wait. *What?*" Afton said. "Someone besides the two people whose faces are on the flyer?"

"Yes, ma'am. There was a sort of blue collar–looking guy with them."

"Blue collar," Max said.

"You know," Huntley said. "Work shirt, trucker cap, blue jeans. Looked like he just got off his shift."

"Would you be able to give a description of this guy if we put you with a sketch artist?" Max asked.

"I think so," Huntley said. "But the other two looked just like the drawings that the police sent out." He glanced at the eight-by-ten-inch flyer that was stuck on the office wall along with a calendar and a bunch of take-out menus. "The drawings that you guys sent out. Anyway, I picked all three of them up at the Radisson hotel in downtown Minneapolis and drove them to Stillwater. Went right up I-35, then east on 36. Made pretty good time, too, considering."

"Where did you take them in Stillwater?" Max asked.

"The Tamarack Hotel. Right downtown by the river."

"Did they have any luggage with them?" Afton asked.

"No."

"Did you go into the hotel with them?" Max asked.

"No, I just stayed in the car. In the hotel's parking lot out back. They said they wouldn't be long and to just wait."

"And how long were they in the hotel? How long did you have to wait for them?"

Huntley thought for a few moments. "Half hour? Forty-five minutes?"

"That's it?" Afton asked. "Short meeting."

"And then they came out of the hotel, climbed in the car, and we drove back here," Huntley said.

"Back to the Radisson on Seventh Street?" Max asked.

Huntley nodded. "That's right."

"Holy crap," Afton said. "It was them, all right."

"What'd they do?" Chase, the dispatcher, asked. He was antsy, scratching his arms and raising red welts, endlessly clearing his throat.

Max quickly related to Chase and Huntley what they knew so far about the helicopter crash along with the murders of Odin and Barber.

"Holy Hannah," Chase said. "These people sound like a regular sleeper cell."

Huntley was more thoughtful. "You know I think I *heard* that crash a couple of nights ago, but I didn't know what it was at the time. It didn't register. I was dropping some folks off at the Fox and Hound Tea Room and it sounded more like, I don't know, when box cars kind of hump together and make that dull, crashing sound. Or a big semi truck having a near miss over on I-94. There are always crashes over there, where 35W and Hiawatha peel off. I didn't know about any helicopter crash until I saw it on the news the next morning."

"This is so awful," Chase said. "Please don't let our company's name get mentioned on TV or in the newspapers on account of this."

"People have been killed and you're worried about your reputation?" Afton asked.

"Damn," Max said, and he really sounded sore. "We missed them by like . . ." He pinched his thumb and forefinger together. "This much. So, Mr. Huntley, did you have any conversation at all with these people? On the ride over or the ride back?"

"Not really," Huntley said. "They were very polite and businesslike. When I picked them up, they just gave me the Stillwater address. And when I dropped them back at the Radisson, they thanked me and paid in cash. Gave me a good tip, too."

"But nothing else," Afton said. "No conversation at all?"

"Well, no," Huntley said. "But I had the partition up. Most clients prefer it that way; they like their privacy. And I was listening to the hockey game."

"I thought hockey was over," Afton said.

"Hockey's never over," Max said.

Huntley nodded. "The Wild. Playoff game against the Blackhawks."

"How'd they do?" Afton asked.

Huntley looked forlorn. "Lost."

Back out on the street, Afton said, "We missed them. They're still in town and we missed them!" She felt so frustrated, she wanted to scream out loud and bang her foot against the curb.

"And they've got some sort of business deal cooking, too," Max said. "Sure as shit they were confabbing with somebody over there."

"But who was it? And what's going on?"

"Could be anything," Max said. "Dope,

diamonds, hookers, fraudulent credit cards . . . who knows? I'm going to jump on the horn with the people at the Tamarack Hotel and then I'll get an investigator with the Stillwater Police to drop by there. If anything blips on the radar, I'll take a run over there myself."

"What do you want me to do?"

"Nothing you can do. Go home."

42

Afton did go home. And since it was Saturday night, she sent out for pizza. One large cheese pizza for the girls, one small pepperoni pizza for her. Lish had tripped out of the house some thirty minutes ago, all gussied up in a slinky dress and boots, on her way to meet a friend (in other words, a date) at the Minneapolis Institute of Art. The museum was holding a combination gallery tour and wine tasting event. Not necessarily in that order.

To counter-balance the heinous crime of serving fast food to her still-growing children, Afton tossed together a fresh garden salad of Bibb lettuce, tomatoes, slivered carrots, cucumbers, and sliced radishes.

When the pizzas arrived, she paid the delivery kid, who looked like he was about twelve years old, gave him a decent tip and an admonition to take care, and then carried the pizzas into the kitchen.

"Pizza," she called out.

Poppy came running in from the living room, all floppy pink sweatshirt, matching tights, and Ugg boots. "Mommy, what's a paternity test?"

Afton whirled on her. "What'd you say? What on earth are you kids watching in there?" She heard a snicker from Tess and stuck her head around the corner. "Turn that thing off."

Tess grabbed the remote control and turned off the TV, then came wandering into the kitchen. "Are you going to tell her, Mom?"

"No," Afton said. "And I don't want you guys thinking about that kind of stuff, okay? Now help yourself to some pizza before it gets cold. Salad, too. Take lots."

"Can I eat in front of the TV?" Poppy asked.

"Yes, you may," Afton said. "In fact, we all can. But only if you don't turn that program back on."

"It's a *Jerry Springer* rerun," Tess said helpfully.

"Right. Well, we'll find something else to watch. Just never mind about him," Afton said.

"Is that what you call trash TV?" Tess asked.

"Because the audience jumps up and trashes the place?" Poppy asked.

Afton slid the cheese pizza toward her. "Something like that, yes."

Tess had grabbed a piece of pizza and was folding it origami-like. "I can't wait for tomorrow," she said.

"For the Jog Your Dog walk?" Afton asked.

Tess nodded. "Bonaparte's all excited about going, too." She broke off a piece of crust and fed it to Bonaparte, who snapped it up immediately.

"Maybe you shouldn't feed pizza to the dog," Afton said.

"That's okay," Poppy said in a matter-of-fact tone. "He'll walk it off tomorrow."

Across town, Terrell was sitting in her silver Mercedes, accompanied by Lester Snell. She had parked down the block from her mother's home, in front of a Frank Lloyd Wright–looking house that some advertising big shot had recently purchased. The night was full-on dark with a lopsided yellow moon glistening through bare treetops.

"You think she's home?" Snell asked.

"Of course she's home," Terrell said. She was gripping the steering wheel tightly as she gazed in the direction of her house. Then, in a crabby voice, said, "Where did you think she'd be? Out at some nightclub on the dance floor? Shaking her money-maker? She's been a widow for, like, two seconds, for Christ's sake. Give her a break."

"Okay," Snell said. "Awright." He was sufficiently cowed. Terrell had a way of making him feel like he'd just driven in from the farm and been kicked off the proverbial turnip truck.

"She'll be feeling sorry for herself and drinking," Terrell said in a more measured, almost analytic tone. "She'll have raided the wine cellar and be in her bedroom sipping the good stuff. Probably a Château Latour or maybe even a Margaux."

"The good stuff," Snell repeated, even though he had no idea what Terrell was talking about. Good stuff to him was booze that came in 1.75-liter bottles from the Liquor Mega-Store.

"I can be in and out in about five seconds."

"You have to be careful," Snell said.

"I will."

For the last few hours, Terrell had been formulating a plan. Now that she was actually working through the final details, she realized the idea had been there all along, hunkered inside her brain for the past couple of days like some kind of cunning, slavering beast. Ever since she'd found the papers in Leland Odin's desk.

Her idea was daring — it was huge with a capital *H* — and once she'd become fixated on it, there was nothing she could do. She couldn't turn it off, she couldn't just stuff her idea away somewhere. No, she was physically itching for this to work, inexorably drawn to it like the mongoose to the cobra.

The next step, of course, had been to explain as much as she could to Snell. She needed his buy-in. Most of all, she needed his muscle and his truck. She'd gotten Snell warmed up to the point where he'd agreed that it was a very cool idea, a monumental plan, if what she'd told him was really true. That's if they weren't caught and arrested first.

"Okay, you wait right here and I'll dash in." Terrell opened the driver's side door and slid out from behind the wheel. "Won't be a minute."

"Be careful," Snell whispered. But Terrell's mind was resolutely made up and she was already running lightly down the street.

43

The faint sound of church bells echoed through the thick stone walls of the casket factory.

"Sunday," Hack said to nobody in particular. "Time to go to meetin'." He stretched, yawned, and scratched his furry stomach where his T-shirt rode up. It had been a long time since he'd set foot inside a church. He just didn't have use for it anymore. Too much Bible thumping and preaching about don't do this and don't do that. Admonitions to follow the Ten Commandments.

Hack figured he'd already broken every one of the commandments in some way, shape, or form. Except for the one about false idols. He wasn't completely sure what that was all about, what exactly constituted a false idol. Maybe like . . . those kids who sang on TV?

Over in the corner, the noodles were cooking again, the aroma drifting through the old factory. Hack thought the crap bubbling in the pot smelled like somebody was boiling an old tennis shoe. Still, it was better than breathing the stink of mouse poop.

Twenty minutes later, everyone having eaten and dressed, Hack rounded up the gang for what he thought of as a serious pep talk. The three Thai guys who'd jetted in yesterday — Chati, Somsak, and the youthful Prasong — didn't speak any English, so Narong had to translate everything for them. Hack would say a couple of sentences, then Narong would repeat everything in Thai. It was slow going, and Hack began to feel like he was some kind of delegate at the freaking UN.

Still, Hack was able to make his message clear. They were all going to drive over to the FTZ site near Highway 280 and Como Avenue. Then, once they made their pickup — Hack didn't say *if they managed* to make their pickup; he was far more optimistic than that — they would rendezvous back here at the casket factory and check in with Mom Chao Cherry. Physically show her the dope. Then they'd cool their heels and, when evening came, make the final push to Detroit. The new Thai guys particularly liked the part where Hack told them the truck wouldn't be armored, but they would.

They were extremely enthusiastic at the idea of carrying guns. They thought it was very American.

Hack was pleased that they were finally going to abandon the old casket factory. It had served them well, but he had no illusion that, given enough time, they wouldn't be discovered. Hell, he knew the cops were already sniffing at their trail, probably stringing together a few clues. But in a couple of hours they'd all be long gone. Vanished.

Hack also knew that Mom Chao Cherry was a crazy old bat who would push her luck and take chances. She still thought she was back in Bangkok, where she could lift a dainty hand and servants would scurry to make things happen. She had no idea how many law enforcement agencies could get involved here in America, and especially right here in the Twin Cities. The Minneapolis Police, Saint Paul Police, ATF, BCA. To say nothing of the various sheriff's departments, DEA, and FBI.

Yup, it was definitely time to get the hell out of Dodge.

Mom Chao Cherry watched the industrial garage door rumble up and the truck full of men pull out. Then the door closed, clanking like chains in a dungeon, and she was alone. She grabbed a cup of tea and hurried upstairs to her second-floor room — must have been a manager's office or something; there was still a desk and an old, rusted fan — and lit her candles. She'd arranged them on a wooden box along with a number of tiny jade statues. Satisfied that she had made a heartfelt appeal to the spirits as well as her dead husband's ancestors, she lit two sticks of sandalwood incense to seal the deal.

Good. Her men were en route and soon they would retrieve her stolen merchandise. All this had been so foolish, she thought. Foolish for the old man to have spread around his bribes and stolen her goods. If he'd left her alone, if he'd even tried to *buy* from her, many lives would have been spared. Retribution wouldn't have been so swift and lethal. On the other hand, Mom Chao Cherry had long since realized that human lives were not all that consequential. Not in her world anyway.

44

Hack was in a good mood as he drove along. In fact, he was feeling so upbeat that he cranked up the radio, and when Rod Stewart came on, singing "Maggie May," he sang right along with good old Rod. Even did a little seat dancing.

"This is popular music?" Narong asked him.

"Kind of a golden oldie," Hack said. He lit a cigarette and added, "I can't tolerate the shit people listen to today. All those whiny teenage girls with their lovesick songs. Plus, the dumb broads need to use Auto-Tune because they can't *carry* a tune. It's a crying shame that the music industry has deteriorated so badly."

"A crying shame," Narong said while Chati, Somsak, and Prasong just nodded.

Hack pointed the truck up Highway 280, burned past the Como exit, and then hung a left on Broadway. They were in a prime industrial area now. Lots of warehouses, truck docks, shippers, and rigging services, and, of course, the Mid-City Industrial Park, where the FTZ was located.

"Almost there," Hack said. For some reason he'd begun to feel nervous. Then again, it was probably just pregame jitters. Hadn't he felt a gut full of apprehension when he and his buddy Duane Sliezak had ripped off that truckload of sheetrock over in Cloquet? Sure, he had. And look how fine that had turned out. They drove the damn stuff out to South Dakota and sold the entire lot to some building-materials wholesaler who didn't care if the shipment was lukewarm or roaring hot.

"Okay," Hack said. He took a final puff on his cigarette and then stubbed it out. He wished he could enjoy a quick toot of coke, but too much was at stake right now. "When we get to the FTZ, everybody stays right here in the damn van and plays dumb, okay?" He glanced over his shoulder, saw the blank faces of the three Thai men, and said, "Jeez, what am I saying? You guys *are* dumb."

"What about me?" Narong asked.

"You don't say or do nothin'," Hack said. "Let me talk to the guys at the gate. I'll show them the paperwork and handle the negotiation."

"Of course," Narong said. He was excited, too. Happy to be finally picking up Mom Chao Cherry's merchandise. Happy to get this strange American ordeal over and done with.

Hack slowed the truck, turned a corner, and headed down a narrow street lined with large gray warehouses. The gate was just ahead, a huge rolling contraption that was gaping open at the moment. A battered pickup truck with a camper on back was just rolling through. Hack eased over to the side of the road to give the truck some room. He turned slightly in his seat to watch it go by and was stunned by what he saw.

"What the hell?" Hack squawked.

The sun was lasering down on the pick-up's windshield just right, perfectly illuminating the faces of the two people who were sitting in the front cab.

Holy crap!

Hack's brain practically exploded with shock. Was he seeing this correctly? Wasn't that the chick he'd just been staring at — kind of fantasizing about — at Leland Odin's funeral? Yes, it was!

Hack's mouth hung open as the truck continued past them and accelerated around the corner.

Now his frantic brain jumped into over-drive.

That's Leland Odin's daughter or stepdaughter or whatever the hell she is!

He'd recognize that girl anywhere . . . with her snooty blond good looks.

But why the hell has she popped up here? Here of all places!

Unless . . .

Oh shit! A double-cross? A really inside-inside job?

Hack made a snap judgment, what he later thought of as a genuinely brilliant decision.

"Hang on, boyo," Hack said to Narong. He pulled the truck forward, then lurched into a hasty K-turn.

"What's wrong?" Narong cried. He was confused and alarmed by this turn of events. "Why are we not going in? What about the paperwork? What about the merchandise?"

"We gotta regroup," Hack said. Even though he had the truck turned around by now, he was feeling unsettled, nervous about having his game plan changed so abruptly.

Narong slapped a hand hard on Hack's shoulder. "What are you doing? We must go back and pick up the goods," he practically shouted. "Now."

Hack shook his head as he tromped down

on the accelerator. "Somebody just beat us to it," Hack said.

"What!" Narong rasped. "Someone stole our shipment?"

Hack continued to accelerate, chasing after the old pickup. "Did you see the truck that came out the gate and whipped past us? The one with the camper on back that's just up ahead of us?"

"What? What?" Narong said. He was still playing catch-up.

"That was Leland Odin's *daughter* in there along with some other asshole."

Now Narong understood. "They took our drugs?" He slapped a hand down on the dashboard, practically in full-blown panic mode.

"They sure as hell did," Hack said.

"Then what . . . ?"

Hack was speeding back up Broadway, bumping over railroad tracks and an ugly mess of potholes. "That's them up ahead. We're going to follow them."

"Follow them," Narong repeated.

"It won't be difficult," Hack said. He was beginning to wrap his mind around this shift in the program. "And maybe . . . maybe if all we have to do is tail those jerks, it might even be easier to hit the jackpot."

It was a piece of cake for Hack to follow along behind the daughter's piece-of-shit truck. Whoever was driving was a fairly cautious driver and rarely broke fifty miles an hour, even when they hit the I-94 freeway. From there it was just a matter of tailing the truck and staying a few cars back in line. It got even easier when the truck turned off onto Dale Street and wended its way through a warren of streets. They twisted and turned, driving through a neighborhood that looked sleepy and quiet. When they passed a fancy church with a large green copper onion dome, Hack wondered if everyone might be crowded inside, heads bowed and praying for . . . what? World peace? A much improved baseball team? Winning the lottery?

Then they turned down a dumpy street and, fifty yards ahead, Hack saw the pickup truck's brake lights flare red. He eased off the gas and coasted over to the curb. From there they all watched as the pickup truck hooked a right and humped down a narrow driveway, where it rocked to a stop behind a shabby little house.

"Looks like we're in business," Hack said.

They watched as two people, a man and a woman, climbed out of the truck and quickly disappeared inside the house.

"That's her," Hack said, his wide eyes reflecting his amazement. "That's the girl." He shook his head. "Ain't that something? Leland Odin's own daughter stealing from her dead old man."

"He stole from us," Narong said bitterly.

"I guess it all comes full circle," Hack said. "Okay, everybody, look sharp now and grab those guns. It's time to go a-knockin' and get this party rockin'." Then, as an aside to Narong, he said, "That probably doesn't translate into Thai all that well. Better just tell your guys to follow behind us, keep their weapons hidden, and for god's sake, don't make any stupid mistakes and shoot us."

Narong gave his instructions as Hack goosed his truck forward and stopped in front of the dingy house. Then they all piled out and powered their way to the front door.

Hack and his merry band of men didn't go a-knockin' at all. Instead, they kicked the front door with such force that they shattered one of the hinges and sent the door crashing down into the living room.

Terrell and Snell were standing next to an old pea-green sofa, shucking off their coats, when the men scrambled over the fallen door and burst in on them.

Terrell screamed loud enough to wake the dead. Snell, with a stupid-surprised look on his face, said, "You can't . . ." and never got a chance to finish his sentence. Hack bounded toward Snell, punched him hard on the jaw, and bounced him backward onto the sofa.

Terrell waved her arms wildly and shrieked again, her voice rising from a high C into operatic territory.

Hack spun around and backhanded Terrell hard across the mouth. Then he pushed her down onto the sofa, where she cowered next to Snell.

"Shut up!" Hack barked. "Just shut the freak up." He pointed his gun directly at Terrell and waggled it in a menacing gesture. "That means you, rich bitch. Open your piehole to make one single peep and, so help me God, I'll put a bullet in your brain."

Eyes big as saucers, Terrell gulped down what was probably going to be a string of epithets. She stared at Hack, who looked like he was deadly serious, and then looked past him, where four Asian men pointed guns at her.

"Okay," she croaked. "Okay."

"I knew it," Snell said in a desperate-sounding whisper. "I knew it was too good to be true."

Hack held out his hand. "Keys. Gimme the keys to your truck."

Snell handed them over.

Hack dashed through the house and out the kitchen door. He opened the pickup truck and did a hasty check within the camper. It was all there. Mom Chao Cherry's drugs. Drugs that had been hijacked and fought over, and had been the cause of several murders. Now they were right here for the taking. All safe and sound.

Back inside the house, Hack rummaged through the junk until he found a bunch of rope and a couple of bandanas. Then he had Narong's men truss up Terrell and Snell like a couple of Thanksgiving turkeys. Once that was accomplished, Hack felt a little more confident. Now he could breathe. He'd shifted gears, snatched victory from the jaws of defeat, and made it all okay again.

Hack turned to Narong. "Can you drive that truck that's parked out back?" He pantomimed shifting gears. "Drive a five-speed?"

Narong bobbed his head. "I can drive that truck, yes. But I have to follow you. I do not know directions."

"No problem," Hack said. "So we'll just split up the team and take both trucks."

Narong gestured at Terrell and Snell, who glared at them from their perch on the sofa. "What about these people? The *robbers*."

Hack gave a nasty chuckle. "I think we'd better take them back to the mother ship with us. As to what their fate will be, well . . . we'll let the old lady decide."

When they rolled into the casket factory some thirty minutes later, Mom Chao Cherry was shocked but also very pleased.

"We picked up your cargo plus a couple of damn crooks," Hack told her. He led her over to the van, where Terrell and Snell were gagged and tied.

"Who are they?" Mom Chao Cherry asked.

Hack tipped a thumb toward Terrell. "The girl there is Odin's daughter."

Mom Chao Cherry sucked at her upper lip and took a step back. "No." Then, "So thievery runs in the family."

"Looks like, ma'am."

Mom Chao Cherry waited a few moments as the large corrugated steel door rolled down, then she carefully inspected the pickup truck. "It is all here? You're quite positive?"

"We have your shipment," Narong assured her.

"Show me."

So Hack and Narong pulled open the back door of the camper and showed her the wooden boxes that were stamped KITCHEN APPLIANCES — KANTANA INDUSTRIAL GROUP.

"Open the boxes," she ordered. "All of them."

"Sure thing," Hack said. He grabbed his pig sticker and pried open every one of the boxes. When they'd finished, they had two hundred plastic bags. All were packed with pure white cocaine and each bag weighed a kilo. Once the dope was cut with laundry detergent or baby laxative and then repackaged into G-rocks, eight balls, or half pieces, the street value would easily be over five million dollars.

Mom Chao Cherry's eyes danced with delight. "Very good. You have done an excellent job." She repeated her words of praise in Thai and the three young men bobbed their heads, pleased that she was so pleased.

"What do you want to do with our two passengers?" Hack asked her.

Mom Chao Cherry gave an imperceptible shrug. "Put them in the basement for now.

I must think about this."

"I could kill them right now," Narong said.

Mom Chao Cherry shook her head. "Just . . . wait."

"Of course," Narong said. "Now we should all rest. Tonight we must drive a long way to make the exchange."

But Mom Chao Cherry was already drifting upstairs, a faint smile on her face.

Once they'd stashed Terrell and Snell downstairs, Narong pulled Hack aside.

"We must go now," Narong said.

Hack stared at him. "What are you talking about? No, man, we ain't supposed to head out until tonight."

"I need to take care of that woman."

Hack touched a hand to his forehead. "Man, oh man. Are you serious?" He'd almost forgotten about the stupid woman. "Can't you let it go?" Now that they had the drugs and had captured the two people, Hack wanted to limit his exposure. After all, the end was almost in sight and he was anxious to get back to Duluth. Without being there to prod his hookers into doing serious business, who knew what would happen? Once, when he was gone for a full week, two of his best girls had run off with a Winnebago full of drunken car salesmen on their way to Canada for a fishing trip.

But Narong was insistent. "You promised."

"Shit."

Narong reached out and touched Hack's shoulder. "Please. You are my friend."

Hack sucked air between his front teeth. "Awright. But we better move fast."

"You still have the address?"

"Yup."

"Then we go now."

They took Hack's car right through downtown and into the Powderhorn Park neighborhood of South Minneapolis.

"Pretty here," Hack said. "Lots of parks and stuff. Imagine how nice it'll be when the trees start to leaf out. Kinda picturesque."

"Too cold," Narong said, giving a little shiver. He'd had it with Minnesota's chilly weather and the strange, bland food Hack seemed to relish from the drive-through places. He was more than ready to head back to Thailand, where the average temperature was a steamy eighty-six degrees and the food had a decent kick to it.

Hack maneuvered down one street, then another, passing a playground and then a neighborhood coffee shop called the Bean

Scene. Two people in North Face parkas were sitting outside on benches drinking coffee.

Finally, they closed in on Afton's house.

"There it is, up ahead," Hack said. "Them's the house numbers I got. The house with the arch over the front door and the white shutters."

"Now we go in and kill her," Narong said. "Kick down another door." He'd very much enjoyed kicking in Snell's door earlier.

"Hold everything," Hack said. He reached over and pressed his hand against Narong's chest to quiet him down. "It looks like we got here too late."

The front door had just opened and two little girls and a small black dog had just emerged. They ran down the front walk, heading for a big black Lincoln Navigator that was parked directly in front of the house.

"Going somewhere," Hack said, as a blond woman in a blue pullover and black yoga pants bounced out the door and locked it behind her. "Looks like we just missed them."

"No," Narong growled. "Looks like we follow them."

45

Bulldogs barked, poodles strutted, Great Danes loped along. And in the midst of all that canine wonderment, Afton, Tess, Poppy, and Bonaparte were having a ball. There had to be at least a hundred people out this early Sunday afternoon for the Jog Your Dog charity walk. Poppy had brushed Bonaparte's black coat until it shone, and Tess had saved up her allowance to buy a snappy red leash.

The day was chilly, only about fifty-five degrees, but a bright yellow sun blazed down. The paved trail they were following wound its way through the verdant Eloise Butler Wildflower Garden, where early blooming wild iris and jack-in-the-pulpit were putting in stellar personal appearances. Then, after making that loop, they crossed Theodore Wirth Parkway and entered something called the Quaking Bog.

"What exactly is a Quaking Bog?" Poppy

asked. She'd worn her mermaid costume, and she shimmered like a little angelfish whenever the sun hit her just right.

"I think it's mostly moss and tamarack trees and ferns," Afton said as they stepped onto a narrow wooden walkway that took them over a water-soaked bog. "According to the sign we just passed, this bog is thirty-seven hundred years old. It's basically a layer of sphagnum moss that's suspended atop a five-acre acid bog."

"Acid sounds dangerous," Tess said.

"I don't think it's that kind of acid," Afton said. "It's more like the proper pH balance that's good for growing wildflowers and saplings and things. So it's perfectly safe. In another month this place will be alive with frogs and dragonflies."

"It is kind of pretty here," Tess said. They were walking single file on the wooden walkway and she was at the back of the line, leading Bonaparte. "And kind of scary, too, like the Haunted Forest in *The Wizard of Oz.*" Towering trees rose up to form a tunnel and they could hear small rustlings in the heavy undergrowth of chaffweed and violet wood sorrel. So far there was no sign of flying monkeys.

"How far do we have to walk?" Poppy asked. "Two miles? Or twenty miles?"

"We're just doing the short track," Afton said. "So that's only a single mile. Think your little legs can handle it?"

"Mermaids don't have legs," Poppy said with all seriousness. "They have fins."

"Then I guess you'll have to swim for it," Afton said.

They stepped off the wooden walkway, plodded their way through a muddy low-lying area, and then were back on another walkway. The woods grew thicker as the wind whooshed through stands of browned cattails. Hunks of fallen trees lay every-where, reminders of a not-so-long-ago ice storm that had pummeled trees all over the area and brought huge branches crashing down.

"I'd say we're earning our money today," Poppy said.

"But the pledges aren't *our* money and the walk is for a good cause," Tess said. "Right, Bonaparte?" She held his leash as she continued to walk along behind Afton and Poppy.

"A good cause for homeless animals," Poppy said. "Because all animals deserve to have a forever home, don't they, Mom?"

"That's for sure," Afton said.

They were looping back toward the last five hundred yards of the winding pathway, heading for the parking lot, where grilled hot dogs and ice cream bars awaited them, when Tess called out, "Hold up a minute."

"What's wrong, honey?" Afton asked. She glanced back to see Tess holding the leash as she hopped around on one foot.

"Got something in my shoe," Tess said.

"Do you need my help? Can you balance okay?"

"No, I got it." Tess slipped off her shoe, shook it, and was about to put it back on when a bird shrieked loudly overhead.

Poppy's eyes went big. "What was that?" she asked. "A vulture?"

"More like an owl," Afton said. She tilted her head back, wondering if she could catch sight of the noisy bird. "Maybe he's got a nest around here."

But there was no more screeching, just the snap of a twig nearby. The sudden quiet of the forest seemed to magnify the noise.

"Mommy, I'm scared," Poppy said.

Afton put a hand on Poppy's shoulder. "There's nothing to be . . ."

The words died on Afton's lips as Narong exploded out of a dense thicket. Dipping his right shoulder, he came at her sideways, hitting Afton with all the power of a freight train. Afton's head snapped backward so hard, she could almost hear an audible *click*

416

in her neck. A jolt of pain shot through her entire body and she was knocked backward, into sticky mud.

"Mommy!" Poppy shrieked.

Afton saw the flash of a knife in Narong's hand and knew she was in terrible trouble. The worst trouble of her life. Then, like an eight-track tape instantly clicking over, she felt paralyzing fear for her kids' lives.

"Run!" Afton screamed at the top of her lungs, even as she was sprawled on her back, kicking wildly, trying to pummel this crazed Asian man with her feet. "Run for help!"

But the kids stood rooted to the spot, transfixed by this strange man who'd sprung from the bushes and knocked their mother flat. He was not only screaming wildly, he was waving a knife and trying his best to get close to their mother so he could stab her.

Go!" Afton shrieked again. "Run!"

But the kids only backed up a few steps, mouths gaping, completely in shock. Narong bent toward Afton, an evil grin twisting his face into a bizarre mask.

Frantic to defend herself, Afton smashed a fist upward as Narong leaned toward her. She connected hard and fast with Narong's nose, the impact stunning him for just a few moments.

That's when Poppy suddenly raced to Narong and began to pummel him with her tiny fists, flailing at him with all her might. Though she was brave, she only served to anger Narong.

"No!" Afton shouted.

Narong grabbed Poppy by her ponytail, spun her around hard, and threw her to the side of the trail.

For Afton, who was still spread-eagled on her back, time stood still. She blinked, like the *click* of a camera's shutter, as quick-cut images registered in her brain. Poppy's small body flying through the air, Narong's maniacal snarl, the flash of cheap sunlight on his steel blade. All this in a split second as hot rage exploded within her.

Afton cranked her head right, saw a gnarly hunk of damp wood, the size of which one might toss in a fire pit, and grabbed it. Holding her breath, she reeled the wood in fast, knowing she might only get this one chance. Then she rocked to a sitting position and whipped the wood forward as hard and fast as she could, mimicking the action her practiced muscles made when driving an ice axe into a frozen waterfall.

Gotta make it count, Afton told herself. She focused all her strength, all her energy, on this one single blow.

Whomp!

Afton was both thrilled and horrified when the wood connected solidly with Narong's forehead and sent him reeling backward.

Gluts of blood flew from his damaged face. Dazed and angry as a scalded cat, he yelped in a language Afton didn't understand.

Afton's last-ditch defense had worked. Sort of. She'd stunned her attacker and bought a miniscule bit of time.

But Narong was fighting hard to shake off the terrible blow and pull himself together. He shook his head, snarled, spit blood, and came at her again for a final, balls-to-the-wall assault.

That's when everything went *kapow* crazy and a growling, black ball of fur launched itself like a rocket-propelled grenade. Bonaparte literally flew through the air, his hackles raised and his sights focused directly on Narong. The little dog's ears were plastered flat against his head, his eyes were black buttons of fury, and his teeth were savagely bared like nothing Afton had ever seen before.

Bonaparte hit Narong hard, causing the man to let loose a high-pitched yodeling scream. The dog was a growling, rolling thunderclap, snarling and battering Narong with his front paws as the man recoiled and wriggled and tried to fight him off.

Then, with one mighty snarl, Bonaparte's jagged teeth clamped down hard on Narong's left arm!

"Ai son teen!" Narong screamed at the top of his lungs. Then, "Get off!" He batted at Bonaparte with his knife hand, stabbing at him, trying to dislodge the beast. But Bonaparte held on tight, sawing down savagely, his bulldog scissors bite as powerful as that of a giant snapping turtle.

That's what turned the tables, of course.

Narong backpedaled a few steps, screaming loudly as Afton came at him again with her hunk of wood. Grasping the wood with both hands, she swung hard and smashed Narong right on the bridge of his nose, hitting both eyes, battering his brain, and causing more blood to spew from his nose. Tree bark, sharp splinters, and bits of green moss flew everywhere. Narong flung his head away in pain, stumbled hard, and started to hobble away. He swore loudly as he swatted helplessly at the brave little dog who refused to let go of his arm.

Afton chased after them, limping down the trail, seeing a flash of silver that marked the line of cars parked nearby. Then, suddenly, Bonaparte dropped off Narong's arm and crumpled to the ground. Afton screamed as she rushed forward, buckthorn and willow branches swatting at her face. She scooped up Bonaparte and clutched the bleeding dog to her chest.

"Brave baby," she cried. Through a veil of tears, she saw Narong, almost a block away now, limping fast toward a red car. There was the sound of an eight-cylinder engine revving up and Afton, still carrying Bonaparte, ran into the street just in time to see the tail end of a faded red car disappear down the road.

"Hey!" a woman yelled at her.

Afton turned to see a woman in jogging clothes with two schnauzers on a leash. The woman was maybe fifty yards off to her left.

"Are you okay?" the woman called out.

"No," Afton said. "I'm not."

Hack and Narong careened onto Highway 55. Hack was driving as Narong shouted angrily in his native Thai language. *"Shia! Shia!"* Damn it! Damn it!

"Did you get her, did you get her?" Hack cried.

Narong's answer was a muddle of Thai and English as he continued to scream and curse at the top of his lungs.

"Take it easy," Hack warned. "Pipe down. We don't want to call attention to ourselves."

Narong held up his arm. "Look at this," he yelped. "Filthy dog." Two sets of bite marks on his lower arm were turning purple. Skin had not only been punctured, it had been ferociously ripped.

Hack glanced at Narong's arm and was stunned by the damage. "Dude, you really got bit. You're gonna get rabies!"

"What are rabies?" Narong asked through clenched teeth.

Hack shook his head. "You get really, really sick and then your jaws, like, lock together so you can't eat."

"I need doctor," Narong said, cradling his arm and looking terrified.

"Yeah, well, let me think about that."

46

Luckily, the Mill City Emergency Veterinary Clinic was just a mile down the road. That's where Afton and the kids took the bleeding and battered Bonaparte. And where, after handing Bonaparte over to a med tech, Afton called Max in a blind panic.

"That asshole came after me!" Afton yelled into her phone. "He came after me and my kids!" She was so mad she was shaking as she stuttered and stammered, trying to explain what had just happened.

Max was stunned. "He was there? That same Asian guy? He attacked you?"

"He attacked me at the Jog Your Dog walk," Afton screamed again.

"Are you hurt?" Max demanded.

"No. Well, I don't think so. Not seriously. Bonaparte got hurt pretty badly."

"Are the *kids* okay? Do they need medical attention?"

"They're okay. We all are. For now anyway."

"What about the dog?"

"Bonaparte was cut by that madman," Afton said, trying to hold back a sob. "On his shoulder. When he came to my rescue. The people here at the vet clinic said he needed emergency surgery."

"Jeez," Max said. "So they're doing it . . . ?"

"Yes. But, Max . . ." Afton gasped for air. "Max, we need to move on this right away! I mean, I saw the car. I . . ." She gulped in another mouthful of air and tried to pull herself back from the brink of panic. She knew she had to think and communicate clearly and not get hysterical just because her kids had been in such terrible danger.

Hold it together, Afton admonished herself. *I will let myself lose it later when all this is over and done with.*

"Wait a minute," Max said. "You actually *saw* the car that the Asian guy drove away in?" There was a sharp intake of breath. "What'd it look like?"

Afton thought hard. "The car was kind of dusty red." She was talking fast now, her brain sorting through bits and slivers of fast-moving images, trying to put it all together into one cohesive thought as she went along.

"I think it was a red car, like the one Sammy Mah told us about, when he saw it over by the noodle factory," Afton said. "The Asian man who attacked me . . . he wasn't driving though, somebody else was."

"Did you catch the plate number?" Max asked.

"No, no, but I saw the sticker on the rear window. That's why I think it was the same car that Sammy Mah saw."

"What did the sticker look like? If you can remember, maybe we can get a bead on it."

"Blue and white. Forming a tower or some sort of bridge." Afton clenched her jaw. "I think. It all happened so fast."

"Give me five minutes," Max said. "I'm gonna call downtown and have somebody look through those books we have. I'll call you right back."

"Okay, okay." Afton hung up, shaking.

"Mommy?" a small voice said.

Afton looked over to see Poppy and Tess sitting on chairs in the waiting room. They were pale and quiet and looked about as scared as she'd ever seen them.

"Kids," she said. She swooped across the waiting room and swept them up in her arms, hugging them tight. "Are you okay?" She didn't wait for an answer. "You're okay, right?" They *had* to be.

425

Tess nodded, Poppy looked a little unsure.

"I'm so sorry this happened," Afton crooned, her voice cracking. "I'm so sorry you had to see that awful man."

"Who was he?" Tess asked.

"One of the bad guys," Afton said.

"What about Bonaparte?" Poppy asked. "He got really hurt when he tried to save you. Do you think he's going to be okay?"

Afton released her grip on them. "I don't know. Let me go check."

She staggered back toward the front desk and managed a shaky smile. "My dog. The French bulldog?"

"He's in surgery," the receptionist said. She wore blue-and-white scrubs with cute little paw prints scattered all over them, and she spoke in a calming manner. "The doctor is working on your little guy right now."

"How long . . . before we know?"

"Probably a couple of hours."

"I need to take my kids home," Afton said.

"Go," the receptionist said. "Take them home. Your dog is in good hands, I guarantee it."

Just as Afton was walking out the door with her kids, Max called back.

"I had Dick Babbitt, who's minding the phones in Homicide today, take a look through the files and he says it sounds an awful lot like the Duluth Port Authority logo."

"No kidding," Afton breathed. Here was something. Maybe.

"Wait," Max said. "He's texting me the image now. Give me a minute and I'll forward it to you."

Afton, Poppy, and Tess all waited outside on the grass, watching a little white poodle get lifted out of a red Jeep and then limp toward the front door of the clinic with its owner.

"Poor dog," Poppy whispered. It had been a horrifying and tragically sobering day for her.

Then Afton's phone dinged and the image was right there in front of her. The logo for the Duluth Seaway Port Authority.

"That's it!" Afton cried when Max came on the line. "That's the exact image I saw on the red car's rear window. What can . . . I mean, what can you find out about this? Maybe run a list of guys from up in Duluth who might have this sticker on their car? The guys who work at the Port Authority?"

"We'll do that," Max said. He sounded calm and in charge. "We're doing it right now."

"Okay, good." Then, "Jeez, I gotta get my kids home. They're really shaken up."

"You go ahead and do that and I'll swing by your house as soon as I can. I'll be there in maybe twenty, twenty-five minutes." Max paused. "You okay to drive? Not too rattled? I can always send a squad."

"I'm okay," Afton said, her voice quavering. "But the dog . . . the dog is bad."

47

Narong was hurting and angry from his dog bites, but it was nothing compared to the ferocity that Mom Chao Cherry leveled at him.

"You went after a police*woman*!" she screamed. "You tried to compromise my *business*! My sole reason for being here." Her flat, dark eyes drilled into Narong, her mouth was an angry slash of red. "I should kill you this instant."

"Khwam metta," Narong said. Mercy. "I please beg your forgiveness." Hack had wrapped a bandana around his wounded hand and now he cradled it, hoping Mom Chao Cherry would see he was in considerable pain.

"You are a stupid boy," she said, her voice practically quavering with anger.

Narong bowed his head contritely. "I am stupid." He wondered what punishment Mom Chao Cherry would inflict upon him?

Would she really kill him? Or would she leave him behind when she returned to Thailand? He was terrified that he would be left by himself in America with Hack as his only friend. Narong cocked his head sideways to risk a quick glance at Hack. Was Hack his friend? The man wasn't saying very much right now.

"Stupid," Mom Chao Cherry muttered again. "So stupid."

Narong flinched, wishing the old lady would snort a line of coke to calm herself down.

"If I could add my two cents here, ma'am," Hack said, finally speaking up.

"No two cents when millions are at stake," Mom Chao Cherry spat at him.

Hack managed to pull his face into a look of self-reproach. It was the same expression that usually worked wonders with his ex-wives, girlfriends, and any other women he was trying to con.

"I suppose you're right," Hack said to Mom Chao Cherry. "But, hell, we was just trying to get a little payback." He ducked his head and tried to inject even more remorse into his voice. And a bit of conviction, too. "You of all people should understand that. Payback, I mean."

Narong squinted at Mom Chao Cherry.

Was she buying into Hack's reasoning? He fervently hoped that she was.

Mom Chao Cherry sighed deeply. "Yes. Payback," she said. "That is something I very much understand." She turned away from Narong and Hack and glanced at the three other men. Chati, Somsak, and Prasong had remained mum, terrified to get involved. As far as Mom Chao Cherry was concerned, these three men were good little soldiers who had followed their marching orders to the letter. They had gone along with Narong and Hack, helped obtain her stolen goods, and brought them back to her.

"Come," Mom Chao Cherry said, waving an imperious hand.

Narong, Hack, and the three men dutifully followed her downstairs into the basement, where their two prisoners were being kept. The minute they hit the bottom step, the wailing started up. Terrell had managed to slip her gag off.

"Let me go, you crazy bitch!" Terrell shouted at Mom Chao Cherry. "You can't *do* this to me. You can't keep me prisoner in this shit hole!"

Mom Chao Cherry led her contingent over to the far wall, where Terrell and Snell were handcuffed to a large iron pipe that disappeared into the cement floor. "You're wrong, child," she said. "I can do anything I wish."

Terrell was about to let loose an unholy shriek again when she thought better of it, caught herself, and snapped her mouth shut. There was something in Mom Chao Cherry's eyes — something ruthless and malevolent — that led Terrell to believe this woman might be savoring her predicament. That she might be enjoying this spectacle a little too much.

Terrell forced herself to take a more modulated tone. "There's absolutely no reason for you to hurt me. My mother is wealthy and will pay you a lot of money for my safe return."

That was Snell's cue to jump in, too.

"Yeah," Snell said. "Terrell's mother is rich. She'll give you a whole bundle of money. All you have to do is let us go."

"Shut up," Terrell spat at him. "Stay out of this."

"Please, Terrell," Snell whined. "Don't be like that, for god's sake. I mean, you can't just leave me behind and let these assholes *kill* me!" He was yammering away, stunned that Terrell would dime him out so easily.

"Shut up," Terrell snarled again. "This is between me and her." She gazed, unblinking, at Mom Chao Cherry.

Mom Chao Cherry moved a step closer. "You are his daughter?"

Terrell shook her head. "No, no way. He wasn't my dad. He just married my mother. I came along for the ride."

"For the ride," Mom Chao Cherry said. "Very interesting the way you phrase that. But you spent the old man's money, did you not?"

Terrell grimaced. Mom Chao Cherry had her there, and she didn't much like it. Didn't like the direction in which this conversation was going either. "Well, maybe," she admitted. "Some of it, I guess."

Mom Chao Cherry stared at Terrell much the same way a lion might observe a lame zebra on the Serengeti. "I will have to think about this," she said finally.

48

To the rest of the Twin Cities, Sunday was an absolute pitch-perfect day. The sun continued to shine down and the last of the snow piles, accumulation from a dozen fierce winter storms, had turned into melting blobs that trickled into storm sewers. With a few kites tossing wildly in the nearby park, thirty-below wind chills were just a fading memory.

But a pall of fear and anxiety hung over Afton's small Minneapolis home.

Inside, Poppy and Tess sat at the kitchen table, stiff and shell-shocked, while Lish rattled around nervously, making hot chocolate and putting out a plate of snickerdoodles. Afton just stood there with her arms wrapped across her chest, observing the scene but feeling chilled to the bone.

Two cookies later, Tess had calmed down, but Poppy was still oozing tears.

"What about Bonaparte?" Poppy asked.

"We'll have to wait and see," Afton said for about the twentieth time. Poppy's questions were tearing her heart out.

"What if he's dead!"

"He's not dead," Tess wheezed angrily. "He can't be. We love him too much!" But she looked scared all over again, unsettled by Poppy's fear.

And it wasn't an irrational fear, Afton told herself. The dog looked like he'd been injured very badly. So who knew what the outcome would be?

A sharp rap sounded on the front door and Max, not waiting for an invitation, came rushing in. He was dressed in a sweatshirt and jeans, as if he'd just come from a softball game, and his expression was almost as stunned as Afton's.

"Are you kids okay?" he asked Poppy and Tess. But he was also asking about Afton.

"We're hanging in there," Afton said. "Though the girls are pretty shaken up."

Tess pursed her lips. "We've been *traumatized,*" she said.

"I know you have," Max said. "And I'm very sorry."

Afton put a hand on her hip as she faced Max. "How did they know I'd be at the park?" A note of hysteria started to creep in. "They must know where I live. They must have *followed* me."

"Damn," Lish said, biting her lip.

"Maybe we should take the kids to Mickey's place?" Afton asked.

"You don't need to do that," Max said. "We've got a couple of squads on the way over here. They'll keep watch over the house. The girls will be completely safe. If you're still worried, we can put a female officer inside."

Afton shook her head. "No. That would be too . . . disruptive."

Max cleared his throat. "I just got off the horn with Thacker. He's called an emergency team meeting."

"Let me guess," Afton said. "And he wants me to come. Now I'm an integral part of the team."

Max flapped a hand. "Hey. I don't make policy."

Lish flew across the kitchen and planted herself directly in front of Max. "You expect Afton to *work* right now?" she asked. "After everything she and the kids have been through?" She shook a warning finger at him.

"We need her now more than ever," Max said. "She's the only one who's gotten a decent look at this asshole."

"You're not supposed to say bad words

like that," Poppy said.

"Sorry." Max's gaze shifted back to Afton. "But you'll come?"

"Yes." Did she have a choice?

Lish stepped over to Afton and pulled her sister into a tight embrace. "Be careful," she cautioned. "If anybody dares come after you again, just step aside and let your lunkhead friend here shoot him. Ask questions later, okay?"

Afton nodded. "Okay."

Max squinted at Lish. "I don't know if you just insulted my character or my shooting skills."

Afton slid into the front seat of Max's car and slammed the door hard. "I hate feeling like this," she muttered.

"Feeling like what?" Max asked. He started the car and pulled away from the curb.

"Vulnerable. Like I don't even know how to keep my kids safe." Every muscle in Afton's body felt taut as a piano wire, and the vestiges of adrenaline still coursing through her veins made her feel buzzy and electric. "I want to get my hands around that asshole's neck and squeeze the life out of him." She balled her hands into fists and brought them crashing down on the dashboard of

Max's car.

"Hey, enough with the violence," Max said. "Five more payments and this sweet ride is mine."

Afton ignored Max and continued to steam. "Coming after me . . . when my *kids* were there. I just want to get my hands on that piece of crap one more time . . ."

"Hey," Max said. "Look . . . look at me."

Afton turned to meet his gaze, her eyes filled with angry tears.

"This guy putting your kids in danger . . . it's like he went after my own kids," Max said. "You know?" He turned his focus back on the road. "Don't think I'm going to rest until we catch this guy. I swear, we're going to nab him and perp walk his ass right through the front door of the station, okay? Throw him in jail and make sure he gets the absolute dumbest public defender we can muster up."

Afton managed a thin smile. "Thanks, Max. But I feel like there's been a dark cloud hanging over me ever since I chased that guy at the hospital. I don't know how to explain it . . . but for the first time in my life I actually want to kill someone. I know that sounds awful, like I'm some kind of sociopath, but there it is. That's the bare naked truth."

"Hey," Max said, "we spend all sorts of time reassuring our kids that monsters don't exist. But they do exist, in all shapes and sizes. You and I, we've come to learn that firsthand. Well, today your kids had the misfortune to meet one of those monsters. And when they're put in that kind of hor-rific danger, we react badly. We lose our shit."

"You think I lost my shit?"

"Well, sure," he said mildly. "But in a *good* way."

They spun down Park Avenue, thinking their private thoughts, not talking for a while.

Finally, Afton said, "How are we gonna catch this guy, Max? And that woman we think he's working with?"

"We keep our eyes open. We press every-one. Tighten the screws on Sunny and the rest of the people around her. Hell, Afton, I even sent the Crime Scene team to that Quaking Bog place you told me about."

"I don't know if there's anything there to find," Afton said. She felt disheartened, as if she should have done more.

"Don't think about it. Just let our guys do their jobs." Max's cell phone buzzed noisily from the bin between the two front seats. "Now, who's that?"

Afton picked up the phone and looked at the caller ID. "Sunny Odin," she said.

A look of annoyance crossed Max's face. "What does *she* want?"

Afton thumbed the On button, put it on speaker, and handed the phone to Max.

"This is Detective Montgomery."

"Detective Montgomery!" Sunny cried. "What have you done with Terrell? You have her, don't you? Please tell me you do."

Max and Afton exchanged glances.

"Whoa," Max said. "Slow down. What exactly are you talking about?"

"You must have her!" Sunny said again. "What have you done with my baby?"

"We don't have your daughter, Mrs. Odin," Max said. "We haven't seen her since Friday night, when we stopped by her boyfriend's house."

"But she's been gone for two days," Sunny sobbed. "Two whole days. I even called the Saint Paul police and they sent a squad to her boyfriend's house. But there was no sign of them. Terrell's car is parked there, but the boyfriend's truck is gone."

"I don't know," Max said. "Maybe they went out for brunch."

"Brunch?" Afton hissed at him. She doubted that Terrell was out guzzling mimosas.

"Isn't that what civilians do on Sundays?" Max said under his breath. "Sit around and eat eggs Benedict and hash browns? Shoot the shit?"

"No," Afton said.

"Please," Sunny implored. "Something's really wrong, I just know there is." The fear was palpable in her voice. "How much more clear do I have to be about this? I desperately need your help."

"Tell you what," Max said. "We can put out a BOLO on Snell's truck. A *be on the lookout for.* Do you happen to know the make and model?"

"I have no idea!" Sunny wailed. "All I know is that Terrell's gone. Probably kidnapped."

"Don't jump to any conclusions," Max said. "Don't ever think the worst."

Along with Max, Afton was turning Sunny's words over in her mind, trying to make sense of Terrell's disappearance.

"Maybe Terrell's up to something," Afton said in a quiet voice. "Or she really did run into the wrong people."

"Hang on a minute," Max said to Sunny. He dropped the phone to his chest, took it off speaker mode, and said, "What are you thinking?"

"I'm not entirely sure," Afton said. "But

these people we've been chasing, they've been picking off Sunny's family and acquaintances like plaster ducks in a shooting gallery."

"True," Max said.

"The other thing is . . . do you remember how well-versed Terrell was when she talked about her stepfather's business? About importing goods and ports of entry and those FTZ trade areas?" Afton asked.

"I guess she knew a bit about it," Max said.

"What if Terrell had some involvement with those Thai people after all?" Afton asked. "Maybe not directly, but what if something happened and she got sucked in?"

"It sounds a little shaky to me," Max said. "It doesn't seem like Terrell and Snell could muster up enough brain cells between the two of them to pull off a decent scheme. Maybe they just got lost on their way home from White Castle."

"Give me the phone," Afton said.

Max handed her the phone.

"Mrs. Odin? This is Afton Tangler. You remember me?"

"Yes, yes," Sunny said.

"What's your daughter's cell phone number?"

Sunny rattled it off to her.

"And who's her carrier?"

"Ah . . . I don't know," Sunny said.

"If you want to find your daughter, you're going to have to focus."

"Maybe . . . Verizon?"

"Are you sure?" Afton asked.

"Yes, yes, that's it," Sunny said. "I just remembered, we have the same carrier. Are you going to trace her phone? Can you do that?"

"We're going to try," Afton said. "Just sit tight and you'll hear back from us." She hung up and said, "Do you think we can get Megan Crowley in the comm center to contact Verizon and have them ping Terrell's phone?"

"We can try," Max said. "Better to give it a shot than have Sunny's friends in high places breathing down our necks. Such as the governor and a couple of senators."

Afton made a quick call to the comm center to determine if Megan was even working today. Turns out she was. Once Afton was routed through, she said, "Megan? Yeah, it's me, Afton. Can you get Verizon to ping a cell phone and see if they can locate the tower for the last call?" She listened and said, "Yes, it's an ongoing investigation I'm working on with Montgomery, the Leland

Odin thing. And yes, we can get you the paperwork ASAP. Okay, sure. Oh, you can? That's great." Afton gave Megan the phone number and carrier. Then she said, "Can you give me any kind of ETA? As you might imagine, this is fairly urgent."

On the other end of the line, Megan replied, "I'll get right on it, but it could take a while."

"Okay," Afton said. "I know you'll do your best." She hung up and said, "You think we should call Sunny back?"

"No, let's give this a little time," Max said. "Assuming the battery hasn't been pulled from Terrell's phone, they might be able to use several towers and triangulate the signal. That'd get us in a lot closer."

"Let's hope so," Afton said. "Because the more I think about this, it's a hell of a strange coincidence for Terrell to go off the grid so soon after her stepfather's murder."

"You're starting to convince me that something really is wrong," Max said. "Here, give me that phone. I'm gonna call Snell's name in so we can get his license and registration and get the squeal out on that BOLO."

They were coasting toward downtown Minneapolis now, just passing the convention center. Some kind of event had just let out and traffic had slowed to a crawl.

"Wouldn't it be something," Max said, "if Terrell and her scuzzy boyfriend were just holed up somewhere doing magic mushrooms?"

"There's always that," Afton said. But she was feeling a tingle. An ominous foreboding that something was very wrong. The question was, could she trust her inner vibe? Did she have that sixth sense that veteran police officers and detectives so often developed? *Huh,* she thought. Probably too soon to tell.

"This traffic sucks," Max said. Now they were stuck behind a huge shiny black bus.

"You got a flasher in your glove box?" Afton asked. She'd like nothing better than to stick that puppy on Max's dashboard and zip through all this congestion.

"Naw," Max said. "It's okay." He glanced at his watch. "We still got time."

They bumped their way slowly down Marquette Avenue, finally making the turn onto Fifth Street, heading for the parking garage attached to the downtown precinct building. As soon as Max turned down the ramp, the phone rang.

Afton grabbed up Max's cell phone. "Hello?" She glanced over at Max. "It's Megan." Then, "Yeah, what have you got?"

445

She grabbed a pen, riffled through the trash on the floor of the car, and found a Burger King receipt. "Okay, go." Afton scratched out an approximation of an address. "And how long has the phone been pinging from that area? Okay, thanks. Thanks so much."

"What have you got?" Max asked, once Afton had hung up. He'd pulled his car into a spot that said RESERVED FOR PRISON VANS ONLY.

"Not an address," Afton said, "because it's impossible to target a single phone that precisely. But a general area."

"And where is this area?"

"Northeast Minneapolis. Best guess, somewhere in the vicinity of Seventeenth Avenue Northeast and Madison Northeast."

"Is that, like, the rail yards?" Max asked.

"I don't know. But I think we should check it out. Northeast Minneapolis is barely ten minutes away."

"Might be a crack house," Max warned.

"And Terrell and her boyfriend could be in serious danger," Afton said.

"We should probably let Thacker know what we're up to."

"So we'll call him on the fly," Afton said. "Look, by the time we go upstairs, lay all this out for Thacker, and get an okay to set up the troops, Terrell and her friend could

446

be dead."

And still Max hesitated. "The shit could hit the fan. I mean, there could be serious blowback . . . on us."

"Come on, Max," Afton urged. "You've got kids. If one of them was in danger what would you do?"

"Okay," Max said, backing out of the parking space and wheeling his car around. "Pop open the glove box and stick that flasher on the dash."

"Now you're talking sense."

49

It was late afternoon and everyone at the casket factory was getting antsy. Under Hack and Narong's supervision, the three Thai men had transferred all the dope from Snell's truck to the rented van. They would all drive to Detroit together, make the transfer, and collect the money.

Hack would drive the van back to Minneapolis, while Mom Chao Cherry would deal with the logistics of getting the cash transferred to one of her overseas accounts. Then, she and her four men would fly back to Thailand. She in first class, the men riding in coach.

"What about this pickup truck?" Narong asked, pointing to Snell's old rust bucket.

"We'll park it a couple of blocks away," Hack said. "Leave the keys in the ignition. With any luck it'll magically disappear by morning." He rubbed the back of his hand against his bristly chin. "And the people downstairs. They need to be dealt with, too."

Narong offered a thin smile. "Mom Chao Cherry has made her decision."

Downstairs, in the stifling darkness, Terrell's eyes darted left and right. She had no idea where she was being held — probably no one else did either — so she was truly on her own. And dear God, she'd seen hooks in the ceiling. What were those for? She shuddered. Perhaps she really didn't want to know.

Snell was no help. Every couple of minutes he mewled like a baby, and every time he hiccupped, strings of snot streamed out his nose. He was no badass; he was just disgusting.

Terrell had tried screaming, but that didn't work. The walls down here were too thick, and every time she opened her mouth to let go a really good bellow, it seemed to just get swallowed up in the cottony darkness. Plus, her jaw was swollen and hurting. She'd been smacked around a lot and now it felt like a couple of teeth had been knocked loose.

And now . . . oh, holy shit, now she heard footsteps creeping down the stairs.

A flashlight winked on in Terrell's face,

startling her and practically blinding her.

"Don't do that," Terrell snapped as more flashlights came on, piercing the darkness like searchlights. "What do you want?" Her knees were shaking and her heart was hammering inside her chest. She was so afraid, she wanted to cower next to Snell, but what would that accomplish? Exactly nothing. Better to throw herself on their mercy. Or try to . . .

"It's time to relocate you folks," Hack said. He sounded pleasant and almost matter-of-fact.

Terrell felt a surge of hope run through her. "We're going somewhere?" she asked. That was good, right? "Did you finally get in touch with my mother? Is she going to pay a ransom?" She prayed that her mother would be particularly generous to these people.

"Not exactly," Hack said.

Overhead, a dim string of lights was turned on and Hack stepped back, watching carefully as Narong and the three men unlocked Terrell and Snell from the metal standpipe. The prisoners tried to struggle, but Narong and his men held on tight.

"We've got orders to move you to a different room," Hack said.

"But you talked to my mother?" Terrell

begged. "Please, if you haven't yet, you've got to call her. She'll pay you a lot of money, I promise!"

"Sorry, kiddo," Hack said. "No can do. That's just not in the cards." He was genuinely regretful. Maybe another time, another place . . . he and this chick could have really gotten it on together. But now . . . well, after all they'd put her through, she wasn't exactly great looking anymore.

Snell started his high, pathetic keening sound again as Narong and his men unceremoniously dragged him and Terrell across the rough concrete floor.

"Wait," Terrell screamed. "Where's the old lady? I want to talk to the old lady. I thought we had a deal!"

"No deal," Narong spat at her.

"If you talk to my mother, she'll pay you to send me back home!"

"Maybe in pieces," Narong said as he grabbed Terrell's arm and jerked her forward.

"What are you doing? Where are you taking us?" Terrell quavered.

It certainly didn't look as if they were headed back upstairs. Instead, the whole lot of them struggled and punched and dragged their way across the expanse of the basement, a moving, writhing pig pile that suddenly converged upon a single narrow door-way.

"Noooo!" Terrell wailed as she and Snell were pushed and shoved inside a small, stone-walled room.

She'd just caught a glimpse of the room's horrific interior.

"Pleeease!" Terrell cried again, thrashing wildly, kicking at her captors, hissing and spitting like a deranged alley cat. And then, finally, going limp with fear.

Three caskets lay inside the room. They were old, covered with an inch of dust, as if they'd been moldering there forever. As if they'd been dragged up from the bowels of Count Dracula's castle.

Terrell and Snell were both shaking so badly, they could barely walk. No matter — the men shoved and dragged them along awkwardly, herding them like cowering, bleating sheep to the abattoir.

Terrell flailed out, practically knocking one of the men off his feet. She managed to touch Hack's arm for just an instant and said in a piteous voice, "For god's sake, no. Don't let them do this to me."

One of the Asian men held up a hand and said, "Wait."

Their sad procession ground to a halt.

"Please?" Terrell said in a small voice

while Snell broke into a wet, burbling whimper.

Then Narong smiled at Terrell, his even white teeth glowing like piano keys in the dark as he slammed a fist directly into her forehead. Her head snapped back, her eyes bulged, and she flew over backward as if buffeted by hurricane winds. From there it was just a matter of the men lifting the creaking lid on the casket and tossing the limp, moaning, barely conscious girl inside.

Stars swam before Terrell's eyes as she felt herself being dropped onto some sort of soft, damp, squishy material. And just before they slammed the lid, the putrid smell of mold rose up to engulf her senses.

50

"Not much to see around here," Max said as they rolled up Seventeenth Avenue. "A few old factories, some depressed-looking homes."

"You're right," Afton said. "It doesn't look like much of anything except maybe a neighborhood that's desperately in need of gentrification." It was a scruffy area. Afton could see that many homes were in need of repair or at least a decent coat of paint. Cars parked on the street were older models, too. Down the block, a blue beater Buick looked like it was terminally jacked up, both its front wheels missing.

"So what do you want to do?" Max asked.

"Maybe just make a couple of loops around the neighborhood and see if anything jumps out at us?"

They drove up Seventeenth, circled left, and then ghosted past a large corrugated tin building surrounded by a high chicken-wire fence. Old sports cars, in various stages of rust and disrepair, sat inside the enclosure. An MGB, the remnants of an old Triumph, the skeleton of a motorbike.

"If Terrell and Snell are hanging out over here," Max said, "Snell's pickup should be parked somewhere."

"You're right. And I haven't seen it."

"I think this is just a funky mix of residential, warehouse, and old-time manufacturing," Max said.

"Except the manufacturing seems to have picked up and cleared out," Afton said. She continued to scan both sides of the street, then cranked her head to the right. "Take a look at that spooky old building over there. A lot of the windows are boarded up, so it must be deserted."

"Hmm?" Max said.

The derelict redbrick building seemed to pull at Afton and hypnotically draw her in. It looked like a pseudo-ancient ruin, a place where a bunch of urban explorers would sneak in for some impromptu exploration.

"What is that place anyway?" Afton asked.

"Dunno," Max said.

"Take a right and swing in closer. I want to get a better look. Jeez, it's huge. And see, there's a painted sign at the top of an old smokestack." Afton blinked as she craned her neck. "Kind of hard to see, though — the paint's all chipped and faded."

Clouds had seeped across the sky, blotting out the sun and turning late afternoon into a gray miasma. The days were still pitifully short.

"But the building itself is kind of interesting," Max said. "Like one of those old breweries that they've turned into . . ."

"Holy shit!" Afton yelped, interrupting Max. "You know what that sign says?"

"No, but I have a feeling you're going to tell me."

They were a half block away from the building now and closing in.

"It says Callahan Casket Company," Afton said.

"Ah, that certainly does lend a creep factor to the neighborhood," Max said.

"But the place looks defunct now. Closed."

"Well, if it's closed, then Terrell and her whacked-out boyfriend probably aren't hanging out there."

"Probably not," Afton said. She hated to admit it, but this errand felt like a bust. "We're going to have to head back pretty soon."

"Got to." Max peered ahead. "I'm gonna

pull into that driveway up ahead and flip a . . ."

"Whoa!" Afton said. She said it in a surprised tone that carried a sharp note of alarm.

"What?" Max asked.

"Stop the car."

Max slammed on his brakes, stopping the car in the middle of the narrow street. "What?" He was glancing around the neighborhood now with cool law enforcement eyes. "What do you see? Tell me."

Afton's throat had gone bone-dry. "Just up ahead," she choked out. "You see that dusty red car parked at the curb?"

"You gotta be shittin' me." Max tapped the gas pedal and eased over to the curb. "You think it's the same car? The one from the noodle factory? The one your asshole got away in today?"

"There's only one way to find out," Afton said. She was trying to tamp down her fear, already grappling for the door handle, ready to jump out and take a look.

Max reached over and grabbed her shoulder. "No, no. If it's your Asian guy, he knows what you look like. Let me go." Max didn't relax his grip on Afton because he didn't trust her judgment right now. She was too hopped up. "Okay?"

Afton thought it over for a couple of seconds, decided that Max was probably right. It was the prudent thing to do. "I guess . . ."

"That means you stay *here*," Max warned. "Don't even try to roll down the window and stick your little head out. If it's the same guy and he's around here . . . well, this might be our only shot at apprehending him."

Max jumped out of the car, walked casually up the street and past the dusty red car. Then he turned around and headed back. Once he climbed back inside his car, he gripped the steering wheel hard and said, "Hot damn, Afton. There's a Duluth Port Authority decal stuck on the back window."

"Oh, dear Lord." Afton was rightfully stunned. "That means he's got them. The Asian man and maybe the old woman he's working with . . . they've got Terrell and Snell."

"We don't know that for a fact," Max said. "But it's a very hinky coincidence. We gotta call it in. This is way too hot to handle by ourselves." He was already punching in numbers on his phone, urgently telling the dispatcher to put him directly through to Thacker. Then Max was practically shouting into the phone, painting the scenario for

Thacker, giving him the details as well as the address.

When Max rang off, Afton said, "Now what?"

"We stay put," Max said. "We sit tight until a SWAT unit arrives. They're armoring up right now. Thacker called for a full-court press."

"We sit here and wait?" Afton said. "But what if Terrell and Snell need help *now*?"

"Can't be helped. Those are our orders."

"Yeah, but . . . oh, jeez." Afton jerked her head forward in disbelief. "We got some major activity going on over there."

"What?" Max focused his sights on the casket factory, where a large garage door had just rolled up.

"You see that?" Afton asked. "Looks like somebody's making a run for it."

"Damn. I hope the shit didn't just hit the fan."

"Still want to sit tight?" Afton wasn't needling Max; she was just anxious. It felt like bugs were crawling through her veins.

"I gotta . . ." Max said.

"You gotta do something. You gotta see what's going on."

But Max was already reaching for his Glock 9mm. Checking it, checking it again.

"You got one of those for me?" Afton asked.

"No way. You stay here."

"Hell no," Afton said. "You can't go in there alone." She could see some sort of van in the building up ahead, but it hadn't backed out yet. "You might need backup."

"Afton . . . no."

"Gimme your extra piece."

"I don't have an extra," Max said.

"The one in the glove box?" Afton was already popping open the glove box, pawing for the gun.

"Damn, woman," Max swore. His shoulders hunched forward and every muscle seemed to tighten. "Okay, but I go in there first. You stay way behind me. If we run into problems, you run like hell and wait for the cavalry to arrive. Is that understood?"

"Perfectly," Afton said.

But Max wasn't finished. "The only way you fire your weapon is if there's a clear and present threat to your person. I can take care of myself. Do not defend me, just run for cover if it all goes to hell." He paused. "You sure you can handle that weapon?"

Afton clicked the clip release, dropped the clip into the palm of her hand, and then slammed it back home. She shoved the slide open and dropped a bullet into the chamber.

"Got it."

The last thing Max said as they climbed out of the car was, "Thacker is really going to be pissed."

Afton's last thought was of her kids.

51

Afton and Max crept up to the casket factory, dodging behind trees, hiding behind
parked cars. The side of the enormous brick
building that faced them had two sets of
garage doors — one yawned open to reveal
a parked van; the other door remained
closed. Down to the far left of the building
was a large cement loading dock and, just
beyond that, a strip of overgrown weeds and
then several sets of train tracks. Afton
figured that some of the tracks were still in
use, while others had fallen into disrepair.

As Max ran on ahead of her, Afton feared
that he was way too exposed. But he managed to trot across the street and then press
himself up against the side of the building
without being noticed. Now he was about
four feet from the garage door opening, hiding behind a brick column that jutted out.

Good. He made it.

Max glanced back at her and shook his

head. He didn't want her to follow him. Well, that was just tough, because there was no way she was going to let him creep into that building all by himself.

Glancing left and then right, Afton ran lightly across the street and joined him, pressing her shoulder up against the brick wall.

"Are you crazy?" Max whispered. "Get out of here. Go around the corner and wait for SWAT to arrive."

But Afton wasn't about to budge.

Just as Max tried to shove her away, there was a jabber of excited voices from inside.

Afton cocked her head, listening. *What?* Several men were all talking at once in a foreign language that sounded like Chinese . . . or Thai.

"Holy shit," Max whispered. "Those people from Bangkok?"

There was the metallic sound of a door being slammed.

"That's a car door," Afton mouthed. "They're getting ready to leave. You have to . . ."

Max pulled his face into a harsh grimace. He knew this was it. He had to make some sort of preemptive move.

Getting up his guts, he eased his way to the opening, his weapon leading the way.

"Police!" Max shouted. "Put your hands in the air!"

There was sudden angry shouting and then the whine of a bullet streaking past Max's head.

"Put down your weapons!" Max shouted. But nobody seemed to be listening, as two more bullets whipped past him.

"Damn," Max said, backing up, practically smashing against Afton.

"You think you can hold them until SWAT arrives?" she shouted, trying to make herself heard above the frantic din inside.

Max shook his head. "I don't know. I think there's four of them in there."

"How many have guns?" she asked.

"I'm guessing maybe . . . two or three?"

The van's engine roared to life and a glut of exhaust fumes blew out the garage door.

"We can't let 'em go," Afton said, gritting her teeth.

Max peeked around the corner again and yelled, "Throw down your weapons!"

"Kill him!" a woman's voice shrieked. "Kill him now!"

"That's gotta be the old woman!" Afton yelled as Max popped around the corner, fast as a serpent's bite, and — BAM! BAM! — fired two more shots.

Inside the garage, mad panic continued.

Shrill voices shouting and arguing in a language Afton and Max were both convinced was Thai.

Then Max dodged inside, pressed himself up against the front grill of the van, and fired two more shots.

"Weapons down!" he ordered. "Everyone put your weapons down!"

Afton peeped around the corner and saw three young Asian men — none of them her attacker — standing there with their hands raised over their heads. They'd placed their weapons on the ground and surrendered. Good, she thought. No shoot-out at the OK Corral. Maybe Max had this under control after all.

But nothing ever comes easy.

A tough-looking hillbilly suddenly leaped out from behind the van, yanking an old lady with him and positioning her in front of him like a human shield. One hand held a gun to her head; the other hand was curled around her throat, squeezing hard. "Out of my way," he bellowed.

"Let go of me, you fool," the old woman gasped. She struggled violently, kicking and trying to twist out of his grasp.

"Shut up, bitch," Hack snarled. "Or I'll crush your windpipe so hard your eyes will pop out like grapes."

The old woman sputtered and struggled, but the hillbilly just gripped her tighter.

"Gaagh!" the old lady croaked, her face blooming bright pink.

"Nobody needs to get hurt," Max said in a level voice. His gun was pointed directly at the hillbilly and the old lady as time seemed to slow down, as if all the participants were mired in wet cement. "Just let her go and we can work this out."

Afton wasn't quite so optimistic. The hillbilly looked like a tough bastard. He didn't look like he had any intention of letting the old lady go. Besides, where was . . . ?

Like a malevolent banshee rising from the forest, the Asian man who'd just attacked Afton some two hours earlier sprang out of the van. His voice was a wild howl as he waved an enormous knife above his head and threw himself at Max like some sort of hellish apparition.

Max fired instantly. There was a loud *pop* and a huge explosion of red, as if an enormous blood bubble had suddenly burst. Then the Asian man made a high-pitched yipping sound and grabbed his wounded hand, the knife clattering to the floor.

"See, now," Max said to the hillbilly. "Now it's your turn to be sensible. Put down your weapon and let the lady go."

A stupid grin creased the hillbilly's face. "No can do, my friend. The two of us are gettin' in that van and driving out of here."

"Let her go *now*," Max pressed. Like a chameleon, Mom Chao Cherry's face had gone from pink to purple and her arms were flailing as if she were trying to teach herself to dog paddle.

Hack dragged Mom Chao Cherry toward the front of the van, bending her backward to cover himself.

"This isn't going to end well," Afton said. Along with Max, she had her gun trained on Hack. But she was also watching her wounded attacker, who glared at her with hate-filled eyes. Weren't wounded animals the most dangerous kind? Sure, they were. Probably wounded people, too.

As if moving in slow motion, Hack eased his way to the van's front door and pulled it open. He would have to scramble inside, mounting a fairly high step as he dragged the woman along with him. Could he manage that? Afton wasn't sure. All she knew was that Max didn't have a clean shot and neither did she.

But Hack had another trick up his sleeve. In one smooth, balletic twirling motion, he reached into the van and pulled out a thin piece of wire. He slipped it over Mom Chao Cherry's head and pulled it tight as a noose.

Mom Chao Cherry let loose another agonized moan. "Agggh!" A thin line of blood appeared around her throat, like a channel-set necklace of bright red rubies.

"SWAT units are on the way," Max threatened. "They'll be here in a few minutes."

Practically lifting the old lady off her feet now, Hack sawed mercilessly at her throat, "Back off or I'll cut her deeper."

"Help!" Mom Chao Cherry cried. She sounded like a garbled crow. "Shooot him!" Blood dripped freely from her throat now, spattering the floor.

"He's killing her," Afton hissed.

"Shut up!" Hack grated. He figured that neither Afton nor Max would risk taking a shot at him. "Just lower your guns while I pull this old bitch into the truck with me."

Afton lowered her gun. Max wavered.

"Come on, now," Hack coaxed as he half pulled, half dragged Mom Chao Cherry into the front seat. "Just stay frosty."

"I'm cool," Max said, lowering his weapon.

"Good," Hack said. "Smart. No need to go off half-cocked."

"Just ease up on her, will you?" Afton asked. "At least let her breathe."

"Whatever," Hack said, flashing a hard, cheesy smile.

Whatever, indeed. It was the instant Mom Chao Cherry was waiting for. Maybe Hack's hand slipped a notch from all that blood bubbling out of her neck. Or he let down his guard because she was practically sitting in his lap.

Like a pissed-off weasel that had been biding its time, she spun all the way around to face him, stretched out her wounded neck, and sank her teeth into Hack's lower lip!

"Aggh!" Hack screamed. The old lady hung on like a rat terrier, tearing and ripping, her dark eyes furious. Hack screamed again, practically yodeling as blood began to seriously spurt from his mouth.

A moment later, Mom Chao Cherry clawed viciously at Hack's eyes. Her long nails, like razor-sharp talons, dug in deep, pulling his eyelids downward until he looked like a melting pumpkin.

"Get off!" Hack screamed. His fist shot up and violently clubbed Mom Chao Cherry on the side of the head.

In that split second, as the old lady released her bite and her head bounced back, Max snapped his gun back up and shot Hack right between the eyes.

"Holy crap!" Afton screamed as blood and

brains blew everywhere. The old woman looked almost quizzical as she raised both hands to paw wildly at her bloody throat. Then she pitched forward and tumbled from the van.

Just for an instant, a fleeting emotion seemed to play across Mom Chao Cherry's lined face. Perhaps it was pain; perhaps it was a sadness that a lifetime of killing and assassinations had come to this. Then it was gone, like the energy expended by a dying firefly, and she hit the cement floor like a sack of flour.

Prasong, the youngest of the three men who'd had his hands raised high, took advantage of the moment that had everyone stunned. He turned and bolted for the doorway, giving it all he had.

Wasting not a millisecond, Narong also spun away from the bizarre scene. He plunged down a long hallway in a full-on mad sprint and disappeared into darkness.

"Damn it!" Afton shouted as she turned and ran after him.

"No!" Max called after her, his voice echoing hollowly in the old building. But there was no stopping her.

Afton sprinted down the hallway, glancing into dirty and dilapidated rooms and work spaces along the way. Most of them had windows that still allowed a small amount of light. One large room held a row of rusted sewing machines where workers had once stitched burial gowns.

But Afton knew Narong wasn't hiding in any of these rooms. She could hear him up ahead of her, breathing heavily, his footsteps drilling hard against the floor. She was determined to catch him. Once she did, she'd beat his brains into the ground as payback.

Droplets of fresh blood from Narong's injured hand spattered the dirty tiles in the hallway as Afton, hot on his heels, followed the trail. The corridor hooked left and, suddenly, there he was. All the way across a debris-strewn room, scrambling up an exterior stone wall like a scuttling spider.

"Stop!" Afton shouted. She dropped into a shooter's stance and pointed her gun at Narong as he leaped up onto a window ledge. Cradling his wounded hand, he screamed at the top of his lungs and kicked frantically at a grimy window, his face as red as fresh liver.

With a growl that came from deep inside her throat, Afton aimed her gun at Narong, meaning to hit him in the leg. To wound him. Cripple him.

He moved at the last second and her shot

missed, kicking up a hail of broken glass and wooden splinters.

With one final, solid kick, Narong shattered the window, shards of glass exploding everywhere. Clambering out onto the ledge, he hesitated for a single moment, and then jumped down.

Afton was right on his heels. With her flexibility, honed from years of rock climbing and running, she sprang through the window and brushed past the broken glass without hesitation. She felt the ground rush up to meet her, put out her hands to cushion her fall, and did a basic somersault into the weeds. Then she was up and running after Narong, still with the gun in her hand, screaming at him, totally lost in fury.

"You tried to kill me!" Afton screamed. "You almost killed my kids!" She ran like there was no tomorrow. Crushed rock bit through the soles of her shoes, and sand burrs clung to her ankles as she pounded after Narong.

Glancing back over his shoulder, Narong flashed a triumphant glance as he raced toward the railroad tracks.

A train was coming, rolling languidly down the tracks.

Damn, Afton thought as the train's whistle broke the silence. *He's going to beat that thing. He's going to jump across the tracks and I'm going to be stuck over here.*

She skidded to a stop and aimed her gun. Sighting the man's back, she placed her finger on the trigger. It would be so easy. A quick flex of her right index finger and this man would be dead. This man who had wantonly killed, who had dared threaten her and her family, would never cause a lick of trouble again. But if she just pulled the trigger and blew him away, it would be cold-blooded murder. Could she live with that?

The green-and-yellow engine pulling three dozen dingy-looking refrigerator cars rolled closer. Afton's gun wavered as she watched Narong sprint for the tracks. He'd be gone in a matter of seconds. Disappeared just like before. But maybe . . . still out there? Maybe still coming after her? Her finger twitched. If she aimed for his right thigh, could she make the shot?

She pulled the trigger just as, with a careless leap, Narong hurled himself in front of the engine.

Narong knew full well that he could make it across, felt smug about cutting off Afton's only chance to catch him.

Narong misjudged.

Maybe it was his wounded hand that caused him to lose focus and stumble, maybe it was fate coming to collect its due.

Steel wheels ground against rails as the train fought to brake. Then a geyser of blood spurted up, an arterial spray that painted the embankment bright red.

Afton watched in horror as Narong's body rolled and twisted like a rag doll as it was dragged down the railroad track for a good five hundred yards. His legs bobbled over wooden railroad ties; sharp red rocks flayed his skin.

Afton looked away, feeling no satisfaction at all.

52

But it wasn't over yet. Shaken to the core by Narong's horrific death, Afton still had the presence of mind to dash back inside the casket factory.

Max was there, of course, maintaining shaky control. His Glock in one hand, his cell phone in the other. Hack was dead, Mom Chao Cherry was bleeding profusely, and the remaining two Asian men had been herded up against a wall and looked like they were ready to cry.

"Where's Terrell?" Afton shouted.

Max shook his head. He was pale as a ghost and looked like he was barely hanging on. Shock.

Afton ripped the scarf from around her neck and went to aid Mom Chao Cherry, who was crouched against the back wheel of the van.

"How bad?" the old woman quavered. "Will I die? I'm not ready to die."

"Let me look." Afton pried the old woman's hand away from her neck and checked the wound. It was deep and still oozing blood but probably not fatal if she got medical attention fairly soon. "If we can get an ambulance here in the next four minutes, I think you'll live."

"Ambulance is two minutes out," Max said. "So is SWAT."

"Okay, then," Afton said. She focused on the old woman. "Where's the girl?"

The old woman shook her head.

"Terrell? Is she here?"

The old woman stared with the black-eyed malice of an angry jackal.

"Come to think of it," Afton said, "that ambulance might be delayed."

A look of fear crossed Mom Chao Cherry's lined face. "Downstairs," she mumbled. "Downstairs."

"Downstairs here?" Afton pulled open the front door of the van and popped open the glove box. When a flashlight rolled out, she grabbed it and turned to glance into the back of the van. "Dope," she said to herself. There had to be a couple hundred plastic-wrapped packets. Then a little louder, so Max could hear her, she said, "This vehicle's packed to the gills with dope."

Max just nodded.

476

Then Afton was racing down a long set of steps into the basement of the casket factory.

It was pitch-dark when she hit the bottom step, so she turned on her flashlight and shone it around. *Lights? Yeah, here they are.*

Afton flipped a switch and a few dim bulbs in wire cages popped on. But there was no Terrell.

So where is she?

Afton did a sort of grid search like she'd seen professional crime-scene investigators conduct. That is, she walked the length of the basement, cut over several feet, and then walked back again. She was searching for something, anything, that would give her a clue as to Terrell's whereabouts.

Three minutes in, she noticed the wooden door. She walked over and butted it hard with her shoulder, putting as much weight behind it as she could. The door grated open slowly to reveal . . . three caskets.

Dear Lord!

Afton flew across the room, her heart in her throat, and landed hard on her knees next to the nearest casket. She flung open the lid and was shocked at the stench that rose out of it. And then was stunned again when a small voice called out, "Momma?"

"Terrell?" Afton said, reaching in to touch

the terrified girl. "Is that you?"

"Help me," Terrell said in a wooden voice.

Afton snaked an arm under Terrell's shoulders and helped her sit upright.

"Are you okay?" Afton asked her.

"No," Terrell said. "After what I just went through, I'll never be okay."

Afton helped Terrell climb out and then hurriedly opened the other two caskets. She found Snell on the second try.

He sat up and started blubbering. "Jeez, it took you long enough."

The SWAT team, two ambulances, three cruisers, and Deputy Chief Thacker arrived minutes later in a blaze of red and blue lights and the *whoop whoop* of sirens.

Thacker looked supremely pissed, but most of that anger drained away when Max gave him a fairly lengthy explanation as to what had just gone down.

For her part, Afton had never been happier to see large, hunky men dressed in riot gear.

Teams of paramedics placed Terrell and Mom Chao Cherry on gurneys and loaded them into the two ambulances. Terrell was handed a cell phone and given the royal treatment. Mom Chao Cherry was stabilized and then handcuffed.

478

Snell wandered around, hoping to score some attention and TLC for himself. Finally, one of the SWAT guys clapped him on the back and said, "Man, you were pretty damn brave. I don't know if I could have handled being slammed inside a casket like that." That seemed to do it for Snell.

Afton looked around at what was basically controlled chaos now. The DEA guys had arrived and practically danced a jig at finding all the dope squirrelled away in the van. Terrell was blubbering into her phone saying, "Mommy? Mommy, I'm here. The cops found me and saved me. But I just want to come home."

The two Thai men had been trundled into the back of a cruiser and driven away. Hack's body remained where he'd fallen.

Still, Thacker kept a tight lid on things. Running everything by the book, informing Afton and Max that they would have to submit formal, detailed reports and might even be required to appear before an incident review board. He made sure the Crime Scene team was given ample time to deal with the body and the building, as well as the carnage on the train tracks.

When Thacker caught Afton's eye, she walked over to him, not sure what he was going to say. All she knew was that he looked as if he wanted to say something.

"So you chased after that guy," Thacker said. "Again."

"He came after me," Afton said. "When I was with my *kids.*" She took a deep breath. "I thought turnabout was fair play."

"Except when it comes to by-the-book police work," Thacker said. "Then it's known as revenge." He cocked an accusatory eye at her. "You've got a lot to learn. Beside the fact that we're going to need a wet-dry vac to scrub that guy up off the tracks."

Afton couldn't tell if Thacker was fiercely angry at her or exhibiting a macabre brand of cop humor. She knew she was treading on very thin ice and decided she'd better work a lot harder on honing that police-intuition thing.

"Are you going to put me on forced leave?" Afton asked him. She was practically holding her breath. "Or fire me?"

After a long, uncomfortable silence, Thacker grunted, "Not today, Liaison Officer Tangler." He turned away from her, took a few steps, and then turned back, offering her a thin sliver of smile. "I've got other plans for you."

53

Prasong was running for his life. He'd squirted out of the door of the casket factory just as the shooting started, then dodged across a narrow street, and ran behind a dingy yellow house. From there he pounded down a back alley past a row of tumbled-down garages and foul-smelling garbage cans. He continued running through backyards and back alleys until he hit a more populated part of town that had shops and restaurants and very tall apartment buildings. Then he jogged across an enormous bridge made of stone arches that took him right into downtown Minneapolis.

Glancing around, Prasong saw a big red-brick building with a red-and-white bull's-eye on its side. Some kind of important sign, he decided. Maybe a government building. That might not be so good. He turned away and searched the city landscape, wondering what to do, where to hide.

Down the street, a group of people was getting ready to climb aboard a shiny blue train. He ran with all his might in that direction and jumped on the train just as the doors were about to snap shut. He fell into a narrow seat, his heart pounding, eyes glancing furtively about, knowing he might be captured at any moment. Much to his surprise, nobody paid any attention to him. He was just another sixteen-year-old kid on his way to wherever.

Okay, Prasong thought. *At least I escaped. I don't know where I am, but at least I got away. Away from the madness, away from a terrible life of servitude under Mom Chao Cherry.*

The train started up and then gathered speed, shuddering and rocking its way through downtown, past many tall office buildings and a giant building with a curved blue glass wall. Then they sped across a bridge that spanned a wide river. Prasong decided it must be the same river that he'd just run across some ten minutes earlier. This big river must snake its way through the city much like the Bang Sue in Bangkok.

The train continued down University Avenue, all the way into the city of Saint Paul.

When Prasong saw a sign printed in his

native language, he jumped off the train and looked around. Saw a family with kids — maybe they were Vietnamese? — who seemed to be headed somewhere. He followed them down a block filled with greengrocers and small shops and ended up in an expansive open-air marketplace. Here, a large group of people — both Caucasians and Asians — milled around together, buying food at dozens of different restaurant stalls. The place reminded him of the Rot Fai night market back in Bangkok. He saw Vietnamese fried fish, Thai noodles, Chinese steamed dumplings, and tiny fish grilled on skewers. Music was playing over loudspeakers, and a man with a refrigerated cart was selling both chocolate ice cream and frozen Thai custard.

When Prasong saw a red-and-gold wooden booth with Thai writing above it, he headed that way. Pressing his nose against the glass, he saw that they were selling some very familiar-looking *sen yai* as well as *khao gang,* his favorite curried rice.

Prasong crossed his fingers, walked over to the harried-looking owner, and asked for a job.

The owner squinted at him. "Cooking?" he asked.

Prasong shook his head.

"Wash dishes?" the owner asked. "Cut fish?" He indicated a large sea bass that was splayed out on a cutting board. *"Pla krapong?"*

This time Prasong nodded. Sure, why not? It was a place to start. A way to meet people and gain a foothold in this new and very different country. Best of all . . . a chance. Working here would certainly be better than killing people and smuggling dope. Prasong shuddered. Anything was better than that.

54

Afton arrived at the emergency veterinary office, scared to death that Bonaparte might be dead by now. She stood at the front desk and managed a half smile at the receptionist. "My dog? Bonaparte? The French bulldog?"

A vet tech who was standing behind the receptionist looked up from her clipboard. "He's out of surgery," she said.

"But how *is* he?" Afton asked. She was terrified that Bonaparte had been too far gone. That he'd lost too much blood. Or that he'd be permanently disabled.

"We don't know," the receptionist said in a kind voice. "Let me call back there. See what the doc says. She's the one who gives the final word."

"Thank you." Afton sat down on a hard plastic chair with one mantra running through her head: *Please be okay, please be okay, please be okay.*

She was aware that she was holding her breath and tried to force herself to relax, to breathe naturally, to hold only good thoughts in her heart.

It wasn't working. The only image in her mind was her dog roaring in to rescue her and then Bonaparte's high-pitched squeal when he'd been cut.

I should have fought harder. Poppy and Tess will be devastated if I don't bring that little dog home to them. Then, *What am I thinking?* I'll *be devastated. Bonaparte's part of our family.*

Afton stared at a poster that hung on the wall. It was a cartoon of a smiling brown dog with a package of heartworm tablets next to it. She looked down at the floor, the dread and worry continuing to build inside of her.

As Afton waited, she was aware of a nearby clock. The seconds ticking away loudly.

She slowly lifted her head. For some reason, the clock sounded more like toenails clicking against the vinyl flooring.

And with that, Bonaparte came limping around the corner of the front desk. He was on a pink leash and being led slowly by one of the veterinarians. His head was bowed, as though he was deep in concentration, and he wore a large bandage around his left shoulder. A white slash of courage against his shiny black coat.

Afton sprang from her chair and went down on her knees. "Bonaparte!" she cried out.

Bonaparte recognized her immediately and wagged his tail. Then he leaned his head against her hip and sighed.

"Oh, dear Lord, you're okay." Afton looked up expectantly at the doctor. "Is he okay?"

The doctor nodded. "He's fine. We debrided and cleaned the wound and then I took fifteen good stitches. He's got a rubber drain in right now, but that will come out in a week. With plenty of rest and some good antibiotics to stave off infection, I anticipate he'll make a full recovery." She smiled. "He's a tough little guy. A real fighter."

With tears in her eyes, Afton nodded. "I know."

Gathering her dog in her arms, Afton kissed him on his forehead and carried him out to her car.

She laid him gently on the front seat, where he settled down immediately.

"Bonaparte," Afton whispered, as more tears began to flow. Then, in the privacy of her car, she thanked him for saving her life.

But, most of all, for saving the lives of Poppy and Tess.

Bonaparte looked up at her with large, intelligent eyes. And Afton knew that the little dog with the big heart understood every single word she'd just spoken to him. And that if Bonaparte ever had to rush to their defense again, he wouldn't hesitate. That was just the kind of dog he was.

ABOUT THE AUTHOR

Gerry Schmitt is the *New York Times* bestselling author of more than forty mysteries, including the Afton Tangler thrillers, as well as the Tea Shop, Scrapbooking, and Cackleberry Club mysteries, written under the pen name Laura Childs. She is the former CEO of her own marketing firm, has won dozens of TV and radio awards, produced two reality TV shows, and invests in small businesses. She and her professor husband enjoy collecting art and traveling, and they have two Shar-Peis.

Find out more at laurachilds.com or become a friend on Facebook.

LP 3/99